Government Printing Office

Report of the Secretary of the Treasury on the State of the Finances

Finances

The Year Ending June 30, 1862

Government Printing Office

Report of the Secretary of the Treasury on the State of the Finances
The Year Ending June 30, 1862

ISBN/EAN: 9783741183430

Manufactured in Europe, USA, Canada, Australia, Japa

Cover: Foto ©Andreas Hilbeck / pixelio.de

Manufactured and distributed by brebook publishing software
(www.brebook.com)

Government Printing Office

Report of the Secretary of the Treasury on the State of the Finances

REPORT

OF THE

SECRETARY OF THE TREASURY,

ON THE

STATE OF THE FINANCES,

FOR

THE YEAR ENDING JUNE 30, 1862.

WASHINGTON:
GOVERNMENT PRINTING OFFICE.
1863.

In the House of Representatives, *December 8*, 1862.

Resolved, That ten thousand extra copies of the Annual Report of the Secretary of the Treasury on the state of the Finances be printed for the use of the present House.

INDEX TO REPORT ON THE FINANCES.

REPORT ON THE FINANCES.

REPORT

OF THE

SECRETARY OF THE TREASURY.

DECEMBER 5, 1862.—Referred to the Committee on Finance, and ordered to be printed.

TREASURY DEPARTMENT, *December* 4, 1862.

SIR: In obedience to the act which requires the Secretary of the Treasury to prepare and lay before Congress, at the commencement of every session, a report on the subject of finance, embracing estimates of receipts and disbursements and plans of revenue, he submits, respectfully, the following views and statements:

The breaking out of the existing rebellion, soon after the incoming of the present administration, demanded the employment of all necessary means for the preservation of the territorial integrity of the republic, and for the maintenance of the constitutional supremacy of the whole people, through their national government, over every State and every citizen.

To authorize and prescribe the employment of these means was the peculiar province of Congress; to call forth and direct the armed force, which might be authorized, belonged to the President, and, under him, to the Departments of War and of the Navy; while to provide the means to meet authorized expenditures in its employment devolved, under the legislation of Congress and the direction of the President, on the Secretary of the Treasury.

Varying exigencies have required adapted measures and demanded unanticipated expenditures. Estimates, correct when made, have been rendered inaccurate by changed circumstances. Such conditions always attend war, whether external or civil, and we could not hope to escape them.

It is not, therefore, matter of surprise that the estimates submitted in July, 1861, for the year ending on the 30th of June, 1862, were exceeded by the actual expenditures, or that those submitted in December, for the year which will end on the 30th of June, 1863, will probably be, in like manner, exceeded.

The estimates of the Secretary must, necessarily, be derived chiefly from information furnished by other heads of departments; and this information, adjusted to existing and probable circumstances, cannot possibly anticipate all the vicissitudes of war or of legislation.

Thus, the estimates for the last fiscal year, submitted at the July session of 1861, were based on estimates from the War Department for an army, including regulars and volunteers, of three hundred thousand men; and from the Navy Department, for a naval force quite inconsiderable in comparison with that afterwards found to be indispensable.   Congress, thinking the proposed military force inadequate, provided for a volunteer army of five hundred thousand men, besides regular troops and special corps, numbering, together, over fifty thousand, and also for considerable additions to various corps, and a large increase of pay and rations.   The estimates of July required, of course, correction in December.

So, also, the estimates for the current fiscal year, submitted at the last session, were framed in substantial accordance with information furnished by the several departments.   The necessities of the war, however, rendered it expedient, in the judgment of the Executive and of Congress, to call for three hundred thousand additional volunteers, and make a draft of three hundred thousand men in addition to these.   The estimates, of course, must again prove inadequate.

The increase of the army, however, did not greatly affect disbursements between the date of the December report and the close of the then current fiscal year.   The increase of debt, therefore, did not exceed the December estimate.   On the contrary, while the estimate anticipated a public debt on the 30th of June, 1862, of $517,372,802 93, its actual amount on that day was $514,211,371 92.   This amount, of course, does not include unascertained claims, but only that debt, the evidences of which exist in the treasury, upon its books, or in the form of requisitions in favor of creditors or of disbursing officers.   It is not probable, however, that at the date named these claims much, if at all, exceeded the balance in the treasury, namely, $13,043,546 81.

But while the public debt on the 1st of July, 1862, did not reach the amount anticipated by the estimates, there is no room for the pleasing hope that the results of the current fiscal year or the next will exhibit a similar proportion.   On the contrary, the estimate of the public debt on the 1st of July, 1863, heretofore submitted, must now be advanced, in view of the unexpected increase of expenditures, authorized and incurred or likely to be incurred, to $1,122,297,403 24; and on the supposition that the war may be continued with undiminished disbursements until the 1st of July, 1864, the debt likely to have been then incurred must be estimated at $1,744,685,586 80.

It has been the care of the Secretary to reduce the cost of the debt, in the form of interest, to the lowest possible amount, and it is a source of real satisfaction to him that he has been able, thus far, to confine it within very moderate limits.   The first loans, being of a magnitude hitherto undreamed of in our market, were necessarily made at an interest which he regarded as high, though lenders strenuously insisted on higher; but large amounts are now obtained at five and four per cent., while the circulation of United States notes constitutes practically a loan from the people to their government without interest.   The average rate on the whole loan is thus reduced to 4⅔ per cent.   Whether a similar result may attend future loans must be determined partly by the legislation of Congress, partly by the conduct of the war, and partly by the condition of the markets for money.

The statements of the actual and estimated receipts and expenditures for the last and the current fiscal year, in comparison with those of the December report, must undergo modifications similar to those of the public debt. Both receipts and expenditures for the current and the following year will be increased: the former by the operations of the augmented tariff and of the internal revenue, and the latter by the exigencies of the war.

The aggregate receipts for the fiscal year 1862, from all sources, including the balance of $2,257,065 80 in the treasury from the preceding year, were $583,885,247 06; and the aggregate expenditures $570,841,700 25; leaving a balance in the treasury on the 1st day of July, 1862, of $13,043,546 81. From the receipts and from the expenditures should be deducted the amounts both received and disbursed within the year on account of permanent and temporary debt, amounting to $96,096,922 09; leaving the total of receipts not applied in payment of debt $487,788,324 97, and the total of current disbursements $474,744,778 16. As the amount of debt, so also the amount of the expenditures for the last year falls short of the estimates.

The actual receipts for the first quarter of the fiscal year 1863, commencing July 1, 1862, appear from the books of the treasury; the receipts for the three remaining quarters can only be estimated on the basis of appropriations made and asked for by the several departments. They have been and are estimated as follows:

For the 1st quarter the actual receipts from customs, internal duties, direct tax, lands, and all other sources, excluding loans, and including the balance, from last year, of $13,043,546 81, were·· $37,208,529 02

For the 2d, 3d, and 4th quarters the estimated receipts from all sources are··············· 143,286,816 58

Making the total of actual and estimated receipts, from ordinary sources and from the direct tax, during the year 1863·················· 180,495,345 60

To this sum must be added sums already realized from loans in all forms, which amounted, during the 1st quarter, to··········$114,458,821 02

And during the months of October and November, estimating for some of the last days of November, to····················· 85,670,895 99

Making an amount already obtained from loans to the 1st of December, and applied in payment of current expenditure and principal and interest of public debt, of························· 200,129,717 01

And there must be added, also, the amount which will probably be hereafter realized from loans in all forms, under existing laws, namely ········ $131,021,197 35

Making the total of receipts, actual and anticipated, under existing laws············ ············ 511,646,259 96

On the other hand—

For the 1st quarter of the fiscal year 1863 the actual expenditures were···················· 111,084,447 40

For the 2d, 3d, and 4th quarters the actual and estimated expenditures, under existing appropriations, including interest on public debt, are 672,843,841 78

And additional appropriations are asked for by the several departments, to meet estimated deficiencies, to the amount of······ ··············· 109,418,032 30

Making the whole amount actually expended or estimated···················· ··············· 893,346,321 48

To which must be added the estimate for payment of principal of public debt during the year, of·· 95,212,456 14

Making an aggregate, for all purposes, of···· 988,558,777 62

It is necessary to observe, however, that in the present state of the law the estimates of the departments always largely exceed expenditures. The law forbids the transfer of any part of an appropriation for one object or class of objects to another. Consequently, when any appropriation happens to be exhausted, expenditures for the objects of it, however important, must be arrested until a further appropriation can be had. Such an occurrence during the recess of Congress might occasion great public inconvenience and injury. Hence it has become usual to make every estimate large enough to cover all possible requirements under it till a session of Congress shall afford an opportunity of providing for any deficiencies which may thereafter occur. Hence there is always a large balance of unexpended appropriations at the end of every fiscal year, which, after two years from the making of them, are carried to the credit of what is called the surplus fund.

It may be safely estimated, therefore, that, of the appropriations made and asked for, there will remain unexpended on the 30th June, 1863, and should, of course, be deducted from the apparent aggregate of expenditures, not less than $200,000,000 00

The deduction of this sum will leave as the true aggregate of expenditures for the year········   788,558,777 62

But of this sum, as already stated, there has been received and may be expected from customs, internal duties, and other ordinary sources········· $180,495,345 60

And from loans in all forms·····   331,150,914 36

Making an aggregate of realized and anticipated resources, to be deducted from the sum of actual and anticipated expenditures for all purposes, of   511,646,259 96

And leaving yet to be provided for the current year by the action of Congress··················   276,912,517 66

The estimates for the fiscal year 1864, commencing on the 1st day of July next, and ending on the 30th day of June, 1864, must, in the present circumstances of the country, be, in great part, conjectural. The estimates of expenditures have been framed by the several departments on the supposition of the continuance of the war—a supposition which, though very properly assumed as the basis of estimates intended to cover all contingencies, is not, it may be confidently hoped, destined to be realized. The estimates of receipts are based upon the operations of recently enacted laws, the working of which cannot be accurately foreseen.

The estimates of expenditures are as follows:

For the civil list, including foreign intercourse and miscellaneous expenses, other than on account of the public debt······················ $25,081,510 08

For the Interior Department, Indians and Pensions   10,346,577 01

For the War Department·····················   738,829,146 80

For the Navy Department····················   68,257,255 01

For interest on public debt··················   33,513,890 50

For principal of public debt·················   19,384,804 16

                                                895,413,183 56

To which sum should be added the expenditures for which appropriations made are estimated as remaining undrawn on the 1st July, 1863······   200,000,000 00

Making the aggregate of expenditures to the 1st July, 1864, for which appropriations are made or asked······································ 1,095,413,183 56

From which should be deducted the probable amount of appropriations which will remain undrawn on the 1st of July, 1864 .... $250,000,000 20

Making the true amount of probable expenditures during the fiscal year, 1864 845,413,18

The estimates of receipts are as follows :

From customs	$70,000,000
From internal duties	150,000,000
From lands	25,000
From miscellaneous sources	3,000,000

Making the aggregate of receipts for the fiscal year 1864 to be deducted from the aggregate of expenditures 223,025,000 00

And leaving the amount of expenditures of the fiscal year 1864 to be provided for 622,388,183 56

The whole amount to be provided by Congress, beyond resources available under existing laws, may, therefore, upon the supposition of the continuance of the war, be stated as follows :

For the fiscal year 1863 .... 276,912,517 66
For the fiscal year 1864 .... 622,388,183 56

Making an aggregate of 899,300,701 22

A tabular statement is submitted with this report, and as part of it, exhibiting clearly the details of the receipts and expenditures of the financial years 1862, 1863, and 1864.

Another table is also submitted, in which may be seen of what particulars the existing debt consists, in what years it was contracted, and when and in what amounts it will become due.

The other tables required by law also accompany this report.

In order to the formation of sound opinions as to the measures required for meeting the demands disclosed by the estimates and yet unprovided for, it may be useful to review, briefly, in connexion with their actual and probable results, the measures already recommended and adopted, or yet under legislative consideration.

With a view to the necessary provision for the expenditures then anticipated, the Secretary proposed to Congress, at its last session, such measures as seemed to him best adapted to the attainment of that object. These were (1st) an increase of duties on various imports ; (2d) an increase of the direct tax ; (3d) the levying of internal duties; (4th) a limited emission of United States notes, convertible into coin ; (5th) the negotiation of loans, facilitated by the organization of banking associations, whose circulation should consist only of notes uniform in character, furnished by the government, and secured, as to convertibility into coin, by United States bonds deposited in the treasury.

At the time these recommendations were submitted, the banks had not suspended specie payments, and there was reason to believe that economized expenditure and decisive military action would secure the means required for the suppression of the rebellion without serious sacrifices on the part of the government, and without resort to any other currency than that of coin and equivalent notes.

Unexpected military delays, however, increased expenditures, diminished confidence in public securities, and made it impossible for the banks and capitalists, who had taken the previous loans, to dispose of the bonds held by them except at ruinous loss, and impossible for the government to negotiate new loans of coin except at like or greater loss.

These conditions made a suspension of specie payments inevitable. The banks of New York suspended on the 30th of December, 1861. Their example was followed by most of the banks throughout the country, and the government yielded to the same necessity in respect to the United States notes then in circulation.

These changed circumstances required a change of measures. The expenditures had already reached an average of nearly a million and a quarter of dollars each secular day; while the revenue from all sources hardly exceeded one-tenth of that sum. It was necessary, therefore, to raise by loans in some form about thirty millions a month, or sixty millions every sixty days.

Careful inquiries satisfied the Secretary that the first $60,000,000 could not be had, in coin, at better rates than a dollar in bonds for eighty cents in money; and that each succeeding loan would involve submission to increasingly disadvantageous terms. To obtain the first $60,000,000 would require, therefore, an issue of bonds to the amount of $75,000,000, and, of course, an increase of the public debt by the same sum; the next $60,000,000 would require, perhaps, $90,000,000 in bonds and debt; and the next $60,000,000, if obtainable at all, would require, perhaps, $120,000,000. It was easy to see that on this road utter discredit and paralysis would soon be reached. The adoption of a plan of finance involving such consequences was not compatible with the Secretary's ideas of public duty.

There remained but one other possible way of raising money by the negotiation of bonds in the usual mode. That way was, to receive in payment of loans the notes or credits of the banks in suspension.

To ascertain what would have been the consequences of a resort to this expedient, it is necessary to remember that the bank circulation of the loyal States amounted, on the 1st day of January, 1861, to $150,000,000; that it had been reduced to $130,000,000 on the 1st day of January, 1862; and that this circulation was diffused throughout the country in all the channels of business. In these circumstances the collection by loans of sufficient amounts to meet the demands upon the treasury in season for prompt payments would be extremely difficult. The negotiation of such loans to the extent required by the public exigencies, would create a demand for the notes which would involve the necessity, at first, of sacrifices not greatly inferior to those attendant on coin loans. If subsequent negotiations should become practicable at seemingly better rates, it would be because the government demand had stimulated the making and issuing of bank notes to an extent far beyond the ordinary needs of business. The increase of circulation thus stimulated would be unlimited, except by the possibility of obtaining interest on loans of it; or, in other words, by the possibility of obtaining credit for it with the community and the government. This limit, certain to be finally reached by all banks improvidently managed, would not, however, be reached immediately, or at the same time by all institutions, or by the same rate of progress in all parts of the country. But an excessive circulation would surely be thrust upon the community, forming a currency, everywhere, but irregularly depreciated, destined in part to become worthless, and certain to tax and derange, beyond measure, the business of the people, and to embarrass, if not arrest, the operations of the government. Loans negotiated in this circulation would be simply exchanges of the debts of the nation, bearing interest and certain to be paid, for the debts of a multitude of corporations, bearing no interest and certain, in part, never to be paid.

This is but a partial representation of the consequences apprehended from the receipt of bank notes for loans to the government. Their character made it impossible for the Secretary to recommend such negotiations, and wholly improbable that Congress would authorize them, if recommended.

No other mode of providing, with any tolerable degree of promptitude, for the wants of the army and navy, and the necessities of other branches of the public service, seemed likely to effect the object with so little public inconvenience and so considerable public advantage as the issue of United States notes adapted to circulation as money, and available, therefore, immediately in government payments.

It was not necessary that the Secretary should recommend this plan to Congress. In his report at the commencement of the session he had pointed out the inconveniences and dangers of a circulation of government notes, even though convertible into specie, and had dwelt especially on the probability that such a circulation would ultimately sink into an irredeemable paper currency. At that time he expected a continuance of specie payments, and hoped that a banking system would be authorized which would at once furnish a sound circulating medium and afford a firm support to the public credit. Neither the expectation' nor the hope, however, had been realized; and a choice was now to be made between a currency furnished by numerous and unconnected banks in various States and a currency furnished by the government which the government could and would, except in a very improbable, not to say impossible, contingency, amply provide for and protect. With these alternatives before him, the Secretary had already declared his unhesitating preference for a circulation authorized and issued by national authority. But the enlightened senators and representatives who composed the financial committees of the respective houses required no new statement of his views on this subject. They saw clearly the necessities created by the suspension, and at once adopted the measure demanded by them. The Secretary, concurring entirely in their judgment, had no duty to perform except that of giving such information and such aid as they called for and he could supply.

An emission of $59,000,000 had been authorized by Congress at the July session, 1861, not with the design of furnishing a general currency, but for the purpose of making good any differences between the amounts obtained by loans and the sums required by the public service. Of these notes $33,460,000 were in circulation at the time of the suspension. Up to that date every note presented for payment had been promptly redeemed in coin. After the suspension an additional emission of $10,000,000 was authorized, on the 12th of last February. Both these issues, amounting together to $60,000,000, were made receivable for all public dues, including customs.

It now became the duty of Congress, not merely to provide the means of meeting the vast demands on the treasury, but to create a currency with which, until the close of the war at least, loans and taxes might be paid to the government, debts to individuals discharged, and the business of the country transacted. Nothing less would satisfy the need of the time.

This duty Congress partially performed by authorizing an emission of $90,000,000 in United States notes, in addition to the $60,000,000 previously authorized, making $150,000,000 in all. The $90,000,000 last issued were made receivable for all national loans and dues, except customs, payment of which was required in specie or notes of the two first issues.

At a later period of the session, in view of the withdrawal of the sixty millions receivable for duties from circulation, and of the expediency of providing a permanent resource for meeting all demands upon temporary deposits in the treasury, Congress authorized a further issue of $150,000,000, of which, however, $50,000,000 were to be reserved from issue until actually required for payment of deposits.

At a still later date Congress, upon the recommendation of the Secretary, authorized the use of postage and revenue stamps as a fractional currency, preferring this expedient to metallic tokens or coins reduced in value below existing standards.

These various acts, taken together, authorized the emission of two hundred and fifty millions of dollars in United States notes, and a further emission of fifty millions, if needed, for the payment of deposits. Of these emissions, the sixty millions receivable for customs were not available as circulation, but might be replaced, as paid in, by notes of the new issues which were thus available, so that, in the end, a total circulation of two hundred and fifty millions might be reached, and, in an improbable contingency, increased by fifty millions more. An emission of fractional currency, as just stated, was also authorized.

In aid of these provisions for public payments, the Secretary recommended, and Congress, by different enactments, authorized, the receipt on temporary deposit, at an interest not exceeding five per cent., of such sums as might be offered, not exceeding, in the whole, one hundred millions of dollars, and the payment, to such creditors as might choose to receive them of certificates of indebtedness, payable in one year and bearing six per cent. interest. Congress also authorized the issue of national bonds to the amount of five hundred millions of dollars, into which the United States notes issued might be converted at the will of the holder. It was provided that these bonds should carry an interest of six per cent. in specie, and be redeemable after five and payable in twenty years. They have received the name of five-twenties or five-twenty-sixes.

These measures have worked well. Their results have more than fulfilled the anticipations of the Secretary. Had other urgent demands on the attention of Congress permitted the consideration and adoption of the suggestions which the Secretary ventured to submit in favor of authorizing the formation, under a proper general law, of banking associations, issuing only uniform notes prepared and furnished by the national government, and of imposing a reasonable tax on the circulation of other institutions, no financial necessity would, perhaps, now demand additional legislation for the current year, except such as experience might suggest for the perfecting of measures already sanctioned.

A short statement will exhibit the practical workings of the laws actually enacted.

To the 1st day of July, 1862, $57,926,116 57 had been received and were remaining on deposit. United States notes to the amount of $158,591,230 had been issued and were in circulation; $49,881,979 73 had been paid in certificates of indebtedness; and $208,345,291 86 had been paid in cash. Not a single requisition from any department upon the treasury remained unanswered. Every audited and settled claim on the government, and every quartermaster's check for supplies furnished, which had reached the treasury, had been met. And there remained in the treasury a balance of $13,043,546 81.

The reverses of June, July, and August, affected, of course, injuriously this financial condition. The vast expenditures required by the large increase of the army, authorized by Congress and directed by the President, made exhausting demands on all available resources. The measures of Congress, however, enabled the Secretary to provide, if not fully yet almost fully, for the constantly increasing disbursements. The actual payments, other than for principal of public debt, during the quarter ending on the 30th of September, were $111,084,446 75; during the month of October they were $49,243,846 04; and during the month of November, $59,847,077 34; while the accumulation of requisitions beyond resources amounted to less than the fourth of the aggregate of these sums, namely, to $48,354,701 22.

It remains to consider what further resources for satisfying the debt now existing in the form of requisitions, and meeting other present and prospective demands upon the treasury, may be provided under existing legislation; and what additional measures may be beneficially adopted for the improvement of the revenue and for the sure establishment of the public credit, by the discharge, with the greatest possible promptitude and punctuality, of all public obligations.

The whole power to borrow money under the act of July, 1861, to authorize a national loan is now exhausted. The only important laws under which means for meeting demands on the treasury can be had are those enacted or modified by Congress at its last session.

These are of two general classes, namely, those which provide revenue from duties and taxes, and those which authorize the obtaining of money by loans in various forms.

The laws of the first class are, (1st,) the several acts imposing duties on imports, and (2d,) the act to provide internal revenue.

The laws of the second class are, (1st,) the act authorizing the issue of United States notes, and of six per cent bonds of the United States, redeemable after five and payable in twenty years, to the amount of five hundred million of dollars; (2d,) the two acts authorizing the issue of certificates of indebtedness and the purchase of coin; (3d,) the act authorizing an additional issue of United States notes; and (4th,) the act authorizing payments in stamps.

The laws of the first class have been too recently enacted, and their practical operation and results are affected by too large a variety of circumstances, to warrant any very confident opinions either as to the particulars in which amendments may be required or the amount of revenue which may be expected from them. The year which will elapse before the next regular session of Congress will allow sufficient time for practical tests, and will doubtless suggest beneficial modifications. It seems already probable that some taxes imposed may be either repealed or reduced in rate at that session, without injury to the public service or the public credit. Possibly, also, some comparatively unimportant changes may be indicated as useful before the close of the present session.

The actual and estimated receipts under these laws for the current fiscal year, as already stated, will amount under the tariff act to $68,041,736 59, and under the internal revenue law to $85,456,303 73. The receipts for all other sources, exclusive of loans, as estimated, will reach $13,953,758 47, making a general aggregate, including $13,043,546 81, balance from last year, of $180,495,345 60, and leaving to be provided from loans, in some form, $608,063,432 02.

The laws of the second class limit the issue of United States notes, exclusive of the contingent reserve for deposits, to $250,000,000; limit the amount receivable on temporary deposit to $100,000,000; and limit the issue of five-twenty sixes to $500,000,000. The issue of certificates of indebtedness and of fractional currency is unlimited by legislation.

The amount of United States notes, including notes receivable for customs, already issued and in circulation or in the treasury to the credit of disbursing officers or of the Treasurer, was on the 1st instant $222,932,111. There yet remains, therefore, under the law an authority to issue the further sum of $27,067,889. The amount received on deposit, including coin and estimating for the last day of November, is $79,798,650. The further sum of $20,201,350 may therefore yet be received. The issue of fractional currency has reached the sum of $3,884,800. The best lights lead to the estimate that before specie payments can be resumed not less than $40,000,000 will be required by the wants of the community. The sum of $36,115,200, not yet issued, may therefore be counted on as an additional resource. It is not easy to determine what further payments can be made in certificates of indebtedness, but it seems probable that payments in that form may be safely carried to the amount of $100,000,000. These payments have already reached $87,363,241 65, and the additional sum of $12,636,758 35 may therefore be paid in that way. What can be justly expected from conversions under the act authorizing the issue of five-twenty sixes, that is to say, from exchanges by holders of United States notes for these bonds, at par, cannot be stated with much certainty. The amount received from this source from the date of the act to the 1st instant, estimating for part of the last week in November, is $23,750,000. It may reasonably be expected that thirty-five millions will be received, if the act remains unmodified, during the remainder of the fiscal year. The aggregate of all these sums, namely, $131,021,197 35, constitutes the total of resources available for the current year under existing laws, except through sales, regarded as impracticable under the act authorizing their issue, of the five-twenties at their market value.

These credit resources, with the actual receipts from like sources, added to revenue in all forms may supply the treasury with $511,646,259 96. There remains a balance of disbursements of $276,912,517 66 to be provided for.

How?

The easiest mode doubtless would be an issue of the required amount in United States notes; but such an issue, especially in the absence of proper restrictions on corporate circulation, would, in the judgment of the Secretary, be as injurious as it would be easy. The addition of so vast a volume to the existing circulation would convert a currency, of which the benefits have thus far greatly outweighed the inconveniences, into a positive calamity. Its consequences would be inflation of prices, increase of expenditures, augmentation of debt, and, ultimately, disastrous defeat of the very purposes sought to be attained by it.

To a certain extent, however, and under certain circumstances, a limited additional issue of United States notes may perhaps be safely and advantageously made.

The Secretary does not concur in the opinion entertained by some, whose ability and experience command deserved respect, that the aggregate currency of the country, composed of United States notes and notes of corporations, is at this moment greatly in excess of legitimate demands for its employment. Much less does he concur in another opinion, not unfrequently expressed, but expressed, in his

REPORT ON THE FINANCES.

judgment, without due consideration, that any actual excess is due
to the issues of United States notes already in circulation.

It is true that gold commands a premium in notes ; in other words,
that to purchase a given amount of gold a greater amount in notes is
required.   But it is also true that, on the suspension of specie payments
and the substitution for coin of United States notes, convertible into
six per cent. specie bonds as the legal standard of value, gold became
an article of merchandise, subject to the ordinary fluctuations of supply and demand, and to the extraordinary fluctuations of mere specu-
lation.   The ignorant fears of foreign investers in national and State
bonds and other American securities, and the timid alarms of
numerous nervous individuals in our own country, prompted large
sacrifices upon evidences of public and corporate indebtedness in our
markets, and large purchases of coin for remittance abroad or hoard-
ing at home.   Taking advantage of these and other circumstances
tending to an advance of gold, speculators employed all the arts of the
market to stimulate that tendency and carry it to the highest point.
This point was reached on the 15th day of October.   Gold sold in
the market at a premium of 37⅜ per cent.

That this remarkable rise is not due wholly, or even in greatest
part, to the increase of the currency, is established beyond reasonable
doubt by considerations now to be stated:

First. The whole quantity of circulation did not, at the time, greatly,
if at all, exceed the legitimate demands of payments.   On the 1st
day of November, 1861, the circulation of United States notes, including credits to disbursing officers and to the Treasurer of the
United States, was $15,140,000.   On the 1st day of November, 1862,
it was, with like inclusions, $210,104,000.   Of corporate notes, on the
1st of November, 1861, the circulation in the loyal States was, according to the best estimates, $130,000,000; on the 1st of November, 1862,
it was $167,000,000.   The coin in circulation, including the coin in
banks, was probably not less, on the 1st of November, 1861, than
$210,000,000.   On the 1st of November, 1862, the coin had been
practically demonetized and withdrawn from use as currency or as a
basis for currency, and is therefore not estimated.   The aggregate
circulation of the loyal States, therefore, was, at the first date,
$355,140,000; and at the second, only $377,104,000.

Secondly. The whole, or nearly the whole, increase in the volume
of the currency which has taken place was, it is believed, legitimately demanded by the changed condition of the country in the year
between the two dates.   The activity in business which, at the close
of that year, had taken the place of the general stagnation which
marked its beginning, and the military and naval preparations and
movements which had vastly augmented the number and amounts of
payments to be made in money, have, it is believed, legitimately
demanded nearly or quite the whole of it.

That such is the case may be reasonably inferred from the fact that
the prices of many of the most important articles of consumption
have declined or not materially advanced during the year.   Wheat,
quoted at $1 38 to $1 45 per bushel on the 1st of November, 1861, was

quoted at $1 45 to $1 50 on the 1st of November, 1862. Prime mess pork, on the 1st of November, 1861, was quoted at $15 to $15 50 per barrel, and on the 1st of November, 1862, at $12 50 to $13. Corn sold on the 1st of November, 1861, at 62 to 63 cents per bushel, and on the 1st of November, 1862, at 71 to 73 cents. A comparison between the prices of hay, beef, and some other staples of domestic produce at the two dates, exhibits similar conditions of actual depression in price or moderate rise.

Thirdly. It is, perhaps, still more conclusive against the theory of great redundancy that on the 15th day of October, when the aggregate actual circulation, national and corporate, was about $360,000,000, the premium on gold was 37⅜; whereas, on the 29th day of November, when the circulation had increased by more than twenty millions, the premium on gold was 29 to 30 per cent.

But if the fact of considerable redundancy in circulation be conceded, it by no means follows that it is the circulation of United States notes which is redundant.

It must be remembered that the law confines national payments and receipts to coin and notes of the United States. Officers of the treasury, officers of the army and navy, all officers of all departments, must observe and enforce this law. For all payments to be made in behalf of the United States, in case of inability to obtain coin, United States notes *must* be issued. It is, indeed, the duty of the legislature to see that the purchasing power of these notes is kept as nearly as possible equal to the purchasing power which gold would have had if specie payments had been maintained; but the issue and use of the notes is unavoidable, and the government can resort to borrowing only when the issue has become sufficiently large to warrant a just expectation that loans of the notes can be had from those who hold or can obtain them at rates not less advantageous than those of coin loans before suspension. The difficulty which the takers of the recent loan of $13,613,450 found in obtaining United States notes with which to meet their engagements to the treasury is very instructive on this head. It points, indeed, directly to the conclusion that loans of United States notes, in sufficient amounts to meet the disbursements of the government, could not now be obtained at rates which a due regard to the interests of the tax-payers would permit the Secretary to accept. Whatever may be said of the aggregate circulation, it cannot, then, be successfully maintained that the circulation of United States notes is excessive. When extended to the limits authorized by existing laws, it will be no larger than the wants of the people and the government imperatively demand.

If there be a considerable redundancy then; if there be a considerable real depreciation of the circulation—which is by no means admitted—what has caused the redundancy and the depreciation?

The cause of all that exists is easily found in the statements of the banking corporations. The circulation of corporate notes increased during the year ending on the 1st of November, 1862, from $130,000,000 to $167,000,000. During the same time the volume of deposits, which answer very many of the purposes of circulation, had swelled from $264,000,000 to $344,000,000. The greater portion of this increase took place within the last seven months.

The augmentation of deposits always accompanies increase of circulation. Together they stimulate loans, and are, in turn, stimulated by the desire of the interest derived from loans. As might have been anticipated, loans increased, though not equally, with the circulation and deposits. From $607,000,000 on the 1st day of November, 1861, they had grown to $677,000,000 on the 1st day of November, 1862.

Here is an obvious and sufficient explanation of whatever undue expansion may have taken place. The Secretary has already expressed the opinion that the circulation is not greatly redundant, and that no considerable depreciation of currency has actually occurred. He thinks it sufficiently proved, however, that whatever there may of either is fairly attributable not to the increase of United States notes, but to the increase of bank circulation and deposits.

It is to be observed that no law compelled and no public necessity required any enlargement of the volume of currency by the banks. On the contrary, there are, in some of the States, positive enactments by which the increase of circulation during suspension is prohibited; and the principle embodied in them is so obviously just that well-managed institutions, when obliged to suspend, almost invariably, without the constraint of any law, reduce their circulation instead of augmenting it. In obedience to this principle, a reduction of bank circulation actually took place after the suspension in December. It was only when United States notes, having been made a legal tender, were diverted from their legitimate use as currency and made the basis of bank circulation, that the great increase of the latter began. It was purely voluntary; prompted, doubtless, by the desire of extending accommodations to business as well as by the expectation of profit. No practical limit upon this increase has as yet been proposed by the parties interested in it.

The Secretary has already shown that the case was far otherwise with the circulation of United States notes. A condition had been created by the suspension which made loans of coin impossible. Loans of corporate notes, objectionable in themselves, were positively prohibited by a law not likely to be repealed. The extension of the United States note circulation, until sufficient in amount to enable the Secretary to obtain it from holders by way of loans, was equally inevitable. A practical limit on its increase is imposed by the judicious legislation of Congress, which makes the notes receivable for loans, and requires that the interest on bonds for loans shall be paid in coin.

Under these circumstances, the path of wisdom and duty seems very clear. It leads to the support of a United States note circulation, and to the reduction of the bank note circulation. A comparatively small reduction of the latter will allow ample room for the whole increase of the former, authorized by existing laws; and as the reduction proceeds the increase may be extended, never, however, passing the point which admits the negotiation of loans at reasonable rates. The Secretary has heretofore advised the imposing of a moderate tax on corporate circulation, and now renews

the recommendation as the best means of reduction and gradual substitution. Such a tax involves no hardships. Notes circulating as
money cost nothing beyond the expense of production and supervision, and yet form a highly accumulative species of property. The
necessities of the war have caused the taxation of almost all forms of
value. Can there be a sound reason for exempting that which costs
the proprietor least and brings him most?

It may be properly added that this desirable substitution of a circulation, uniform in description and value, for a circulation varying
widely in both, may, perhaps, be more easily and beneficially effected
now than at any other time. The circulation of United States notes
may greatly facilitate the payments to the banks through which their
own notes must be withdrawn; and thus, not only protect the community from the inconveniences, but the banks from the losses which
might otherwise attend reduction.

It may also be added that when the substitution shall have been
accomplished, and, perhaps, if circumstances favor, at an earlier
period, payments in specie of United States notes may be resumed
with less cost and less injury to business than would attend a like
resumption in payment of corporate notes. With comparatively
trivial sacrifice, the government can, whenever its expenditures are
reduced to its revenue, provide, by loan or otherwise, all the coin
needed to commence and maintain the resumption.

While the Secretary thus repeats the preference he has heretofore
expressed for a United States note circulation, even when issued directly by the government, and dependent on the action of the government for regulation and final redemption, over the note circulation of
the numerous and variously organized and variously responsible
banks now existing in the country; and while he now sets forth,
more fully than heretofore, the grounds of that preference, he still
adheres to the opinion expressed in his last report, that a circulation
furnished by the government, but issued by banking associations,
organized under a general act of Congress, is to be preferred to
either. Such a circulation, uniform in general characteristics, and
amply secured as to prompt convertibility by national bonds deposited
in the treasury, by the associations receiving it, would unite, in his
judgment, more elements of soundness and utility than can be combined in any other.

A circulation composed exclusively of notes issued directly by the
government, or of such notes and coin, is recommended mainly by
two considerations:—the first derived from the facility with which it
may be provided in emergencies, and the second, from its cheapness.

The principal objections to such a circulation as a permanent system are, 1st, the facility of excessive expansion when expenditures
exceed revenue; 2d, the danger of lavish and corrupt expenditure,
stimulated by facility of expansion; 3d, the danger of fraud in management and supervision; 4th, the impossibility of providing it in sufficient amounts for the wants of the people whenever expenditures
are reduced to equality with revenue or below it.

These objections are all serious. The last requires some elucidation. It will be easily understood, however, if it be considered that a government issuing a credit circulation cannot supply, in any given period, an amount of currency greater than the excess of its disbursements over its receipts. To that amount, it may create a debt in small notes, and these notes may be used as currency. This is precisely the way in which the existing currency of United States notes is supplied. That portion of the expenditure not met by revenue or loans has been met by the issue of these notes. Debt in this form has been substituted for various debts in other forms. Whenever, therefore, the country shall be restored to a healthy normal condition, and receipts exceed expenditures, the supply of United States notes will be arrested, and must progressively diminish. Whatever demand may be made for their redemption in coin must hasten this diminution; and there can be no reissue; for reissue, under the conditions, necessarily implies disbursement, and the revenue, upon the supposition, supplies more than is needed for that purpose. There is, then, no mode in which a currency in United States notes can be permanently maintained, except by loans of them, when not required for disbursement, on deposits of coin, or pledge of securities, or in some other way. This would convert the treasury into a government bank, with all its hazards and mischiefs.

If these reasonings be sound, little room can remain for doubt that the evils certain to arise from such a scheme of currency, if adopted as a permanent system, greatly overbalance the temporary though not inconsiderable advantages offered by it.

It remains to be considered what results may be reasonably expected from an act authorizing the organization of banking associations, such as the Secretary proposed in his last report.

The central idea of the proposed measure is the establishment of one sound, uniform circulation, of equal value throughout the country, upon the foundation of national credit combined with private capital.

Such a currency, it is believed, can be secured through banking associations organized under national legislation.

It is proposed that these associations be entirely voluntary. Any persons, desirous of employing real capital in sufficient amounts, can, if the plan be adopted, unite together under proper articles, and, having contributed the requisite capital, can invest such part of it, not less than a fixed minimum, in United States bonds, and, having deposited these bonds with the proper officer of the United States, can receive United States notes in such denominations as may be desired, and employ them as money in discounts and exchanges. The stockholders of any existing banks can, in like manner, organize under the act, and transfer, by such degrees as may be found convenient, the capital of the old to the use of the new associations. The notes thus put into circulation will be payable, until resumption, in United States notes, and, after resumption, in specie, by the association which issues them, on demand; and if not so paid will be redeemable at the treasury of the United States from the proceeds of the bonds pledged in security. In the practical working of the plan, if sanc-

tioned by Congress, redemption at one or more of the great commercial centres, will probably be provided for by all the associations which circulate the notes, and, in case any association shall fail
in such redemption, the treasurer of the United States will probably,
under discretionary authority, pay the notes, and cancel the public
debt held as security.

It seems difficult to conceive of a note circulation which will com-
bine higher local and general credit than this. After a few years no
other circulation would be used, nor could the issues of the national
circulation be easily increased beyond the legitimate demands of
business. Every dollar of circulation would represent real capital,
actually invested in national stocks, and the total amount issued could
always be easily and quickly ascertained from the books of the
treasury. These circumstances, if they might not wholly remove
the temptation to excessive issues, would certainly reduce it to the
owest point, while the form of the notes, the uniformity of devices,
the signatures of national officers, and the imprint of the national seal
authenticating the declaration borne on each that it is secured by
bonds which represent the faith and capital of the whole country,
could not fail to make every note as good in any part of the world as
the best known and best esteemed national securities.

The Secretary has already mentioned the support to public credit
which may be expected from the proposed associations. The importance of this point may excuse some additional observations.

The organization proposed, if sanctioned by Congress, would require within a very few years, for deposit as security for circulation,
bonds of the United States to an amount not less than $250,000,000.
It may well be expected, indeed, since the circulation, by uniformity
in credit and value, and capacity of quick and cheap transportation,
will be likely to be used more extensively than any hitherto issued, that the demand for bonds will overpass this limit. Should
Congress see fit to restrict the privilege of deposit to the bonds
known as five-twenties, authorized by the act of last session, the
demand would promptly absorb all of that description already issued
and make large room for more. A steady market for the bonds would
thus be established and the negotiation of them greatly facilitated.

But it is not in immediate results that the value of this support would
be only or chiefly seen. There are always holders who desire to sell
securities of whatever kind. If buyers are few or uncertain, the
market value must decline. But the plan proposed would create a
constant demand, equalling and often exceeding the supply. Thus a
steady uniformity in price would be maintained, and generally at a
rate somewhat above those of bonds of equal credit but not available
to banking associations. It is not easy to appreciate the full benefits
of such conditions to a government obliged to borrow.

Another advantage to be derived from such associations would be
found in the convenient agencies which they would furnish for the
deposit of public moneys.

The Secretary does not propose to interfere with the independent
treasury. It may be advantageously retained, with the assistant

treasurers already established in the most important cities, where the customs may be collected as now, in coin or treasury notes issued directly by the government, but not furnished to banking associations.

But whatever the advantages of such arrangements in the commercial cities in relation to customs, it seems clear that the secured national circulation furnished to the banking associations should be received everywhere for all other dues than customs, and that these associations will constitute the best and safest depositaries of the revenues derived from such receipts. The convenience and utility to the government of their employment in this capacity, and often, also, as agents for payments and as distributers of stamps, need no demonstration. The necessity for some other depositaries than surveyors of ports, receivers, postmasters, and other officers, of whose responsibility and fitness, in many cases, nothing satisfactory can be known, is acknowledged by the provision for selection by the Secretary contained in the internal revenue act; and it seems very clear that the public interest will be secured far more certainly by the organization and employment of associations organized as proposed than by any official selection.

Another and very important advantage of the proposed plan has already been adverted to. It will reconcile, as far as practicable, the interests of existing institutions with those of the whole people.

All changes, however important, should be introduced with caution, and proceeded in with careful regard to every affected interest. Rash innovation is not less dangerous than stupefied inaction. The time has come when a circulation of United States notes, in some form, must be employed. The people demand uniformity in currency, and claim, at least, part of the benefit of debt without interest, made into money, hitherto enjoyed exclusively by the banks. These demands are just and must be respected. But there need be no sudden change; there need be no hurtful interference with existing interests. As yet the United States note circulation hardly fills the vacuum caused by the temporary withdrawal of coin; it does not, perhaps, fully meet the demand for increased circulation created by the increased number, variety, and activity of payments in money. There is opportunity, therefore, for the wise and beneficial regulation of its substitution for other circulation. The mode of substitution, also, may be judiciously adapted to actual circumstances. The plan suggested consults both purposes. It contemplates gradual withdrawal of bank note circulation, and proposes a United States note circulation, furnished to banking associations, in the advantages of which they may participate in full proportion to the care and responsibility assumed and the services performed by them. The promptitude and zeal with which many of the existing institutions came to the financial support of the government in the dark days which followed the outbreak of the rebellion is not forgotten. They ventured largely, and boldly, and patriotically on the side of the Union and the constitutional supremacy of the nation over States and citizens. It does not at all detract from the merit of the act that the losses, which they feared but unhesitatingly risked, were transmuted into unexpected gains. It is a solid recommendation of the suggested

plan that it offers the opportunity to these and kindred institutions
to reorganize, continue their business under the proposed act, and
with little loss and much advantage, participate in maintaining the
new and uniform national currency.

The proposed plan is recommended, finally, by the firm anchorage
it will supply to the union of the States. Every banking association
whose bonds are deposited in the treasury of the Union ; every indi-
vidual who holds a dollar of the circulation secured by such deposit ;
every merchant, every manufacturer, every farmer, every mechanic,
interested in transactions dependent for success on the credit of that
circulation, will feel as an injury every attempt to rend the national
unity, with the permanence and stability of which all their interests
are so closely and vitally connected.   Had the system been possible,
and had it actually existed two years ago, can it be doubted that the
national interests and sentiments enlisted by it for the Union would
have so strengthened the motives for adhesion derived from other
sources that the wild treason of secession would have been impossible ?

The Secretary does not yield to the phantasy that taxation is a
blessing and debt a benefit ; but it is the duty of public men to ex-
tract good from evil whenever it is possible.   The burdens of taxation may be lightened and even made productive of incidental benefits
by wise, and aggravated and made intolerable by unwise, legislation.
In like manner debt, by no means desirable in itself, may, when circumstances compel nations to incur its obligations, be made by discreet
use less burdensome, and even instrumental in the promotion of public and private security and welfare.

The rebellion has brought a great debt upon us.   It is proposed to
use a part of it in such a way that the sense of its burden may be
lost in the experience of incidental advantages.   The issue of United
States notes is such a use ; but if exclusive, is hazardous and temporary.   The security by national bonds of similar notes furnished to
banking associations is such a use, and is comparatively safe and permanent; and with this use may be connected, for the present, and
occasionally, as circumstances may require, hereafter, the use of
the ordinary United States notes in limited amounts.

No very early day will probably witness the reduction of the public
debt to the amount required as a basis for secured circulation.   Should
no future wars arrest reduction and again demand expenditures beyond
revenue, that day will, however, at length come.   When it shall arrive.
the debt may be retained on low interest at that amount, or some
other security for circulation may be devised, or, possibly, the vast
supplies of our rich mines may render all circulation unadvisable
except gold and the absolute representatives and equivalents, dollar
for dollar, of gold in the treasury or on safe deposit elsewhere.   But
these considerations may be for another generation.

The Secretary forbears extended argument on the constitutionality
of the suggested system.   It is proposed as an auxiliary to the power
to borrow money; as an agency of the power to collect and disburse
taxes; and as an exercise of the power to regulate commerce, and of

the power to regulate the value of coin. Of the two first sources of power nothing need be said. The argument relating to them was long since exhausted and is well known. Of the other two there is not room nor does it seem needful to say much. If Congress can prescribe the structure, equipment, and management of vessels to navigate rivers flowing between or through different States as a regulation of commerce, Congress may assuredly determine what currency shall be employed in the interchange of their commodities, which is the very essence of commerce. Statesmen who have agreed in little else have concurred in the opinion that the power to regulate coin is, in substance and effect, a power to regulate currency, and that the framers of the Constitution so intended. It may well enough be admitted that while Congress confines its regulation to weight, fineness, shape, and device, banks and individuals may issue notes for currency in competition with coin. But it is difficult to conceive by what process of logic the unquestioned power to regulate coin can be separated from the power to maintain or restore its circulation, by excluding from currency all private or corporate substitutes which affect its value, whenever Congress shall see fit to exercise that power for that purpose.

The recommendations, now submitted, of the limited issue of United States notes as a wise expedient for the present time, and as an occasional expedient in future times, and of the organization of banking associations to supply circulation secured by national bonds and convertible always into United States notes, and after resumption of specie payments, into coin, are prompted by no favor to excessive issues of any description of credit money.

On the contrary, it is the Secretary's firm belief that by no other path can the resumption of specie payments be so surely reached and so certainly maintained. United States notes receivable for bonds bearing a secure specie interest are next best to notes convertible into coin. The circulation of banking associations organized under a general act of Congress, secured by such bonds, can be most surely and safely maintained at the point of certain convertibility into coin. If, temporarily, these associations redeem their issues with United States notes, resumption of specie payments will not thereby be delayed or endangered, but hastened and secured; for, just as soon as victory shall restore peace, the ample revenue, already secured by wise legislation, will enable the government, through advantageous purchases of specie, to replace at once large amounts, and, at no distant day, the whole, of this circulation by coin, without detriment to any interest, but, on the contrary, with great and manifest benefit to all interests.

The Secretary recommends, therefore, no mere paper money scheme, but, on the contrary, a series of measures looking to a safe and gradual return to gold and silver as the only permanent basis, standard, and measure of values recognized by the Constitution— between which and an irredeemable paper currency, as he believes, the choice is now to be made.

No country possesses the true elements of a higher credit—no country, in ordinary times, can maintain a higher standard of currency and payment than the United States.

The government is less costly than that of most other great powers. The expenditures of the current fiscal year, excluding those of the War and Navy Departments, can hardly equal those of the last year, which amounted to $24,511,476 66. Estimating those of these departments at double the expenditures of the last year before the rebellion, they would for the current year, had the war ended before last midsummer as was anticipated at the date of the last report, amount to the sum of $55,845,834 48. The interest on the public debt is for the current year estimated at $25,041,532 07, and will not probably go over that sum. The whole expenditures of the government for the current year, on the supposition of peace, would, therefore, not exceed $105,371,843 21. This aggregate must be increased hereafter by the addition of interest on the loans of the current and future years and by pensions, the precise amount of which cannot be foreseen. Estimate the former at fifty, and the latter at ten millions a year, and the total annual expenditures in peace will reach, omitting fractions, to $165,000,000. The expenditures of Great Britain during the year ending March 31, 1862, were $364,436,682; those of France for 1862, according to French official estimates, will reach $421,823,900, and the annual expenses of Russia, according to the best accessible information, do not fall short of $230,000,000.

To meet our annual expenditures, and to assure beyond contingency the punctual discharge of the interest of the public debt, and the creation of a sinking fund for its reduction, Congress has provided a revenue from customs even now reaching nearly seventy millions a year, and a revenue from internal duties which will not probably fall short of one hundred and fifty millions a year.

Without reckoning any other resources than those already provided, the revenue, therefore, will annually exceed the expenditures by fifty-five millions, which sum may be used for the reduction of the public debt. If, then, the war shall be continued, contrary to hope and expectation, to midsummer of 1864, and the public debt shall reach the utmost limit now anticipated of seventeen hundred and fifty millions of dollars, the excess of revenue will reduce that debt, during the first year of peace, more than three per cent.

But the American republic possesses immense resources which have not yet been called into contribution. The gold-bearing region of the United States stretches through near eighteen degrees of latitude, from British Columbia on the north to Mexico on the south, and through more than twenty degrees of longitude, from the eastern declivities of the Rocky mountains to the Pacific ocean. It includes two States, California and Oregon; four entire Territories, Utah, Nevada, New Mexico, and Washington; and parts of three other Territories, Colorado, Nebraska, and Dakota. It forms an area of more than a million of square miles, the whole of which, with comparatively insignificant exceptions, is the property of the nation. It is rich not only in gold, but in silver, copper, iron, lead, and many other valuable minerals. Its product of gold and silver during the current year will not probably fall very much, if at all, short of $100,000,000; and it must long continue gradually, yet rapidly, to increase. If this product be subjected to a reasonable seignorage, as suggested by some, or if, as suggested by others, the mineral lands be subdivided and sold in convenient parcels, with proper reservations in favor of the miners now in occupation of particular localities, a very considerable revenue may, doubtless, be obtained from this region without hardship to the actual settlers and occupiers.

And there are other mines than those of gold or silver, or copper or iron, in the wide territory which includes the public lands of the United States. Every acre of the fertile soil is a mine which only waits for the contact of labor to yield its treasures; and every acre is opened to that fruitful contact by the Homestead Act. When the opportunities thus offered to industry shall be understood by the working millions of Europe, it cannot be doubted that great numbers will seek American homes, in order to avail themselves of the great advantages tendered to their acceptance by American law. Every working man who comes betters the condition of the nation as well as his own. He adds in many ways, seen and unseen, to its wealth, its intelligence, and its power. It is difficult to estimate the contribution which immigration, properly encouraged by legislation and administration, will make to revenue; but, directly and indirectly, it cannot be reckoned as less than that which may be expected from the metallic products of the gold-bearing region.

With such resources at the disposal of the republic, no one need be alarmed lest the United States may become unable to pay the interest on its debt, or to reduce the principal to whatever point the public interest may indicate. The republic is passing through the pangs of a new birth to a nobler and higher life. Twice already she has paid off a national debt contracted for the defence of her rights; the obligations of that which she now incurs for the preservation of her existence will be not less sacredly fulfilled.

But while resources are thus ample, it is not the less the dictate of prudence and of good faith to a generous people that the greatest pains should be taken to reduce the public burdens to the lowest point compatible with justice to honest public creditors. Prodigality may exhaust the amplest resources and impair the firmest credit. To retrench superfluity; to economize expenditures; to adjust accurately measures to objects; to infuse resolute vigor and a just sense of responsibility into every department of public activity are not less important to credit and revenue than to general success in administration.

It has been already stated that the amount to be provided, beyond resources available under existing laws, is, for the current year, $276,912,517 66, and for the ensuing year, $627,388,183 56.

To provide these amounts loans in some form must be negotiated.

The Secretary has already expressed the opinion, with great deference to the superior wisdom of Congress, that it will be unwise, unless conditions greatly change, to authorize the increase of United States notes beyond the limit now fixed by law. Should any vacuum be created by the withdrawal of bank note circulation, that vacuum should, doubtless, be filled by United States notes. Should Congress adopt the measures proposed by the Secretary, it is not improbable that an additional issue of fifty millions may be required for that purpose within the year, and an equal additional issue during the following year. And it may well be hoped that military successes, reestablishing the authority of the United States in large districts of the insurgent region, will call for further issues to supply the place of the worthless currency which the rebellion has forced upon the people. Should it be deemed expedient to invest the Secretary with any discretionary power, in view of these contingencies, it should be so limited as to allow no increase of aggregate circulation beyond the clear demands of real business.

A considerable additional sum may probably be obtained by removing the limit on temporary deposits. The amount of these deposits has steadily increased, notwithstanding large repayments to depositors. The treasury of the government has been made the savings bank of the people. Should the restriction be removed, there is reason to believe that twenty-five millions may be received beyond the maximum now fixed, during the year.

But the chief reliance, and the safest, must be upon loans. Without any issues of United States notes beyond the amount now authorized, it seems certain that loans for the whole amount required for the current year can be readily obtained at fair rates ; and it may be confidently hoped that before its close the resources of the country will be so well understood, and the restoration of its territorial integrity so well assured, that capitalists will not hesitate to supply whatever may be needed for the subsequent year.

But in order to the advantageous negotiation of loans the action of Congress is necessary.

As an important element of facility in negotiation, the plan for banking associations has been already considered. Little direct aid is, however, to be expected from this plan during the present, nor very much, perhaps, during the next year. The operation of associations organized under it must, at first, be restricted mainly to investing United States notes in bonds; issuing a circulation based on these bonds; and transacting ordinary business. As the notes received for the bonds cannot be reissued without injurious inflation of the circulation, they must necessarily be withdrawn and cancelled. The aggregate circulation of government United States notes withdrawn will be replaced by the amount of national circulation furnished to the associations. The immediate advantage to the government will be found in the market created for bonds, and the support thereby given to the national credit. The more general advantages which have been described must attend the gradual organization of banking associations, and will only be fully apparent when the national circulation furnished to them shall become the established and sole note circulation of the country.

Other legislation is therefore needed.

The act of last session authorized the Secretary to issue bonds of the United States, already often mentioned as five-twenties, to the amount of five hundred millions of dollars, and to dispose of them for coin or United States notes at the market value thereof. In the same act authority was given to issue $150,000,000 in United States notes, which authority was afterwards enlarged to $250,000,000; and it was provided that any holder of such notes to the amount of fifty dollars, or any multiple of fifty, might exchange them for five-twenty bonds, at par.

The effect of these provisions was to make negotiations of considerable amounts impossible; for considerable amounts are seldom taken, except with a view to resales at a profit, and resales at any profit are impossible under the law. Negotiations below market value are not allowed, and if not allowed the taker of the bonds can expect no advance, unless a market value considerably below par shall become established. The act makes advance above par impossible, by authorizing conversion of United States notes into bonds at that rate.

The Secretary respectfully recommends the repeal of both these provisions. The first imposes, it is believed, a restriction which Congress did not intend; and the second has been followed by the inconveniences which were feared, rather than by the benefits which were expected. Convertibility by exchange at will is of little or no advantage to the holder of the notes; for the clauses which secure their receivability for all loans make them practically convertible. Whenever the volume of notes reaches a point at which loans can be effected at rates fair to the country and desirable to takers, loans will, of course, be made, and ample opportunities for conversion offered.

Should Congress, however, be of opinion that these clauses should be retained, it will be necessary to provide for other loans, at rates more favorable to the takers than convertibility into five-twenties. This can be done either by authorizing bonds at longer time, or by increasing the rates of interest offered.

The Secretary cannot recommend either course except as an alternative to no provision at all.

As such an alternative he would prefer the issue of 7.30 three years bonds, convertible into five-twenty sixes at or before maturity, and of smaller notes bearing an interest of 3.65 per cent., as proposed in his first report.

A discretionary power may, perhaps, be advantageously conferred on the Secretary, to be exercised as exigencies may require or allow. He does not covet the responsibilities belonging to such a power, but would not shrink from such exercise of it as, in his best judgment, the public good would require. He believes it, however, to be unnecessary. He believes that the time and rate of the five-twenty loan authorized were judiciously determined, and he believes that if the suggested changes are made in the law, the needed supplies can be obtained through these loans. No prudent legislator, at a time when the gold in the world is increasing by a hundred millions a year, and interest must necessarily and soon decline, will consent to impose on the labor and business of the people a fixed interest of six per cent on a great debt, for twenty years, unless the necessity is far more urgent than is now believed to exist. The country has already witneseed the results of such measures in the payment, in 1856, of more than four and a half millions of dollars for the privilege of paying a debt of less than forty-one millions, some twelve years, averaged time, before it became due.

The general views of the Secretary may therefore be thus briefly summed:

He recommends that whatever amounts may be needed beyond the sums supplied by revenue and through other indicated modes be obtained by loans, without increasing the issue of United States notes beyond the amount fixed by law, unless a clear public exigency shall demand it. He recommends, also, the organization of banking associations for the improvement of the public credit and for the supply to the people of a safe and uniform currency. And he recommends no change in the law providing for the negotiation of bonds except the necessary increase of amount and the repeal of the absolute restriction to market value and of the clauses authorizing convertibility at will.

If Congress shall concur in these views, the Secretary, though conscious of the great difficulties which vast, sudden, and protracted expenditures impose on him, ventures to hope that he may still be able to maintain the public credit and provide for the public wants.

The report of the director of the mint contains the usual information relative to the coinage for the past year, and makes several suggestions, to which I respectfully invite your attention.

The net amount of bullion received was $45,423,231 01. The amount coined was: of gold coins, $45,532,386 50; of silver coins, $2,812,401 50; of cent coins, $116,000; of gold bars, $16,144,190 05; and of silver bars, $418,680 01; making a total coinage of $65,023,658 06.

Of the bullion deposited, $26,188,863 87 was received at the assay office in New York. Of the gold bars $16,094,768 44, and of silver bars $415,633 57, in value, were stamped at the same office.

At the branch mint in San Francisco the gold deposits were $16,136,622 96, and the silver deposits and purchases $749,114 14, in value. The value of the gold coined was $15,545,000; of silver coined, $641,700; and of silver bars, $1,278 65.

Soon after the authority of the Union was re-established at New Orleans a special agent was appointed to examine the condition of the branch mint in that city, and its machinery. The machinery proved to have been greatly injured, and portions of it were found distributed and secreted in various parts of the city. The portions were collected and replaced in the mint, and the necessary repairs are in progress. The operations of the branch mint, however, have not been, and for the present, at least, will not be, resumed.

By the act of April 24, last, a branch mint was directed to be established at Denver, in the Territory of Colorado, and an appropriation of $75,000 was made to carry the act into effect. A mint had already been established there by individuals engaged in assaying and stamping, on private account, the bullion produced in that region. A commission was appointed to ascertain and report as to the value of this establishment and the comparative expediency of purchasing it or erecting a new one; and, upon their recommendation, the existing mint, with all its apparatus, was purchased for $25,000.

The Secretary respectfully commends to the consideration of Congress the expediency of establishing an assay office or branch mint at some convenient point in Nevada Territory.

In his last report the Secretary took occasion to invite the attention of Congress to the importance of uniform weights, measures, and coins, and to the worth of the decimal system in the commerce of the world. He now ventures to suggest that the present demonetization of gold may well be availed of for the purpose of taking one considerable step towards these great ends. If the half eagle of the Union be made of equal weight and fineness with the gold sovereign of Great Britain, no sensible injury could possibly arise, from the change; while, on the resumption of specie payments, its great advantages would be felt in the equalization of exchange and the convenience of commerce. This act of the United States, moreover, might be followed by the adoption by Great Britain of the federal decimal divisions of the coin, and thus a most important advance might be secured towards an international coinage, with values decimally expressed.

Under the provisions of the several acts of Congress relative to trade and commerce between the loyal States and those States and parts of States declared to be in insurrection, general regulations have been issued prescribing the conditions under which that trade and commerce, to a limited extent, may be conducted. This trade has been authorized only with sections of the country in which, since the proclamation of the President, the authority of the government has been re-established by military occupancy. No licenses or permits have been granted for commerce with inhabitants of insurrectionary districts beyond the limits of such occupancy. Under the provisions of the fifth section of the act of July 13, 1861, special agents have been appointed whose duty has been to carry out the authorized instructions of the department, and it is anticipated that the expenses of their agency will be defrayed from moderate charges for permits granted under their supervision.

The collection of cotton, rice, and other abandoned property, and the superintendence of laborers and plantations which, at the date of my last report, was committed to agents of this department, has since been transferred, as more properly belonging to his department, to the control of the Secretary of War.

The report of the Solicitor of the Treasury, and the suggestions made by him, are entitled to consideration.

During the last session the Secretary had the honor of transmitting the draft of a bill for the detection and prevention of fraudulent entries at the custom-houses, and he adheres to the opinion that the provisions therein embodied are necessary for the protection of the revenue. That invoices representing fraudulent valuations of merchandise are daily presented at the custom-houses is well known, and for the past year the collector, naval officer, and surveyor of New

York have entertained suspicions that fraudulent collusions with some of the customs-officers existed. Measures were taken by them to ascertain whether these suspicions were well founded. By persistent vigilance facts were developed which have led to the arrest of several parties and the discovery that a system of fraud has been successfully carried on for a series of years. These investigations are now being prosecuted under the immediate direction of the Solicitor of the Treasury for the purpose of ascertaining the extent of those frauds and bringing the guilty parties to punishment. It is believed that the enactment at the last session of the bill referred to would have arrested, and that its enactment now will prevent hereafter, the frauds hitherto successfully practiced.

The increased and increasing labors and responsibilities devolved upon the collector at New York suggest the expediency of appointing an additional officer at that port, to be denominated the assistant collector and authorized to act for the collector, during his necessary absence, and to perform such other duties as may be prescribed or approved by the Secretary of the Treasury. Provision should be made that his authentication of any lawful document shall entitle it to the same effect in the courts and elsewhere as the signature of the collector, and that his acts shall not impair the responsibility of the collector or of his sureties, to the government.

The Exchange building in the city of New York, leased for three years for use as a custom-house, has been altered, and for some time partially occupied. The complete removal to it of the customs-officers will soon be accomplished. The whole of the old custom-house building will be required by the assistant treasurer; and it will be necessary, therefore, either to purchase the rented building or to erect another for custom-house purposes. It is believed that it would be impossible to purchase an equally eligible site and erect an equally suitable edifice for the price fixed in the lease of the Exchange; and it is therefore recommended that the option to purchase at that price be availed of.

The administration of the hospital fund has been looked to with great care, and the expense of its distribution, it is believed, reduced to the most economical point. As has been before reported, the number of hospitals is in excess of the legitimate requirements of the seamen, and the Secretary repeats his recommendation of December last, that those least advantageously situated be disposed of on the most favorable terms. During the past year all the hospitals under the control of this department have, in whole or in part, been placed at the disposal of the War Department for the use of sick and disabled soldiers. This use, not originally contemplated, has been most opportune and beneficial.

Under the act authorizing payments in stamps an arrangement was made with the Postmaster General for a supply of postage stamps to be distributed for use in such payments. It was soon discovered, however, that stamps prepared for postage uses were not adapted to the purposes of currency. Small notes of equal amounts were therefore substituted, and the Secretary assumed the charge of preparation and distribution. With utmost efforts it was found impossible to

keep pace with the public demand for this currency; and, although
the daily issue has been rapidly increased to $100,000 and is being
extended as fast as practicable to twice that amount, the supply is
yet largely deficient. The whole demand, however, will be fully met
as soon as possible.

With a view to test the practicability and economy of engraving
and printing United States notes at the department under the act of
July 11, 1861, the Secretary has contracted for paper, and has authorized the preparation of small notes as substitutes for revenue
stamps, substantially like the small notes now substituted for postage
stamps, and indulges the hope that results will commend his action to
the approval of Congress, and that the necessary modification of the
provisions relating to stamps and engraving will receive its sanction.

Some difficulties have been encountered in the practical execution
of the act of last session, directing the monthly instead of quarterly
rendition of disbursing officers' accounts, and their direct transmission to the accounting officers of the treasury, without preliminary
examination by the chiefs of the administrative bureaus; and these difficulties, though not insuperable, may require some further legislation
for their removal. But the reform sought by the act is important,
and the purpose of accomplishing it should not be relinquished.

Statements in detail of the operations of the department will
be found in the reports of the heads of the several bureaus, to
whom the Secretary gladly acknowledges his obligations for most
faithful and assiduous labors, by which the multiform business under
his general charge, increased tenfold in consequence of the insurrection, has been carried on with a degree of success hardly believed
to be attainable. The unprecedented increase in the volume and
variety of accounts must necessarily require more clerical force and
more room in order to the prompt settlement indispensably necessary
to the protection of honest creditors, and to the security of the government from fraud. These great objects, it is believed, may also
be promoted by a modification of the existing arrangement of the
bureaus, so as to bring all the accounts of each department into one
bureau instead of dividing them between several, as is now directed.

The Bureau of Internal Revenue has been organized under the act
of last session, and is now actually engaged in the labors assigned to
it. Collectors and assessors have been appointed in all the districts
of the loyal States, and the revenue from the duties imposed by the
law is steadily and rapidly increasing. In the absence of any statu-
tory directions, he has assigned the settlement of the accounts of the
bureau to the Fifth Auditor and First Comptroller.

The Secretary invites particular attention to the remarks of the
Third Auditor relative to payments for property lost or destroyed in
the military service. He also respectfully suggests that authority be
given to the Secretary to appoint commissioners to examine and
audit the claims of the several States now referred to that office for
settlement.

The favorable consideration of Congress is respectfully invited to
the requests of the Treasurer and of the Register of the Treasury

for the appointment of a deputy in each of their bureaus. Of the necessity for such appointments no doubt is entertained.

The action of the supervising inspectors of steamboats, collectively as a board, and individually in their respective districts, merits the approval of Congress. Their report, to which the Secretary invites attention, gives evidence of the value of their labors, while the comparative immunity from accidents secured by their vigilance attests the wisdom of the act under which their work is prosecuted.

The regulations directing the examination of applicants for appointment in the revenue cutter service, and making certificates of competency from the board of examiners pre-requisites to commissions, tend manifestly to the improvement of the service, and will be adhered to. This service has become an essential arm of the department in the execution of the laws. Its highest vigor and activity will especially be demanded so long as the present high rates of duty shall be required by the exigencies of the country. The Secretary hopes to be able to place it on a footing of the utmost efficiency, without permitting its cost to exceed appropriations already made. The great demand by other departments for shipwrights and machinery has not, as yet, permitted advantageous contracts for the additional revenue steamers authorized by Congress. Careful specifications, however, have been prepared, and the work will be proceeded with as soon as practicable.

Full details of the operations of the Coast Survey will appear in the report of the Superintendent.

The services by which its great value was strikingly illustrated during the earlier months of the rebellion have been continued with undiminished zeal and fidelity to the present time, and its general work has been prosecuted with as much activity and success as the peculiar demands made upon it by the circumstances of the country would allow.

Within the year 43,000 copies of maps and charts have been furnished for naval vessels, and 2,000 to captains and pilots of government transports on their personal application.

Its accustomed vigilant superintendence has been exercised by the Light-house Board over the light-houses, light-ships, beacons, and buoys on the northern and Pacific coasts, and especial attention has been directed to the restoration of those destroyed by the rebel enemies of the country. Numerous lights and beacons have been re-established on the coast of the insurgent region, and the re-establishment of others will keep pace with the progress of the fleets and armies of the republic. A confident expectation is indulged that along the whole coast will soon shine the old unbroken chain of lights for the guidance of the mariner and the security of commerce.

All which the Secretary most respectfully submits to the indulgent consideration of Congress.

S. P. CHASE,
Secretary of the Treasury

Hon. H. HAMLIN,
 Vice President of the United States and
   President of the Senate.

No. 1.

RECEIPTS AND EXPENDITURES

For the fiscal year ending June 30, 1862.

RECEIPTS.

The total receipts, including a balance on hand July 1, 1861, of $2,257,065 80 were $583,885,247 06, as follows:

From customs	$49,056,397 62	
From lands	152,203 77	
From miscellaneous sources	931,787 64	
From direct tax	1,795,331 73	
		$51,935,720 76
From loans—		
For 3 years 7.30 bonds	122,037,585 34	
For 5.20 years 6 per cent. bonds	13,990,600 00	
For Oregon war bonds	1,000,700 00	
For 20 years' bonds, 6 per cent., at par, for $50,000,000 7 per cents	46,303,129 17	
For 2 years' treasury notes, under act of June 22, 1860, and March 2, 1861	14,019,034 66	
For 60-day treasury notes, under act of March 2, 1861	12,896,350 00	
For treasury notes, under acts February 8 and March 2, 1861	3,500 00	
Under loan act February 8, 1861	55,257 50	
For United States notes, acts July 17 and August 5, 1861, and February 12, 1862	60,030,000 00	
For United States notes, act February 25, 1862	98,620,000 00	
From temporary loan, act February 25, 1862	66,479,324 10	
From certificates of indebtedness, acts March 1 and 17, 1862	49,881,979 73	
From temporary loan, in anticipation of popular subscription	44,375,000 00	
		529,692,460 50
Aggregate receipts		581,628,181 26
Balance in treasury		2,257,065 80
Total resources		583,885,247 06

EXPENDITURES.

The aggregate expenditures were $570,841,700 25
From which, to show the actual current expenditures of the government, should be deducted the payments of *principal* of the public debt, the repayment of temporary loans, and substitution of United States notes, under acts February 25, 1862; for United States notes, under acts July 17 and

August 5, 1861, and February 12, 1862, retired from circulation, amounting, altogether, to $96, 096, 922 09

Which leaves, as current expenditures for the support of the government and of the war, *including* the interest on the public debt, in all forms, the aggregate sum of 474, 744, 778 16

More fully stated, as follows:

For the civil list	$21, 408, 491 16	
For pensions and Indians	3, 102, 985 50	
For interest	13, 190, 324 45	
		$37, 701, 801 11
For the War Department ....;........		394, 368, 407 36
For the Navy Department		42, 674, 569 69

Aggregate current expenditures $474, 744, 778 16

And on account of *public debt and loans*, deducted as above:

Old funded debt	3 06	
Redemption of purloined treasury notes, act April 10, 1846	51 50	
Redemption treasury notes, under acts prior to July 22, 1846	50 00	
Redemption treasury notes, under acts December, 1857, December, 1860, and March 2, 1861	43, 110, 000 00	
Repayment of temporary loan from banks, made in anticipation of popular subscription ...... :............	44, 375, 000 00	
Repayment on account of temporary loan, under acts February 25 and March 17, 1862	8, 553, 207 53	
United States notes, act July 17, 1861, retired by substitution	58, 610 00	
		96, 096, 922 09

	570, 841, 700 25
Leaving balance in treasury July 1, 1862, of	13, 043, 546 81
	583, 885, 247 06

RECEIPTS AND EXPENDITURES

For the year ending June 30, 1863.

The receipts and expenditures, as submitted for the current year, show the actual transactions for the quarter ending 30th September last, and are estimated for the three remaining quarters. The basis of estimated expenditures is the appropriations already made and those asked for. From the aggregate amount is deducted the probable balance that will remain undrawn on the 1st July next, by which the amount actually required during the year is more accurately shown than it would otherwise be.

RECEIPTS.

Actual, first quarter, and estimated for three quarters of the year ending June 30, 1863.

From customs :

First quarter, (actual)	$23,041,736 59	
Second, third, and fourth quarters, (estimated)	45,000,000 00	
		$68,041,736 59

From lands :

Actual, one quarter	22,181 04	
Estimated, three quarters	66,543 12	
		88,724 16

From miscellaneous sources :

Actual, one quarter	561,079 08	
Estimated, three quarters	1,683,237 24	
		2,244,316 32

From the direct tax :

Actual, one quarter	83,681 77	
Estimated, three quarters	11,537,036 22	
		11,620,717 99

From internal duties :

Actual, one quarter	456,303 73	
Estimated, three quarters	85,000,000 00	
		85,456,303 73

Aggregate receipts, actual and estimated, from all sources other than from loans for the year	167,451,798 79
Balance in treasury July 1, 1862	13,043,546 81
	180,495,345 60

EXPENDITURES.

The estimates being based upon appropriations made and asked for the current year, and including the balances of former appropriations unexpended on the 1st July last :

For the civil service, foreign intercourse, and miscellaneous :

First quarter, (actual)	$4,436,907 32	
Second, third, and fourth quarters, appropriated	27,697,497 94	
Appropriations asked for,(deficiency)	677,137 97	
		$32,811,543 23

For Interior Department, pensions and Indians :

First quarter, (actual)	1,046,906 42	
Second, third, and fourth quarters, appropriated	4,925,350 88	
Appropriations asked for,(deficiency)	10,649 13	
		5,982,906 43

Ex. Doc. 1——3

For the War Department :

First quarter, (actual)	$90, 869, 850 88	
Second, third, and fourth quarters, appropriated	547, 759, 732 90	
Appropriations asked for,(deficiency)	108, 730, 245 20	
		$747, 359, 828 98

For the Navy Department :

First quarter, (actual)	10, 076, 353 91	
Second, third, and fourth quarters, appropriated	72, 101, 156 86	
		82, 177, 510 77

For interest on public debt :

First quarter, (actual)	4, 654, 428 87	
Second, third, and fourth quarters required	20, 360, 103 20	
		25, 014, 532 07

Aggregate from all sources other than for principal of public debt	893, 346, 321 48
Of this amount of $893,346,321 48 it may be safely estimated that there will remain undrawn on the 30th of June next the sum of	200, 000, 000 00
Making the estimated aggregate amount required during the year, ending June 30, 1863, for the support of the government and of the war, the sum of	693, 346, 321 48

Add for public debt due and becoming due during the year, as follows :

Treasury notes, under various acts	$2, 849, 111 64	
Loan of 1842	2, 883, 364 11	
Certificates of indebtedness	49, 881, 979 73	
Temporary loan	9, 913, 510 66	
U. S. notes, act Feb. 25, (retired)	2, 000, 000 00	
Three years' bonds	2, 000 00	
U. S. notes, act 17th July, (retired)	27, 682, 490 00	
		95, 212, 456 14

Aggregate for the year	788, 558, 777 62
Deduct actual and estimated receipts from all sources other than loans for the year	180, 495, 345 60
And there remains to be provided	608, 063, 432 02

In addition to the sum of $180,495,345 60, the actual and estimated receipts for the year from sources other than loans, there has been received from loans and applied to current expenditures and payment of public debt during the quarter ending September 30, 1862 :

For 2 year 6 p. c. treasury notes, under act March 2, 1861	$1, 500 00
For 3 year 7.30 bonds .	3, 550, 000 00
For 5.20 year 6 p. cent. bonds	2, 539, 803 45

For Oregon war bonds.	$145,050 00	
For U. S. treas'y notes, act Feb. 25, 1862...	72,436,000 00	
For temporary loan, act February 25.......	22,813,843 14	
For certificate indebt'ss	12,184,824 43	
For fractional currency	787,800 00	
		$114,458,821 02

And during October and November:		
For 3 year 7.30 bonds..	13,613,450 00	
For 5.20 year 6 p. cent. bonds...........	7,219,596 55	
For U. S. notes, under act Feb. 25, 1862...	21,587,211 00	
For fractional currency.	3,097,000 00	
For certif's indebt'ss ..	31,181,437 39	
For temporary loan....	8,972,200 95	
		85,670,895 99
		$200,129,717 01

Leaves still to be provided......................	407,933,715 01
The estimated additional receipts from sources under existing laws are...	131,021,197 35
Showing a deficiency of.............................	276,912,517 66

With the interest accruing on that sum.

RECEIPTS AND EXPENDITURES

As estimated for the year ending June 30, 1864.

RECEIPTS.

From customs.......................................	$70,000,000 00
From lands	25,000 00
From miscellaneous sources..........................	3,000,000 00
From internal duties................................	150,000,000 00
Aggregate.................................	223,025,000 00

EXPENDITURES.

Balance of former appropriations estimated to be unexpended July 1, 1863...	$200,000,000 00
For civil service, foreign intercourse, and miscellaneous...	25,081,510 08
For Interior Department, Indians, and pensions.........	10,346,577 01
For the War Department.............................	738,829,146 80
For the Navy Department............................	68,257,255 01
For interest on public debt	33,513,890 50
Principal of public debt.............................	19,384,804 16
	1,095,413,183 56

Of this amount of $1,095,413,183 56, it may be safely esti-
mated that there will remain undrawn on the 30th June,
1864, the sum of.................................... $250, 000, 000 00

Aggregate for the year............................... 845, 413, 183 56
The estimated receipts, as before stated, for that year are
placed at... 223, 025, 000 00

Leaving to be provided for by loans the sum of 622, 388, 183 56

No. 2.

Statement of duties, revenues, and public expenditures during the fiscal year ending June 30, 1862, agreeably to warrants issued, exclusive of trust funds.

The receipts into the treasury during the fiscal year ending June 30, 1862, were as follows:

From customs, viz:

During the quarter ending September 30, 1861.	$7,198,602 55	
During the quarter ending December 31, 1861..	8,309,066 47	
During the quarter ending March 31, 1862.....	14,618,558 44	
During the quarter ending June 30, 1862......	18,930,170 16	
		$49,056,397 62

From direct tax, viz:

During the quarter ending June 30, 1862......................		1,795,331 73

From sales of public lands, viz:

During the quarter ending September 30, 1861.	36,967 03	
During the quarter ending December 31, 1861..	39,658 46	
During the quarter ending March 31, 1862.....	27,019 74	
During the quarter ending June 30, 1862......	49,558 54	
		152,203 77
From miscellaneous and incidental sources...........................		931,787 64

From loans, treasury notes, and certificates of indebtedness, viz:

Loan under act of February 8, 1861..............	55,257 50	
Loan of November 16, 1861.....................	46,303,129 17	
Stock for the Washington and Oregon war debt.	1,000,700 00	
$\frac{7}{10}$ years bonds, per act of February 25, 1862...	13,990,600 00	
Three years bonds, at 7 $\frac{3}{10}$ per cent...........	166,412,585 34	
Temporary loan, per act of February 25, 1862..	66,479,324 10	
Treasury notes issued under act of June 22, 1860, as authorized by act of March 2, 1861.......	14,019,034 66	
Sixty days' treasury notes issued per act of March 2, 1861	12,896,350 00	
United States notes payable on demand.........	50,030,000 00	
Treasury notes issued per acts of February 8 and March 2, 1861...............................	3,500 00	
Treasury notes issued per act of February 25, 1862.	98,620,000 00	
Certificates of indebtedness authorized by acts of March 1 and 17, 1862.................	49,881,979 73	
		529,692,460 50

Total receipts...:.............................		581,628,181 26
Balance in the treasury on July 1, 1861.................		2,257,065 80
Total means.................................		583,885,247 06

The expenditures during the fiscal year ending June 30, 1862, were as follows:

LEGISLATIVE, EXECUTIVE, JUDICIAL, &C.

For Congress, including books......................	$2,516,852 76	
For executive......................................	1,958,410 96	
For judiciary	958,464 56	
For governments in the Territories.................	216,785 78	
For officers of mint, branch San Francisco, and assay office, New York.............................	90,925 00	
For assistant treasurers and their clerks...........	48,104 02	
For supervising and local inspectors, &c...........	57,756 08	
For surveyors general and their clerks.............	91,710 13	
Total civil list..		5,939,009 29

FOREIGN INTERCOURSE.

For salaries of ministers	$326,950 14
For salaries of secretaries and assistant secretaries of legation	41,697 83
For salaries of secretaries of legation to China and Turkey acting as interpreters	1,130 60
For salaries of consuls	352,829 39
For salaries of interpreters to consuls in China	5,139 47
For salaries of marshals for consular courts in Japan, &c	2,583 05
For interpreters, guards, and other expenses of consulates in Turkish dominions	1,965 27
For intercourse with the Barbary powers	345 38
For contingent expenses of all missions abroad	50,275 31
For contingent expenses of foreign intercourse	79,303 96
For loss by exchange on drafts of consuls and commercial agents	14,976 37
For office rent to those consuls who are not allowed to trade	21,981 14
For purchase of blank books, stationery, &c., for consuls	27,672 75
For preservation of the archives of the several consulates	3,747 62
For relief and protection of American seamen	166,233 48
For bringing home from foreign countries persons charged with crime	5,188 36
For rent of prisons for American convicts in Japan, &c	4,239 36
For bringing from Sidney eight seamen belonging to the ship "Junior," charged with the crimes of mutiny and murder, &c	12,770 46
For expenses in acknowledging the services of masters and crews of foreign vessels in rescuing American citizens from shipwreck	4,000 00
For defraying the expenses of the Japanese embassy	259 01
For expenses incident to the execution of the neutrality act	7 50
For carrying out stipulations, &c., in the treaty between the United States and Hanover	44,497 06
For compensation of commissioner, &c., to carry into effect convention between United States and republics of New Granada and Costa Rica	8,499 92
For compensation of commissioner, &c., to run and mark boundary between United States and British possessions bounding on Washington Territory	15,029 00
For expenses of the representation of the industrial interests of the United States at the exhibition of all nations at London in 1862	2,000 00
For awards under the convention between the United States and republics of New Granada and Costa Rica	146,387 92
Total foreign intercourse	$1,333,710 35

MISCELLANEOUS.

For mint establishment	526,116 75
For contingent expenses under the act for the safe-keeping of the public revenue	48,120 33
For compensation to persons designated to receive and keep the public revenue	938 65
For compensation to special agents to examine books, &c., in the several depositories	2,128 23
For building vaults as additional security to the public funds in 66 depositories	1,281 96
For expenses of engraving, &c., treasury notes and certificates of stock	39,239 69
For defraying the expenses of a national loan, &c	507,318 67

For premium on the purchase of coin	$9,312 50
For survey of the Atlantic and Gulf coasts of the United States	199,900 00
For survey of the western coast of the United States.	111,000 00
For survey of the Florida reefs and keys	18,000 00
For fuel and quarters of officers of the army serving on coast survey	1,000 00
For publishing observations made in the progress of the survey of the coast of the United States	5,000 00
For pay and rations of engineers of steamers used in the coast survey	8,000 00
For repairs of vessels used in the coast survey	10,000 00
For running a line to connect the triangulation on the Atlantic coast with that on the Gulf of Mexico	1,000 00
For completing the works of the exploring expedition	1,220 05
For putting the plates of the exploring expedition in order for preservation	1,500 00
For paying arrears due authors and artists of exploring expedition	4,796 51
For payment for horses and other property lost or destroyed in the military service of the United States.	9,819 67
For claims not otherwise provided for	2,645 01
For expenses of the Smithsonian Institution, per act of August 10, 1846	30,910 14
For mail services performed for the several departments of government, per 12th section act of March 3, 1847	200,000 00
For further compensation to the Post Office department for mail services performed for the two houses of Congress, &c., per act March 3, 1851	250,000 00
For supplying deficiencies in the revenues of the Post Office Department	2,932,596 43
For transportation of mails between the United States and foreign countries	65,382 12
For carrying the mails from New York, via Panama, to San Francisco	113,750 00
For continuation of the Treasury building	294,511 46
For building post offices, court-houses, &c., including purchase of sites	23,454 85
For public buildings in the Territories	7,217 20
For expenses of collecting the revenue from customs	3,264,724 63
For repayments to importers the excess of deposits for unascertained duties	1,642,940 35
For debentures or drawbacks, bounties or allowances.	637,224 20
For debentures and other charges, per act October 16, 1837	6,918 05
For salaries of special examiners of drugs and medicines	4,122 41
For additional compensation to collectors, naval officers, &c.	6,355 89
For refunding duties on fish, &c., under reciprocity treaty with Great Britain	2,609 88
For refunding duties on arms imported by States	65,173 50
For support and maintenance of light-houses, &c.	621,575 81
For building light-houses, &c., and for beacons, buoys, &c.	42,599 68
For life-boats, compensation of keepers of stations.	16,935 29
For marine hospital establishment	290,447 41
For building marine hospitals, including repairs	5,226 78
For building custom-houses, including repairs	26,066 26
For expenses of collecting revenue from sales of public lands	170,912 22
For survey of the public lands	92,480 03
For survey of public and private land claims in California	12,985 20

For resurvey of lands in States where the offices are closed...	$1,978 01
For services of special counsel, &c., in defending the title to public property in California...............	3,365 03
For rent of surveyors general's offices, &c............	15,781 56
For repayment for lands erroneously sold............	30,336 39
For indemnity for swamp lands sold to individuals...	138,404 40
For distribution of the proceeds of the sale of public lands...	41,657 00
For supplying newly created offices, &c., with full sets of Statutes at Large.............................	2,901 25
For running and marking the boundary line between the United States and Texas.......................	5,312 68
For suppression of the slave trade...................	222,528 39
For expenses of taking the eighth census............	557,386 00
For United States Capitol extension.................	30,000 00
For new dome of the United States Capitol..........	35,000 00
For Patent Office building.........................	17,530 97
For alterations and repairs of public buildings in Washington, improvement of grounds, &c.............	31,124 99
For compensation of public gardener, gate-keepers, laborers, watchmen, &c..........................	23,659 98
For salaries and other necessary expenses of the metropolitan police...................................	85,530 00
For lighting the President's House, Capitol, &c. with gas...	54,942 40
For fuel, &c., for President's House.................	2,874 25
For refurnishing President's House..................	19,359 14
For collection of agricultural statistics.............	70,000 00
For asylum for insane of District of Columbia and army and navy of the United States..............	52,611 00
For Columbian Institute for deaf, dumb, and blind of District of Columbia..............................	9,034 10
For support and care of transient paupers in the District of Columbia..................................	4,381 15
For penitentiary in the District of Columbia........	36,696 14
For Potomac and Eastern Branch bridges, compensation of draw-keepers, &c.........................	37,327 13
For patent fund....................................	168,340 26
For expenses of packing and distributing congressional journals and documents.......................	20,000 00
For preservation and distribution of the collections of exploring expeditions...........................	8,000 00
For making cases, &c., in Patent Office building to receive copyright books, &c......................	4,200 00
For the relief of sundry individuals.................	21,453 53
For sundry items...................................	18,192 24
For preparing unfinished records of public and private surveys, to be transferred to the State authorities..	5,435 72
Total miscellaneous..............................	$14,129,771 52

UNDER THE DIRECTION OF THE INTERIOR DEPARTMENT.

For Indian department.............................	$2,223,402 27
For pensions, military..............................	731,693 68
For pensions, naval................................	118,388 28
For relief of sundry individuals....................	29,501 27
Total under Interior Department..................	3,102,985 50

UNDER THE DIRECTION OF THE WAR DEPARTMENT.

For army proper, &c................................	$13,329,477 97
For transportation of the army, volunteers and regulars...	46,942,467 24

For clothing of the army, volunteers and regulars...	$56,724,952 05
For purchase of horses for cavalry, &c., volunteers and regulars...................................	13,748,297 79
For quartermaster's department, &c., volunteers and regulars..	42,875,758 76
For medical and hospital department, volunteers and regulars..	2,309,112 58
For purchase of arms, ordnance, and ordnance stores, volunteers and regulars.............................	27,499,238 36
For pay and subsistence of volunteers and militia, &c.	175,918,867 34
For Military Academy..............................	117,717 30
For armories, arsenals, ordnance, &c...............	7,658,936 68
For fortifications and other works of defence........	3,558,884 84
For construction of roads, bridges, &c.............	22,967 79
For improvement of rivers, harbors, &c............	30,318 95
For gunboats on western rivers....................	2,089,422 69
For relief of sundry individuals and miscellaneous...	1,533,047 04

Total under War Department........................... $394,368,407 36

UNDER THE DIRECTION OF THE NAVY DEPARTMENT.

For pay and subsistence of the navy, &c.............	$11,246,091 87
For contingent expenses	1,888,231 48
For increase, repairs, &c...........................	13,009,393 52
For six first class steam-frigates...................	50,176 42
For five sloops-of-war.............................	64,106 83
For seven sloops-of-war, second class..............	1,946,011 10
For twelve side-wheel steamers....................	1,172,349 58
For armored ships and floating batteries............	1,596,562 56
For seven steam-sloops and one side-wheel steamer...	85,021 93
For temporary increase of the navy	3,000,000 00
For ordnance, ordnance stores, and small arms......	5,148,294 71
For fuel..	1,349,763 75
For hemp...	300,458 53
For Naval Academy	47,584 32
For navy yards...................................	535,719 50
For magazines	29,587 31
For hospitals.....................................	7,330 61
For marine corps, including marine barracks........	920,174 54
For relief of sundry individuals and miscellaneous...	277,711 13

Total under the Navy Department..................... 42,674,569 69

Total expenditures, exclusive of the public debt......... 461,554,453 71

PUBLIC DEBT.

For old funded debt	$3 06
For interest on public debt, including treasury notes.	13,190,324 45
For reimbursement of treasury notes, per act prior to July 22, 1846	50 00
For redemption of treasury notes which have been purloined	51 50
For payment of treasury notes, issued per act of December 23, 1857	2,567,700 00
For payment of treasury notes, issued per act of December 17, 1860	9,936,150 00
For payment of treasury notes, issued per act of March 2, 1861	30,606,150 00
For reimbursement of temporary loan, per acts of July 17 and August 5, 1861..........................	44,375,000 00

For reimbursement of temporary loan, per acts of February 25 and March 17, 1862...................... $8,553,207 53

For redemption of United States notes, issued under act of July 17, 1861............................. 58,610 00

Total public debt.. $109,287,246 54

Total expenditures.. 570,841,700 25

Balance in the treasury July 1, 1862................... 13,043,546 81

L. E. CHITTENDEN, *Register.*

TREASURY DEPARTMENT, *Register's Office, November* 29, 1862.

No. 3.

Statement of the receipts and expenditures of the United States for the quarter ending September 30, 1862, exclusive of trust funds.

RECEIPTS.

From customs		$23,041,736 59
From sales of public lands		22,181 04
From direct tax		83,681 77
From internal revenue		456,303 73
From incidental and miscellaneous sources		561,079 08
From two years' 6 per cent. treasury notes, per act of March 2, 1861	$1,500 00	
From 7 3/10 three years' coupon bonds, per acts of July 17 and August 5, 1861	3,550,000 00	
From United States notes issued per act of February 25, 1862	72,436,000 00	
From 5/20 years' bonds, per act of February 25, 1862	2,539,803 45	
From certificates of indebtedness, per acts of March 1 and 17, 1862	12,184,824 43	
From temporary loan, per acts of February 25 and March 17, 1862	22,813,843 14	
From stock for Washington and Oregon war debt	145,050 00	
From United States postage stamps	787,800 00	
		114,458,821 02
		138,623,803 23

EXPENDITURES.

Civil, foreign intercourse, and miscellaneous		$4,436,907 32
Interior, (pensions and Indian)		1,046,906 42
War		90,869,850 23
Navy		10,076,353 91
Interest on the public debt, including treasury notes	$4,654,428 87	
Reimbursement of treasury notes, per act prior to July 22, 1846	50 00	
Payment of treasury notes issued per act of December 23, 1857	14,300 00	
Payment of treasury notes issued per act of December 17, 1860	4,500 00	
Payment of treasury notes issued per act of March 2, 1861	22,550 00	
Redemption of 7 3/10 coupon bonds, per act of July 17, 1861	2,000 00	
Redemption of United States notes issued per act of July 17, 1861	27,682,490 00	
Redemption of United States notes issued per act of February 25, 1862	2,000,000 00	
Redemption of certificates of indebtedness, per acts of March 1 and 17, 1862	5,885,000 00	
Reimbursement of temporary loan, per acts of February 25 and March 17, 1862	9,913,510 66	
		60,178,829 53
		156,608,847 41

L. E. CHITTENDEN, *Register.*

TREASURY DEPARTMENT,
  Register's Office, November 29, 1862.

No. 4.

Statement showing the amount of public debt of the United States on July 1, 1862.

Loan of 1842	$2,883,364 11	
Do...1847	9,415,250 00	
Do...1848	8,908,341 80	
Do...1858	20,000,000 00	
Do...1860	7,022,000 00	
Do...1861, act of February 8, 1861	18,415,000 00	
Do...1861, act of July 17, 1861	50,000,000 00	
Do...1862	9,907,850 00	
Texan indemnity	3,461,000 00	
Oregon war debt	998,690 00	
Texas debt	112,092 59	
Old funded and unfunded debt	114,115 48	
		$131,237,613 98
Treasury notes issued under acts prior to 1857	104,611 64	
Treasury notes issued under act of December 23, 1857	18,500 00	
Treasury notes issued under act of December 17, 1860	6,300 00	
Treasury notes issued under acts of June 22, 1860, and February and March, 1861, 2 years	2,716,700 00	
Treasury notes issued under act of March 2, 1861, 60 days	3,000 00	
		2,849,111 64
Three years' bonds, dated August 19, 1861, issued under act of July 17, 1861	53,004,300 00	
Three years' bonds, dated October 1, 1861, issued under act of July 17, 1861	69,832,250 00	
		122,836,550 00
United States notes issued under acts of July 17, 1861, and February 12, 1862	53,040,000 00	
United States notes issued under act of February 25, 1862	96,620,000 00	
		149,660,000 00
Temporary loan under act of February 25, March 17, and July 11, 1862		57,746,116 57
Certificates of indebtedness issued under act of March 1, 1862		49,881,979 73
		514,211,371 92

No. 5.

MINT OF THE UNITED STATES,
Philadelphia, October 27, 1862.

SIR : I have the honor to present the following report of the operations of the mint and its branches for the fiscal year ending June 30, 1862 :

The coinage of the mint and branches for that period has been large, but not equal to that of the preceding year. Various causes contributed to this reduction ; the principal one being the disturbed condition of our country, which not only affected the financial and commercial relations of the nation, but embarrassed and retarded operations in the mining districts, and limited the supply from these sources. The quantity of foreign coin and bullion deposited was not large, amounting only to $11,268,710 71.

The amount of bullion received at the mint and branches during the year was as follows : Gold, $67,118,544 56; silver, $4,098,673 14; total deposits, $71,217,217 70. From this total must be deducted the re-deposits of bullion, or bars made at one institution and deposited at another, for coinage. This deduction made, the amount will be $45,423,231 01.

The coinage for the same period was as follows : Gold coins, $45,532,386 50; fine gold bars, $16,144,190 05; silver coins, $2,812,401 50; silver bars, $418,680 01 ; cent coins, $116,000 ; total coinage, $65,023,658 06 ; number of pieces of all denominations of coin, 28,296,899.

The distribution of the bullion received and coined at the mint and branches was as follows : At Philadelphia, gold deposits, $26,287,009 77 ; gold coined, $29,987,386 50 ; fine gold bars, $49,421 61 ; silver deposits and purchases, $1,855,606 96 ; silver coined, $2,170,701 50 ; silver bars, $116,000. Total deposits of gold and silver, $28,142,616 73 ; total coinage, $32,274,088 ; number of pieces, 25,951,899.

At the branch mint, San Francisco, the gold deposits were $16,136,622 96 ; gold coined, $15,545,000 ; silver deposits and purchases, $749,114 14 ; silver coined, $641,700 ; silver bars, $1,278 65. Total coinage of gold and silver, $16,187,978 65 ; number of pieces, 2,345,000.

The assay office in New York received during the year $24,694,911 83 in gold bullion and $1,493,952 04 in silver. Fine gold bars stamped at that office, 3,867 ; value, $16,094,768 44 ; silver bars, 2,164 ; value, $415,603 57. Total value of gold and silver bullion, $26,188,863 87.

No reports have been received from the branches at New Orleans, Dahlonega, or Charlotte.

Although New Orleans is now, and has been for some months, in the possession of the Union forces, yet the operations at the branch mint in that city have not been resumed, nor is it expedient or necessary that they should be. After the suppression of the rebellion, and the pacification of the country, the branch located there might again be successfully and usefully operated ; till then it should remain closed. No consideration, of public or private interest, would, under the most favorable circumstances, justify the reopening of the branches at Dahlonega or Charlotte. They ought not to have been established ; and, having been the source of useless expenditure, they should not, even in the event of the States in which they are respectively located returning to their allegiance, be again employed for minting purposes.

Whether gold or silver coins were struck at any of the defected branches of the mint during the past year I have not been able to ascertain with certainty. If any, the amount was small. Prior to the defection of the branch at New Orleans, the dies in that institution were defaced or destroyed by some of the loyal employés, under the direction of one of the officers who remained true to his duty and to his country. This destruction of the dies must have delayed, if not altogether prevented, any coinage at that branch.

The mines of the United States continue to yield large amounts of the precious metals. Most of the gold and silver deposited at the mint and branches was the product of these mines. The sum of $30,976,593 24 in gold and $1,032,264 45 in silver was received from this source. As heretofore, much of the domestic silver was obtained by separating it from the gold deposits in which it is found. The mines of the Washoe region exhibit a gratifying increase in quantity. The gold mines of other portions of our country yield largely, and their capacity is almost unlimited. The deposits of gold from Colorado Territory or Pike's Peak have largely increased, and the daily developments of the mineral wealth of that region would seem to indicate that, before many years, the production from the mines there will rival in amount that of California.

The receipts from the State of Oregon during the year amounted to $888,205 against $3,181 last year—an increase full of encouragement to the miner.

The yield of gold and silver from Nevada, in the form of mixed bullion—one third of the value of which is in gold—has largely increased during the last nine months, and increased supplies of the precious metals from that region may be confidently expected.

Gold deposits from Washington Territory have also been received, and the indications of a large increase are favorable.

The deposits of gold and silver bullion at the mint and branches, during the year, from the mines of the United States, notwithstanding the disturbed condition of public affairs and the troubles on our western borders, were only $2,800,000 less than the amount of the preceding fiscal year. The decrease was in the amount received from California, and must be attributed to other causes than diminished yield of the mines of that State. The reports from the gold and silver regions of our country are highly satisfactory and promise an abundant and increasing yield.

The places whence the deposits of gold and silver were obtained, and the amount from each locality, are set forth in the tabular statements attached to this report.

The exchange of nickel for the old copper cents was continued during the year. The number of the old cents is rapidly diminishing, and that coin will soon disappear altogether from the circulation. The demand for the nickle cent has largely increased. The disappearance of the small silver coins from circulation has caused the new cent to be extensively used, and every effort has been made to meet the demand. Large amounts have been sent to every part of the country, and orders, beyond our ability to fill, are constantly forwarded to the mint. The profits of the cent coinage have been fully adequate to meet all expenses of material, production and transmission to the parties ordering them.

The coinage of the past was of a more general character than that of the preceding year. A greater variety of all the gold and silver coins was produced, and among them an unusual number of the smaller gold coins.

The distinct and unequivocal recognition of the divine sovereignty in the practical administration of our political system is a duty of the highest obligation. History unites with divine revelation in declaring that "happy is that people whose God is the Lord." In the exercise of political sovereignty our nation should honor him; and now, in this hour of peril and danger to our country and its liberties, it is becoming to acknowledge his power and invoke his protection. Our national coinage in its devices and legends should indicate the Christian character of our nation, and declare our trust in God. It does not do this. On the contrary, ancient mythology, more than Christianity, has stamped its impress on our coin. It is, however, gratifying to know that the proposition to introduce a motto upon our coins, expressing a national reliance on divine support has been favorably considered by your department, and will no doubt be approved by an intelligent public sentiment. The subject is under the control of Congress; and without a change in existing laws, no alteration in the legends and devices of most of our national coins can be made; a motto, however, may be added without additional authority or violation of the present law.

The 13th section of the act of January 18, 1837, prescribes the following devices and legends for our coinage: "Upon one side of each of the said coins there shall be an impression emblematic of liberty, with an inscription of the word *Liberty*, and the year of the coinage; and upon the reverse of each of the gold and silver coins there shall be the figure or representation of an eagle, with the inscription *United States of America*, and a designation of the value of the coin, but on the reverse of the dime and half dime the figure of the eagle shall be omitted." The provisions of this act being still in force, except as to the silver coins of less denomination than the dollar, the *character* of the devices upon the coins referred to in the section cited, viz: the eagle, half eagle, quarter eagle and silver dollar, cannot be altered unless authority therefor be given by an act of Congress. The same remark applies to the double eagle. The coins not included in the provisions of the act referred to are the three dollar piece, gold dollar, and siver coins of less denomination than the dollar, also the cent coin. The figure of the eagle is omitted on the reverse of the gold dollar, and the device thereon, as well as for the obverse and reverse of the three dollar piece and silver coins last referred to, having been fixed by the Secretary of the Treasury, may be altered by the same authority.

In consideration of the legal provisions referred to, it will be necessary, in attempting to introduce a motto on the face of our coins, to interfere as little as possible with the present legal devices. The first difficulty to be encountered is the necessary condensation. The idea should be unmistakebly expressed in our own language, and at the same time the letters should be distinctly and easily legible. To unite these desiderata within the limits presented on the face of the the coin, in connexion with the required arrangement of the legal devices, demands much reflection. The motto "In God is our trust," which has become familiar to the public mind by its use in our national hymn the "Star Spangled Banner," would be an appropriate one, but it contains too many letters to insert in the place of the *crest*, without crowding too much for good taste. For greater brevity we may substitute the words, "God our trust," which convey the same idea, in a form of expression according with heraldic usage, and as readily understood as the more explicit form of the other. The most appropriate place for this motto is found in connexion with the national inscription, which on all our larger coins is on the reverse, the device of which is an eagle, with the heraldic accompaniments appropriate to the *arms* of the Union as adopted by law, dispensing at present with the motto (E Pluribus Unum) and the *crest*, except on the double eagle. The place of the *crest* offers the best position for inscribing a motto, as on all the other coins which are large enough to admit of such an addition this space is now vacant, and therefore a motto, if sufficiently brief, may be introduced with the least disturbance of the device as now arranged. The adoption on our coin of the motto "God our trust," or some other words expressive of national reliance upon divine support, would accord fully with the sentiment of the American people, and it would add to the artistic appearance of the coins.

I would again call the attention of the department to the anomalous character of the silver dollar of the United States, and respectfully refer to the observations on this subject contained in my last annual report, also to the propriety and expediency of enlarging the limit of the legal tender for silver. The limit, with great propriety and advantage to public and private interests, might and ought to be extended to fifty or one hundred dollars.

PRICE OF SILVER AND GOLD.

There is some reason, from present experience, to fear a continuous advance of gold and silver, as compared with the legal tender currency issued by the government. That fear may be much abated by considering the amazing production of the gold fields of the world, to which there has been no parallel in past history. It is very much to the purpose to consider that at the era of the great Napoleonic war the supply of precious metals was chiefly maintained by the mines of Mexico and South America, the washings of the gold coast of Africa, and some initial developments in Russia, altogether not exceeding twenty-five millions of dollars, by a literal estimate annually for a series of years. During the most critical part of this era the premium on gold in England reached forty-one per cent., as against Bank of England notes, but was generally much less; and in three years, from 1813 to 1816, fell from the highest point to par with bank paper. Since those times it is almost unnecessary to say the stock of gold has been immensely re-enforced; and we have now the gold fields of California and adjacent territories, Colorado or Pike's Peak, Australia, New Zeland, Russia, Nova Scotia, and the very promising silver regions of Washoe and Arizona. Adding together all the sources of supply, both gold and silver, we may safely estimate an annual yield, in these times, of one hundred and seventy-five millions of dollars, or seven times the amount produced annually for some years prior to the peace of 1815.

There is, therefore, much reason to hope that the price of gold and silver, as compared with actual currency, cannot go on rising indefinitely and ruinously, and that the return of peace will bring a returning tendency to specie payments. The civilized world does not want a mere metallic currency, but it must have a sufficient metallic support for its bills of credit, and it is easy to see that only five years addition of gold and silver from the mines will exert a vast influence. Once out of the ground and put in an available shape, they are, setting off the mere abrasion of coins, a perpetual addition to the machinery of trade and the wealth of the world.

ABRASION OF COINS.

Very remarkable statements have from time to time been published as to loss by abrasion or wear of coins, making the amount so great as almost to cast discredit upon metallic currency. Thus we are told by one writer that the annual loss, in a country where both gold and silver circulate, is one part in 420; by another, one in 300; by a third, one in 200; and one "gentleman of great accuracy and acuteness" (cited by Jacobs) says that the loss on coined silver is full one per cent. per annum. A more recent and alarming estimate, from British sources, would lead to the expectation that silver pieces of the size of their shilling, or our quarter dollar, would in less than ten years be worn so much as to be no longer passable. Every one knows the value of such statements on this side of the water.

We have recently had occasion to make a thorough re-examination of this important subject, and have ascertained what is the average annual loss on each size of gold coin, and on the silver promiscuously. Not to enter into details here, it may be stated that the silver coin averages a loss of one part in 630; the half eagle one in 3,550; the double eagle one in 9,000; and that, by a cautious estimate as to the proportions of the various sizes of coin actually among us, the average annual loss by abrasion does not exceed one part in 2,400; that is, in times when specie is current at par with bank paper, and not lying idle. Let it be observed that all experiments hitherto made, in regard to abrasion, seem to have been based upon pieces not higher in value than the sovereign or half eagle. This has rendered expedient a new examination, because the great preponderance of our specie is in large pieces, which, being less exposed by circulation, must be judged by a law of their own. While one double eagle is lying quiet, five or ten smaller pieces are passing from hand to hand.

SMALL CHANGE.

In regard to our minor currency, usually called "small change," it is difficult to realize the fact that, with over forty-five millions of dollars in silver coin now in the country, we should be driven to a substitute, which, however useful as a temporary measure, cannot enter into comparison, in point of convenience and durability, with small coin, not to speak of intrinsic value. Why cannot silver change be issued on a basis somewhat similar, yet more favorable than that on which the copper coin is issued, namely, not to give a full bullion value, but to afford a public benefit? The cent we issue costs the government scarcely half a cent; but for its purposes, and with the stamp of authority, it is worth its nominal value to everybody: it is largely sought after, notwithstanding so many have been issued, and would purchase no more if it were three times as heavy. Would the half dime, dime, or quarter dollar be any less acceptable if, it were, say three-fourths of the present weight of those coins? At all events, we could most safely and seasonably issue ten millions of dollars in five and ten cent pieces, of the present nineteenths fineness, but of reduced weight, and of legal tender to the amount of five or ten dollars. The new pieces would, of course, be not worth that much abroad, but they would be at home, which is all we are concerned about. A legal provision to this effect, prospective perhaps, to follow the wearing out of the stamp currency, would at once bring to the mint a supply of the old coin, and of silver bullion from the Washoe mines and other sources, by holders desirous of realizing a premium and of accommodating their own business. So much of the gain as would be necessary to draw the material should go in that direction; the remainder would pay expenses of recoinage and transportation. The three-cent pieces already out, and considerably coined, might be left to fulfil their mission, without calling them in or adding to their number, the cents being sufficient to fill the space between one cent and five. It would be best at present to limit the new issue to the dime and half dime, leaving the larger coins for future consideration, or, probably, to return to their par value on the return of better times.

STATEMENT OF FOREIGN COINS.

This statement, as required by law, will be found appended to the report. The additions are few, but there are alterations in the silver occasioned by the raising of the mint price. In gold, we find the sovereign of the mint of Sydney, Australia, by the trial of a much larger lot than has been hitherto procurable, a little higher in average weight, and a little lower in average fineness, than reported last year. It may be well to state here that an inquiry has been raised in England as to the propriety of making Australian coin pass everywhere concurrently with the British sovereign, being, in fact, of equal value, though quite different in devices and in color. We have not seen the printed documents on this subject, but as the coinage of the Sydney mint is large, it is worth while to bring the matter to public notice.

There are also several varieties of private coinage at Pike's Peak, Colorado Territory, which, not being foreign nor legal, cannot claim a place in our coinage statistics; and yet, being issued in considerable amounts, and current in the far west, ought to receive attention. They are all of a pale color, and more highly alloyed than our lawful coinage, making up in some cases by increase of weight. Thus we have the ten-dollar piece of Clark, Graber & Co., ranging from 768 to 832 thousandths fine, and of course, as various in weight; but they all appear

Ex. Doc. 1——4

to be about ten dollars in value, (a few cents more or less,) by computing the value of the silver contained and charging for the parting. The ten-dollar piece of J. J. Conway & Co. is only 630 thousandths fine, by a single trial, being largely alloyed with the silver actually present. The net value of gold and silver is $7 25. The five-dollar piece of John Parson & Co., by a single trial, is 751 thousandths fine, and its net value $4 20. The trials in these latter cases are not sufficient for a fair average valuation, but they will give an idea as to the deficiency.

In silver we have added, from a recent assay, the Maria Theresa thaler of Austria, which is coined specially for the Levant trade, but always bears the date of 1780, no matter when struck. We have lately had a good opportunity to make an average of old and new pieces, many being of the latter sort. They fully maintain their original standards, and are, in fact, a little better than we reported them twenty years ago.

In January of the present year the mint price of silver was raised from 121 to 122½ cents per ounce troy, of standard fineness. This requires an entire change in the column of values of silver coins, and the change has accordingly been made.

NATIONAL MEDALS.

The medal department of the mint has become a most important and interesting part of the institution. The reproduction of national and other American medals of historic interest has been received with great favor by all who are interested in numismatics, and by all who desire the development of native genius and skill in this branch of the arts. Medals of honor for the navy, in recognition of noble and patriotic services in defence of the nation's honor and life, have been prepared here, which reflect the highest credit on the artists and workmen engaged in their preparation.

Rare and valuable coins and medals have been added to the mint cabinet during the year. The cabinet has become a very attractive place, and the daily crowds of intelligent visitors attest its value and importance as a numismatic collection.

LIST OF TABLES IN APPENDIX.

A.—Statement of bullion deposited at the mint of the United States and branches during the fiscal year ending June 30, 1862.

B.—Statement of the coinage at the mint of the United States and branches during the fiscal year ending June 30, 1862.

C.—Statement of gold and silver of domestic production deposited at the mint of the United States and branches during the fiscal year ending June 30, 1862.

D.—Coinage of the mint and branches from their organization to the close of the fiscal year ending June 30, 1862. (Eleven tables.)

E.—Gold of domestic production deposited at the mint of the United States and branches to June 30, 1862. (Seven tables.)

F.—Statement of the amount of silver coined at the mint of the United States and branches at San Francisco and New Orleans, under the act of February 21, 1853.

G.—Statement of the amount of silver of domestic production deposited at the mint of the United States and its branches from January, 1841, to 30th June, 1862.

H.—Statement of amount and denominations of fractions of the Spanish and Mexican dollar deposited at the mint of the United States for exchange for the new cent to June 30, 1860.

I.—Amount of fractions of the Spanish and Mexican dollar purchased at the mint of the United States, the branch mint at New Orleans, and assay office, New York, to June 30, 1862.

J.—Cents of former issue deposited at the United States mint for exchange for the nickel cent to June 30, 1862.

K.—Statement of the weight, fineness, and value of the foreign gold coins.

L.—Statement of the weight, fineness, and value of foreign silver coins.

Very respectfully, your obedient servant,

JAMES POLLOCK,
Director of the Mint.

Hon. S. P. CHASE,
Secretary of the Treasury, Washington City.

A.

Statement of deposits at the mint of the United States, the branch mint at San Francisco, and assay office, New York, during the fiscal year ending June 30, 1862.

Description of bullion.	Mint of the U. States, Philadelphia	Branch mint, San Francisco.	Assay office, New York.	Total.
Fine bars	$24,172,885 33			$24,172,885 3
United States bullion	1,435,890 45	$15,754,262 96	$13,786,439 83	30,976,593 2
United States coin	386,302 24		4,836 00	391,138 2
Jewellers' bars	75,973 04		233,244 00	309,217 0
Foreign coin	199,846 38	48,400 00	9,685,280 00	9,933,526 3
Foreign bullion	16,112 33	333,960 00	985,112 00	1,335,184 3
Total gold	26,287,009 77	16,136,622 96	24,694,911 83	67,118,544 5
Fine bars	1,620,143 36		958 00	1,621,101 3
Jewellers' bars	37,202 19		62,055 00	99,257 1
United States bullion	38,334 31	749,114 14	244,816 00	1,032,264 4
United States coin, (o. s.)	75,804 18		33,604 00	109,408 1
Foreign coin	77,283 05		972,019 04	1,049,302 0
Foreign bullion	6,839 87		180,500 00	187,339 8
Total silver	1,855,606 96	749,114 14	1,493,952 04	4,098,673 1
Total gold and silver	28,142,616 73	16,885,737 10	26,188,863 87	71,217,217 7

Less redeposits at the different institutions: Gold, $24,172,885 33; silver, $1,621,101 36 .... 25,793,986 6

45,423,231 0

Statement of the coinage at the mint of the United States, the branch mint, San Francisco, and assay office, New York, during the fiscal year ending June 30, 1862.

Denomination.	Mint of the United States, Philadelphia.		Branch mint, San Francisco.		Assay office, New York.	Total.	
	Pieces.	Value.	Pieces.	Value.	Value.	Pieces.	Value.
GOLD.							
Double eagles	1,052,375	$21,047,500 00	760,600	$15,200,000 00		1,819,375	$36,247,500 00
Eagles	79,999	799,990 00	18,000	180,000 00		97,999	979,990 00
Half eagles	639,432	3,197,160 00	18,000	90,000 00		657,432	3,287,160 00
Three dollars	5,785	17,355 00				5,785	17,355 00
Quarter eagles	1,952,949	3,133,192 50	30,000	75,000 00		1,982,949	3,208,192 50
Dollars	1,799,259	1,799,259 00				1,799,259	1,799,259 00
Fine bars		49,421 61			$16,094,768 44		16,144,190 05
Total gold	4,829,399	30,036,868 11	826,000	15,545,000 00	16,094,768 44	5,655,399	61,676,576 55
SILVER.							
Dollars	1,750	1,750 00				1,750	1,750 00
Half dollars	2,391,350	1,195,675 00	1,179,500	589,750 00		3,570,850	1,785,425 00
Quarter dollars	2,803,750	700,937 50	120,000	30,000 00		2,923,750	730,937 50
Dimes	1,584,550	158,455 00	219,500	21,950 00		1,584,050	158,405 00
Half dimes	2,352,550	117,627 50				2,352,550	117,627 50
Three cents	608,550	18,256 50				608,550	18,256 50
Bars		1,797 79		1,278 65	415,603 57		418,680 01
Total silver	9,502,500	2,172,499 29	1,519,000	642,978 65	415,603 57	11,041,500	3,231,081 51
CENTS	11,600,000	116,000 00				11,600,000	116,000 00
Total coinage	25,951,899	32,274,068 00	2,345,000	16,187,978 65	16,510,372 01	28,296,899	65,023,658 06

C.

Statement of gold and silver of domestic production deposited at the mint of the United States, the branch mint at San Francisco, and assay office at New York, during the fiscal year ending June 30, 1862.

Description of bullion.	Mint of the United States, Philadelphia.	Branch mint, San Francisco.	Assay office, New York.	Total.
GOLD.				
California	$244,259 81	$14,029,759 95	$19,580,647 63	$33,854,667 39
Colorado	1,122,332 50	680 00	912,403 00	2,035,416 50
North Carolina	81 38		2,232 00	2,313 38
Georgia	135 40		1,469 00	1,604 40
Washington Territory	215 70			215 70
Vermont			3,293 00	3,293 00
Nevada		13,000 00	40,846 00	53,846 00
New Mexico			1,983 00	1,983 00
Arizona			391 00	391 00
Santa Fé, New Mexico			260 00	260 00
Virginia			316 00	316 00
South Carolina			2,065 00	2,065 00
Oregon		868,000 00	205 00	868,205 00
Parted from silver	68,864 66	822,823 01	241,029 00	1,132,716 67
Total gold	1,435,890 45	15,734,262 96	13,786,439 83	30,976,593 44
SILVER.				
Lake Superior	12,597 38		8,769 00	21,366 38
Nevada	3,618 37	655,911 23	98,617 00	757,446 60
California			6,294 00	6,294 00
Arizona			105 00	105 00
Parted from domestic gold	22,118 56	93,202 91	129,101 00	245,122 47
Total silver	38,334 31	749,114 14	244,816 00	1,032,254 45
Total gold and silver of domestic production	1,474,224 76	16,503,377 10	14,031,255 83	32,008,857 69

Coinage of the mint and branches from their organization to the close of the fiscal year ending June 30, 1862.

1. MINT OF THE UNITED STATES, PHILADELPHIA.

Period.	GOLD COINAGE.						
	Double eagles.	Eagles.	Half eagles.	Three dollars.	Quarter eagles.	Dollars.	Fine bars.
	Pieces.	*Pieces.*	*Pieces.*	*Pieces.*	*Pieces.*	*Pieces.*	*Value.*
1817............	....	132,592	845,909	....	22,197	....	....
1837............	....	....	3,087,925	..?........	879,903	....	....
1847............	....	1,227,759	3,269,921	....	345,526	....	....
1857............	8,122,526	1,970,597	2,260,390	243,015	5,544,900	15,348,608	$33,612,140 46
....	468,504	13,690	32,633	13,059	113,097	208,724	21,088 10
....	98,196	8,600	20,718	11,524	76,562	231,873	49,286 59
....	188,615	16,013	19,724	13,402	13,721	78,743	170,275 34
....	2,341,921	44,005	56,526	6,072	121,376	13,955	66,434 76
....	1,052,375	79,299	639,432	5,785	1,253,249	1,799,259	49,421 61
Total............	12,272,137	3,492,555	10,233,178	272,857	8,370,531	17,681,162	33,968,646 86

1. MINT OF THE UNITED STATES, PHILADELPHIA—Continued.

Period.	SILVER COINAGE.						
	Dollars.	Half dollars.	Quarter dollars.	Dimes.	Half dimes.	Three cents.	Bars.
	Pieces.	*Pieces.*	*Pieces.*	*Pieces.*	*Pieces.*	*Pieces.*	*Value.*
1793 to 1817..........	1, 439, 517	13, 104, 433	650, 280	1, 007, 151	265, 543	....	....
1818 to 1837..........	1, 000	74, 793, 560	5, 041, 749	11, 854, 949	14, 463, 700	....	....
1838 to 1847..........	879, 873	20, 203, 333	4, 952, 073	11, 387, 995	11, 093, 235	....	....
1848 to 1857..........	350, 250	10, 691, 088	41, 072, 280	35, 172, 010	34, 368, 520	37, 778, 900	$32, 355 5
1858	....	4, 028, 000	10, 600, 000	690, 000	4, 000, 000	1, 266, 000	843 3
1859	73, 500	2, 636, 000	4, 996, 000	1, 760, 000	2, 840, 000	1, 380, 000	9, 341 0
1860	315, 530	349, 800	909, 800	576, 000	870, 000	548, 000	21, 656 3
1861	164, 900	741, 300	3, 034, 200	1, 573, 000	2, 787, 000	265, 000	2, 624 3
1862	1, 750	2, 391, 350	2, 803, 750	1, 364, 550	2, 352, 550	608, 550	1, 797 7
Total..........	3, 226, 320	128, 938, 864	74, 060, 132	65, 385, 655	73, 040, 548	41, 846, 450	68, 618 4

1. MINT OF THE UNITED STATES, PHILADELPHIA—Continued.

Period.	COPPER COINAGE.		TOTAL COINAGE.				
	Cents.	Half cents.	Number coined.	Value of gold.	Value of silver.	Value of copper.	Total value coined.
	Pieces.	*Pieces.*	*Pieces.*				
to 1817	29,316,272	5,235,513	52,019,407	$5,610,957 50	$8,268,295 75	$319,340 28	$14,198,593 53
to 1837	46,554,830	2,205,200	158,882,816	17,639,382 50	40,566,897 15	476,574 30	58,682,853 95
to 1847	34,967,663	....	86,327,378	29,491,010 00	13,913,019 00	349,676 63	43,753,705 63
to 1857	51,449,979	544,510	244,908,562	256,950,474 46	22,365,413 55	517,222 34	279,833,110 35
....	23,400,000	....	44,833,766	10,221,876 60	4,971,823 37	234,000 00	15,427,699 97
....	30,700,000	....	44,833,111	2,660,646 59	3,009,241 08	307,000 00	5,976,887 67
....	34,200,000	....	38,099,348	4,354,576 84	857,076 30	342,000 00	5,553,653 14
....	10,166,000	....	21,315,255	47,963,145 76	1,601,324 37	101,660 00	49,666,130 13
....	11,600,000	....	25,951,899	30,036,808 11	2,172,499 29	116,000 00	32,274,088 00
Total	272,354,744	7,985,223	719,171,542	404,928,878 36	97,725,589 86	2,763,473 55	505,366,722 37

2. BRANCH MINT AT SAN FRANCISCO.

Period.	GOLD COINAGE.							
	Double eagles.	Eagles.	Half eagles.	Three dolls.	Quarter eagles.	Dollars.	Unparted bars.	Fine bars.
	Pieces.	Pieces.	Pieces.	Pieces.	Pieces.	Pieces.	Value.	Value.
1854	141,468	123,826	268		246	14,632	$5,641,504 05	$5,863 16
1855	859,175	9,000	61,000	6,600			3,270,594 93	88,782 50
1856	1,181,750	73,500	94,100	34,500	71,120	24,600	3,047,001 29	12,136 55
1857	604,500	10,000	47,000	5,000	20,000			
1858	885,940	27,800	58,600	9,000	49,200	20,000	816,295 65	
1859	689,140	2,000	9,720		8,000	15,000		19,871 68
1860	579,975	10,000	16,700	7,000	28,800	13,000		
1861	614,300	6,000	8,000		14,000			
1862	760,000	18,000	18,000		30,000			
Total	6,316,248	280,126	313,388	62,100	221,366	87,232	12,775,395 92	236,653 89

2. BRANCH MINT AT SAN FRANCISCO—Continued.

Period.	SILVER COINAGE.					TOTAL COINAGE.			
	Dollars.	Half dollars.	Quarter dolls.	Dimes.	Bars.	No. of pieces.	Gold.	Silver.	Total.
	Pieces.	*Pieces.*	*Pieces.*	*Pieces.*	*Value.*		*Value.*	*Value.*	*Value.*
	....	....	....	....	....	282,712	$9,731,574 21	....	$9,731,574 21
	....	121,950	412,400	....	....	1,471,272	20,957,677 43	$164,075 00	21,121,752 43
	....	211,000	286,000	....	$23,609 45	1,977,559	28,315,537 84	200,609 45	28,516,147 29
	....	86,000	28,000	....	....	800,500	12,490,000 00	-50,000 00	12,540,000 00
	....	218,000	63,000	30,000	19,752 61	1,362,028	19,276,095 65	147,502 61	19,423,598 26
	15,000	463,000	172,000	20,000	29,469 87	1,463,893	13,906,271 68	327,969 87	14,234,241 55
	5,000	693,000	24,000	40,000	211,411 52	1,417,475	11,889,000 00	572,911 52	12,461,911 52
	....	350,000	52,000	100,000	71,485 61	1,144,300	12,421,000 00	269,495 61	12,690,485 61
	....	1,179,500	120,000	219,500	1,278 65	2,345,000	15,545,000 00	642,978 65	16,187,978 65
Total....	20,000	3,322,450	1,157,400	479,500	357,007 71	12,264,739	144,532,156 81	2,375,532 71	146,907,689 52

3. BRANCH MINT, NEW ORLEANS.

Period.	GOLD COINAGE.					
	Double eagles.	Eagles.	Half eagles.	Three dollars.	Quarter eagles.	Dollars.
	Pieces.	*Pieces.*	*Pieces.*	*Pieces.*	*Pieces.*	*Pieces.*
1838 to 1847................................	....	1,026,342	709,925	....	550,528	....
1848 to 1857................	730,500	534,250	108,100	24,000	546,100	1,004,000
1858...........................	47,500	21,500	13,000	....	34,000	....
1859...........................	24,500	4,000	....	....	....	....
1860...........................	4,350	8,200	....	....	....	....
1861, (to January 31)	9,600	5,200	....	....	....	....
Total......................	816,450	1,599,492	831,025	24,000	1,130,628	1,004,000

D.—*Coinage of the mint and branches*—Continued.

3. BRANCH MINT, NEW ORLEANS.—Continued.

riod.	SILVER COINAGE.							TOTAL COINAGE.			
	Dollars.	Half dollars.	Quarter dollars.	Dimes.	Half dimes.	Three cents.	Bars.	Number of pieces.	Value of gold.	Value of silver.	Total value coined.
	Pieces.	*Pieces.*	*Pieces.*	*Pieces.*	*Pieces.*	*Pieces.*	*Value.*				
47.........	59,000	13,509,000	3,973,500	6,473,500	2,739,000	....	....	28,300,695	$15,180,365	$6,418,700 00	$93,606,065 00
57.........	40,000	21,406,000	4,586,000	5,690,000	5,170,500	780,000	....	43,538,250	23,934,250	12,681,100 00	35,815,350 00
....	....	4,514,000	1,416,500	1,540,000	4,540,000	....	....	10,996,000	1,315,000	2,942,900 00	4,257,000 00
....	200,000	4,910,000	544,000	440,100	1,060,000	....	$324,996 47	7,144,500	630,000	3,923,896 47	3,753,896 47
....	280,000	3,212,000	388,000	370,000	1,060,000	....	25,422 33	4,322,550	169,000	1,598,422 33	1,767,422 33
Jan'y 31)..	395,000	898,000	....	....	....	....	15,818 31	1,237,800	244,000	825,818 33	1,069,818 33
al.........	974,000	47,481,000	10,177,500	14,513,500	15,619,000	780,000	377,937 13	94,900,695	40,381,615	29,890,037 13	70,271,659 13

4. BRANCH MINT, DAHLONEGA.

Period.	GOLD COINAGE.					
	Half eagles.	Quarter eagles.	Three dollars.	Dollars.	Total pieces.	Total value.
	Pieces.	*Pieces.*	*Pieces.*	*Pieces.*		
1838 to 1847	576, 553	134, 101	....	....	710, 654	$3, 218, 017
1848 to 1857	478, 392	60, 605	1, 120	60, 897	601, 014	2, 607, 729
1858	19, 256	900	....	1, 637	21, 793	100, 167
1859	11, 404	642	....	6, 957	19, 003	65, 582
1860	12, 800	1, 602	....	1, 472	15, 844	69, 477
1861, (to February 28)	11, 876	....	....	1, 566	13, 442	60, 946
Total	1, 110, 281	197, 850	1, 120	72, 529	1, 381, 750	6, 121, 919

D.—*Coinage of the mint and branches*—Continued.

5. BRANCH MINT, CHARLOTTE.

Period.	GOLD COINAGE.				
	Half eagles.	Quarter eagles.	Dollars.	Total pieces.	Total value.
	Pieces.	*Pieces.*	*Pieces.*		
to 1847	269, 424	123, 576	....	393, 000	$1, 656, 060 00
to 1857	500, 872	79, 736	103, 899	684, 507	2, 807, 599 00
....	31, 066	9, 056	....	40, 122	177, 970 00
....	39, 500	....	5, 235	44, 735	202, 735 00
....	23, 005	7, 469	....	30, 474	133, 697 50
(to March 31)	14, 116	....	....	14, 116	70, 580 00
Total	877, 983	219, 837	109, 134	1, 206, 954	5, 048, 641 50

6. ASSAY OFFICE, NEW YORK.

Period.	Fine gold bars.	Value.	Silver bars.	Value.	Total pieces.	Total value.
1854	822	$2,888,059 18	....	....	822	$2,888,059 1
1855	6,182	20,441,813 63	....	....	6,182	20,441,813 6
1856	4,727	19,396,046 89	52	$6,792 63	4,779	19,402,839 5
1857	2,230	9,335,414 00	550	123,317 00	2,780	9,458,731 0
1858	7,052	21,798,691 04	894	171,961 79	7,946	21,970,652 8
1859	3,295	13,044,718 43	1,985	272,424 05	5,280	13,317,142 4
1860	....	6,831,532 01	....	222,226 11	....	7,053,758 1
1861	4,816	19,948,728 86	1,089	187,078 63	5,905	20,135,807 5
1862	....	16,094,768 44	....	415,603 57	....	16,510,372 0
Total	29,124	129,779,772 50	4,570	1,399,403 78	33,694	131,179,176 2

D.—*Coinage of the mint and branches*—Continued.

7. SUMMARY EXHIBIT OF THE COINAGE OF THE MINT AND BRANCHES TO THE CLOSE OF THE YEAR ENDING JUNE 30, 1862.

Mints.	Commencement of coinage.	Gold coinage.	Silver coinage.	Copper coinage.	Entire coinage.	
		Value.	*Value.*	*Value.*	*Pieces.*	*Value.*
...iladelphia	1793	$404,928,878 36	$97,725,589 86	$2,763,473 55	719,171,542	$505,417,941 77
...n Francisco	1854	144,532,156 81	2,375,532 71	....	12,264,739	146,907,689 52
...w Orleans, (to January 31, 1861)	1838	40,381,615 00	29,890,037 13	....	94,900,695	70,271,652 13
...arlotte, (to March 31, 1861)	1838	5,048,641 50	....	....	1,206,954	5,048,641 50
...hlonega, (to February 28, 1861)	1838	6,121,919 00	....	....	1,381,750	6,121,919 00
...say office, New York..	1854	129,779,772 50	1,399,403 78	....	33,694	131,179,176 28
Total...........		730,792,983 17	131,390,563 48	2,763,473 55	828,959,374	864,947,020 20

Statement of gold of domestic production deposited at the mint of the United States and branches to the close of the year ending June 30, 1862.

1. MINT OF THE UNITED STATES, PHILADELPHIA.

Period.	Parted from silver.	Virginia.	North Carolina.	South Carolina.	Georgia.	Tennessee.	Alabama.	New Mexico.
1804 to 1827			$110,000 00					
1828 to 1837		$427,000 00	2,519,500 00	$397,500 00	$1,763,900 00	$12,400 00		
1838 to 1847		513,594 00	1,303,636 00	159,366 00	566,316 00	16,499 00	$45,493 00	
1848 to 1857		534,491 56	467,237 00	55,626 00	44,577 50	6,664 00	9,451 00	$48,397 00
1858		16,377 00	15,175 00	300 00	16,365 00			
1859		15,720 00	9,305 00	4,675 00	20,190 00	240 00		975 00
1860		17,402 62	8,450 11		7,556 41	595 88		
1861		7,900 29	7,522 80		15,049 41		92 76	
1862			81 38		135 40			
Total		1,538,485 41	4,440,908 29	540,467 00	2,438,989 72	36,403 88	55,036 76	48,672 00

Period	Parted from silver.	California.	Oregon.	Colorado.	Arizona.	Washington Ter.	Other sources.	Total.
1804 to 1827								$110,000 00
1828 to 1837							$13,200 00	5,063,500 00
1838 to 1847							21,037 00	2,623,541 00
1848 to 1857		$226,829,591 62	$54,985 00				7,218 00	228,067,473 62
1858		1,373,506 07	3,600 00					1,426,323 07
1859		959,191 79	2,960 00	$145 00				1,012,701 79
1860		683,369 02	2,750 16	346,604 05			1,402 61	1,048,160 98
1861		426,387 81		607,592 06	$3,048 37		1,507 96	1,068,622 48
1862		$68,864 66	244,259 81		1,120,333 50		$215 70	1,435,890 45
Total	68,864 66	230,505,676 12	63,695 16	2,076,674 63	3,048 37	215 70	44,364 97	241,858,532 67

E.—*Statement of gold of domestic production*—Continued.

2. BRANCH MINT, SAN FRANCISCO.

Period.	Parted from silver.	California.	Colorado.	Nevada.	Oregon.	Total.
....	....	$10,842,281 23	....	....	....	$10,842,281 23
....	....	20,860,437 20	....	....	....	20,860,437 20
....	....	29,209,218 24	....	....	....	29,209,218 24
....	....	12,526,826 93	....	....	....	12,526,826 93
....	....	19,104,369 99	....	....	....	19,104,369 99
....	....	14,098,564 14	....	....	....	14,098,564 14
....	....	11,319,913 83	....	....	....	11,319,913 83
....	....	12,206,382 64	....	....	....	12,206,382 64
....	$822,823 91	14,029,759 95	$680 00	$13,000 00	$888,000 00	15,754,262 96
Total..............	822,823 01	144,197,754 15	680 00	13,000 00	888,000 00	145,922,257 16

E.—*Statement of gold of domestic production*—Continued.

3. BRANCH MINT OF NEW ORLEANS.

Period.	North Carolina.	South Carolina.	Georgia.	Tennessee.	Alabama.	California.	Colorado.	Other sources.	Total.
1838 to 1847	$741 00	$14,306 00	$37,365 00	$1,772 00	$61,903 00			$3,613 00	$119,699
1848 to 1857		1,911 00	2,317 00	947 00	15,379 00	$21,606,461 54		3,677 00	21,630,692
1858			1,560 00	162 12		448,439 84			450,163
1859						93,272 41			93,272
1860					661 53	97,135 00	$1,770 39		89,566
1861, (to January 31)						19,932 10	1,666 81		21,598
Total	741 00	16,217 00	41,241 00	2,883 12	77,943 53	22,255,240 89	3,437 20	7,290 00	22,404,993

E.—*Statement of gold of domestic production*—Continued.

4. BRANCH MINT, CHARLOTTE, NORTH CAROLINA.

Period.	North Carolina.	South Carolina.	California.	Total.
1838 to 1847	$1,529,777 00	$143,941 00		$1,673,718
1848 to 1857	2,503,412 68	222,754 17	$87,321 01	2,813,487
1858	170,560 33	5,507 16		176,067
1859	182,489 61	22,762 71		205,252
1860	134,491 17			134,491
1861, (to March 31)		65,558 30		65,558

5. BRANCH MINT, DAHLONEGA.

iod.	Utah.	North Carolina.	South Carolina.	Georgia.	Tennessee.	Alabama.	California.	Colorado.	Other sources.	Total.
1847.....	....	$64,351 00	$95,427 00	$2,978,353 00	$32,175 00	$47,711 00	....	....	....	$3,218,017 00
1857....	....	23,278 62	174,811 91	1,159,420 98	9,837 42	11,918 92	$1,294,719 89	....	$951 00	2,059,991 87
....	....	....	33,329 58	57,691 45	107 33	....	5,993 58	....	....	95,614 58
....	....	2,656,88	4,810 35	57,023 12	....	....	609 19	$813 70	....	65,073 24
Feb.23.)	....	3,483 70	2,004 36	35,588 92	....	....	1,097 37	24,906 86	....	67,085 21
....	$145 14	812 79	2,086 91	22,162 14	....	....	4,219 79	32,772 28	....	62,193 05
....	145 14	99,585 19	311,242 81	4,310,459 61	42,119 75	59,629 92	1,936,016 69	57,763 84	951 00	6,117,913 95

6. ASSAY OFFICE, NEW YORK.

riod.	Parted from silver.	Virginia.	North Carolina.	South Carolina.	Georgia.	Alabama.	New Mexico.	California.	Colorado.	Utah.	Arizona.	Oregon.	Nevada.	Other sources.	Total.
....	....	$167 0	$3,916 00	$395 00	$1,242 00	....	....	$9,291,457 00	....	....	....	....	....	$1,600 00	$9,297,177 00
....	....	2,370 00	3,750 00	7,690 00	13,100 00	$350 00	....	25,025,896 11	....	....	....	....	....	....	25,054,686 11
....	....	6,928 00	805 07	4,092 49	41,101 28	323 62	....	16,529,008 90	....	....	....	....	....	....	16,582,129 16
....	....	1,531 00	1,689 00	2,863 00	10,451 00	1,545 00	....	9,899,557 00	....	....	....	....	....	27,563 00	9,917,836 00
....	....	501 00	7,007 00	6,354 00	12,951 00	2,181 00	....	19,690,521 48	....	....	....	$5,581 00	....	405 00	19,732,629 46
....	....	430 00	20,109 00	700 00	14,755 00	569 00	....	11,694,879 23	$3,944 00	....	....	9,966 00	....	....	11,738,094 25
....	....	4,204 00	9,755 00	....	19,358 00	....	....	5,093,628 36	248,081 00	$4,080 00	$1,100 00	....	....	....	6,311,804 36
....	$241,029 00	3,869 00	2,753 00	670 00	6,900 00	918 00	$50,714 00	19,277,659 14	1,449,105 00	73,734 00	16,871 00	3,181 00	....	....	20,702,334 14
....	....	216 00	2,833 00	2,055 00	1,462 00	....	1,543 00	13,380,647 83	912,403 00	....	391 00	205 00	$40,846 00	3,293 00	15,754,962 96
al........	241,029 00	20,920 00	52,029 07	24,819 29	121,338 28	5,720 62	8,257 00	129,863,857 49	2,614,424 00	78,414 00	18,452 00	11,833 00	40,846 00	32,891 00	135,101,553 44

E.—*Statement of gold of domestic production*—Continued.

7. SUMMARY EXHIBIT OF THE ENTIRE DEPOSITS OF DOMESTIC GOLD AT THE UNITED STATES MINT AND BRANCHES TO JUNE 30, 1862.

Mint.	Parted from silver	Virginia.	North Carolina.	South Carolina.	Georgia.	Alabama.	Tennessee.	California.	Colorado.
Philadelphia	$68,264 66	$1,538,485 41	$4,449,908 99	$540,467 00	$9,436,089 72	$55,036 78	$56,403 88	$930,595,676 19	$9,075,674 63
San Francisco	339,823 01							144,197,754 15	680 00
New Orleans			741 00	16,917 00		41,941 00	3,883 12	92,955,940 89	3,437 00
Charlotte			4,590,730 79	480,593 31				87,321 01	
Dahlonega			99,585 19	311,242 81	4,310,459 61	59,829 92	48,119 75	1,938,016 69	57,763 84
Assay office	241,099 00	20,320 00	52,099 07	94,519 29	191,338 94	5,720 04		199,983,657 95	3,514,194 00
Total	1,132,716 67	1,558,805 41	9,113,994 34	1,352,969 44	6,909,198 61	198,330 83	81,406 75	589,145,865 91	4,753,049 67

Mint.	Parted from silver.	Utah.	Arizona.	Nebraska.	New Mexico.	Oregon.	Nevada.	Other sources.	Total.
Philadelphia		$1,507 96	$3,048 37	$1,402 01	$46,672 00	$63,625 16		$41,670 70	$941,856,532 67
San Francisco						856,000 00	$13,000 00	7,890 00	145,932,357 16
New Orleans									93,404,993 74
Charlotte									5,068,575 14
Dahlonega		145 14						851 00	6,117,913 96
Assay office		78,414 00	18,452 00		8,237 00	11,833 00	40,846 00	32,831 00	133,133,730 31
Total		80,067 10	21,500 37	1,402 01	56,929 00	963,458 16	53,846 00	82,739 70	554,506,009 97

ment of the amount of silver coined at the mint of the United States and its branches at San Francisco and New Orleans under the act of February 21, 1853.

Year.	United States mint at Philadelphia.	Branch mint, San Francisco.	Branch mint, New Orleans, to Jan. 31, 1861.	Total.
....	$7, 806, 461 00	....	$1, 225, 000 00	$9, 031, 461 00
....	5, 340, 130 00	....	3, 246, 000 00	8, 586, 130 00
....	1, 393, 170 00	$164, 075 00	1, 918, 000 00	3, 475, 245 00
....	3, 150, 740 00	177, 000 00	1, 744, 000 00	5, 071, 740 00
....	1, 333, 000 00	50, 000 00	....	1, 383, 000 00
....	4, 970, 980 00	127, 750 00	2, 942, 000 00	8, 040, 730 00
....	2, 926, 400 00	283, 500 00	2, 689, 000 00	5, 898, 900 00
....	519, 890 00	356, 500 00	1, 293, 000 00	2, 169, 390 00
....	1, 433, 800 00	198, 000 00	414, 000 00	2, 045, 800 00
....	2, 168, 941 50	641, 700 00	....	2, 810, 641 50
Total...........................	31, 043, 512 50	1, 998, 525 00	15, 471, 000 00	48, 513, 037 50

G.

Statement of the amount of silver of domestic production deposited at the mint of the United States and its branches, from Januar[y] 1841, to June 30, 1862.

Year.	Parted from gold.	Nevada.	Arizona.	Sonora.	North Carolina.	Lake Superior.	California.	Total.
1841 to 1851.	$768,509 00							$768,509 0
1852	404,494 00							404,494 0
1853	417,279 00							417,279 0
1854	328,199 00							328,199 0
1855	333,053 00							333,053 0
1856	321,938 38							321,938 3
1857	127,256 12							127,256 1
1858	300,849 36					$15,623 00		316,472 3
1859	219,647 34				$23,398 00	30,122 13		273,167 4
1860	138,561 70	$102,540 77	$13,357 00	$1,220 00	12,257 00	25,880 58		293,797 0
1861	364,724 73	213,420 84	12,260 00		6,233 00	13,372 72		610,011 2
1862	245,122 47	757,446 60	105 00			21,366 38	$3,224 00	1,032,264 4
Total	3,969,634 10	1,073,408 21	25,722 00	1,220 00	41,888 00	106,364 81	8,224 00	5,226,441

H.

Statement of the amount and denomination of fractions of the Spanish and Mexican dollar deposited at the mint of the United States for exchange for the new cent to June 30, 1860.

Year.	Quarters.	Eighths.	Sixteenths.	Value by tale.
1857	$78,295 00	$33,148 00	$16,602 00	$128,045 00
1858	68,644 00	64,472 00	32,085 00	165,201 00
1859	111,589 00	100,080 00	41,930 00	263,059 00
1860	182,330 00	51,630 00	24,105 00	258,065 00
Total	440,858 00	249,330 00	114,182 00	814,370 00

I.

Statement of the amount of fractions of the Spanish and Mexican dollar purchased at the mint of the United States, the branch mint, New Orleans, and assay office, New York, to June 30, 1862.

Year.	Mint of U. S., Philadelphia.	Branch mint, N. Orleans, to Jan. 31, 1861.	Assay office, New York.	Total.
1857	$174,485 00	$1,360 00	$112,502 00	$288,347 00
1858	326,033 00	17,355 00	147,453 00	490,841 00
1859	165,115 00	19,825 00	110,564 00	295,504 00
1860	58,353 74	9,075 00	62,072 00	129,500 74
1861	36,572 05	5,680 00	10,474 00	52,726 05
1862	20,585 95		11,401 00	31,986 95
Total	781,144 74	53,295 00	454,466 00	1,288,905 74

J.

Statement of cents of former issue deposited at the United States mint for exchange for cents of the new issue to June 30, 1860.

Year.	Value by tale.
1857	$16,602 00
1858	31,404 00
1859	47,235 00
1860	37,500 00
1861	95,245 00
1862	53,365 00
Total	281,351 00

A statement of foreign gold and silver coins prepared by the director of the mint, to accompany his annual report, in pursuance of the act of February 21, 1857.

EXPLANATORY REMARKS.

The first column embraces the names of the countries where the coins are issued; the second contains the name of coin, only the principal denominations being given. The other sizes are proportional; and when this is not the case, the deviation is stated.

The third column expresses the weight of a single piece in fractions of the troy ounce carried to the thousandth, and in a few cases to the ten thousandths of an ounce. The method is preferable to expressing the weight in grains for commercial purposes, and corresponds better with the terms of the mint. It may be readily transferred to weight in grains by the following rule: Remove the decimal point; from one-half deduct four per cent. of that half, and the remainder will be grains.

The fourth column expresses the fineness in thousandths—*i. e.*, the number of parts of pure gold or silver in 1,000 parts of the coin.

The fifth and sixth columns of the first table expresses the valuation of gold. In the fifth is shown the value as compared with the legal content or amount of fine gold in our coin. In the sixth is shown the value as paid at the mint after the uniform deduction of one-half of one per cent. The former is the value for any other purposes than recoinage, and especially for the purpose of comparison; the latter is the value in exchange for our coins at the mint.

For the silver there is no fixed legal valuation, the law providing for shifting the price according to the condition of demand and supply. The present price of standard silver is 1.22½ cents per ounce, at which rate the values in the fifth column of the second table are calculated. In a few cases, where the coins could not be procured, the data are assumed from the legal rates, and so stated.

K.

GOLD COINS.

Country.	Denomination.	Weight.	Fineness.	Value.	Value after deduction.
		Oz. dec.	Thous.		
Australia	Pound of 1852	0.281	916.5	$5 32.37	$5 29.71
Do	Sovereign of 1855–'60	0.256.5	916	4 85.58	4 83.16
Austria	Ducat	0.112	986	2 28.28	2 27.04
Do	Souverain	0.363	900	6 75.35	6 71.98
Do	New union crown, (assumed)	0.357	900	6 64.19	6 60.87
Belgium	Twenty-five francs	0.254	899	4 72.03	4 69.67
Bolivia	Doubloon	0.867	870	15 59.25	15 51.46
Brazil	Twenty milreis	0.575	917.5	10 90.57	10 85.12
Central America	Two escudos	0.209	853.5	3 68.75	3 66.91
Chili	Old doubloon	0.867	870	15 59.26	15 51.47
Do	Ten pesos	0.492	900	9 15.35	9 10.78
Denmark	Ten thaler	0.427	895	7 90.01	7 86.06
Ecuador	Four escudos	0.433	844	7 55.46	7 51.69
England	Pound or sovereign, new	0.256.7	916.5	4 86.34	4 83.91
Do	Pound or sovereign, average	0.256	915.5	4 84.48	4 82.06
France	Twenty francs, new	0.207.5	899.5	3 85.83	3 83.91
Do	Twenty francs, average	0.207	899	3 84.69	3 82.77
Germany, north	Ten thaler	0.427	895	7 90.01	7 86.06
Do	Ten thaler, Prussian	0.427	903	7 97.07	7 93.09
Do	Krone, (crown)	0.357	900	6 64.20	6 60.88
Do south	Ducat	0.112	986	2 28.28	2 27.14
Greece	Twenty drachms	0.185	900	3 44.19	3 42.47
Hindostan	Mohur	0.374	916	7 08.18	7 04.64
Italy	Twenty lire	0.207	898	3 84.26	3 82.34
Japan	Old cobang	0.362	568	4 44.0	3 41.8
Do	New cobang	0.280	572	3 57.6	3 55.8
Mexico	Doubloon, average	0.867.5	866	15 52.98	15 45.22
Do	Doubloon, new	0.867.5	870.5	15 61.05	15 53.25
Naples	Six ducati, new	0.245	996	5 04.43	5 01.91
Netherlands	Ten guilders	0.215	899	3 99.56	3 97.57
New Granada	Old doubloon, Bogota	0.868	870	15 61.06	15 53.26
Do	Old doubloon, Popayan	0.867	858	15 37.75	15 30.07
Do	Ten pesos, new	0.525	891.5	9 67.51	9 62.68
Peru	Old doubloon	0.867	868	15 55.67	15 47.90
Portugal	Gold crown	0.308	912	5 80.66	5 77.76
Prussia	New union crown, (assumed)	0.357	900	6 64.19	6 60.87
Rome	2½ scudi, new	0.140	900	2 60.47	2 59.17
Russia	Five roubles	0.210	916	3 97.64	3 95.66
Spain	100 reals	0.268	896	4 96.39	4 93.91
Do	80 reals	0.215	869.5	3 86.44	3 84.51
Sweden	Ducat	0.111	975	2 23.72	2 22.61
Tunis	25 piastres	0.161	900	2 99.54	2 98.05
Turkey	100 piastres	0.231	915	4 36.93	4 34.75
Tuscany	Sequin	0.112	999	2 31.29	2 30.14

L.

SILVER COINS.

Country.	Denomination.	Weight.	Fineness.	Value.
		Oz. dec.	*Thous.*	$
Austria	Old rix dollar	0. 902	633	$1 02. 37
Do	Old scudo	0. 836	902	1 02. 64
Do	Florin before 1858	0. 451	833	51. 14
Do	New florin	0. 397	900	48. 63
Do	New union dollar	0. 596	900	73. 01
Do	Maria Theresa dollar, 1780	0. 895	838	1 02. 12
Belgium	Five francs	0. 803	897	98. 04
Bolivia	New dollar	0. 643	903. 5	79. 07
Do	Half dollar	0. 432	667	39. 22
Brazil	Double milreis	0. 820	918. 5	1 02. 53
Canada	Twenty cents	0. 150	925	18. 87
Central America	Dollar	0. 866	850	1 00. 19
Chili	Old dollar	0. 864	908	1 06. 79
Do	New dollar	0. 801	900. 5	98. 17
Denmark	Two rigsdaler	0. 927	877	1 10. 65
England	Shilling, new	0. 182. 5	924. 5	22. 96
Do	Shilling, average	0. 178	925	22. 41
France	Five franc, average	0. 800	900	98. 00
Germany, north	Thaler before 1857	0. 712	750	72. 67
Do....north	New thaler	0. 595	900	72. 89
Do....south	Florin before 1857	0. 340	900	41. 65
Do....south	New florin, (assumed)	0. 340	900	41. 65
Greece	Five drachms	0. 719	900	88.08
Hindostan	Rupee	0. 374	916	46. 62
Japan	Itsebu	0. 279	991	37. 63
Do	New itzebu	0. 279	890	33..80
Mexico	Dollar, new	0. 867.5	903	1 06. 62
Do	Dollar, average	0. 866	901	1 06. 20
Naples	Scudo	0. 844	830	95. 34
Netherlands	2½ guild	0. 804	944	1 03. 31
Norway	Specie daler	0. 927	877	1 10. 65
New Granada	Dollar of 1857	0. 803	896	97. 92
Peru	Old dollar	0. 866	901	1 06. 20
Do	Dollar of 1858	0. 766	909	94. 77
Do	Half.dollar of 1835–'38	0. 433	650	38. 31
Prussia	Thaler before 1857	0. 712	750	72. 68
Do	New thaler	0. 595	900	72. 89
Rome	Scudo	0. 864	900	1 05. 84
Russia	Rouble	0. 667	875	79. 44
Sardinia	Five lire	0. 803	900	98. 00
Spain	New pistareen	0. 166	899	20. 31
Sweden	Rix dollar	1. 092	750	1 11. 48
Switzerland	Two francs	0. 323	899	39. 52
Tunis	Five piastres	0. 511	898. 5	62. 49
Turkey	Twenty piastres	0. 770	830	86. 98
Tuscany	Florin	0. 220	925	27. 70

A.

TREASURY DEPARTMENT,
First Auditor's Office, October 30, 1862.

SIR: I have the honor to submit the following report of the operations of this office for the fiscal year ending June 30, 1862:

RECEIPTS.

Accounts adjusted.	No. of accounts	Amount.
Collectors of customs.	1,163	$47,201,589 29
Collectors under steamboat act	314	24,022 65
Aggregate receipts	1,477	47,225,611 94

DISBURSEMENTS.

Collectors and disbursing agents of the treasury	691	$3,863,311 21
Official emoluments of collectors, naval officers, and surveyors.	884	823,696 86
Additional compensation of collectors, naval officers, and surveyors	18	5,573 49
Accounts for duties illegally exacted, and in satisfaction of judgments rendered in United States circuit courts	42	106,595 69
Accounts for net proceeds of unclaimed merchandise, duties exacted on damaged merchandise, and for storage and fees illegally exacted	306	238,481 53
The judiciary	835	945,021 67
Interest on the public debt	12	10,582,132 07
Treasury notes for redemption, and received in payment of duties and other public dues	1,377	45,618,552 26
Reimbursing temporary loan of August 19, 1861, from associated banks	1	8,875,000 00
Reimbursement of temporary loan	142	9,216,040 15
Temporary loans, act of February 25, 1862	3	960,650 00
Certificates of indebtedness	1	615,961 63
Demand treasury notes destroyed	5	8,250,000 00
Money in lieu of bounty land	2	200 00
Property lost in the military service of the United States	58	9,829 53
Inspection of steam vessels, for travelling expenses, &c	103	13,626 39
Life-saving stations, coasts of Long Island and New Jersey	7	5,795 80
Support of insane asylum of Washington	5	44,489 31
Columbia Institution for deaf, dumb, and blind	9	6,746 60
Superintendent of Public Printing	68	371,293 17
Designated depositaries for additional compensation	6	942 94
Commissioner of Public Buildings	382	230,896 97
Contingent expenses of the Senate and House of Representatives of the United States, and of the departments of the government	417	1,329,329 95
Support of the penitentiary of the District of Columbia	8	52,148 41
Bounty for the capture of slaves, under act of March 3, 1819.	374	58,385 99
Mints and assay offices	29	87,298,420 39
Territories	56	112,506 63
Coast survey	24	590,239 80
Salaries of officers of the civil list, paid directly from the treasury	794	332,418 68
Disbursing clerks for paying salaries	235	1,876,753 15
Disbursing agent, California land claims	3	2,869 22
Withdrawal of applications in appeal cases	4	15,926 66

A—Continued.

Accounts adjusted.	No. of accounts.	Amount.
Treasurer of the United States, for general receipts and expenditures..	4	$164,983,859 58
Superintendents of lights.................................	280	421,769 74
Agents of marine hospitals................................	380	256,214 05
Miscellaneous..	341	4,427,008 86
Total	7,906	352,564,687 88

Number of reports and certificates recorded..........................	7,997
Number of letters recorded	1,065
Acknowledgments of accounts written	4,770
Total	13,832

T. L. SMITH, *Auditor.*

Hon. S. P. CHASE,
   Secretary of the Treasury.

B.

Statement of the operations of the Second Auditor's office during the fiscal year ending June 30, 1862, showing the number of money accounts settled, and the amount of the expenditures embraced therein, and, in general, the other duties pertaining to the business of the office; prepared in obedience to instructions of the Secretary of the Treasury.

The number of accounts settled is 9,606, embracing an expenditure of $37,111,957 47, under the following heads, viz:

Pay department		$4,181,276 33
Indian affairs		3,335,885 23
Ordnance department, viz:		
Expended by disbursing officers	$3,730,064 66	
Private claims, including expenditure under appropriation for purchase, &c., of arms, &c.	23,340,549 47	
		27,070,614 13
Quartermaster's department, expended on account of "contingencies of the army," medical and hospital and ordnance appropriations		79,026 15
Medical and hospital department, viz:		
Expended by disbursing officers.............	$791,865 64	
Private claims, including accounts of contract surgeons, &c.............................	899,787 56	
		1,691,653 20
Expenses of recruiting		217,088 97
Arrears of pay, &c., to discharged and deceased officers and soldiers..		249,180 64
Contingencies of the army, expended by disbursing clerk of the War Department		78,961 66

Purchase of book of tactics, &c., for volunteers.............	$37,255 74
Miscellaneous claims, including contingencies, collecting, drilling and organizing volunteers, Harper's Ferry armory, &c.	64,694 32
Police of Baltimore......................................	99,326 48
Removing stables around Washington Infirmary............	4,588 22
Expenses of commanding general's office	2,237 16
Contingent expenses of adjutant general's department	169 24
Property accounts examined and adjusted	5,021
Requisitions registered, recorded, and posted, ...	5,589
Letters, claims, &c., received, briefed, and registered	37,473
Letters written, recorded, indexed, and mailed	14,584
Private claims suspended or rejected...........................	822
Army recruits registered	18,007
Dead and discharged soldiers registered.......................	7,510
Certificates of military service issued to Pension Office............	206

In addition to the foregoing, various statements and reports have been prepared and transmitted from this office, as follows:

Annual statement of disbursements in the department of Indian affairs for the fiscal year ending June 30, 1862; prepared for Congress, comprised in 580 manuscript pages, foolscap.

Annual statement of the recruiting fund; prepared for the adjutant general of the army.

Annual statement of the contingencies of the army; prepared in duplicate for the Secretary of War.

Annual statement of the contingent expenses of this office; transmitted to the Secretary of the Treasury.

Annual report of balances on the books of this office remaining unaccounted for more than one year; transmitted to the First Comptroller.

Annual report of balances on the books of this office remaining unaccounted for more than three years; transmitted to the First Comptroller.

Annual statement of the clerks and others employed in this office during the year 1861, showing the amount paid to each on account of salary; transmitted to the Secretary of the Treasury.

Statement showing all payments made to the Pottawatomie Indians, either in money or goods, under the various treaties with those tribes, beginning with the treaty of Greenville, in 1795, and embracing the treaty of 5th and 17th June, 1846. By an act of Congress approved 2d March, 1861, it became the duty of the Second Auditor to prepare this statement. The only process for accomplishing the work was that of a careful examination of the accounts of the numerous superintendents, agents, and sub-agents disbursing moneys appropriated for the fulfilment of the treaty stipulations. The records of the office furnish reliable data as to the payments made to the Indians from 1813 to 1860, embracing a period of forty-eight years. The necessary routine in obtaining from the files the proper accounts for examination involved much time and labor. The treaties in the case, numbering thirty or more, were first to be strictly examined, and each article and its requirements set forth. The annual appropriations were then to be traced; the agents who drew the money from the treasury ascertained; and the dates of the settlements of their accounts sought from the books in which they are recorded. The number of settlements duly examined in this investigation was but little short of five hundred. There are three clerks in the office employed in the examination and adjustment of Indian accounts. One of these has the management of the property book; the other two that of the money accounts. To one of the latter class was assigned the duty of preparing the statement in question. The time unavoidably occupied in the performance of the work was some eight or nine months, subtracting to that extent from the current operations of this branch of the public service during the last fiscal year.

Monthly reports of the clerks in this office, submitted each month to the Secretary of the Treasury, in compliance with his instructions of the 17th August and 11th September, 1861, together with a tabular statement showing the amount of business transacted in the office during the month, and the number of accounts remaining unsettled at the close of the month.

The bookkeeper's register shows the settlement of 5,574 ledger accounts, which have been regularly journalized and posted in the ledgers which, as well as those for the appropriations, have been duly kept up. The payments made to officers by paymasters of the army have been entered in the officers' and company pay-books of both the regular and volunteer service.

E. B. FRENCH, Auditor.

TREASURY DEPARTMENT,
   Second Auditor's Office, October 24, 1862.

C.

TREASURY DEPARTMENT,
Third Auditor's Office, November 8, 1862.

SIR : I have the honor to submit the following report of the operations of this bureau during the fiscal year ending June 30, 1862.

From the bookkeeper's statement it appears that requisitions have been drawn by the Secretary of War on the Secretary of the Treasury during the fiscal year, on such of the appropriations for the military service as are entered on the books of this office, to the amount of $232,655,673 35.

The principal appropriations drawn upon, as above, were for the following objects :

For quartermaster's department	$29, 591, 150 63
For incidental expenses, quartermaster's department	13, 986, 778 79
For army transportation	47, 213, 457 83
For barracks and quarters	2, 522, 107 55
For purchase of horses	13, 773, 745 84
For clothing of the army	56, 549, 985 14
For subsistence of the army, three months militia, and two and three years volunteers	48, 695, 360 86
For refunding to States expenses of volunteers	7, 645, 825 99
For gunboats on western rivers	2, 159, 922 69

Counter requisitions were drawn on sundry persons for transfers in settlements treasury drafts cancelled, and deposits in treasury, to amount of $1,448,216 98

The accounts audited in this office, and reported to the Comptroller, of advances made to disbursing officers and agents, claims settled and paid, including amounts due contractors, unclaimed pensions, and of persons under special acts of Congress, involved the sum of $32,277,710 64.

A more detailed statement of the number and description of accounts examined in the various divisions of the office will be found appended to this report.

Although it appears that the amounts involved in the accounts, claims, &c., examined and audited during the last fiscal year are large beyond precedent, yet a mere inspection of the figures affords but an imperfect idea of the increased labor· and responsibility devolved on this office during the year, and which will be increased in a still greater ratio during the present year.

. For many years the amounts involved in expenditures, the accounts for which were audited in this office, averaged but little more than ten·millions of dollars per annum, and during the last ten years the largest amount of settlements in any one year involved less than sixteen millions. After the Mexican war it was estimated that the excess of expenditures for the entire army for three years, viz : from April 1, 1846, till April· 1, 1849, over those for the three years immediately preceding the war, amounted to $58,853,993 41, being an average of less than twenty millions per annum. A large portion· of this, viz : for pay, ordnance, hospital, and clothing supplies, was settled in the Second Auditor's office. Notwithstanding the comparatively small increase in the· expenditures, this office at that time fell largely in arrear, and it was not until 1853 that the arrearages were brought up. In the years 1850–'51–'52, respectively, there remained on hand 1,820, 1,900, and 2,359 unsettled accounts. So far, however, this office has prevented an undue accumulation of business, so that at the close of the last fiscal year there remained on hand and unadjusted only 593 accounts, many of which could not be settled, for the reason that explanations and further evidence were required before an adjustment could be made. These accounts involved an expenditure of upwards of twenty millions of dollars, but during the first quarter of the present fiscal year fully that amount of accounts have been adjusted and reported to the Comptroller ; other accounts, however, have in the meantime been received ; thus leaving the balance on hand, on the 30th ultimo, about the same amount, and which is equivalent to about one quarter's work.

Under the act of March 3, 1849, " to provide for the payment of horses and other property lost or destroyed in the military service of the United States." 392 claims have been presented at this office during the fiscal year, and 56 awards were made on which the sum of $9,869 19 was· allowed and paid. These claims are accumulating. During the first quarter of the present fiscal year 285 claims have been received, amounting to $65,062 41, and 45· awards have been made, on which the sum of $8,617 14 was allowed and paid. At the end of the quarter there remained on file 579 claims, arising under the act since the present war, involving the sum of $110,798 63. Some old claims for losses during the Mexican war still remain unadjusted, but the claimants nearly all reside in the so-called· seceded States, or in States a portion of whose citizens are in rebellion against the government. It has been deemed advisable, under the circumstances, to let them rest at present, giving a preference to claims arising out of recent losses. It is believed that but a very small portion of these old claims would be allowable at any rate. Of the claims now being allowed, nearly all are for·horses actually killed in battle. A considerable number have been filed for losses occasioned by capture, both horse and rider being taken, and the officer or private afterwards deprived of his horse by the enemy. No action has been taken on claims of this description. Some claims have also been filed, under the second section of the law, for " boats," in the service by contract, and lost, by unavoidable accident, or abandonment, or destroyed by order of the officers in command. No action has been taken on any of these claims. If the word " boat," as used in that section, be held to include *steamboats*, there·is no estimating the number and amount of claims that may arise under the law. I respectfully recommend that some other provision be made by Congress for the settlement of claims of this description. When the act was passed; it was not anticipated that such an immense amount of claims would at any time be placed exclusively under the ·jurisdiction of the Third Auditor. And·from what has already been seen, it is manifest that, as at present situated, it is next·to impossible for him· to devote that time and investigation necessary to their proper adjudication.

The extended military operations have had the effect of increasing the claims

Ex. Doc. 1——6

of a miscellaneous character, such as for arrearages of pay due deceased team-
sters and other employés of the quartermaster's department, and claims for subsistence or property furnished to the service under certain circumstances, but
which, not being paid by the officers contracting the liability for want of funds,
are referred to the treasury for settlement. All such receive the administrative
examination and approval of the proper military bureau before being acted on
by the accounting officers. Some large claims for clothing purchased and for
railroad transportation have been in this way paid through the Treasury Department, instead of through the quartermaster or other disbursing officer. The
aggregate amount of 520 claims presented during the year (including 20, in
which no specific sum was claimed) was $4,880,739 14. Of these, 378 have
been acted on, and payment, to the amount of $4,354,724 06, has been made.
Of the remaining 151 claims, some have been reported to the Comptroller, others
have been referred to the appropriate military bureaus for examination, and not
returned, a few have been withdrawn, and the remainder have not been acted
upon.

Claims of States for reimbursement of expenses incurred by them in "enrol-
ling, subsisting, clothing, supplying, arming, equipping, paying, and transport-
ing" their troops "employed in aiding to suppress the present insurrection
against the United States," provision for the settlement of which was made by
the act of July 27, 1861, have been filed in this office during the year and up
to the present time, to the amount of $23,941,834 49. The Secretary of the
Treasury, in his report to Congress at the commencement of the last session,
stated that, "as the law did not seem to contemplate the continued action of
State officers for federal objects, but confined the appropriation made by it to
expenses incurred, leaving expenses to be incurred to the action of federal
officers within their respective spheres of duty, the Secretary has not thought
himself authorized to settle in the unusual mode provided by the act, except
for advances actually made, or, at least, contracted for prior to its passage."
At the last session of Congress, however, an amendatory act was passed directing that the said act "shall be construed to apply to expenses incurred as well
after as before the date of the approval thereof." Hence, the claims filed include expenditures incurred from the date of the first proclamation of the President up till the date of filing the claims. The claims of Vermont and Virginia,
and parts of the claims of Iowa, Illinois, and New Jersey, have been reported
to the Second Comptroller. The claims of Maine, Connecticut, New York,
Michigan, Pennsylvania, Wisconsin, Indiana, New Hampshire, Ohio, and Minnesota have been taken up for examination, some of which are nearly ready to
report, and others are awaiting additional information or evidence from the
State authorities before they can be finally acted on. At an early period the
Secretary consented to make advances, or partial payments, to the State authorities to the amount of forty per centum on amounts expended by them, and such
payments have been made to the amount of $7,645,825 99 up till 1st October.

In the "act to provide increased revenue from imports, to pay interest on the
public debt, and for other purposes," approved August 5, 1861, a direct tax of
$20,000,000 was levied on the States, agreeably to an apportionment therein
made, and it was provided that a deduction of fifteen per centum should be made
on such parts of said tax as might be paid into the treasury of the United
States on or before the last day of June, in the year to which such payment
relates, and it was further provided that the amount of such tax apportioned to
any State should be liable to be paid and satisfied, in whole or in part, by the
release of such State, duly executed to the United States, of any liquidated
and determined claim of such State, and that in case of such release such State
should be allowed the same abatement of the amounts of such tax as would be
allowed in case of payment of the same in money. By the act of May 3, 1862,
this provision was directed to be so construed as to apply to all such claims of

States for reimbursement, as above, as should be filed with the proper officer of the United States before the 30th of July, and the abatement of fifteen per cent. was directed to be made on such portion of the tax as might be paid by the allowance of such claims, in whole or in part, the same as if the final settlement and liquidation thereof had been made before the last day of June.

The quotas of direct tax apportioned to the States which have filed their claims for reimbursement as above, amount, in the aggregate, to $13,086,849 62; deduct fifteen per centum, there will remain a net amount due the United States of $11,123,822 18. To this add the amount of advances, or partial payments, already made, and we have an aggregate of $18,769,648 17; being only $5,172.186 32 less than the total amount of claims presented. But these claims will be more or less reduced on final settlement, so that I am inclined to think the sum of the amounts allowed will not greatly exceed the amount of tax. In certain of the States the volunteers are paid a monthly pay, for themselves or families, in addition to the regular army pay of the United States, and they have charged this in their claims for reimbursement. All such payments will be disallowed.

The whole amount of Oregon and Washington Indian war claims filed under the act of March 2, 1861, is $3,946,555. At the date of my last annual report claims to amount of $1,093,465 88 had been acted on, and awards made thereon amounting to $501,671 66. Since then claims to amount of $1,692,267 12 have been acted on, and awards made amounting to $963,251 83. Total amounts acted on, $2,785,733, on which the sum of $1,464,923 49 has been awarded for payment. There, therefore, remain in the office claims involving the sum of $1,160,822, on which, when acted on, between $500,000 and $600,000 will probably be allowed and paid. It is hoped that before long these claims will be disposed of.

By the act of March 2, 1861, an appropriation was made of $400,000, or so much thereof as shall be necessary to defray the expenses incurred by the State of California in the suppression of Indian hostilities therein in the years 1854, '55, '56, '58, and '59, and the Third Auditor was directed to audit the accounts of the State for the services of volunteers, and for supplies, transportation, and personal services, agreeably to certain rules prescribed in the act. On the 2d of November, 1861, the books, papers, rolls, &c., relating to said claim were filed by the agents of the State in this office, the amount claimed being $449,605 74. The claims relating to the various expeditions have been examined and investigated according to the best lights and information attainable, and the sum of $229,987 67 appears to be allowable. An award has not yet been made, but will be prepared and executed in a short time.

Whilst I feel justified, therefore, in saying that, considering the circumstances and the difficulties under which this office has labored, the business committed to its charge is in a satisfactory condition, I cannot omit observing that, with all the industry and effort of which the present force is capable, it will be impossible to keep up with the demands of the service and prevent an accumulation of business. The advances from the treasury to disbursing officers, on requisitions from the Secretary of War registered in this office during the last fiscal year, amounted to $227,253,952 94. During the first quarter of the present fiscal year the advances on similar requisitions amounted to $65,294,044 85, or at the rate of $260,000,000 for the year. Add to this the amounts involved in claims of States, accounts of other disbursing officers, and business arising under special acts of Congress, and we have an aggregate quadrupling the entire expenses of the government for civil, legislative, judicial, army, navy, &c., &c., in former years.

The accounts audited and on hand unaudited amounting in the aggregate to less than $70,000,000, while the advances amounted to $227,000,000, it follows that accounts for disbursements to the amount of, say, $150,000,000, are yet outstanding, or, having been rendered to the proper military bureau, have not yet reached this office. It is known that a large number of accounts are on hand in the military bureaus undergoing "administrative scrutiny," and these will, in due course, reach the treasury officers. Presuming that the necessary measures have been or will be taken there to keep pace with the increased demands of the service, this accumulation must necessarily be transferred to the treasury. It is only a question of time, as eventually these accounts must all find their way to the treasury. Thus it will be seen that, great as have been the increased demands on this office, much greater remain in store. Looking to this probable accumulation, and with a view of taking some precautionary measures to meet it, in my last annual report I recommended that authority be obtained for the employment of ten additional clerks. About the first of May last ten clerks who had been on temporary duty in the office of the Secretary of the Treasury were transferred to this office and have since been employed therein. These added to the regular force will make seventy-one clerks. In the estimates just made for the next fiscal year I have submitted an estimate for twenty additional clerks; and I have no hesitation in saying that their services will be absolutely necessary, and the authority for their employment should be obtained as soon as practicable. The total force of the office will then be ninety-one clerks. It is proper to state here that in point of fact this increase will only about restore the number of clerks legally attached to this office and appropriated therefor prior to July 1, 1860. At that time, not anticipating such a condition of affairs as has since transpired, by my recommendation twenty-nine clerks who were legally attached to the office, and whose salaries were charged to its appropriations but were temporarily doing duty in other offices, were permanently transferred to those offices, thus reducing the appropriations for clerks in the office in the sum of $39,200, and the number of clerks from ninety to sixty-one.

But, as before remarked, a mere reference to the vast increase in the expenditures, as compared with former years, affords no adequate idea of the unprecedented difficulties and responsibilities devolved upon the officers of this department who are charged with the settlement of these accounts. Previous to the breaking out of the rebellion the military establishment consisted of about fifteen thousand men, so organized as to be capable of considerable expansion without materially affecting or requiring much addition to the disbursing departments. The officers were generally experienced in their line of duty, and perfectly familiar with the laws and regulations applicable to the various branches of the service. The total number of officers disbursing in the quartermaster's and commissary departments, and having accounts to render, averaged less than four hundred for several years prior to 1861, and a large portion of these were acting for short periods of time, and disbursing small amounts of money. By the Army Register for 1860 there were but thirty-six officers regularly commissioned in the quartermaster's department, and but twelve in the subsistence department. By a late official report from the commissary general I am advised that for the second quarter of the present year there were twelve hundred and four officers having accounts to render in the subsistence department; and a similar report from the quartermaster general advises me that there were seven hundred and thirty-three officers in his department who will have accounts to render for the same quarter. Add to these the commissaries and quartermasters appointed or to be appointed for the troops received or to be received into service under the late calls, and I think the number may be safely estimated at twenty-five hundred. When it is remembered that the large proportion of these officers are but recently appointed, mostly taken from the walks of civil life, inexperienced, ignorant alike of their duties and the laws and regulations applicable to the branches of service in which they are engaged, in some cases incompetent or otherwise unfitted for the position, it may well be expected that many irregularities will take place, the proper forms often be not observed, unauthorized expenditures incurred, and, indeed, violations of express regulations, and errors of every description—of omission as well as com mission—occur. All these things complicate and render more difficult the investigation and settlement of the accounts, necessarily increase the labor of the accounting officers, and, besides involving the disbursing officers in difficulties growing out of the suspension or disallowance of their vouchers, often result in losses to the treasury impossible to be reclaimed. And the inexperience of the disbursing officers above referred to is not the sole cause of such irregularities, for they are not unfrequently led into them by their superior officers, from the same inexperience on their part, and want of knowledge of the laws and regulations. There is a regulation which provides that "an officer shall have credit for an expenditure of money or property made in obedience to the order of his commanding officer. If the expenditure is disallowed, it shall be charged to the officer who ordered it." This regulation is held up as a shield of protection for unauthorized expenditures by disbursing officers, made upon the approval or under the order of the commanding officer; and whilst it does often relieve the officer so paying, it only transfers the liability to the officer giving the order, thus giving rise to a controversy between him and the government as to the legality or propriety of the expenditure. Cases of this description are of not unfrequent occurrence. By some officers this regulation would seem to be regarded as recognizing in them a sort of general and unlimited authority to direct the payment of claims and liabilities of every description, provided they appear to be just and meritorious, without regard to whether such payments are authorized by law or regulations, or embraced in any of the appropriations made by Congress. Of this character are claims for damages for property destroyed or injured by troops, or impressed into the public service, &c. Many such payments are believed to have been made; and all vouchers therefor must necessarily be rejected at the treasury, however meritorious or equitable they may appear to be. Congress will no doubt at some period make provision for the investigation and payment of all proper claims for losses or damages growing out of the military operations, under such rules and regulations as may be deemed just and right. Until such provision is made, or some appropriation made for payment of such claims, disbursing officers are not authorized, nor have commanding officers any right, to require them to pay them out of moneys in their hands belonging to any of the appropriations specifically made for the support and maintenance of the army and the various branches of the service connected with it. And so with regard to other departures from law or regulations. In short, the accounting officers feel it their duty to require conformity to the *laws* and *regulations* in force, and until changed by competent authority, adhering also to established rules and principles, the more necessary and important now, when the legitimate expenditures have reached such a vast amount, and so many opportunities offer for incurring unauthorized expenditures.

The system of accountability for public money placed in the hands of officers for disbursement that was suited to a state of peace and a small military establishment may need some revision to meet the condition of things arising from the present state of the country. Officers who had not heretofore disbursed more than a few thousands or hundreds of thousands of dollars per annum are now disbursing as many millions in a single quarter of the year. The security and check provided for faithful performance of duty and to guard against improvident expenditures which were considered ample may now be inadequate. In such an emergency, in the hurry and confusion incident to the bringing into the field such immense armies, it was impossible to avoid irregularities in the purchasing, contracting, &c., growing out of the inexperience or unfaithfulness of agents employed for the purpose. Such abuses readily disclose themselves, however, and the remedy can be easily applied. In the formation of a system such as shall afford the greatest possible security against fraud, peculation, or improvidence in expenditures, and also secure the faithful application of the public money to the specific purpose for which it is raised and set apart, every provision possible should be made for the most rigid scrutiny and strict accountability. The system now in force, in the main, is well adapted to secure these objects. All accounts for disbursements receive a triple examination; first, by the military bureau under whose direction the expenditures were made; next, by this office, where the formal report and statement are made; and, finally, by the Comptroller who revises the settlement. It is believed that, for fidelity in the performance of their duties, the disbursing officers of the army have compared favorably hitherto with those in any other branch of the government. While this is the case, however, it is not doubted that some improvements might be made by the adoption of safeguards and restrictions not hitherto necessary, but now rendered essential by the changed circumstances of the time. Take, for instance, the quartermaster's department. This is one of the most extensive branches of the military service. It is the duty of this department to make the purchases of clothing for the army, horses, wagons, equipments, forage; to provide means of transportation for troops and supplies, &c.; and advances of money are made to its officers directly from the treasury upon requisitions of the Secretary of War in their favor. The disbursements of this branch of the service during the past year amount to more than one hundred and sixty millions of dollars.

The fifth section of the act "regulating the accountability for clothing and equipage issued to the army of the United States, and for the better organization of the quartermaster's department," provides "that each officer appointed under this act shall, before he enters upon his duties, give bond, with sufficient surety, to be approved by the Secretary of War, in such sum as the President shall direct, with condition for the faithful performance of the duties of his office." The bonds of quartermasters now in the service have been executed at various periods, some of them a number of years ago, and were doubtless fixed in amount with reference to the then existing state of affairs, and the amounts of money and property for which they would probably become accountable. None of them, as far as I am advised, exceed thirty thousand dollars; for the most part they seldom exceed ten thousand dollars. There are disbursing officers whose bonds do not exceed the latter sum, who have been accountable for and disbursed at least that many millions of dollars during the past year. Now, it is true that the security for faithful performance of duty does not depend merely on official bonds, and, therefore, the amount of penalty in a bond is, after all, only secondary to that greater security, the personal integrity of the officer; nevertheless, all experience has shown the necessity of requiring bonds for amounts in some degree commensurate with the responsibilities imposed. These remarks apply equally to officers disbursing in the commissary department. It is, therefore, respectfully suggested whether some of these bonds should not be renewed as well as increased in amount. Furthermore, the exigencies of the service frequently require that *acting* assistant quartermasters or commissaries be appointed, and who are charged with the same duties that devolve upon the regular quartermasters and commissaries, and in like manner receive money for disbursement either directly from the treasury or from other officers having money in their hands. In such cases I am not aware that any security is given or required. It is true these appointments are generally only for a temporary purpose, or a short period of time; although I believe instances are not unfrequent where they have been continued for a considerable time, during which large amounts of money have been in their possession.

It is believed that some looseness has prevailed in the mode of transacting business by some disbursing officers, especially in the matter of taking receipts for payments not actually made, such receipts sometimes being used as vouchers in the settlement of their accounts. The modes by which credits may thus be obtained for money not actually paid, or for a sum greater than the actual con tract price, are numerous. It is true, the law makes offences of this kind embezzlement, but the difficulty lies in detecting the transaction and establishing the fact. Officers may also, in times like the present, have on hand large sums of money not actually needed for current demands upon them, which are thus exposed to risk of loss, as well as affording temptation for use or employment for their personal benefit and advantage. Various modes have been suggested to provide against this. It has been suggested that advances of money should not be made directly to the officers, but that they should have credits for specified amounts with the United States Treasurer, or assistant treasurers, and be required to draw checks or drafts in payment of all liabilities incurred by them. Some legislation has been had on this subject, but it does not seem to have entirely accomplished the purpose. It is believed, however, that a system might be devised upon this principle which could be carried into practical execution and enforced. Not the least among the advantages of such a system would be the retaining in the treasury of several millions of dollars, which otherwise remain in the hands of disbursing officers. And the difficulty which sometimes exists in collecting balances in the hands of officers when ceasing to disburse, or when going out of the service by death, resignation, or otherwise, would be avoided

The act of 3d March, 1817, providing for the settlement of accounts and prescribing the duties of the Comptrollers and Auditors, made it the duty of the Second Auditor to "receive all accounts relative to the pay and clothing of the army, the subsistence of officers, bounties and premiums, military and hospital stores, and the contingent expenses of the War Department;" and of the Third Auditor to receive "all accounts relative to the subsistence of the army, the quartermaster's department, and generally all accounts of the War Department other than those provided for," said Auditors to examine the accounts, respectively, and certify the balance and transmit the accounts, with the vouchers and certificate, to the Second Comptroller for his decision thereon." In the army appropriation act, approved March 3, 1857, a certain sum was appropriated for the purchase of clothing for the army, camp and garrison equipage, and it was provided that "hereafter all the accounts and vouchers of the disbursing officers of the quartermaster's department of the army shall be audited and settled by the Third Auditor of the Treasury." Under the operation of this provision the class of accounts known as the accounts of officers of the "purchasing department," for disbursements on account of clothing and equipage, which had previously been settled by the Second Auditor, were transmitted through the Quartermaster General's office to this office, leaving to the Second Auditor the settlement of accounts pertaining to the pay of the army, arms, &c., hospital stores and contingencies of the army and War Department. The purchasing officers of clothing, camp and garrison equipage relieve themselves from accountability by producing the receipt of the military storekeeper of the post that the property has been "received by him in store." The accounts of the military storekeepers show the issue and application to the public service, and these accounts are settled by the Second Auditor. I think all the accounts, both of money and property expended and issued under one appropriation, should be adjusted in the same office. Military storekeepers having in charge clothing, camp and garrison equipage, but no money for disbursement, may not be regarded, strictly, as "disbursing officers" of the quartermaster's department, but are intimately connected and blended therewith in the particulars mentioned. It is, therefore, recommended that such further legislation be had on the subject as will require all accounts relating to the purchase and issue of clothing, camp and garrison equipage to be settled in one office. Indeed, it has been heretofore recommended by the Secretaries of the Treasury and War Departments that *all* accounts relative to the army should be settled in one office. In his report on the finances for the year 1853, Secretary Guthrie recommended that all accounts of the Interior Department should be sent to the Second Auditor, and all accounts of the War Department to the Third Auditor.

By the second section of "An act concerning the disbursement of public money," approved January 31, 1833, it is provided: "That every officer or agent of the United States who shall receive public money which he is not authorized to retain as salary, pay, or emolument, shall render his accounts quarter yearly to the proper accounting officers of the treasury, with the vouchers necessary to the correct and prompt settlement thereof, within three months at least after the expiration of each successive quarter, if resident within the United States, and within six months if resident in a foreign country." The army regulations require, in addition, certain reports and returns to be made to the military bureaus, monthly or otherwise, whereby the bureau and the department may be advised of the transactions of the subordinate officers, their contracts and purchases; and the regulations also provide that "every officer intrusted with public money or property shall render all prescribed returns and accounts to the bureau of the department in which he is serving, where all such returns and accounts shall pass through a rigid administrative scrutiny before the money accounts are transmitted to the proper officers of the Treasury Department for settlement." The long established practice has been for the disbursing officers to send their quarterly accounts to the chief of the military bureau, by whom, after the accounts have been examined and approved, or otherwise, they are sent to the treasury for settlement. This course of proceeding, although in some respects desirable, necessarily involves some delay, and, latterly, in consequence of the great press of business in the military bureaus, has prevented the transmission of many accounts within the time limited by the law. At the last session of Congress an act was passed providing that from and after its passage (July 17, 1862) all such accounts should be rendered monthly instead of quarterly, as heretofore, and "such accounts, with the vouchers necessary to the correct and prompt settlement thereof, shall be rendered *direct* to the proper accounting officer of the treasury and be mailed or otherwise forwarded to its proper address within ten days after the expiration of each successive month," with authority to the Secretary of the Treasury, if in his opinion the circumstances of the case require it, to extend the time prescribed for the rendition of accounts.

The intention of Congress in passing this act was, manifestly, to secure more promptitude in the rendition of accounts, as well as early settlement thereof. The law, it will be observed, requires the accounts to be rendered "*direct*" to the proper accounting officer of the treasury, instead of to the "bureau of the department" in which the officer is serving, as required by the army regulation before referred to. The law, therefore, nullifies the regulation in that respect. Hence, too, the "administrative scrutiny" of the military bureau with regard to the character of the expenditures made by the subordinate officers will not be obtained, unless it should be by other means. In my opinion this administrative action is desirable, not only as fully apprising the chiefs of the military bureaus of the precise character of the expenditures made by their subordinates, disbursing under their direction, but also fixing the responsibility which their approval of such expenditures carries. The rule of this office is to pass no voucher to which objection has been made in the administrative examination of the military bureau; but the fact of a voucher having passed the bureau without objection does not preclude the accounting officers from raising such objections as their examination may render necessary. Such objections are raised, notwithstanding the approval of the bureau.

In the absence of any law or regulation on the subject I shall feel disposed to refer all accounts for disbursements to the head of the proper military bureau for his administrative scrutiny and approval, and for my own advisement in the premises, before taking them up for settlement. Such a course it seems to me is eminently proper, for the information of the bureau as well as the accounting officers. I am of opinion, however, that the intention of the law, in requiring the accounts to be sent *direct to the treasury*, was not to *avoid* or *prevent* the administrative action of the bureau, but merely to secure a more prompt and frequent rendition of accounts, leaving such further administrative action as might be desirable and necessary to be obtained after the accounts have been rendered. A different construction would appear to have been put on this act in some of the departments, and in consequence thereof uniform action has not been obtained. The quartermaster general has, by a circular order, directed all officers disbursing in his department to take their receipts or vouchers in triplicate, instead of in duplicate, as heretofore, one copy of which, with the necessary returns, abstracts, &c., comprising his account, to be sent to the quartermaster general, another to the proper accounting officer, viz: the Third Auditor, and the third to be retained by the officer. It is believed the same course has been substantially adopted in the subsistence department, and in some cases two accounts from the same officer for the same period have been received at this office, one through the commissary general and the other from the officer himself. The law has not yet got fairly into practical operation, but a comparatively small portion of the officers having accounts to render having sent their accounts to this office. It is important that some definite and uniform action should be obtained on this subject.

The accounts for expenditure of property, issues of supplies, &c., have become of great magnitude, and involve many questions, for the proper investigation and determination of which it would seem some further authority should be obtained or regulations made. The abandonment or destruction by the officers in charge, or capture by the enemy, of property and supplies, have become of frequent occurrence, and the losses resulting therefrom are believed to be immense. In all such cases there should be an investigation had immediately of the facts and circumstances connected with such abandonment, destruction, or capture, and the evidence collected showing the quantities and descriptions of property lost or destroyed, together with the conclusions arrived at as the result of such investigation, should be made of record and filed in the proper office for its information and government as to the propriety of releasing the accountability of the officer or officers in whose charge such property was at the time. The only regulation on this subject is to the following effect: "Public property lost or destroyed in the military service must be accounted for by affidavit, or the certificate of a commissioned officer, or other satisfactory evidence." This appears to contemplate some action; but if the officer accountable neglects or fails to take the proper steps to account for the property, or to furnish evidence of the facts and circumstances connected with the loss, there is no provision made for any investigation. In fact, the whole matter appears to rest with the officer himself; and if he does nothing he simply remains charged with the property, and there is no evidence to show whether he should be relieved or not. It may not unreasonably be presumed that, in the worst cases of delinquency, there will be the least effort made to provide the affidavits, certificates, or other satisfactory evidence concerning the loss. The same may be said with regard to property "captured from the enemy." The regulations provide that "a return of all property captured will be made by the commanding officer of the troops by whom such capture was made to the adjutant general at Washington, in order that it may be disposed of according to the orders of the War Department." Whatever returns or disposition may have been made of property captured, the accounts and returns, so far as received at this office, show but little acquisition, either as property captured and applied to the service or as proceeds of sales thereof.

By a provision of the act of August 3, 1861, the army ration was considerably increased, and by subsequent regulation of the subsistence department "all *sound* articles of subsistence saved by troops or employés, by an economical

use of the ration," was directed to be purchased at cost price, and paid for by
the subsistence department, the bills to be "presented for payment by commanders of companies, officers in charge of bakeries," &c. This regulation embraces "savings of companies, of bakeries, and all savings from the army ration
made by an organized command." The object sought to be accomplished by
this change was praiseworthy, but it may well be doubted whether, practically,
it has resulted in benefit, either to the soldier or the government. On the contrary, I am inclined to the belief that it has opened up a prolific source of fraud
on both, at the same time materially increasing the cost of supplies, besides
complicating the accounts. At least this is the impression that has obtained in
this office, by examination of the bills for savings of company rations purchased
as authorized.

Finally, it is respectfully suggested whether the accounting officers of the
treasury should not be clothed with some further and specific authority, by
themselves or agents, to make investigations and inquiry where in their opinion,
such investigation is necessary in the examination of accounts sent to them for
settlement. Their investigation is, in a great degree, limited to the papers transmitted with the accounts, or such other evidence or information as the records
of the government afford, and which may be within their reach. It is my
opinion that the employment of one or more special agents, if the right kind of
men were appointed, would greatly aid in detecting unfaithful officers, if any
there be, and bringing them to punishment. Such additional precautionary
measures involve no impeachment or disparagement of the integrity of the officers connected with the service.

With great respect, your obedient servant,

R. J. ATKINSON, *Auditor.*

Hon. S. P. CHASE,
    Secretary of the Treasury.

---

*Summary statement of the principal operations of the Third Auditor's office
during the fiscal year ending 30th June,* 1862.

841 quartermasters' accounts settled, involving the sum of....	$15,084,545 51
815 commissaries' accounts settled, involving the sum of......	10,412,017 93
130 pension agents' accounts settled, involving the sum of....	725,095 67
81 engineers and topographical engineers' accounts settled, in-
volving the sum of....................................	542,853 73
378 miscellaneous claims, involving the sum of.............	4,354,724 06
56 claims for horses lost or destroyed, involving the sum of...	9,869 17
Oregon and Washington Indian war claims settled..........	1,148,604 72
2,867 bounty land claims examined and reported to Pension Office.	
18 half-pay pension claims.	
7,734 letters written and recorded.	
554 property accounts examined and adjusted.	
4,094 requisitions registered, recorded and posted.	

D.

TREASURY DEPARTMENT,
Fourth Auditor's Office, October 21, 1862.

SIR: I have the honor to acknowledge the receipt of your communication of
the second instant, requesting me to prepare, prior to the 1st proximo, a report
of the operations of this bureau for the fiscal year ending June 30, 1862, to accompany your annual report on finance.

In conformity with these instructions, I respectfully submit the subjoined statistics for the past fiscal year and germane remarks :

First. The total number of accounts audited during the year and transmitted to the Second Comptroller of the Treasury for his revision is nine hundred and sixty-two, (962,) embracing the accounts of paymasters, assistant paymasters, acting assistant paymasters, naval storekeepers, navy agents, the disbursing officers of the marine corps, the agents for the payment of pensions, and other officers in the service, involving an aggregate expenditure of $18,294,429 53, distributed, principally, under the following heads of appropriation :

Pay of the navy, &c.	$17,474,517 20
Pay of marine corps	661,398 93
Pay of provisions	158,513 40

Second. The number of requisitions for drafts for the naval service issued during the year is eighteen hundred and seventeen, (1,817,) amounting in gross to $43,293,259 ; for the pension service, fifty-one, amounting to $120,272 54.

Third. The number of official letters received during the year is twelve thousand four hundred and twenty-six, (12,426,) and the number written, thirteen thousand six hundred and twenty-seven, (13,627,) exclusive of reports.

Fourth. The official reports furnished are twenty-three (23) in number.

Fifth. The number of allotments, or half-pay tickets, granted and entered upon the books of this office is five thousand nine hundred and ninety-three (5,993.)

Sixth. The number of bounty-land cases, pension cases, and reports for naval asylum is ninety-three (93.)

At the close of each quarter of the year a report was made to the Second Comptroller, exhibiting the names of those disbursing agents of the Navy Department who had failed to render their accounts within the period prescribed by the act of January 31, 1823, showing also the nature and extent of the default in each case,

Quarter-annual reports are made to the honorable Secretary of the Navy, showing the amount which has been passed to the credit of the navy hospital fund on the books of this office.

A report has also been made to the honorable Secretary of the Navy, showing, in detail, the items of expenditures charged to the appropriation of the contingent expenses of the navy.

A statement is now in preparation and will be transmitted to that functionary, setting forth the amount of money received during the year by each officer of the navy and marine corps on account of pay, rations, travel, servants' hire, forage, &c., under the provisions of the statute of February 16, 1843.

Applications by seamen for admission into the naval asylum at Philadelphia were numerous. As a service of twenty years is required to entitle an applicant to such privileges, and as the services, in many instances, performed at intervals of time, extend through a period of thirty-five or forty years, much time has been occupied in the examination of such cases.

Upon a careful comparison of these statistics, explanatory of the business transactions of the office, with those of the previous annual report which I had the honor to transmit on the 28th of November, 1861, you will observe that the aggregate amount disbursed and audited in this office for the past fiscal year exceeds that of the prior year some $7,000,000.

This increase, however, does not include the disbursements of officers whose cruises had not terminated sufficiently early for settlement within the fiscal year; such additional accounts, in all probability, would have exhibited an outlay much larger than the above-mentioned sum.

In the commencement of the present administration the total number of disbursing officers in the navy was about one hundred, (100.) By reference to the Navy

Register published on the 1st of September, it will be found that the number has increased to about two hundred and seventy-five, (275.)

One of these agents alone has drawn from the treasury, during the last fiscal year, the sum of $14,688,000, for which he has, in compliance with the law, produced his vouchers now in process of adjustment.

By reference to this report you will also perceive that the correspondence of the office has very nearly triplicated, the number of letters written falling somewhat short of fourteen thousand, (14,000,) and, in fact, each division of labor has, to some extent, correspondingly increased.

The entire moneyed transactions of the navy, as you are aware, are adjusted in this office, either through the accounts of paymasters, navy agents, or special agents, including the purchase and charter of vessels, and the large important contracts therewith connected.

The number of public vessels now afloat is about three hundred and seventy-five, (375,) excluding such as are on the stock, for which bills are constantly being paid, also receiving and store ships in this and foreign countries.

It may not be irrelevant for me to state, in this connexion, that the bonds of naval disbursing officers are at present no larger than they were some few years since, when the receipts and disbursements of such officers were comparatively small. Navy agents give $75,000 bonds, and paymasters $25,000. The disbursements of one of these officers for the past fiscal year amounted to nearly $15,000,000.

I have already respectfully presumed to call the attention of the honorable Secretary of the Navy to the necessity, in my opinion, of an increase in the amount of the bond.

The increased clerical force granted under the act of May 20, 1862, I conceive to be sufficiently large to meet the increased duties of the office, which have been so greatly augmented by the enlargement of the navy and the immense disbursements of its agents. Acquaintance with the ordinary routine of business and familiarity with the laws and regulations governing the pay and emoluments of officers, and the purchase of material, can only be perfectly attained by study and assiduity. The plan you have instituted of exacting monthly reports from each clerk in the employ of the department transmitted with the report of the head of the bureau, is well calculated to incite a healthy ambition in the discharge of official duty.

I have the honor to be, respectfully, your obedient servant,

HOBART BERRIAN.

Hon. S. P. CHASE.
   Secretary of the Treasury.

E.

TREASURY DEPARTMENT,
Fifth Auditor's Office, November 6, 1862.

SIR: I have the honor to report that during the fiscal year ending June 30, 1862, the necessities of the public service created by the rebellion and the change and increase of foreign ministers and consuls have made the labor of this office nearly double that of the preceding year. Without any increase of our clerical force, however, we have promptly settled all accounts presented with proper and sufficient vouchers. We have also given considerable aid to our associates in other branches of this department in signing and issuing treasury notes, in counting and burning coupons and demand notes, in starting the new Bureau of Internal Revenue, and in all other requirements upon this office.

Schedule A, accompanying this report, shows the cost of the diplomatic service as settled in this office for the fiscal year, and that the twenty-nine legations therein mentioned have been paid the sum of ($323,506 90) three hundred and twenty-three thousand five hundred and six dollars and ninety cents.

Schedule B shows that the one hundred and seventy-five consulates therein mentioned, in the eighteen months including the last fiscal year and the last half of the year preceding, in salaries and exchange on salary drafts, have cost us ($432,141 39) four hundred and thirty-two thousand one hundred and forty-one dollars and thirty-nine cents, and that the fees collected at the consulates and placed to the credit of the government during the same time amounted to ($125,371 64) one hundred and twenty-five thousand three hundred and seventy-one dollars and sixty-four cents.

Schedules C, D, and E show that the support of disabled seamen at all the consulates, together with their transportation and passage home, and the arrest of criminal seamen and sending them home, has cost the treasury within the fiscal year ($226,858 82) two hundred and twenty-six thousand eight hundred and fifty-eight dollars and eighty-two cents, and that sixty thousand one hundred and thirty-four dollars and eighty-three cents ($60,134 83) were collected during the same time as extra wages at the several consulates.

This last amount exceeds the sum collected the preceding year by about fifty per cent., and in the present condition of our commerce affords evidence of increasing diligence in our consuls.

Our consular system is, as will be seen by the foregoing statements, a burden upon the treasury, and to save it from destruction retrenchment and reform are needed.

When, by the act of Congress of March 1, 1855, salaries were substituted for fees to our consuls, the fees were greatly reduced. Experience has shown the reduction to have been a financial mistake; and if the consular system is to be anything like self-sustaining, it seems to me the fees, collected for the pretended purpose of paying salaries, should be raised to the old standard.

The mode of paying consuls, in consequence of the derangement of our currency and the extravagant rates of foreign exchange, now daily becoming worse and worse, and in many instances causing a loss of from forty to sixty per cent. in the payment of salaries abroad, demands correction.

I can think of no better way than to stop the payment of all differences of exchange, and pay our European consuls, as we do our ministers, in London; those of Eastern Asia at the legation in China, and all others in New York. Should drafts for salary be negotiated by ministers and consuls at their own cost, I feel confident that foreign bankers and brokers would make much less profit out of the business than under the present mode of negotiation, and the loss to our ministers and consuls would be much less than that now cheerfully borne by the public servants at home in accepting payment of their salaries in a currency thirty per cent. below the standard of coin. If, under the troubles brought upon us by the rebellion, any of the gentlemen who represent us abroad should be dissatisfied with the proposed change, I have no doubt competent and worthy citizens could easily be found willing to relieve them of their official responsibilities.

These changes, like the one mentioned in my last report, which the honorable Secretary thought worthy of his recommendation to Congress, I am aware might require some action on the part of the national legislature.

With great respect, your obedient servant,

                                    JOHN C. UNDERWOOD,
                                                    Auditor.

Hon. S. P. CHASE,
    Secretary of the Treasury.

SCHEDULE A.

Statement of expenses of all missions abroad for salaries, contingencies, and loss by exchange, from the 1st of July, 1861, to the 30th of June, 1862, as shown by accounts adjusted in this office, other than which may have been paid by the disbursing clerk of the Department of State.

	Salary.	Contingencies.	Loss by exchange	Total.
GREAT BRITAIN.				
Chas. F. Adams, minister.				
From July 1, 1861, to June 30, 1862	$17,500 00			
From May 16, 1861, to June 30, 1862 ...	....	$358 61		
Chas. L. Wilson, secretary of legation.				
From July 1, 1861, to June 30, 1862	2,625 00			
Benj. Moran, assistant secretary of legation.				
From July 1, 1862, to June 30, 1862	1,500 00			
	21,625 00	3,581 61	....	$25,206 61
FRANCE.				
Wm. L. Dayton, minister.				
From July 1, 1861, to June 30, 1862	17,500 00			
From May 19, 1861, to June 30, 1862 ...	....	2,492 32		
From October 1, 1861, to June 30, 1862..	....	....	$49 73	
Wm. L. Dayton, jr., secretary of legation.				
From July 1, 1861, to June 30, 1862	1,500 00			
From July 3, 1861, to March 31, 1862...	....	....	10 40	
W. S. Pennington, secretary of legation.				
From July 1, 1861, to June 30, 1862	2,625 00			
Loss on drafts, October 1, 1861, and March 31, 1862......................	....	....	16 02	
	21,625 00	2,492 32	76 15	24,195 47
RUSSIA.				
John Appleton, minister.				
From July 1 to July 8, 1861.............	280 86			
Cassius M. Clay, minister.				
From July 1, 1861, to June 30, 1862	12,000 00			
From April 11, 1861, to June 30, 1862...	....	1,277 72		
	12,280 86	1,277 72	....	13,558 58

Statement of expenses of all missions abroad, &c.—Continued.

	Salary.	Contingencies.	Loss by exchange	Total.
PRUSSIA.				
Joseph A. Wright, minister.				
From July 1, 1861, to August 8, 1861 ...	$1,271 74			
Norman B. Judd, minister.				
From July 1, 1861, to June 30, 1862	12,000 00			
From April 20, 1861, to June 30, 1862...	....	$870 38		
From July 6, 1861, to June 30, 1862	....	....	$86 11	
H. Kreissman, secretary of legation.				
From July 1, 1861, to June 30, 1862				
Loss on drafts, dated July 6, 1861, and January 2, 1862	....	....	10 27	
	15,071 74	870 38	96 38	$16,038 50
AUSTRIA.				
J. Glancey Jones, minister.				
From July 1, 1861, to December 15, 1861.	5,478 26			
From July 1, 1861, to December 15, 1861.	....	205 20		
J. Lothrop Motley, minister.				
From August 10, 1861, to June 30, 1862.	10,695 65			
From August 10, 1861, to June 30, 1862.	....	335 60		
	16,173 91	540 80	....	16,714 71
SPAIN.				
Wm. Preston, minister.				
From July 1 to July 4, 1861	130 43			
Carl Schurz, minister.				
From July 1, 1861, to September 30, 1861.	3,000 00			
From March 28, 1861, to Sept. 30, 1861..	....	978 40		
Horatio J. Perry, secretary of legation and chargé d'affairs.				
From July 1, 1861, to June 30, 1862....	4,208 15			
From July 1, 1861, to June 30, 1862....	....	1,212 34		
From January 1, 1862, to June 30, 1862.	....	....	6 91	
	7,338 58	2,190 74	6 91	9,536 23

Statement of expenses of all missions abroad, &c.—Continued.

	Salary.	Contingencies.	Loss by exchange	Total.
MEXICO.				
Jno. B. Weller, minister.				
From July 1 to August 8, 1861, home transit	$1,271 74			
Thomas Corwin, minister.				
From July 1, 1861, to June 30, 1862	12,000 00			
From March 22, 1861, to June 30, 1862..	....	$1,748 09		
W. H. Corwin, secretary of legation.				
From July 1, 1861, to June 30, 1862	1,800 00			
	15,071 74	1,748 09	....	$16,819 83
BELGIUM.				
H. S. Sanford, minister.				
From July 1, 1861, to March 31, 1862...	5,625 00			
From March 20, 1861, to March 31, 1862.	....	1,412 72		
From Sept. 30, 1861, to April 1, 1862 ...	....	....	$5 89	
Aaron Goodrich, secretary of legation and chargé d'affaires ad interim.				
From July 1, 1861, to November 22, 1861.	1,477 57			
	7,102 57	1,412 72	5 89	8,521 18
BRAZIL.				
J. Watson Webb, minister.				
From July 3, 1861, to March 31, 1862...	8,934 78			
From July 3, 1861, to March 31, 1862 ...	....	931 61		
Loss on draft, June 30, 1861	....	....	25 00	
A. L. Blackford, secretary of legation and chargé d'affaires.				
From July 1, 1861, to October 4, 1861...	1,473 91			
C. L. Lazarus, acting secretary of legation.				
From October 8, 1861, to January 7, 1862.	450 76			
Loss on draft, January 7, 1862..........	....	....	35 75	
	10,859 45	931 61	60 75	11,851 81

Statement of expenses of all missions abroad, &c.—Continued.

	Salary.	Contingén-cies.	Loss by exchange	Total.
CHINA.				
A. Burlingame, minister.				
From July 1, 1861, to March 31, 1862....	$9,000 00			
Loss on draft, January 6, 1862..........	....	....	$21 45	
S. Wells Williams, interpreter.				
From July 1, 1861, to December 31, 1861.	2,500 00			
Loss on draft, September 30, 1861.......	....	....	3 77	
G. W. Heard, secretary of legation.				
From July 1, 1861, to December 31, 1861.	1,500 00			
	13,000 00	....	25 22	$13,025 22
PERU.				
Christopher Robinson, minister.				
From July 1 to July 7, 1861, awaiting instructions.....................	190 22			
From December 10,1861, to June 30, 1862.	5,597 83			
From December 10,1861, to June 30, 1862.	....	$415 75		
Chas. Easton, secretary of legation.				
From May 2, 1862, to June 30, 1862	247 25			
Loss on draft, July 21, 1862...........	....	....	22 40	
	6,035 30	415 75	22 40	6,473 45
TURKEY.				
E. Joy Morris, minister.				
From July 1, 1861, to June 30, 1862......	7,500 00			
From June 8, 1861, to June 30, 1862......	....	2,429 83		
From October 1, 1861, to January 4, 1862.	....	....	123 00	
Amount allowed from former report.....	....	....	220 58	
John P. Brown, secretary of legation and dragoman.				
From July 1, 1861, to September 30, 1861.	750 00			
From July 1, 1861, to March 31, 1862	2,250 00			
From July 1, 1861, to August 8, 1862, as chargé d'affaires	211 96			
From July 1, 1861, to March 31, 1862	....	667 49		
From October 1, 1861, to February 26, 1862.	....	....	85 54	
James Williams, minister.				
From July 1 to July 30, 1861	611 41			
	11,323 37	3,097 32	429 12	14,849 81

EX. DOC. 1——7

Statement of expenses of all missions abroad, &c.—Continued.

	Salary.	Contingencies.	Loss by exchange	Total.
SWEDEN AND NORWAY.				
J. S. Haldeman, minister.				
From July 1, 1861, to March 31, 1862....	$5,625 00			
From March 16, 1861, to March 31, 1862 .	....	$241 66		
Loss on draft, December 31, 1861	....	....	$17 04	
	5,625 00	241 66	17 04	$5,883 70
DENMARK.				
Bradford R. Wood, minister.				
From July 1, 1861, to June 30, 1862	7,500 00			
From March 22, 1861, to June 30, 1862 ..	....	314 78		
	7,500 00	314 78	....	7,814 78
GUATEMALA.				
E. O. Crosby, minister.				
From July 1, 1861, to June 30, 1862	7,500 00			
From March 23, 1861, to June 30, 1862...	....	247 23		
	7,500 00	247 23	....	7,747 23
SWITZERLAND.				
Theodore S. Fay, minister.				
From July 1 to 30, 1862, home transit ...	611 41			
From July 1, 1861, to June 30, 1862	7,500 00			
From May 14, 1861, to June 30, 1862	....	506 26		
	8,111 41	506 26	....	8,617 67
PORTUGAL.				
George W. Morgan, minister.				
From July 1, 1861, to September 4, 1861 .	1,345 11			
James E. Harvey, minister.				
From July 1, 1861, to June 30, 1862	7,500 00			
From April 30, 1861, to June 30, 1862	....	921 71		
From March 31, 1862, to April 21, 1862 ..	....	....	40 60	
	8,845 11	921 71	40 60	9,807 42
PONTIFICAL STATES.				
John P. Stockton, minister.				
From July 1 to July 21, 1861............	427 99			
Loss on draft, August 13, 1861	....	....	3 56	
	427 99	....	3 56	431 55

Statement of expenses of all missions abroad, &c.,—Continued.

	Salary.	Contingencies.	Loss by exchange	Total.
NETHERLANDS.				
James S. Pike, minister.				
From July 1, 1861, to June 30, 1862	$7,500 00			
From March 28, 1861, to June 30, 1862...	....	$611 13		
Loss on draft, April 24, 1862............	....	....	$6 46	
	7,500 00	611 13	6 46	$8,117 59
NICARAGUA.				
A. B. Dickinson, minister.				
From July 1, 1861, to June 30, 1861 .....:	7,500 00			
From April 29, 1861, to June 30, 1861 ...	....	1,031 44		
	7,500 00	1,031 44	....	8,531 44
NEW GRANADA.				
George W. Jones, minister.				
From July 1, 1861, to December 20, 1861.	3,525 81			
From July 1, 1861, to December 20, 1861.	....	257 87		
A. A. Burton, minister.				
From July 1, 1861, to June 30, 1862	7,500 00			
From May 29, 1861, to June 30, 1862	....	348 73		
G. W. Davis, secretary joint commission with New Granada.				
From September 11, 1861, to March 10, 1862	1,333 33			
From September 11, 1861, to March 10, 1862	....	2,639 89		
	12,359 14	3,246 49	....	15,605 63
HONDURAS.				
J. R. Partridge, minister.				
From February 10, 1862, to June 30, 1862.	2,916 66	....	....	2,916 66
ARGENTINE CONFEDERATION.				
R. M. Palmer, minister.				
From July 1, 1861, to April 26, 1862	6,160 76			
From April 16, 1861, to April 26, 1862 ...	....	559 07		
From February 27, 1862, to April 8, 1862.	....	....	220 57	
Robert C. Kirk, minister.				
From March 4, 1862, to June 30, 1862....	2,334 69			
From April 9, 1862, to June 30, 1862	....	45 00		
	8,495 45	604 07	220 57	9,320 09

Statement of expenses of all missions abroad, &c.—Continued.

	Salary.	Contingencies.	Loss by exchange	Total.
CHILI.				
John Bigler, minister.				
From July 1, 1861, to December 1, 1861..	$4,184 79			
From July 1, 1861, to December 1, 1861..	....	$165 26		
Thomas H. Nelson, minister.				
From July 1, 1861, to June 30, 1862	10,000 00			
From June 17, 1861, to June 30, 1862....	....	895 20		
C. S. Rand, secretary legation.				
From July 1, 1861, to June 30, 1862	1,500 00			
	15,684 79	1,060 46	....	$16,745 25
PARAGUAY.				
C. A. Washburn, commissioner.				
From July 1 to July 7, 1861, (partial transit).........................	142 66			
From July 27, 1861, to March 31, 1862 ...	5,095 11			
From June 8, 1861, to March 31, 1862....	....	172 64		
From October 19, 1861, to February 28, 1862	....	....	$59 34	
	5,237 77	172 64	59 34	5,469 75
HAWAIIAN ISLANDS.				
Thomas J. Dryer, commissioner.				
From July 1, 1861, to June 30, 1862	7,500 00			
From June 5, 1861, to June 30, 1862	....	423 65		
	7,500 00	423 65	....	7,923 65
LONDON.				
John Miller, despatch agent.				
From July 1, 1861, to October 31, 1861....	....	1,486 75	....	1,486 75
ECUADOR.				
C. R. Duckalew, minister.				
From July 1, 1861, to August 30, 1861 ...	1,263 58			
From April 1, 1861, to August 30, 1861...	....	139 76		
F. Hassaurek, minister.				
From July 1, 1861, to June 30, 1861	7,500 00			
From March 23, 1861, to June 30, 1861...	....	315 69		
From July 24, 1861, to June 30, 1861	....	....	358 63	
	8,763 58	455 45	358 63	9,577 66

Statement of expenses of all missions abroad, &c.—Continued.

	Salary.	Contingencies.	Loss by exchange	Total.
VENEZUELA.				
E. A. Turpin, minister.,				
From July 1, 1861, to January 15, 1862...	$4,082 50			
From April 1, 1861, to January 15, 1862..	....	$68 15		
H. T. Blow, minister.				
From July 1 to July 7, 1861, (partial transit)	142 66			
From October 5, 1861, to May 22, 1862...	4,739 91,			
From October 5, 1861, to May 22, 1862...	....	60 40		
	8,945 07	128 55	....	$9,073 62
COSTA RICA.				
C. N. Riotti, minister.				
From July 1, 1861, to March 31, 1862	5,625 00			
From June 8, 1861, to March 31, 1862....	....	276 40		
Loss on draft, September 30, 1861	....	....	$10 33	
	5,625 00	276 40	10 33	5,911 73
BARING BROTHERS & CO., UNITED STATES BANKERS, LONDON.				
Amount of loss by exchange on remittances made by the treasurer from January 8 to June 19, 1862.................	6,400 00			
Amount of gain by exchange on remittances made by the treasurer from July 1 to December 31, 1862................	666 67			
Loss by exchange	5,733 33	....	....	5,733 33
)				323,506 90

SCHEDULE B.

Statement of the amount for salaries and loss by exchange paid to and fees received from the consular officers of the United States, mentioned in schedule B and C, of the act of August 18, 1856, "to regulate the diplomatic and consular systems of the United States," for the year ending December 31, 1861.

No.	Consulate—where located.	Salaries.	Loss by exchange.	Fees.
1	Acapulco*	$2, 108 68	....	$662 60
2	Aix la Chapelle	2, 930 01	$58 19	802 00
3	Alexandria*	289 73	....	....
4	Amoor river	500 00	....	7 45
5	Amoy	3, 495 64	3, 136 56	165 66
6	Amsterdam*	1, 013 58	....	233 33
7	Autwerp	3, 044 35	61 60	1, 548 73
8	Apia*	....	....	....
9	Aspinwall	3, 012 25	....	1, 498 98
10	Athens*	1, 059 76	35 43	4 00
11	Aux Cayes	815 20	....	309 00
12	Antigua*	....	....	....
13	Beirut	2, 000 00	116 70	51 45
14	Basle	2, 305 00	76 32	883 50
15	Batavia	1, 385 76	....	106 53
16	Bay of Islands	1, 000 00	11 48	275 73
17	Belfast	2, 277 18	....	971 97
18	Buenos Ayres	2, 163 04	....	1, 734 13
19	Bremen	2, 052 85	160 63	206 00
20	Bristol†	342 38	....	6 00
21	Barbadoes*†	....	....	....
22	Bermuda	236 41	....	34 52
23	Barcelona†	277 18	....	107 28
24	Balize*†	....	....	....
25	Bahia	1, 000 00	....	215 55
26	Cardiff†	362 76	....	188 00
27	Cork	2, 253 46	14 71	413 83
28	Calcutta*	4, 916 65	17 25	1, 978 41
29	Cape Town	1, 000 00	75 07	155 15
30	Cadiz†	1, 803 08	93 70	582 49
31	Curaçoa*	334 23	....	154 63
32	Candia	589 67	....	....
33	Cyprus	1, 125 00	74 78	1 61
34	Canton	4, 000 00	1, 030 44	449 74
35	Cape Haytien	1, 277 16	....	172 63
36	Callao*	3, 833 88	....	774 43
37	Cobija	500 00	....	41 95
38	Constantinople	3, 387 31	625 03	185 43
39	Carthagena	500 00	....	215 48

° Returns incomplete.   † Compensation established by act of 1861.

Statement of the amount of salaries, &c.—Continued.

No.	Consulate—where located.	Salary.	Loss by exchange.	Fees.
40	Demarara	$2,598 66	$22 72	$339 84
41	Dundee	2,103 67	....	514 09
42	Elsinore	1,830 16	212 14	81 40
43	Frankfort-on-the-Main*	2,983 14	12 50	201 00
44	Funchal	1,740 48	32 04	11 81
45	Foo-Choo	7,737 36	2,099 22	234 88
46	Fayal	750 00	....	351 54
47	Florence*	....	....	....
48	Falkland Islands*	500 00	....	....
49	Gaspé Basin†	216 02	....	....
50	Genoa	1,896 26	16 21	765 39
51	Glasgow*	3,554 33	....	2,538 68
52	Geneva*	1,565 21	24 19	98 00
53	Gaboon*	....	....	....
54	Guayaquil*†	152 65	....	31 11
55	Gottenburg†	228 25	78 15	....
56	Halifax*	2,163 36	....	732 93
57	Havre	7,298 50	11 49	5,658 93
58	Hamburg	2,313 48	4 71	1,365 32
59	Havana	6,083 13	....	4,521 23
60	Honolulu*	5,315 44	148 52	1,571 96
61	Hong Kong*	1,921 19	....	2,790 04
62	Jerusalem	2,057 05	119 35	13 00
63	Kingston	2,418 20	3 85	583 90
64	Leipsic	1,581 91	57 77	506 75
65	La Rochelle	1,499 99	125 51	190 17
66	La Guayra	1,499 99	....	256 69
67	Leeds	2,250 00	53 06	1,050 00
68	Lyons	1,754 26	72 47	306 00
69	Lahaina	3,594 40	120 07	150 40
70	Lanthala*	500 00	....	7 36
71	Leghorn*	840 71	25 93	121 02
72	Liverpool*	1,324 71	20 21	949 96
73	London	8,450 06	....	6,534 98
74	Lisbon*†	....	....	....
75	La Paz*†	....	....	....
76	La Union*†	....	....	....
77	Montreal	4,330 50	116 57	362 09
78	Munich	1,232 81	26 80	78 00
79	Malaga*	1,607 38	97 04	356 67
80	Marseilles	2,877 73	72 58	1,083 34

* Returns incomplete.   † Compensation established by act of 1861.

Statement of the amount of salaries, &c.—Continued.

No.	Consulate—where located.	Salary.	Loss by exchange.	Fees.
81	Manchester	$2,206 59	....	$376 00
82	Moscow*	2,048 91	$198 88	1 00
83	Monrovia	1,000 00	....	110 17
84	Montevideo*	....	....	....
85	Maranham	1,000 00	23 52	60 68
86	Mauritius	2,500 00	172 24	857 84
87	Melbourne	4,293 47	405 90	1,113 76
88	Maracaibo†	578 79	....	14 42
89	Matanzas	2,797 69	....	1,731 01
90	Messina	1,500 00	143 26	346 42
91	Mexico	1,163 04	....	314 00
92	Macao*†	....	....	....
93	Matamoras*	163 04	....	....
94	Manzanillo†	52 99	....	....
95	Malta†	619 56	81 90	116 53
96	Nassau	1,648 04	....	484 04
97	Naples	1,557 06	....	489 24
98	Ningpo	4,705 52	1,431 27	63 77
99	Nantes†	256 78	5 19	....
100	Napoleon Vendee†	....	....	....
101	Nice†	171 19	....	....
102	Nagasaki*	....	....	....
103	Oporto*	576 37	32 18	59 79
104	Omoa	1,000 00	....	20 63
105	Odessa	992 70	....	115 56
106	Panama	3,880 83	....	644 22
107	Ponce	1,500 00	....	441 52
108	Para	1,000 00	....	230 36
109	Prince Edward's Island	1,150 81	14 28	98 80
110	Paso del Norte*	250 00	....	10 00
111	Palermo	1,622 27	79 15	519 64
112	Port au Prince	2,386 57	....	219 51
113	Paris	5,244 56	17 20	2,285 00
114	Pernambuco	2,000 00	....	779 81
115	Paita*	....	....	....
116	Paramaribo*	....	....	....
117	Rotterdam	2,387 65	82 29	926 42
118	Revel	2,266 29	392 92	30 36
119	Rio Janeiro	7,399 30	225 34	3,679 54
120	Rio Grande del Sul*†	750 00	12 49	276 19
121	Rio Grande	....	....	....
122	San Juan, P. R	2,413 03	....	229 42
123	Stettin	1,174 26	66 47	103 30
124	Spezzia	1,146 73	6 90	2 67

° Returns incomplete.　　　　　† Compensation established by act of 1861.

Statement of the amount of salaries, &c.—Continued.

No.	Consulate—where located.	Salary.	Lost by ex-change.	Fees.
125	Stuttgart*	$1,074 95	$12 48	$157 00
126	St. Thomas..............	5,110 84	22 79	1,834 21
127	San Juan del Norte.......	2,296 09	....	53 59
128	Singapore	2,500 00	210 56	1,080 25
129	St. Jago de Cuba.........	2,673 62	....	388 33
130	St. Domingo city.........	1,683 90	72 75	91 66
131	Shanghai................	4,815 21	91 66	1,623 93
132	Smyrna..................	2,331 51	369 06	229 74
133	Sabanillo................	500 00	....	303 00
134	St. Paul de Loando	1,000 00	....	117 12
135	St. Croix...............	....	....	....
136	St. Petersburg	2,213 73	....	68 75
137	Santos	529 88	....	....
138	St. Catherine's	415 70	....	....
139	Santiago	750 00	....	23 46
140	San Juan del Sur.........	2,570 63	....	30 00
141	Southampton*	1,439 97	....	40 62
142	St. Marc*	353 15	....	11 47
143	Trieste	2,538 33	35 33	262 40
144	Turks' Island...........	2,593 09	....	243 55
145	Tampico	750 00	....	300 09
146	Tumbez*................	500 00	....	736 52
147	Trinidad de Cuba.........	2,983 22	....	343 22
148	Talcahuana..............	1,082 54	45 93	650 72
149	Tabasco	925 28	....	82 69
150	Tangier*................	244 56	....	....
151	Tripoli*.................	2,307 52	....	....
152	Tunis*..................	1,500 00	....	....
153	Tahiti*	750 00	24 26	39 09
154	Trinidad†	293 47	....	48 03
155	Tehuantepec*†	....	....	....
156	Vienna	1,687 49	22 35	720 00
157	Vera Cruz...............	3,341 98	44 49	337 89
158	Valparaiso....,.........	2,741 82	98 52	1,436 05
159	Venice..................	1,173 22	88 39	21 89
160	Zanzibar	1,000 00	114 76	65 81

* Returns incomplete. † Compensation established by act of 1861.

Salaries	$276,067 93
Loss by exchange...	13,795 69
	289,863 62

Fees returned by consuls	$77,590 21
Balance paid by treasury	212,273 41
	289,863 62

Statement of the amount for salaries and loss by exchange paid to and fees received from the consular officers of the United States mentioned in schedules B and C of the act of August 12, 1856, "to regulate the diplomatic and consular systems of the United States," for the first two quarters of the year 1862.

No.	Consulate—where located.	Salaries.	Loss by exchange.	Fees.
1	Acapulco................	$1,000 00	....	$452 65
2	Aix la Chapelle..........	1,250 00	$54 83	448 00
3	Alexandria*.............	....	....	....
4	Amoor river*............	....	....	....
5	Amoy..................	1,499 99	724 21	187 94
6	Amsterdam..............	500 00	16 30	163 61
7	Antwerp...............	1,250 00	....	856 39
8	Ancona†............	851 89	86 56	11 37
9	Aspinwall..;..........	1,250 00	60 72	640 87
10	Athens............	500 00	55 25	6 25
11	Aux Cayes*.....	375 00	....	91 57
12	Algiers†................	125 00	....	....
13	Antigua*†..............	....	....	....
14	Beirut...... ....;....	1,000 00	58 05	25 00
15	Basle............	1,000 00	46 42	610 00
16	Batavia................	499 99	48 34	263 08
17	Bay of Islands..........	500 00	66 56	201 30
18	Belfast................	1,000 00	....	1,027 14
19	Buenos Ayres...........	1,549 25	....	1,062 76
20	Bremen................	1,500 00	113 07	136 00
21	Bahia*................	520 32	....	47 26
22	Bristol................	750 00	23 83	330 78
23	Barbadoes†.............	250 00	....	97 17
24	Bermuda.....:.........	750 00	....	374 26
25	Barcelona†.............	750 00	....	138 26
26	Balize*†................	....	....	....
27	Bilboa†................	281 59	....	....
28	Bergen†................	525 00	32 11	50
29	Cardiff†............	750 00	17 47	736 26
30	Cork..................	1,000 00	21 45	278 51
31	Calcutta...............	2,500 00	17 25	1,410 73
32	Cape Town.............	334 91	....	12 36
33	Cadiz*................;	25 00	....	....
34	Curaçoa†...............	750 00	....	216 79
35	Candia*................	....	....	....
36	Cyprus.......	1,000 00	29 64	6 00
37	Canton.,....	2,000 00	450 51	202 46
38	Callao.................	1,750 00	....	626 51
39	Cobija................	250 00	....	18 00
40	Constantinople..........	1,500 00	107 52	138 20
41	Carthagena.............	405 34	....	90 27

* Returns incomplete.   † Compensation established by act of 1861.

Statement of the amount of salaries, &c.—Continued.

No.	Consulate—where located.	Salaries.	Loss by exchange.	Fees.
42	Demarara............	$1,000 00	$92 15	$91 65
43	Dundee....	1,000 00	....	526 00
44	Elsinore.....	816 65	91 73	8 77
45	Frankfort-on-the-Main.....	1,500 00	94 92	155 00
46	Funchal..............	750 00	51 69	100 22
47	Foo-Choo.............	1,750 00	418 96	97 12
48	Fayal.................	350 00	....	264 53
49	Florence*†...............	....	....	....
50	Falkland Islands*........	....	....	....
51	Genoa.....	750 00	....	485 98
52	Glasgow..........	1,250 00	....	1,175 00
53	Geneva*.............	375 00	5 85	11 00
54	Guayaquil.............	303 57	....	33 64
55	Gaboon*............	125 00	....	....
56	Galatza*†...............	....	....	....
57	Gaspé Basin†.....	750 00	7 50	....
58	Gottenburg†............	750 00	....	40 99
59	Halifax..............	1,000 00	....	379 49
60	Havre................	3,000 00	115 08	1,439 88
61	Hamburg...........	1,000 00	32 41	765 17
62	Havana..............	3,000 00	....	2,585 45
63	Honolulu.............	2,000 00	43 59	574 48
64	Hong Kong............	1,750 00	....	3,353 73
65	Jerusalem............	750 00	45 76	11 00
66	Kingston.............	500 00	....	148 80
67	Kanagawa†	2,147 14	1,010 65	82 64
68	Leipsic.....	750 00	46 57	276 75
69	La Rochelle*..........	375 00	....	50 00
70	La Guayra.....	1,064 38	....	129 53
71	Leeds.....	1,000 00	35 47	596 80
72	Lyons	750 00	10 78	384 00
73	Lahaina...............	1,500 00	186 99	24 00
74	Lanthala*............	250 00	....	33 75
75	La Union*†.............	....	....	....
76	Leghorn,.............	750 00	....	279 29
77	Liverpool.....	3,750 00	....	4,960 12
78	London.......	3,750 00	18 14	2,586 97
79	Lisbon*†................	....	....	....
80	La Paz*†.........	....	....	....

* Returns incomplete. † Compensation established by act of 1861.

*Statement of the amount of salaries, &c.—*Continued.

No.	Consulate—where located.	Salaries.	Loss by exchange.	Fees.
81	Montreal..................	$2,000 00	....	$168 18
82	Munich......	567 93	$29 37	24 50
83	Malaga...................	750 00	125 88	71 02
84	Marseilles................	1,250 00	20 56	613 37
85	Manchester...............	1,000 00	47 10	356 50
86	Moscow......ρ.......... ...	1,000 00	139 65	2 50
87	Monrovia*...............	250 00	....	....
88	Montevideo*..............	83 33	....	....
89	Maranham................	500 00	6 91	48 26
90	Mauritius................	981 10	147 89	315 61
91	Melbourne*...............	1,604 39	24 66	358 06
92	Maracaibo†...............	750 00	....	186 12
93	Matanzas.................	1,250 00	....	1,147 12
94	Messina....	750 00	29 46	249 49
95	Mexico*..................	250 00	....	30 54
96	Macao*...................	....	....	....
97	Matamoras................	172 22	....	9 75
98	Manzanillo†..............	70 83	....	....
99	Malta†....	750 00	107 60	87 45
100	Martinique†..............	842 16	.......†..	34 82
101	Nassau*......	....	....	....
102	Naples*..................	659 34	....	177 85
103	Ningpo*..................	....	....	....
104	Nantes†..................	750 00	69 44	34 19
105	Napoleon Vendee*†.......	....	....	....
106	Nice†....................	620 83	55 70	25 00
107	Nagasaki*†...............	....	....	....
108	Newcastle†.....	533 38	....	145 17
109	Oporto...................	850 00	55 77	136 09
110	Omoa*......	250 00	....	4 75
111	Odessa*..................	375 00	....	....
112	Otranto†.................	737 49	....	....
113	Panama...................	1,750 00	....	311 64
114	Ponce....................	750 00	....	324 48
115	Para*....................	332 41	....	629 02
116	Prince Edward's Island....	750 00	17 97	33 42
117	Paso del Norte*..........	....	....	....
118	Palermo.......	750 00	38 99	438 40
119	Port au Prince............	1,000 00	....	249 85
120	Paris....................	2,500 00	36 16	1,976 00
121	Pernambuco..............	1,242 91	29 09	313 49
122	Paita*...................	....	....	....
123	Pictou†......	375 00	....	....
124	Paramaribo*..............	....	....	....

* Returns incomplete.   † Compensation established by act of 1861.

*Statement of the amount of salaries, &c.—*Continued.

No.	Consulate—where located.	Salaries.	Loss by exchange.	Fees.
125	Port Mahon†	$504 16	$22 52	....
126	Rotterdam	1,000 00	33 18	$527 02
127	Revel	1,097 83	102 90	2 00
128	Rio de Janeiro.	3,000 00	71 83	861 13
129	Rio Grande de Sul*	....	....	....
130	Rio Grande*†	....	....	....
131	San Juan, P. R.	1,000 00	21 18	161 22
132	Stettin	500 00	32 42	24 50
133	Spezzia	500 00	....	2 75
134	Stuttgart	500 00	27 02	89 00
135	St. Thomas	2,000 00	32 80	1,356 81
136	San Juan del Norte	1,000 00	....	36 54
137	Singapore	625 00	108 44	259 87
138	St. Jago de Cuba	1,250 00	....	358 02
139	St. Domingo City	750 00	58 48	52 46
140	Shanghai	1,613 88	161 95	176 14
141	Smyrna*	1,081 84	163 66	102 85
142	Sabanilla*	....	....	....
143	St. Paul de Loando	500 00	....	35 67
144	St. Croix*	....	....	....
145	St. Petersburg	1,000 00	....	8 25
146	Stockholm†	563 50	32 84	38 65
147	Santos†	750 00	38 08	28 66
148	Santiago†	750 00	51 77	5 15
149	San Juan del Sur*	500 00	....	61 18
150	Southampton	1,000 00	....	93 51
151	St. John's, N. B.†	504 16	....	316 75
152	St. John's, N. F.†	350 77	6 69	13 10
153	Swatow*	....	....	....
154	Santander†	487 56	36 54	....
155	Scio†	491 65	65 37	....
156	St. Marc*†	375 00	....	10 77
157	Trieste	1,000 00	....	106 51
158	Turk's Island	1,000 00	....	79 07
159	Tampico	750 00	....	55 25
160	Tumbez	125 00	....	7 65
161	Trinidad de Cuba*	625 00	....	117 17
162	Talcahuano*	250 00	....	189 99
163	Tabasco*	....	....	....
164	Tangier*	513 73	....	....
165	Tripoli*	....	....	....
166	Tunis*	....	....	....
167	Tahiti*	....	....	....

* Returns incomplete.   † Compensation established by act of 1861.

Statement of the amount of salaries, &c.—Continued.

No.	Consulate—where located.	Salaries.	Loss by exchange.	Fees.
168	Trinidad	$750 00	....	$126 21
169	Tehuantepec*†	....	....	....
170	Vienna	750 00	$47 54	353 00
171	Vera Cruz................	1,750 00	....	277 35
172	Valparaiso...............	1,500 00	....	678 05
173	Venice	871 82	20 86	8 58
174	Valencia†	748 63	....	63 56
175	Zanzibar*	250 00	....	34 34

* Returns incomplete.   † Compensation established by act of 1861.

Amount of salaries $135,827 87
Amount of loss by exchange.............................   6,449 90

                                142,277 77

Amount of fees returned by consuls...................... $47,781 43
Balance paid by treasury...............................   94,496 34

                                142,277 77

NOTE.—At some of the consulates the amount paid exceeds the fixed salary; in every case this is in consequence of a change of consular officer, the new consul being paid for time while receiving instructions and making the transit to his post of duty, the retiring consul, in the meantime, receiving salary at the consulate. Again: the retiring consul receives compensation for time of making the transit home, after the new consul has entered upon his duties and receives pay at the consulate.

SCHEDULE C.

Statement showing amount of money allowed for relief of destitute seamen at the several consulates of the United States in foreign countries, together with the extra wages and money collected by consular officers on account of such seamen; also amount allowed as loss by exchange on drafts of consuls to cover said disbursements, for the fiscal year ending June 30, 1862.

Name of consulate.	Disbursements.	Loss by exchange.	Receipts.
Acapulco	$26 00	....	$90 00
Amoy, (2 quarters)	110 28	....	40 00
Antwerp*	260 40	....	348 00
Aspinwall	1, 502 25	$60 50	37 50
Apia	264 50	....	72 00
Aux Cayes	152 90	....	....
Bahia	224 00	....	252 00
Barbadoes, (3 quarters)	58 08	....	54 00
Barcelona	52 60	....	....
Batavia	574 61	....	144 00
Bathurst	113 59	....	75 00
Bay of Islands	2, 223 49	200 61	1, 332 25
Belfast	411 92	....	594 00
Bermuda	776 89	7 51	122 40
Bombay	503 40	....	841 69
Bremen*	566 98	....	546 45
Bordeaux	....	....	48 00
Bristol	1, 094 90	....	581 80
Buenos Ayres*	2, 048 65	65 94	1, 057 29
Cadiz	136 80	7 72	48 00
Calcutta	1, 567 35	....	1, 824 00
Callao	12, 818 72	....	3, 199 50
Cape Haytien	216 93	....	48 00
Cape Town	98 50	....	....
Cardiff	284 17	....	....
Cienfuegos	160 50	....	....
Constantinople	356 78	55 10	58 73
Cork	644 19	....	40 09
Curaçoa	342 00	....	513 00
Demarara	303 54	4 18	267 00
Dublin	95 42	1 39	98 00
Falmouth	491 64	....	48 00
Fayal	2, 988 92	....	1, 561 66
Funchal	772 80	....	45 00
Genoa*	2, 118 12	....	2, 992 82
Gibraltar	199 85	....	39 18
Glasgow	278 94	....	343 82

Statement showing amount of money allowed, &c.—Continued.

Name of consulate.	Disbursements.	Loss by ex-change.	Receipts.
Gottenberg*	$52 68		$375 00
Guayaquil	569 20		$375 00
Guaymas	290 75	$7 75	6 00
Hakodadi	105 50		531 00
Halifax	340 45		20 00
Hamburg	130 08		421 38
Havana	2,918 56		3,464 70
Havre	1,540 92	41 54	837 65
Hilo	1,462 50		333 93
Hobart Town	286 74		401 14
Hong Kong	1,679 46		1,024 19
Honolulu	33,780 72	1,737 53	° 6,479 69
Kingston, Jamaica	8 44		
Lahaina	20,827 00	2,552 46	324 00
Lanthala	126 12		108 00
Leeds	56 53	2 23	
Leghorn	21 26		31 98
Lisbon	478 44		521 72
Liverpool	6,717 59	177 21	2,967 05
London	2,631 93		1,000 00
Londonderry	60 36		
Malaga	61 15	4 60	
Manilla, (premium $45 89)	323 50		78 00
Maranham	152 00		228 00
Marseilles	1,429 93	34 57	630 00
Martinique	123 74		
Matanzas	599 80	7 52	228 02
Mazatlan	2,728 75		36 00
Melbourne, (3 quarters)	237 30		411 47
Montevideo	1,222 66		1,657 93
Montreal	21 25		
Nagasaki	8 00		
Naples	107 44		129 43
Newcastle-upon-Tyne	130 38		
Oporto*	182 61	2 27	189 00
Paita, (1 quarter)	2,433 50		210 00
Panama	975 40		108 00
Palermo	126 25	14 45	
Pernambuco	2,796 35	113 60	1,455 87
Plymouth	4 60		
Port Louis, (Mauritius)	1,128 52	42 90	1,009 50

O.—*Statement showing amount of money allowed, &c.*—Continued.

Name of consulate.	Disbursements.	Loss by exchange.	Receipts.
Port au Prince*	$97 15		
Rio Grande de Sul, (2 quarters)	330 00		$1,749 00
Rio de Janeiro, (3 quarters)	1,452 00		2,298 00
Rotterdam	83 73	$2 11	12 00
San Juan del Norte	129 33		
San Juan, P. R., (3 quarters)	682 12		200 00
Santos			80 00
Shanghai	1,755 98		1,938 00
Singapore	5,735 87	79 05	3,695 43
Sierra Leone	57 48		49 56
Southampton	326 82		
Stettin	6 00		
St. Croix	21 62		45 00
St. Catherine	7 20		72 00
St. Domingo City	111 00		
St. Helena	1,589 73		515 00
Smyrna	404 50	87 10	
St. John, N. B.*	322 16		
St. John, N. F.*	125 80		186 00
St. Petersburg	52 50		87 00
St. Thomas	797 03	7 61	429 00
Sydney, N. S. W.	4,383 08	753 84	1,557 00
Tahiti	749 50	76 95	
Talcahuano	13,198 20	905 78	1,887 00
Teneriffe	1,168 00	194 51	
Trieste	504 81		
Tumbez, (premium $757 57)	7,984 00		1,020 00
Turk's Island	64 00		
Valparaiso	8,075 67		814 55
Vera Cruz	149 75		
Venice	8 90	98	
Zanzibar	90 00		115 00
Total	174,182 90	7,249 41	60,134 83

NOTE.—Those consulates marked thus ° include expenditures made prior to July 1, 1861, but reported with accounts subsequent to that time, and not included in the report of the finances for 1861.

Synopsis of the above.

Total disbursements $174,182 90
Total loss by exchange 7,249 41
                                           $181,432 31
Total receipts—of extra wagés, moneys, and premium 60,134 83

Excess of expenditures over receipts 121,297 48

The following allowances have also been made out of the fund for the relief of seamen as balances of extra wages or arrear wages due estates of deceased seamen, viz:

Name of deceased.	Consulate at which he died.	Amount allowed.
John Brewer	Santiago de Cuba	$5 26
John Stanton	Liverpool	23 42
Robert Ammon	Honolulu	96 00
Francis Weeks	Sydney	80 00
S. C. Currant	Hilo	19 93
Meyer Godman	Arica	242 00
John Anderson	Havana	34 81
		502 42

The following sums have also been allowed as wages refunded to seamen directly from the United States treasury, out of the "fund for the relief," &c.:

Name of seaman.	Consulate where discharged.	Amount allowed.
James Hayden	Liverpool	$31 00
George H. Armstrong	Sydney	100 00
John S. Percival	Calcutta	80 00
James Ridgeway, assignee for seven seamen	Cork	237 80
J. T. Johnson	Cork	54 29
James Ralph	Cork	21 60
John Merrill	Cork	21 60
Henry Price	Cork	36 00
Harman Damnen	Cork	21 60
Lewis Kavanagh	Cork	3 60
John M. Luskie	Cork	8 10
Ronald McDonald	Cork	48 50
James Wilson	Cork	21 60
		685 72

The following sums were allowed for relief to seamen picked up at sea, viz:

To John Henderson & Co., owners of the ship Edward Everett, for relief to their own crew..............................	$163 24
To Peter Rogerson & Son, owners of the British brig Jessie, for rescuing the crew of the ship Northumberland, in 1856......	11,683 12
To James Fulton, paymaster United States navy, for expenses incurred in rescuing two of the crew of ———, near Shanghai, in 1860	50 00
Total	11,896 36

There was allowed the further sum of $269 75 to W. B. Boggs, United States navy, for expenses for copying, &c., in the investigation of the Sandwich Islands hospitals.

Recapitulation.

Disbursements by consuls in excess of moneys received by them..	$114,048 07
Loss in exchange on same	7,249 41
Paid estates of deceased seamen.............................	502 42
Wages refunded to seamen	685 72
Paid parties, other than consuls, for relief to seamen*	11,896 36
Paid for copying, &c...................................	269 75
Total	134,651 73

---

* Of this sum $11,683 12 was paid for rescuing the crew of the ship Northumberland by authority of an act of Congress.

SCHEDULE D.

Statement showing the number of "destitute American seamen" sent to the United States from their several consulates during the fiscal year ending June 30, 1862, and the amount paid for their passage.

Consulate.	Remarks.	No. of seamen.	Amount.
Acapulco		7	$70 00
Almeria	4 at $10 each, and 1 at $20, in a foreign ship.	5	60 00
Amoor River		3	30 00
Antigua		6	60 00
Antwerp		3	30 00
Aspinwall		63	630 00
Barbadoes		9	90 00
Bathurst		3	30 00
Bay of Islands		2	20 00
Bermuda	23 at $10 each, and 8 at $12 each, in British ships.	31	326 00
Bordeaux		1	10 00
Bremen		1	10 00
Bristol		1	10 00
Buenos Ayres		3	30 00
Cadiz		13	130 00
Callao		4	40 00
Cardenas		1	10 00
Cardiff		2	20 00
Cape Haytien		11	110 00
Cape Town		1	10 00
Cienfuegos		6	60 00
Constantinople		1	10 00
Demerara		4	40 00
Falmouth		2	20 00
Fayal	28 at $10 each, 6 at $35 each, and 5 at $18 each, in foreign ships; 5 at $20 each, 36 at $18 each, and 4 at $30 each, being in excess of the lawful number.	84	1,448 00
Fortune Island		8	80 00
Funchal	To Messina	1	25 00
Genoa		3	30 00
Gibraltar		7	70 00
Glasgow		2	20 00
Guaymas		27	270 00
Halifax		44	410 00

D.—*Statement showing number of destitute American seamen, &c.*—Continued.

Consulate.	Remarks.	No. of seamen.	Amount.
Havana		21	$210 00
Havre	15 at $10 each ; 1 at $100, and 1 at $60—sick.	17	310 00
Hilo		1	10 00
Hong Kong		7	70 00
Honolulu		100	1,000 00
Inagua		1	10 00
Jacmel		1	10 00
Jeremie		3	30 00
Kingston, (Jamaica)		5	50 00
Lisbon		7	70 00
Liverpool	135 at $10 each, and 1 at $40, in a British ship.	136	1,390 00
London		69	690 00
Malaga		3	30 00
Marseilles		1	10 00
Martinique	2 at $10 each, and 1 at $25, in a foreign vessel.	3	45 00
Matanzas		7	70 00
Mazatlan	27 at $10 each, and 1 at $20, in a foreign ship.	28	290 00
Messina		3	30 00
Montevideo		2	20 00
Montreal		2	20 00
Montego Bay		3	30 00
Naples		2	20 00
Nassau	22 at $10 each, and 49 at $12 each, in foreign ships.	71	808 00
Nuevitas		5	50 00
Panama		5	50 00
Palermo		1	10 00
Pernambuco		45	450 00
Paramaribo		1	10 00
Port Elizabeth		1	10 00
Puerto Cabello		8	80 00
Rio de Janeiro		5	50 00
Sagua la Grande		1	10 00
San Juan, (P. R.)		5	50 00
Singapore		3	30 00

*D.—Statement showing number of destitute American seamen, &c.—*Continued.

Consulate.	Remarks.	No. of seamen.	Amount.
Sydney, (N. S. W.).		2	$20 00
Smyrna.........	Insane seaman........	1	200 00
Southampton......		2	20 00
St. Jago de Cuba...		4	40 00
St. Helena. .'......		12	120 00
St. John's, (N. B.).		11	83 50
St. Thomas, (W. I.).		36	360 00
Sidney, (N. S.).....		2	14 00
Talcahuano........		4	40 00
Trieste..........		2	20 00
Tumbez.........		1	10 00
Turk's Islands.....		16	160 00
Valparaiso........		4	40 00
Vera Cruz.........		16	160 00
Yarmouth, (N. S.)..		4	28 00

MISCELLANEOUS.

Crew of the ship Silver Star, wrecked on Jarvis's island, Pacific ocean, and brought to Honolulu by the brig Josephine..........................		27	270 00
Crew of the wrecked schooner Mississippi, brought to Philadelphia by the bark Eliza Ann..........		5	21 00
Crew of the wrecked schooner Maryland, brought to Philadelphia by the brig William Butcher........		5	50 00
Crew of the wrecked brig Citizen, brought to New York by the brig Ianthe......................		11	99 00
Crew of the wrecked brig Granada, brought to New York by the British schooner Greyhound........		4	40 00
Crew of the wrecked bark B. Hallett, brought into Glasgow by the British bark Annie Hall........		10	33 00
Crew of the wrecked ship Eagle Speed, brought into Calcutta by the British steamer Burniah..........		13	268 13
Part of the crew of the wrecked ship Star of Hope, brought to Philadelphia by the ship Monterey.....		3	73 50
Total..............................		1,127	12,402 13

SCHEDULE E.

Statement showing the amount expended in arresting American seamen in foreign countries, charged with the commission of crime on American vessels, together with the expenses attending the examination of the same by the consul, and the expenses of sending them to the United States for trial, with the witnesses, during the fiscal year ending June 30, 1862.

Consulate where the expense originated.	No. of men.	Amount expended.	Remarks.
Batavia	3	$76 46	
Bordeaux........	1	47 55	
Cadiz	2	200 00	
Cardiff	2	110 22	
Havana	2	49 75	
Havre	1	22 99	
Liverpool	14	2,553 93	
London	2	411 36	
Loanda..........	1	10 00	
Mayagues	1	50 00	
Montevideo	1	150 00	
Palermo	1	10 00	
Rotterdam	1	47 86	
Singapore	4	1,000 00	
St. Thomas	1	8 16	
Sydney	8	14,921 85	Special appropriation in case of mutineers of ship "Junior," 1858.
	45	19,670 13	

Whole amount adjusted for fiscal year ending June 30, 1862 ... $19,670 13
Amount expended under special appropriation in case of ship
    "Junior".. 14,921 85

Leaving the ordinary expenses for the year........... 4,748 28

F.

OFFICE OF THE AUDITOR OF THE TREASURY
FOR THE POST OFFICE DEPARTMENT,
October 31, 1862.

SIR: To present in detail the financial affairs of the Post Office Department, and the extensive, diversified, and complicated operations of this bureau for the fiscal year ending June 30, 1862, would swell this report beyond convenient limits. I therefore beg leave to submit only a brief outline of the principal labors performed by the office. All that relates to the financial transactions of the Post Office Department, as exhibited by the books and accounts of this bureau, will fully appear in my report to the Postmaster General.

The efforts of the office in collecting the scattered revenues of the Post Office Department have been crowned with unusual success, notwithstanding the wide-spread pecuniary embarrassment occasioned by the existing unhappy rebellion against the integrity of the government. The sum collected within the fiscal year from late postmasters alone amounts to $476,447 39, which exceeds the amount collected from the same class of debtors during the fiscal year 1861 by the sum of $179,212 23; is $296,907 73 greater than the amount collected in the fiscal year 1860 by my predecessor; and is very largely in excess of the collections made in any previous fiscal year since the organization of the bureau. There has also been collected by drafts of this office from present postmasters the sum of $48,241 25, a description of labor not hitherto performed by the office. To the untiring industry and extraordinary labors of the clerical force are to be attributed these gratifying results.

During the fiscal year two hundred and sixty-one suits were instituted by the office for the recovery of sums due to the government, amounting, in the aggregate, to $76,468 62. Of these suits one hundred and twenty-eight have been tried, and all except two decided in favor of the United States.

Within the fiscal year the important and complicated accounts between the United States and foreign governments have been considerably augmented, but they have been promptly and satisfactorily adjusted.

The number of changes of postmasters reported by the Post Office Department requiring the final adjustment of their accounts during the fiscal year was	7,336
The number of late postmasters' accounts in charge of the office	37,638
The number of present postmasters' accounts in charge of the office	19,652
The number of quarterly accounts of postmasters adjusted, audited, and registered	77,109
The number of accounts of mail contractors audited and reported to the Postmaster General for payment	14,740
The number of accounts of special and route agents audited and reported for payment	4,605
The number of accounts of special contractors and mail messengers audited and reported for payment	15,988
The number of miscellaneous accounts audited and reported for payment	165
The number of accounts of United States attorneys, and marshals, and clerks of United States courts adjusted and reported for payment	143
The number of accounts for paper and printing post office blanks	21
The number of accounts for advertising	124
The number of "collection orders" issued to mail contractors	61,083
The number of "collection drafts" issued	8,300
The number of "department drafts" countersigned and registered	15,314
The number of "department warrants" countersigned and registered	4,970

The number of letters received 117, 317
The number of letters prepared, recorded, and mailed 82, 875
The number of folio post pages of correspondence recorded in the
  "miscellaneous" letter book................................. 895
The number of pages recorded in the "collection" letter book 4, 315
The number of pages recorded in the "suit" letter book........... 476
The number of pages recorded in the "report" letter book......... 203
The number of accounts on the ledgers..................... ..... 75, 981
The number of corrected quarterly accounts of postmasters copied, re-
  stated, and mailed..................................... ...... 20, 500
The number of stamp and stamped envelope accounts examined, com-
  pared, and restated...,................................. ...... 79, 616

By comparing the foregoing brief summary with that contained in my last
annual report, it will be seen that the aggregate amount of labor performed by
this office within the fiscal year 1862 greatly exceeds that accomplished in the
fiscal year 1861.

It affords me great pleasure, in conclusion, to state that the entire business
of the bureau is now in a very satisfactory condition, and that the accuracy,
promptness, and ability with which it has been discharged during the fiscal year
reflects the highest credit on the clerical corps employed in the office.

I have the honor to be, very respectfully,

Hon. S. P. CHASE,   G. ADAMS, Auditor.
    Secretary of the Treasury.

G.

TREASURY DEPARTMENT,
First Comptroller's Office, October 28, 1862.

SIR: I submit herewith an abstract of the business of this office for the fiscal
year ending June 30, 1862.

The following named warrants of the Secretary of the Treasury have been
countersigned, entered in blotters, and posted, to wit:

Stock warrants ....,..................................\.............. 1, 718
Quarterly salary warrants..................................... 1, 955
Treasury (proper) warrants........................... ....:... 2, 070
Treasury interior warrants.................................... 2, 401
Treasury customs warrants.................................... 1, 945
War pay warrants.. 8, 735
War repay warrants.. 552
Navy pay warrants..,....................................... 1, 948
Navy repay warrants.. 357
Interior pay warrants... 823
Interior repay warrants:...................................... 362
Treasury appropriation warrants............................... 25
Interior appropriation warrants................................ 20
Customs appropriation warrants....,.............:........:. 16
War appropriation warrants............................,..... 20
Navy appropriation warrants..,.............................. 17
Texas debt warrants.,....................;................,... 3
Land covering warrants............................ ......,.. 225
Customs covering warrants................................... 762
Miscellaneous covering warrants.............................. 1, 327

                                                          25, 281

The accounts described as follows, reported to this office by the First and Fifth Auditors and the Commissioner of the General Land Office, have been revised and certified to the Register of the Treasury, to wit:

I. From the First Auditor:

Judiciary.—Embracing the accounts of marshals for expenses of the United States courts, of district attorneys, of clerks of the United States circuit and district courts, and of United States commissioners, for per diems and fees, and rent of court-rooms 774

Public debt.—Embracing accounts for redemption of United States stock and treasury notes, the interest on the public debt, the United States Treasurer's accounts, temporary loans, the United States assistant treasurers' accounts, and other matters properly belonging thereto ... 1,637

Salaries.—Embracing accounts for salaries of United States supreme, district, and territorial judges, attorneys, marshals, local inspectors, officers of the executive departments, &c 1,055

Public printing.—Embracing accounts for public printing, binding, and paper 84

Mint and branches.—Embracing accounts of gold, silver, and cent bullion, of ordinary expenses, repairs, wages of employés, &c 31

Territorial.—Embracing accounts of governors of the Territories for contingent expenses, erection of public buildings, of the secretaries of Territories for legislative and contingent expenses, &c 50

Miscellaneous.—Embracing accounts of the Coast Survey, of the Commissioner of Public Buildings, the insane asylum, the penitentiary, for the suppression of the slave trade, for horses lost in the military service of the United States 873

Congressional.—Embracing the accounts of the Secretary of the United States Senate and the Clerk of the House of Representatives 97

II. From the Fifth Auditor:

Diplomatic and consular.—Embracing accounts of foreign ministers for salary and contingent expenses, of United States secretaries of legation for salary, of consuls general, of consuls, and commercial agents for salary and for disbursements for relief of destitute American seamen, for passage from foreign ports to the United States of destitute and criminal American seamen and witnesses, of United States commissioners under reciprocity treaty, of accounts under treaty for foreign indemnity, of contingent expenses of consulates 1,860

Patent Office.—Embracing accounts for contingent and incidental expenses, salaries, &c 18

Census Office.—Embracing accounts of the disbursing clerk for salaries and all other expenses 2

III. From the Land Office:

Embracing accounts of receivers of public money, of receivers acting as disbursing agents, of surveyors general and deputy surveyors, of lands erroneously sold, of the several States for percentage on lands sold within their limits 1,795
                                                                    ====

Aggregate of accounts revised:
From First Auditor 4,601
From Fifth Auditor 1,880
From Commissioner of the General Land Office 1,795
                                                            ——— 8,276
Bonds entered, filed, and indexed 375
Letters written upon matters appertaining to the business of the office .. 4,459
Decisions recorded, amounting to, pages 96

There have been also regularly entered, filed, and indexed with the proper briefs, all letters and communications received in the office.

The semi-annual emolument returns made by the United States marshals, district attorneys, and clerks of courts, in pursuance of the third section of the act of February 26, 1853, have been examined, entered, and properly filed; also the requisitions made, from time to time, for advances to United States marshals, territorial officers, treasurers of mint and branches, to disbursing officers and agents, &c., have been examined and reported upon in all cases.

There are many miscellaneous duties to be performed, arising from the necessary business of the office, which need not here be particularized. These require, in many instances, much time and labor, and have been attended to as they were presented, from day to day.

Very respectfully,

ELISHA WHITTLESEY,
Comptroller.

Hon. S. P. CHASE,
Secretary of the Treasury.

H.

TREASURY DEPARTMENT
Second Comptroller's Office, November 19, 1862.

SIR: Pursuant to instructions, I have the honor to submit the following report of the operations of this office during the fiscal year ending the 30th June last:

The number of accounts of disbursing officers, agents, &c., received, acted on, passed, and recorded during the fiscal year was as follows:

Reported by the Second Auditor... 5,572
Reported by the Third Auditor... 3,092
Reported by the Fourth Auditor... 476

Whole number... 9,140

The expenditures accounted for in the settlements of the Second Auditor embrace moneys appropriated by Congress for the use of the pay department of the army; the recruiting service; medical and hospital department; ordnance service, armories, arsenals, ordnance stores, purchase of arms, &c.; expenses of collecting, drilling, and organizing volunteers; contingencies of the army; as also the disbursements of the Indian department.

The accounts reported by the Third Auditor cover a very large field of public expenditure, embracing the quartermaster's department, construction of gunboat fleet, and steam rams; clothing of army, subsistence of army, engineer department, fortifications, military pensions; the settlement of State disbursements under acts of 17th and 27th July, 1861, and other expenditures of the War Department, for details of which I have, respectfully, to refer to the Auditor's official report.

The Fourth Auditor's accounts were for expenditures of the naval establishment, comprising disbursements by paymasters of the navy and marine corps, navy agents, naval storekeepers and navy pensions, prize money, &c.

Many of these settlements embraced a large number of vouchers, and included very heavy expenditures, and not only required time but a high degree of official capacity and experience in their investigation.

All undergo here a critical revision in reference to the legality and correctness of the payments, as well as that they were authorized in pursuance of appropriations duly made by law.

I have reason to believe that the work thereon has been promptly and satisfactorily performed.

The total amount embraced in these settlements was $87,684,097 64, viz:

Second Auditor's	$37,111,957 47
Third Auditor's	32,277,710 64
Fourth Auditor's	18,294,429 53

Additional to the above, there has been reported to and examined in this office a large number of another class of settlements, being "certificate accounts" or claims for balance due officers who have resigned, died, &c., and to soldiers who have been discharged or died in the service with pay and bounty due; and of seamen, their heirs, administrators, &c.

The amount, when duly investigated and found from the official rolls and records to be due upon such "certificate" settlements, is made payable by disbursing officers of the army and navy, according to the branch of military or naval service to which the party for whose services the claim is allowed properly belonged.

To this class of settlements by the accounting officers of the treasury, with the concurrence of the War Department, I have, within the past year, added the payment of private physicians or citizen surgeons duly employed by the medical and hospital department.

It became matter of necessity to adopt this mode of settlement to avoid overtasking the Secretaries of War and Treasury, and other officers of both departments, for record, signature, and counter signatures to adjustments of mere monthly stipends, for the payment of which it happened that proper disbursing officers were not duly provided by other authority of law or regulation.

"Certificate" settlements originate in the offices of the Second and Fourth Auditors, respectively, and were during the last fiscal year thus reported to and acted upon in this office, in number as follows:

Accounts reported by the Second Auditor	3,019
Accounts reported by the Third Auditor	539
Making a total of	3,558

The number of requisitions upon the Secretary of the Treasury received, examined, countersigned, and recorded upon the books of this office was as follows:

Drawn by the Secretary of the Interior:

Pay or advance requisitions	806
Refunding requisitions	143

Drawn by the Secretary of War:

Pay or advance requisitions	8,465
Refunding requisitions	558

Drawn by the Secretary of the Navy:

Pay or advance requisitions	2,046
Refunding requisitions	328
Whole number	12,346

There were received and filed during the fiscal year 1861-'62, 874 letters upon official business, the answers to which cover 574 pages folio post of the letter book.

All the annual statements for Congress required by the law of May 1, 1820, have been promptly transmitted in duplicate to the Secretaries of Interior, War, and Navy. These statements exhibited the balances of the several appropriations remaining upon the books on the 1st of July, 1860; the appropriations for the War and Navy Departments and for the Indian and Pension branches of the Interior Department made by Congress for the fiscal year 1860-'61; the repayments and transfers in that year; the amount applicable under each appropriation, and the amount drawn by requisitions during the same period; and, finally, the balances remaining unexpended on 30th June, 1861, with such appropriations as were carried to the surplus fund.

All other prescribed duties of this office—embracing decisions on cases specially reported from the Second, Third, and Fourth Auditors, or from the bureaus and officers of the War, Navy, and Interior Departments; filing official bonds and the numerous contracts received from those departments; the supervision of transcripts for suit, &c.—have received prompt attention, the business here having, by great exertion, been well kept up, so that no material part of it is as yet in arrears.

I feel it my duty to declare my conviction that the accounting officers of the treasury have not realized the immense amount of labor hereafter to be devolved upon them. It is only necessary to call attention to the military and naval expenditure of the past as compared with the immense increase of appropriations rendered necessary by the present war.

Time has still to be allowed for the rendition from the administrative bureaus of the War and Navy Departments of the accounts of the various disbursing officers to whom public moneys have been recently advanced, and the increasing number to whom advances are being daily made.

In fact, the very great number of these officers and agents to whom public funds will be and are intrusted must be commensurate with the wide field of operations and the magnitude of the appropriations and necessary expenditure.

That irregularities and abuses under such circumstances will occur, I submit is inevitable. It becomes, however, the duty of the accounting officers closely to analyze and scrutinize all such accounts presented to the treasury for settlement. Their labors and responsibilities are thus increased in a greater degree than by the mere ratio of increased appropriations. Nor this alone : some new precedents and authorizations of expenditure have grown out of the necessities of the present occasion.

Recent laws have been found to conflict, or, separately, to so authorize expenditures for the same purpose as not to designate a sufficient dividing line to prevent certain classes of military expense being paid for under two or three different appropriations by different disbursing officers.

Thus, without extraordinary vigilance and experience on the part of the disbursing officers, duplicate or triplicate payments may in some instances have occurred, by fraud, or in conflict with right or the intention of law.

To this subject the Secretary of the Treasury early called the attention of the accounting officers of his department.

Fully aware of the possibilities injurious to the interest of the government that might be realized from the looseness of hurried legislation, I have exercised every power or prerogative intrusted to this office to guard against and to stop at the treasury all such double or triplicate payments.

Thus, in the detection of many cases of fraud I have been successful, and double payments, made in different shapes, for the same services, under color of existing laws, have been disallowed at this office.

I have, nevertheless, to submit that this class of payments, made by disbursing officers of separate bureaus of the War Department, do not reach the knowledge of the accounting officers of the treasury until long after the erroneous disbursement has been made, and reclamation becomes difficult, impracticable, or impossible.

The labor of investigation into different accounts, settlements, and returns necessary to trace and discover these unauthorized payments, inevitably tasks the time and attention of the accounting officers at a period when all their efforts are strained to keep up with the current business of their offices.

I had the honor to suggest for your consideration a provision by which the accounting officers would be greatly relieved of the responsibility and labor of the adjustment of State accounts, under acts of 17th and 27th July, 1861. This, I believe, could not be properly effected without corresponding legislation, and meanwhile the labor is being performed, I trust, faithfully and satisfactorily, adding, however, to the large aggregate of duty imposed on this and the Third Auditor's office.

In many of the settlements of military and naval expenditures, the provisions of the tax law will, certainly for the present, require vigilant co-operation with the Commissioner of Revenue, until the laws, details, and instructions are so perfected as to place the whole subject entirely under the control of the Commissioner.

Payment of damages in the military and naval service, and all questions of expenditure unauthorized by law, will, as heretofore, not be affirmed by the passage of vouchers therefor, but will have, before allowance at the treasury, to await authorization by Congress.

I have, on several occasions, had the honor to suggest that doubts, amounting to reasonable conviction, have so arisen as to the fidelity and good faith which occasionally attend the presentation of vouchers for disbursements, that a local examination should be had by some proper agent of the treasury.

In some cases of absolute fraud here discovered, local investigation of its extent and means of proper punishment should be so provided for as to deter future attempts of the kind on the treasury.

Property accounts, involving the distribution, application to necessary use of supplies, &c., purchased, loss, damage, capture, &c., embrace a heavy responsibility, which, in my opinion, should rest with the administrative bureaus of the War and Navy Departments, as, indeed, in contemplation of the laws creating those offices I believe has been ordained. Hence, the examination of all such returns accompanying money accounts should be under the supervision of the different military and naval bureaus, for administrative advisement to the accounting officers of their correctness.

Obstacles have been found to exist to the strict execution of the act of July 17, 1862, entitled "An act to provide for the more prompt settlement of the accounts of disbursing officers."

By a provision of the law, modifications are authorized, at your discretion, as to the extension of time for the rendition of accounts therein provided for.

At your suggestion, the recommendation of the different branches of War, Interior, and Navy Departments has been submitted to you, with report from this office thereon.

In the naval branch of the service, the modification thus recommended has been approved by you. That suggested for the War and Interior I have no doubt will meet the entire acquiescence of those departments, and thus will be conserved the salutary and essential purpose of the law.

I would avoid the extension of this paper, by respectfully referring you to the separate reports of the Second, Third, and Fourth Auditors for details and suggestions.

With the addition of duties which those officers anticipate, and with the increase of clerical force recommended by them, this office inevitably shares.

In this connexion I do but follow out the suggestions of my predecessors, as well as my own convictions, in recommending that the clerical increase of this office should be in ratio of one revising clerk here to three given additionally to each of the Auditors of the War and Navy for the purpose of stating accounts.

Further, I may be permitted to add, that the measure of ability, as of salary, should, as has hitherto been invariably urged by my predecessors, be higher in this office.

If further experience of the increasing magnitude of labor and responsibility devolving on this office shall, in my opinion, justify me in recommending other provisions of law, I will, at the proper time, venture to call your attention to the subject, rather than undertake a task which may be impossible faithfully to be executed by any one, however able or experienced.

With great respect your obedient servant,

J. MADISON CUTTS, *Comptroller.*

Hon. SALMON P. CHASE,
    Secretary of the Treasury.

I.

TREASURER'S OFFICE, *November* 27, 1862.

SIR: The following summary of the business of the treasury for the fiscal year ending the 30th June, 1862, together with suggestions in regard to needful changes in this office, is respectfully submitted:

The amount paid into the treasury during said year, and covered by thirty-three hundred and forty-three warrants, was—

From customs, lands, and miscellaneous sources	$583, 317, 631 42
War Department	3, 271, 609 67
Navy Department	2, 434, 195 21
Interior Department	173, 981 42
Total	589, 197, 417 72

The preceding amounts include repayments into the treasury for adjusting balances. The aggregate payments into the treasury for the fiscal year ending June 30, 1861, were only $88,694,572 03.

The payments during the fiscal year ending on the 30th June last, made upon 21,296 drafts issued upon 21,282 warrants, were—

For civil, diplomatic, miscellaneous, and public debt	$132, 333, 453 19
War Department	397, 640, 017 03
Navy Department	45, 102, 472 30
Interior Department	3, 300, 300 27
Total	578, 376, 242 79

The above sums include transfers for adjusting balances.

For the fiscal year ending June 30, 1861, the total payments from the treasury were only $90,012,449 79.

The amount received for the use of the Post Office Department, from postmasters and others, for the fiscal year, including a balance of $57,684 03 in the treasury at the commencement of the year, was

	$3, 683, 688 20
Paid on 4,310 post office warrants $3, 644, 381 62	
Less amount of cancelled warrants 5, 858 90	
	3, 638, 522 72
Leaving at the close of the year, subject to draft	45, 165 48

The sum of $197,740,177 20 was transferred, by means of 472 transfer orders, from one depository to another, to facilitate disbursements for the public service.

In addition to the "transfer account" with the assistant treasurer at New York, like accounts have been opened during the past year with the assistant treasurers at Boston and Philadelphia, that have greatly benefited public creditors and facilitated business operations at this office. Nearly forty millions has been paid through the medium of those accounts.

The practice of holding moneys to the credit and subject to the draft of disbursing officers continues to work advantageously to them and with safety to the government, but at the expense of largely increased labor and responsibility thrown upon those employed in that branch of the public service. These deposits of disbursing officers have increased at this office, during the year, from a little over eight millions to more than one hundred and ninety millions of dollars.

The business of the treasury proper, embracing aggregate receipts and disbursements at all the offices of the department, has increased over the preceding year, as six and a half to one. The transactions of this office have, however, increased over those of last year in the ratio of nearly twenty-three to one. The subjoined statements for the last two fiscal years will present a full and clear idea of the money movements at the office in this city, and, by comparison, the great accumulation of labor incident to the increase of business transactions.

Statement of the receipts and disbursements at the treasury of the United States for the fiscal year ending June 30, 1861.

Cash in treasury June 30, 1860	$604,598 97
Coin by express	3,965,500 00
New York transfer drafts	3,934,984 74
Receipts on loans	2,863,794 16
Receipts for use of Post Office Department	17,972 14
Sundry receipts	1,144,985 38
Agency deposits	8,130,834 21
Total	20,662,669 60
Disbursements to July 1, 1861	19,691,430 16
Cash in treasury July 1, 1861	971,239 44
Total	20,662,669 60

Statement of receipts and disbursements at the treasury of the United States for the fiscal year ending June 30, 1862.

Cash in treasury July 1, 1861	$971,239 44
Coin received by express	9,570,000 00
New York transfer checks	39,351,553 73
Receipts on national loan	4,272,602 40
Receipts for Post Office Department	200,380 31
Receipts on 6 per cent. 5.20 United States bonds	190,896 77
Receipts on 4 per cent. temporary loan	92,523 40
Sundry receipts	756,961 94
United States notes, old issue	60,030,000 00
United States notes, new issue	100,620,000 00
Certificates of indebtedness	44,888,979 73
Old issue United States notes returned to be burned	8,696,700 00
New issue United States notes returned	4,000,000 00
Oregon war bonds issued	1,010,750 00
Deposits	190,104,209 47
Reimbursement for old issue United States notes burned	58,610 00
Total	464,815,407 19

Disbursements to July 1, 1862, viz:

Paid on depositors' checks, treasury drafts, post office warrants, interest on public debt, &c.	$248, 348, 084 03
Redemptions.—Certificates of indebtedness	5, 384, 574 11
4 per cent. temporary loan	1, 624 51
old issue United States notes destroyed	6, 990, 000 00
new issue, destroyed	2, 000, 000 00
Paid members of Congress	870, 365 70
Transfers and credits	195, 016, 105 66
Cash in treasury	6, 204, 653 18
Total	464, 815, 407 19

The first entire month that the office was in my charge, April, 1861, the total receipts and disbursements, exclusive of balances, was $3,007,832 21.

The same items for April, 1862, amounted to $331,165,816 81, or more than one hundred and ten times as much as for the same month last year. Although many items in the above amounts are represented three or four times, thereby increasing totals in both months, yet all these transfers of money and entries upon books became necessary to the correct transaction of business, and involved corresponding risks and responsibilities. The correspondence of the office for the month of April, 1861, exclusive of letters containing remittances, numbered *fifty-four;* in April, 1862, the number of written letters was *five hundred and twenty.*

At the close of the fiscal year ending June 30, 1861, there were upon the books *eighty* open accounts of disbursing officers; at the close of the last fiscal year those accounts had increased to *two hundred and thirty-two.*

Depositors' checks in the former year	22,430
Depositors' checks in the latter year	81,150
Transfer checks, drawn in the former year	1,484
Transfer checks, drawn in the latter year	8,158

A glance at the facts and figures set forth will show the *necessity* for an entire reconstruction of the *personnel* of this office. As at present organized, the force employed and the room occupied are inadequate to the proper transaction of the public business, although it is believed that the multifarious duties and labors appertaining to the bureau have been thus far discharged with exactness and promptitude. The work has been performed by devoting not only almost every hour of each day, (Sundays not excepted,) but many hours of night, to continuous labor beyond the endurance of most men. The compensation of those employed in this office, with the present cost of living, is too small for the services rendred, and not enough to maintain such as have families. It is less than one-half that paid to employés of the same grade in the office at New York, who have like duties, perform no more labor, and incur no greater responsibilities It has been only by personal appeals to their patriotism, and holding out the hope that Congress would do them justice, that some of the best clerks have been induced to remain in this office. Others, unable to endure the hard and long-continued labor, have succumbed and left the office. There are at present more temporary than regular clerks employed here, yet nearly the whole force is overworked to a degree that *cannot be continued.* Under former regulations, thirty-six hours' labor per week was required, but seldom had of clerks. There are persons now in this office who work faithfully and efficiently full threefold that time, and even the Sabbath has brought to

Ex. Doc. 1——9

them no period of rest. It is right and proper that such faithfulness and industry, united with suitable talents and integrity, receive reward in a substantial form.

The public exigencies and the business of the office require that there be a deputy treasurer, with all the powers of the Treasurer of the United States. The number of clerks should also be increased; and as a high order of ability and moral character is required, and great responsibilities must rest on them, they should be paid at least as well as clerks of like grade, and discharging similar duties, in other offices.

Very respectfully, your obedient servant,

F. E. SPINNER,
Treasurer of the United States.

Hon. S. P. CHASE,
  Secretary of the Treasury.

J.

TREASURY DEPARTMENT,
Solicitor's Office, November 17, 1862.

SIR: I have the honor herewith to transmit a report of the operations of this office for the fiscal year ending June 30, 1862, embraced in five tabular statements.

In the first four of these statements the proceedings are classified, as far as it can be conveniently done, so as to present as distinctly as possible all that has been done in each of the judicial districts, and in each particular class of business; to which is added a general summary of the whole, viz:

No. 1.—Statement of suits on transcripts of the official settlements of the accounts of defaulting public officers, contractors, &c., adjusted by the accounting officers of the Treasury Department.

No. 2.—Statement of suits brought during the year for the recovery of fines, penalties, and forfeitures for violations of the revenue laws, and for other causes, including prize cases and cases arising under the act of July 13, 1862.

No. 3.—Statement of suits on warehouse transportation bonds for duties on imported goods.

No. 4.—Statement of miscellaneous suits, which includes all suits brought during the year which are not embraced in the three preceding tables.

No. 5.—A general summary showing the aggregates of the foregoing tables.

From this general summary it appears that the whole number of suits of all descriptions brought during the year is 1,072, of which 10 were of class 1, for the recovery of $66,517 88; 843 of class 2, for $1,322,996 93; 29 of class 3, for $40,704 74; and 190 of class 4, for $28,010.

Of these suits, 544 have been disposed of during the year, as follows, viz: 358 decided for the United States; 55 decided against the United States; 98 settled and dismissed, and 33 remitted by the Secretary of the Treasury; leaving still pending and undecided 528. Of the whole number remaining undecided, 233 are in the southern district of New York; and I am informed that the chief cause of their not having been brought to trial has been the inability of the judges sitting within that district to hear and determine the immense number of cases brought before them.

Of the suits on the docket of the office which were instituted previous to the commencement of the last fiscal year, 148 have been disposed of during the year, viz: 26 decided for the United States; 50 decided against the United States, and 72 settled and dismissed.

The aggregate number of suits of all descriptions decided and otherwise disposed of during the year is 692. The gross amount of judgments obtained, exclusive of those *in rem*, is $66,342 29; and the whole amount collected from all sources is $461,438 87.

The following table presents a general comparative view of the business under the charge of the office, so far as the same is exhibited in the foregoing statements and summary for the last fiscal year, and for the year immediately preceding the last:

Year.	SUITS BROUGHT DURING THE FISCAL YEAR.								
	Total amount reported sued for.	Total amount of judgments for United States.	Total amount reported collected.	Decided for United States.	Decided against United States.	Settled and dismissed.	Remitted.	Pending.	Total number of suits brought.
1861.	$444,279 16	$75,683 59	$113,787 74	112	23	39	35	327	529
1862.	1,463,229 55	35,757 45	339,433 63	356	55	98	33	536	1,072

Year.	SUITS BROUGHT PRIOR TO THE FISCAL YEAR.						Whole number of judgments in favor of United States during fiscal year.	Whole amount of judgments in favor of United States during fiscal year.	Whole amount collected from all sources during fiscal year.
	Amount of judgments in old suits.	Decided for United States.	Decided against United States.	Settled and dismissed.	Total number disposed of.	Amount collected in old suits.			
1861.	$61,734 76	66	5	51	122	$229,558 72	178	$136,818 35	$343,346 46
1862.	30,584 84	96	50	72	148	122,005 25	384	66,342 29	461,438 87

By reference to this table it will be perceived that the business of the last year was fully double that of the year next preceding, and, I will add, there seems to be no prospect of its diminution, but, on the contrary, there is every reason for believing that it will undergo still further and greater increase.

Very soon after I entered upon the duties of this office my attention was attracted by the large amount of outstanding judgments in favor of the United States which is evidenced by its books, and I have caused investigations to be made with a view to determine the amount of these judgments; the causes which have led to their immense accumulation, and whether it is not practicable to devise means of greatly reducing the amount now outstanding, and of preventing such accumulations in future.

By reference to statements herewith transmitted, showing the character and condition of these judgments, in detail, and to a summary exhibiting the gross amount, and the amount outstanding in each judicial district, it will be perceived that the aggregate of these uncollected judgments within the districts at present under the control of the national government reaches the large sum of $8,685,157 47.

I am persuaded that one of the chief causes of so large an accumulation of uncollected judgments has been the state of the law relating to the compensation of district attorneys. Their compensation has been, and still is, altogether inadequate, and it is, in my judgment, regulated by defective, artificial, and unwise provisions. It is measured by a fee bill which falls far short of apportioning the compensation in accordance with the amount of service rendered.

Especially, *no* allowance is made, by way of percentage or otherwise, for the collection of money due to the government. There is a fee for the prosecution of the suit for the money to judgment, and that is all. For anything that may be done afterwards—and experience shows that often the greater difficulties of realizing for the government what is due to it remain to be surmounted after judgment—the district attorney receives absolutely no compensation whatever. With the rendition of the judgment, therefore, all his personal interest in the proceeding terminates. He files his precipe for execution, it is true, and the execution issues; but the marshal may not readily discover property wherewith to satisfy it, and he, too often prematurely, abandons all effort to do so, and returns "*nulla bona.*" Often, too, an execution will not reach property which is known to exist, and further proceedings are requisite, in order to enforce the judgment. The district attorney is pressed with other duties; the return of the marshal is not questioned; the additional proceedings are not taken; every day's delay increases the difficulties in the way of collection; perhaps the district attorney goes out of office, and is succeeded by another incumbent, who has had no responsibility in connexion with the case, knows nothing of it, and receives no compensation for anything he may do in relation to it. The result is, the judgment remains year after year uncollected, though, by the use of the requisite means, it might have been, and, in many cases, might still be, enforced.

I consider it vain to expect any other result, so long as the present system of compensating district attorneys remains in operation. The adoption by them of the necessary measures for enforcing a judgment would, in many cases, involve them in personal expense, for the reimbursement of which no provision is made, and, in almost all cases of any difficulty, would impose upon them much labor, for which, as I have already said, they receive no compensation.

I feel confident, however, that by a change of the law in this respect, and the adoption of some other means, which I will point out, a large portion of these outstanding judgments may still be collected. For this purpose, I would recommend—

1st. That, in addition to the compensation now allowed by law, district attorneys be allowed a commission upon all moneys collected for the United States in suits under their care; making the commission larger where the moneys are collected upon judgments obtained by their predecessors than when collected on such as are obtained by themselves.

2d. That the Solicitor of the Treasury be authorized, under the direction and with the approbation of the Secretary of the Treasury, to employ special attorneys and agents, upon such terms as the Secretary and Solicitor may deem reasonable and proper, to collect any outstanding judgments in favor of the United States, for the collection of which they may consider it expedient to resort to such means.

3d. That the Secretary of the Treasury be authorized, upon a full report by the proper district attorney of the facts and circumstances connected with any judgment, and the terms upon which it is proposed to compromise the same, and upon the concurrent recommendation of the district attorney and of the Solicitor of the Treasury, to compromise such judgment accordingly.

I would recommend the allowance of such a commission to district attorneys as a matter of justice to those officers; but, independent of all such considerations, I would most earnestly recommend it as a measure of the clearest policy, as I entertain no doubt whatever that its adoption would result in advantage to the government. I do not conceive it to be necessary for me to say anything by way of explanation or enforcement of the proposition to authorize the Solicitor to employ special agents and attorneys. With reference to the power of compromising judgments, I will say that, while it is a power which has been held to be vested in the Solicitor of the Treasury, it is one concerning the exercise of which I should feel great hesitation, and which I certainly should not exercise without the advice and approbation of the Secretary of the Treasury. Still, I think it is a power which ought to exist as well for the interest of the government as for the sake of judgment debtors, since it is often practicable to obtain a portion of a judgment by compromise when nothing could be obtained by compulsory measures; and I know of no place where such a power could be so appropriately lodged as with the head of the Treasury Department.

Another subject which has received from me very considerable consideration is that of frauds in the importation of foreign merchandise. On the 14th of March last I had the honor of addressing you upon this subject, on the occasion of returning to you a printed communication in relation thereto, which had been addressed to you by a gentleman of New York, and which you had caused to be transmitted to me for examination, and for an expression of my views upon the suggestions contained therein. In the letter which I then addressed to you I used the following language : " I have no doubt that extensive frauds have been committed, and that their commission is still persisted in. I am persuaded that the revenue suffers loss to large amounts annually from this cause, and that every consideration of interest and of morals requires that it should be suppressed. The treasury needs all that is due to it, and the cause of morality is served by visiting violations of it with due punishment. Besides, it is due to honest merchants to protect them against the practices of the unscrupulous." Recent developments, and further examination and reflection have only served to deepen the convictions thus expressed, and I beg to call your attention to the letter to which I refer, and to the printed communication by which it was accompanied, for a more full exposition of this subject than I shall attempt in this report.

In that letter I stated, and I take the liberty of here repeating, that first in order among the means of preventing a continuance of these frauds, I would place vigorous and unrelaxing efforts to detect and punish those which have already been committed, since nothing would have a better tendency to deter persons from committing frauds in the future than perceiving that the government is earnestly engaged in prosecuting those committed in the past. For this purpose I think that special agents, to be employed as detectives in this branch of the government service, might be employed with advantage, as well abroad as at home.

But I am of opinion that prospective measures of prevention may be adopted with the most salutary results. The first great object in all efforts of this character must be to secure the disclosure, in an authentic and permanent form, of the actual terms of all purchases of foreign merchandise imported into this country, and the deposition and retention of the evidence thereof in positions safe and accessible, and convenient alike for the purpose of estimating the duty and of detecting any error or fraud.

For this purpose it seems to me that the following requirements could not fail to have a most beneficial effect :

1st. To require every invoice of foreign merchandise to be signed by the seller or his authorized agent, and accompanied by an affidavit or solemn declaration that it exhibits the actual terms of the purchase to which it relates, including the currency or other consideration actually paid for the merchandise.

2d. That such invoice shall be deposited, within a limited and short time after the purchase, with some officer of the government of the United States, as the consul or commercial agent, in the country of the purchase. This should be done in order to guard against the possibility of changing the invoice between the time of the purchase and the time of making the entry of the goods, and to afford ready means of comparing the prices stated therein with the markets of the country, and in connexion with the next requirement which I shall suggest, for still another and not less important purpose, viz.; that of preventing the possibility of the loss or destruction of the invoice by collusion or otherwise.

3d. The exhibition and deposit with the revenue officers of a duplicate of the invoice, verified by the certificate of the consul or other officer, stating that the original has been deposited with him, and showing the time when such deposit was made.

4th. The affidavit of the importer as to the genuineness and truthfulness of the invoice in every respect.

In addition to these measures, I think it highly important that the whole subject of the prevention, detection, and prosecution of violations of the revenue laws be placed under the general supervision of some officer of the Treasury Department. This seems to me alike necessary for the energy and the uniformity of the measures to be adopted; and I am confident that it would prove alike conducive to the interests of the government and of importers. As a large portion of those measures are now, and must remain, under the direction of the Solicitor of the Treasury, it would seem that there is no other officer to whom the remainder could be so appropriately assigned as to him. For the very considerable increase in labor and responsibility which would be the result, he might be allowed a very small percentage—probably one-half of one per cent. would be sufficient—upon the moneys collected under his supervision. While such an allowance would be sufficient for his compensation, it would be too small in any particular case to excite his cupidity, and thereby cloud his judgment, or unduly influence his action.

In conclusion, I have to say that fully persuaded, as I am, that the adoption of the several measures which I have thus indicated would redound to the advantage of the government, I beg most earnestly to recommend that they be adopted, and that Congress be asked to make such legislative provisions as may be requisite to that end. Though some of these measures would confer incidental benefits upon certain officers of the government, I feel assured that any such special advantages would be outweighed by those which would accrue to the government itself a hundredfold.

I have the honor to be, with high respect,

EDWARD JORDAN, *Solicitor.*

Hon. S. P. Chase,
    Secretary of the Treasury.

Statistical summary of business under charge of the Solicitor of the Treasury during the fiscal year ending June 30, 1862.

	SUITS BROUGHT DURING THE FISCAL YEAR ENDING THE THIRTIETH DAY OF JUNE, A. D. 1862.															
Judicial districts.	Treasury transcripts.		Fines, penalties, and forfeitures.		Miscellaneous.		Warehouse transportation bonds.		Total amount (reported) sued for.	Total amount (reported) judgm'ts for United States.	Total amount (reported) collected.	Decided for United States.	Decided against U. States.	Settled and dismissed.	Remitted.	Pending.	Total number of suits brought.
	No.	Amount sued for.	No.	Amount sued for.	No.	Amount sued for.	No.	Amount sued for.									
mpshire			27	$4,309 44	1				$4,309 44	$5,983 23	$6,983 21	3		1	4	15	28
			3		2											5	5
uetts	1	$13,996 60	57		1				13,996 60		33,996 49	17		9		33	59
cut			4		2						625 00	4		2			6
land			6		9						805 40	5		2		1	22
rk, northern district			8		13	$6,350 00	1	$287 00	6,637 00		107,281 67	7			15	15	375
rk, southern district	1	21,879 96	302	85,197 86	57		15	3,608 64	110,686 46		720 14	67	52	11	12	223	375
sey			14								107,367 57	8		1	3	4	14
ania, eastern district			108	35,292 53	3				35,292 53	4,624 29		40		5	4	62	111
ania, western district	1	11,905 34							11,905 34							1	1
c			2	578 10					576 10							2	2
d			90	4,100 00	1	3,000 00			7,100 00		7,659 61	28	1	20	4	36	91
of Columbia																	
eastern district																1	1
western district	1	6,044 36							6,044 36								
arolina																	
arolina																	
northern district																	
southern district			39	1,166,746 00					1,166,746 00		33,996 78	29			10	39	
a, northern district																	
a, middle district																	
a, eastern district																	
a, western district																	
ppi, northern district																	
ppi, southern district																	
eastern district																	
s, eastern district																	
western district																	
s, eastern district			3	600 00	1		3	149 20	749 20		149 20	3				6	9
se, western district																	
se, eastern district																	

	SUITS BROUGHT DURING THE FISCAL YEAR ENDING THE THIRTIETH DAY OF JUNE, A. D. 1862.															
Judicial districts.	Treasury transcripts.		Fines, penalties, and forfeitures.		Miscellaneous.		Warehouse transportation bonds.		Total amount (reported) sued for.	Total amount (reported) judgments for United States.	Total amount (reported) collected.	Decided for United States.	Decided against U. States.	Settled and dismissed.	Remitted.	Pending.	Total number of suits brought.
	No.	Amount sued for.	No.	Amount sued for.	No.	Amount sued for.	No.	Amount sued for.									
Tennessee, middle district	....	....	....	....	....	....	....	....	....	....	....	....	....	....	....	....	33
Tennessee, western district	....	....	....	....	....	....	....	....	....	....	....	....	....	....	....	....	32
Kentucky	2	$4,138 36	29	....	2	$5,000 00	....	....	$9,138 36	....	$9,581 19	94	....	....	....	9	16
Ohio, northern district	....	....	17	....	13	9,000 00	3	$6,161 40	6,161 40	....	2,947 35	17	....	7	....	8	52
Ohio, southern district	....	6,456 87	13	$500 00	3	9,000 00	....	....	6,956 87	....	2,146 93	10	....	....	....	6	17
Indiana	....	....	44	....	8	....	5	10,335 50	19,995 50	....	2,147 00	24	....	13	1	14	39
Illinois, northern district	....	....	....	....	12	2,560 00	....	....	....	....	....	5	....	....	....	12	11
Illinois, southern district	....	....	39	....	....	....	....	....	....	....	10,940 16	31	1	4	....	3	10
Michigan	4	2,096 39	1	6,000 00	6	7,000 00	....	....	15,096 39	....	5 00	1	....	1	2	5	2
Wisconsin	....	....	9	6,980 00	1	2,000 00	....	....	8,980 00	....	9,078 50	2	....	1	....	....	....
Iowa	....	....	....	....	....	....	3	95,170 00	95,170 00	$95,170 00	....	2	....	....	....	....	....
Minnesota	....	....	....	....	....	....	....	....	....	....	....	....	....	....	....	91	55
Kansas	....	....	1	....	54	....	....	....	....	....	....	19	....	15	3	10	23
California, northern district	....	....	93	13,100 00	....	....	....	....	13,100 00	....	4,540 50	5	1	4	....	....	11
California, southern district	....	....	....	....	....	....	....	....	....	....	....	....	....	....	....	6	....
Oregon	....	....	....	....	....	....	....	....	....	....	....	4	....	1	....	....	....
Washington Territory	....	....	2	300 00	2	....	....	....	300 00	....	....	....	....	....	....	....	....
Utah Territory	....	....	....	....	....	....	....	....	....	....	....	....	....	....	....	....	....
Nebraska Territory	....	....	....	....	....	....	....	....	....	....	....	....	....	....	....	....	....
Dakota Territory	....	....	....	....	....	....	....	....	....	....	....	....	....	....	....	....	....
Colorado Territory	....	....	....	....	....	....	....	....	....	....	....	....	....	....	....	....	....
Nevada Territory	....	....	....	....	....	....	....	....	....	....	....	....	....	....	....	....	....
New Mexico Territory	....	....	....	....	....	....	....	....	....	....	....	....	....	....	....	....	....
Total	10	66,517 8d	843	1,322,996 93	190	26,010 00	99	45,704 74	1,463,929 55	35,757 45	332,433 63	356	65	98	33	528	1,072

Statistical summary of business under charge of the Solicitor of the Treasury, &c.—Continued.

Judicial districts.	SUITS BROUGHT PRIOR TO THE PRESENT FISCAL YEAR.						Whole number of judgments rendered in favor of United States during the year.	Whole amount of judgments rendered in favor of United States during the fiscal year ending June 30, 1862.	Whole amount collected from all sources during the fiscal year ending June 30, 1862.
	Amount of judgments in all old suits this year.	Decided for the United States.	Decided against United States.	Settled and dismissed.	Total number of suits disposed of.	Amount collected in all old suits this year.			
...ampshire	....	......	....	4	4	....	8	$5,963 23	$6,963 21
...tt.	....	......	....	......	......	....	......	....	....
...husetts	....	1	....	......	1	$554 60	16	....	32,951 29
...ticut	....	......	....	......	......	....	4	....	....
...sland	....	1	....	......	......	....	5	....	025 00
...ork, northern district	....	1	......	......	......	399 77	8	....	1,205 17
...ork, southern district	....	14	48	58	120	53,561 55	81	....	160,843 22
...rsey	....	......	....	......	......	....	6	....	790 14
...vania, eastern district	....	1	2	1	4	9,439 07	41	4,894 22	109,926 54
...ivania, western district	....	......	....	......	......	....	......	....	....
...re	....	......	....	......	......	....	......	....	....
...nd	....	......	....	......	......	....	28	....	7,659 01
...of Columbia	....	......	....	2	2	659 00	......	....	659 00
...a, eastern district	....	......	....	......	......	....	......	....	....
...a, western district	....	......	....	......	......	....	......	....	....
...Carolina	....	......	....	......	......	....	......	....	....
...a	....	......	....	......	......	....	......	....	....
..., northern district	....	......	....	......	......	....	......	....	....
..., southern district	....	......	....	......	......	13,361 37	29	....	46,938 15
...na, northern district	....	......	....	......	......	....	......	....	....
...na, western district	....	......	....	......	......	....	......	....	....
...na, middle district	....	......	....	......	......	....	......	....	....
...ah, eastern district	....	......	....	......	......	....	......	....	....
...ah, western district	....	......	....	......	......	....	......	....	....
...ippi, northern district	....	......	....	......	......	....	......	....	....
...ippi, southern district	....	......	....	......	......	....	......	....	....
...eastern district	....	......	....	......	......	....	......	....	....
...western district	....	......	....	......	......	....	......	....	....
...as, eastern district	....	......	....	......	......	....	......	....	....
...as, western district	....	......	....	......	......	....	......	....	....
...ri, eastern district	....	......	....	......	......	....	3	....	149 20

Judicial districts.	Amount of judgments in all old suits this year.	Decided for the United States.	Decided against United States.	Settled and dismissed.	Total number of suits disposed of.	Amount collected in all old suits this year.	Whole number of judgments rendered in favor of United States during the year.	Whole amount of judgments rendered in favor of United States during the fiscal year ending June 30, 1862.	Whole amount collected from all sources during the fiscal year ending June 30, 1862.
Missouri, western district									
Tennessee, eastern district									
Tennessee, middle district									
Tennessee, western district									
Kentucky						$651 14	24		$9,581 12
Ohio, northern district	$4,500 00	1			1	5,271 27	18	$4,500 00	3,548 49
Ohio, southern district		3		5	8	557 50	13		7,417 49
Indiana		1			2	1,271 59	23		2,704 50
Illinois, northern district	11,090 95	3			3	1,271 59	8	11,090 95	1,271 59
Illinois, southern district							31		10,940 16
Michigan							1		5 00
Wisconsin						4,470 00	2		6,548 50
Iowa						7,161 09	2	25,170 00	7,161 09
Minnesota									
Kansas	14,648 93						19	14,648 93	
California, northern district	344 96	1			1	39,097 10	6	344 96	43,637 90
California, southern district									
Oregon									
Washington Territory							4		
Utah Territory									
Nebraska Territory				1	1				
Dakota Territory									
Colorado Territory									
Nevada Territory									
New Mexico Territory									
Total	30,584 84	26	50	72	148	129,005 25	364	66,342 29	481,438 87

K.

TREASURY DEPARTMENT,
Register's Office, November 20, 1862. '

SIR: There is probably no bureau connected with the government the operations of which are brought to your attention so seldom as that of the Register. It is for this reason, and because I believe some congressional action indispensable, if its constantly increasing duties are to be properly performed, that I desire to bring to your notice, somewhat more fully than is usually done, a statement of what has been performed during the last fiscal year, and to make some suggestions in relation to the future.

The Register's bureau is divided into three departments or divisions, which are commonly known as the divisions of "*Loans*," "*Receipts and Expenditures,*" and "*Commerce and Navigation.*" I shall refer to them in the order in which they are named.

LOANS.

In this division is transacted the business pertaining to the public debt. It is the transfer office for registered and coupon bonds. In it are received daily the certificates of stock for transfer, and new certificates are made out, recorded, and issued. All the evidences of assignable indebtedness against the United States, except the United States notes, are recorded in this division, and from it all are issued, except these and the three years bonds, bearing $7\frac{3}{10}$ interest. The proper authority for making the issue to each party is received from the office of the Secretary of the Treasury, the certificates and bonds are prepared, returned to the office of the Secretary to be entered and sealed, are then returned and transmitted to the parties entitled to receive them. In all cases of transfer, the authority to do it is examined and passed upon, and as this is often done by attorneys and corporations, questions are almost daily presented requiring an examination and decision upon legal principles. Schedules of the semi-annual interest upon all the registered bonds, with estimates of the interest falling due upon coupon bonds, are prepared for the Treasurer and the different assistant treasurers. All the interest coupons, when paid, are returned here, and having been assorted and counted, are placed in their regular order in books for permanent preservation. The redeemed and cancelled treasury notes are assorted, arranged, and filed away.

During the last fiscal year the original issues of United States stock have been as follows:

Loan of Feb'y 8, 1861.	$75,000, embraced in bonds or certificates, No..	75
Loan of July 17, 1861.50,000,000,....do........do........do........		41,300
Oregon war debt.....	998,600,....do........do........do........	3,159
Loan of 1862, or $\frac{7}{10}$,..	9,908,850,....do........do........do........	13,164
	60,982,450	57,698

An issue of nearly seventy millions of dollars, requiring the filling up, recording and signing of fifty-seven thousand six hundred and ninety-eight bonds or certificates.

The transfers have been as follows:

Loan of 1842.,.......	117 transfers, certificates	317, amounting to	$680,100
Loan of 1847........	201...do...,....do....	563....do.....	1,074,500
Loan of 1848........	75,..do.......do....	235....do.....	707,900
Loan of 1858........	23...do.......do.,,,	34....do.....	245,000

Loan of 1860........	44 transfers, certificates 268 amounting to	$273,000
Loan of Feb'y 8, 1861	758...do.......do....2,742....do......	6,404,000
Loan of July 17, 1861	488...do.......do....1,933....do......	7,540,000
Loan of ⁵⁄₂₀s.........	1...do.......do.... 1....do......	1,000

1,707 transfers, certificates 6,093, amounting to 16,925,500

These transfers, amounting to sixteen millions nine hundred and twenty-five thousand five hundred dollars, required six thousand and ninety-three certificates.

These transfers have required journal and ledger entries to the number of six thousand eight hundred and twenty-eight, and the opening of over six hundred new accounts.

Seventy-nine thousand eight hundred and eighty-nine paid coupons have been counted, trimmed, and numerically arranged, twenty-thousand of which have been pasted in books prepared for that purpose.

The business of this division has required the writing and copying of three thousand two hundred and fifty-seven letters.

Ninety thousand two years' treasury notes have been signed by the Register and entered upon the books, and sixteen thousand two hundred and fifty-six certificates of deposit for treasury notes or bonds have been examined, entered, and checked.

Schedules of dividends have been forwarded semi-annually to the Treasurer and assistant treasurers at Washington, Baltimore, Philadelphia, New York and Boston, covering one hundred and eighty-eight large pages of account paper, containing five thousand six hundred and forty names.

All the powers of attorney (and the number is very large, requiring a separate ledger) for the collection of interest have been examined, decided upon, and recorded, and a copy made for the First Auditor; and the proper assistant treasurers have been furnished with a copy of each entry as it is made upon the books.

All the unclaimed dividends have been recorded in a book, a copy of which has been furnished to the Treasurer.

In addition to what I have stated, there has been a large amount of labor performed which cannot be put into tabular form, such as making statements, answering calls from the Secretary, Congress, and individuals, preparing and numbering books for the entry of notes, coupons, &c.

This labor alone would probably very nearly equal the whole labor of this division in former years.

The fact that this large amount of business has been promptly performed, without the slightest error or complaint from any quarter which has reached me, is due to the fidelity and industry of the clerks in charge. John Oliphant, the head of the division, and John R. Nourse, the principal clerk in it, have been unremitting in their attention to it. Stock received for transfer by the morning mail is invariably transferred and transmitted to the parties by return mail, and the remaining part of the business is transacted with great promptness. Very numerous evidences are constantly received from parties and corporations interested that this promptness is not unappreciated.

Great as has been the increase in the business of this division during the last fiscal year, the ratio of increase since the close of the year has been greater still. It has now reached a magnitude not at all pleasant to contemplate. I have no hesitation in saying that this division alone should be made a separate bureau, and that its proper supervision would furnish sufficient employment for a competent officer. If the ratio of increase is to continue, and the evidence is conclusive that it must for some time to come, the transaction of its business with the promptness which has hitherto characterized it is a simple impossibility. It would be almost superfluous to remark that the issue and transfer of evidences of the public debt must be promptly made, if the interests either of the government or those dealing with it are to be consulted and protected.

RECEIPTS AND EXPENDITURES.

This division is the counting-house of the treasury. In it are kept the accounts with all agents, disbursing or receiving officers, as well as separate accounts with all the appropriations; warrants for receipts into, and disbursements from, the treasury are signed and recorded; all accounts connected with the treasury are entered after having passed the Comptroller, and, with their vouchers, are deposited in the files room. Most of the accounts showing a balance against the United States are copied, and the copies, properly certified, are transmitted to the office of the Secretary of the Treasury, where warrants are made for their payment. Quarterly settlements are made by the greater number of the disbursing officers; others are made monthly, and some of the assistant treasurers have accounts settled daily. As a basis for most of these settlements, this division furnishes a certificate to the proper Auditor showing the balance upon the last settlement and the advances since in items. To this division the estimates of appropriations are sent by all the departments, and here they are digested, condensed, and put in proper form to be submitted by the Secretary of the Treasury to Congress. A volume is annually published, showing in detail the receipts and expenditures of the government. This volume, which costs much time and labor, it appears to me possesses sufficient importance to deserve a more general circulation throughout the country. The law now allows the publication of only five hundred copies, and these are so distributed that few outside of the departments are aware of its existence. It shows the receipts from all sources, except those connected with the Post Office Department, the districts in which they are collected, with the names of the officers collecting them. It exhibits also the aggregates of expenditures under each head of appropriation, and the names of the officers or persons making the disbursements. The last report comprises 560 closely printed pages, and in order to prepare it a statement is made in detail of the covering and pay warrants, with the appropriations on account of which they are drawn. This statement requires more labor and time in its preparation than the contents of the report itself, which comprises the aggregates of the details contained in the statement. My reasons for suggesting the propriety of publishing a larger number of copies are briefly these: Congress and the country would thus be advised of the nature and extent of the receipts and expenditures from all sources, and the persons through and by whom they are made, and the necessity would be obviated for a large proportion of the calls for statements and information upon this department. These calls are numerous upon this and all the other divisions of this bureau. The labor of weeks is required to answer some of them, which occasions many serious interruptions to the business of the office. As many of them relate to the receipts and expenditures of the government, it is believed that a general circulation of the annual reports showing them would materially reduce the number which would be made in future.

There have been received during the year ending June 30, 1862, and entered under their appropriate heads—

Accounts from the various accounting offices, which are twice registered and filed.. 11,267
There were entered in the several journals and posted to the ledger.. 3,802
Such as showed balances against the government were copied, certified by the Register, and transmitted to the Secretary of the Treasury for pay warrants. The number of these was 9,000

The number of treasury expenditure warrants issued was.. 10, 076
    (All these were copied, and entered in the different jour-
    nals, which is equivalent to a second copy.)
Treasury warrants for receipts, customs, &c.............. 2, 314
Expenditure warrants issued from Interior, War, and Navy
    Departments...................................... 11, 193
Repayment warrants issued (Interior, War, and Navy) 1, 022
                                                    —————
                                                    24, 605

    Making an aggregate of............................... '48, 674

  Many of these warrants contain more than one appropriation, and each item
of appropriation requires a distinct entry in several books, and as much entering
as if there was but one in the warrant, so that, in the entry of 24,605 warrants
issued during the year, more than one hundred thousand separate entries were
required.

The number of certificates from the books, showing the balances at
    the last settlement and the advances since, furnished to the account-
    ing offices was...'. 5, 525
The number of accounts open on the several ledgers on the 30th of
    June, 1862, was 4, 145
And the number of pages occupied by the entry of 3,802 accounts,
    10,076 treasury expenditure warrants, and 2,314 treasury receipt
    warrants, was 1, 856
The drafts issued upon pay warrants are all recorded in this division.
    The number was.. 21, 268
The certificates of indebtedness issued under the acts of 1817 and March,
    1862, are recorded and in part filled up. The number up to June 30,
    1862, was 26, 256

  Much preparatory work for the balancing of the several ledgers has been done
during the past year, and there is much time and labor expended in the performance
of various services which, from their nature, cannot be specifically enumerated.
These alone would probably occupy the time of two or more clerks during the
whole year.

  This division has for many years been under the general charge and direction
of B. F. Rittenhouse. I can only repeat in regard to him the expressions
which have been so many times reported in his favor by my predecessors. He
has met the demands upon his time and industry, created by the extraordinary
increase of the business of his division, faithfully and promptly. I am not
aware of any division in the Treasury Department the duties of which are more
complicated or important, or which have been more largely increased by the
war. I feel that I am only performing an act of justice in urging the propriety of making him some additional compensation. He is almost daily called
upon to perform duties which do not properly belong to his division, but
which his thorough knowledge of the receipts and expenditures of the government for many years enables him to discharge. Nothing but unremitting attention during the whole year, joined to an unusual capacity for business, could
have enabled him to accomplish so much.

  It will be seen at once that the business of this division must increase in exact
proportion with the receipts and expenditures of the government. It has been accomplished during the past year by an increased activity and industry on the part
of the clerks in this division, instead of a corresponding increase in their number.

COMMERCE AND NAVIGATION.

From this division the annual report of commerce and navigation is issued, and its duties are, the receiving, from the various collection districts and other sources, returns and statements showing the value and descriptions of the various articles imported and exported, whether in American or foreign vessels; the rate and amount of duties; the countries from and the districts into which the imports, and the districts from and the countries to which the exports are made; the correction of these returns, and their entry into suitable books, and their compilation for the annual report; the compilation of statements for Congress and others; the making of estimates and statements for new tariffs; the preparation of forms for returns of imports and exports, duties and tonnage, for the collection districts; the statements and tables for the financial report of the Secretary of the Treasury; the superintendence of the printing and proof-reading of the annual report and other statements issued, with the official correspondence relating to these several subjects.

There are, at present, seventy-two collection districts, which make quarterly returns of the business done in each district. These returns consist of—

Imports in American vessels ....
Imports in foreign vessels .... } Four abstracts of each, one
Exports of foreign merchandise in American } under each tariff, to be rendered
vessels .... } each quarter.
Exports of foreign merchandise in foreign
vessels ....

Exports of domestic produce in American }
vessels .... } One abstract each, each quarter.
Exports of domestic produce in foreign vessels }

Imports under the reciprocity treaty with Great }
Britain in American vessels .... } One abstract each, each quarter.
Ditto in foreign vessels .... }

Indirect trade in American vessels .... }
Indirect trade in foreign vessels .... } One abstract each, each quarter.

Tonnage of American vessels entered ...... }
Tonnage of American vessels cleared ...... } One abstract each, each quarter.

Tonnage of foreign vessels entered .... }
Tonnage of foreign vessels cleared .... } One abstract each, each quarter.

These abstracts have each to be examined, and if found to be incorrect, which, for the past year, has been rather the rule than the exception, the collector of the district from which the incorrect return was received is written to, and the correction made. If correct, or when made so, the return is entered in the books of the division by countries, by districts, and in the aggregates, or footings, of the abstracts. To have these returns entered requires, for—

Imports:
In American vessels.............. 10 books, of 5 forms each, of 58 pages.
In foreign vessels 7   do.   5   do.   58 "
    Exports of foreign merchandise:
In American vessels................ 9   do.   5   do.   58 "
In foreign vessels 10   do.   5   do.   58 "
    Exports of domestic produce:
In American vessels............... 4   do.   20   do.   12 "
In foreign vessels 2   do.   22   do.   12 ".

making a great increase by reason of the changes in the tariff from ad valorem to specific rates of duty.

In consequence of the changes in the tariff, it is necessary to keep separate and distinct books of the imports and exports of foreign merchandise, under the several acts of March 3, 1857, March 2, August 5, and December 24, 1861—four different sets of books. This great increase of the work has made it impossible to enter the returns from the several collectors and balance the books of the division as early as heretofore.

By the passage of the act of March 2, 1861, the work upon the report for the year ending June 30, 1861, was increased from 684 pages for the report of 1860, to 1,093 pages for that of 1861—a difference of 409 pages. By the passage of the acts of August 5 and December 24, 1861, the work has been materially increased over that of last year, and will make about 1,500 pages of printed matter. These changes in the tariff have rendered new "forms" of returns of imports and exports of foreign merchandise necessary, and an increase in the number and character of the books of the division. Last year one of the two sets of books covered a period of only *three months;* this year two sets, each covering the entire year—the third set from the 5th of August, and the fourth set from the 24th of December, 1861. As the fiscal year begins on the first day of July, the third set covers nearly the whole year.

During the past year ending June 30, 1862, there have been *two* changes made in the "form" of return of imports and exports, in addition to the forms of last year. Under the act of March 3, 1857, the "form" contained 34 pages; under the act of March 2, 1861, 56 pages; under the act of August 5, 58 pages. The act of July 14, 1862, the "form" under which was required to be made up during the work on the report for 1862, and now in the hands of the public printer, will have about 80 pages.

There is a separate office connected with the division of commerce and navigation, in which the tonnage accounts are kept, which has, for many years, been conducted by Mr. Lowndes. It receives from the various collection districts ninety-five accounts each quarter, in which are embraced abstracts of permanent and temporary registers and enrolments. These accounts are examined and compared with the vouchers presented with them, and the proper entries are made in the several books containing the tonnage accounts. These accounts require much correction, and involve an extensive correspondence with the collectors.

During the year there have been prepared and distributed—

Signed and sealed registers	3,515
Enrolments	4,300
Licenses	5,550

Duplicate registers issued in the several districts in the year 1860, in number 2,956, and duplicate enrolments issued in 1859, in number 7,518, duplicate enrolments issued in 1860, in number 8,499, have been recorded in detail; many calls from Congress, the State and other departments, have been promptly answered, and more than sixty thousand returned registers have been placed in suitable books for preservation.

The work in the division of commerce and navigation has been done under the general supervision of D. W. Haines. It is highly probable that, in order to bring out the annual report at the time provided by law, in future an addition will be required to its clerical force. I have refrained from asking this increase for the reason that as many changes in the tariffs as have been made during the past year will not probably again occur, and the labor may be expected to assume a more definite and uniform character, and I have thought it better that a temporary delay should be suffered now than to ask for a permanent increase in the number of clerks, which might turn out to be unnecessary.

A very large increase of the labor of the Register's office has been occasioned by the destruction of the demand notes issued during the year 1861. These after having been counted in the Treasurer's office are cut in two, and the upper halves sent to the Register's office, where they are counted and compared with the Treasurer's statement, and if found correct are destroyed under the direction of a committee appointed by you for that purpose. The amount thus destroyed up to the date of this report exceeds *forty millions of dollars.* This business has been transacted under the general direction of John A. Graham, the chief clerk in this office. This with his other complicated duties have been performed with his customary promptness and fidelity.

I ought specially to call your attention to the files room of the Register's office, in which are received and properly disposed of the accounts coming from various sources, through the offices of the First Comptroller and Commissioner of Customs. Some idea of the magnitude and number of these accounts may be given by the statement that they require for their accommodation a room 120 feet in length by over 20 feet in width, which is closely filled with iron cases, all which are being rapidly filled up. Notwithstanding their great number and complication, any account can be produced with the delay of a few minutes, or in default of it, the evidence showing where or in whose custody it is. Daily reference is had to these accounts by the various bureaus of the government, and in the course of the year thousands are temporarily withdrawn by departments having authority, receipted for and returned. In this room the transcripts of accounts for suit and other purposes are prepared. It would afford me pleasure to say of all the other departments of my office what I can of this, that I do not see wherein it is susceptible of improvement. The credit of this is due to Messrs. Smith and Wannal, the clerks in charge, who seem to have endeavored so to construct and arrange their department that if put into the hands of a stranger, the system is so simple and effective, that a few hours only would suffice to enable him to perform the duties which these clerks discharge.

In an emergency like the present the government may rightfully require the highest degree of diligence and industry from every person in its service. During the past year this requirement in the Register's office has been fully answered, and the utmost exertion on the part of the Register and his clerical force has barely accomplished the performance of the necessary business of the office. If this business was not to be increased, I should hesitate long before I undertook to go through with it for another year. But the evidence is conclusive that it must be very largely increased, and I make this report with the clear conviction that it will be physically impossible for any one man to perform during the current year the duties required of the Register under existing laws and regulations. These have existed without any substantial alteration, so far as this bureau is concerned, for more than thirty years. It must be manifest that the force and capacity of an office like this which would be ample when the receipts and expenditures of the government amounted to fifty or sixty millions of dollars per year, would be very insufficient under an expenditure of that sum monthly. With the present unremitting pressure of current business the Register has not a moment to give to the examination of the details of labor in the several divisions, or to any attempts to improve their efficiency. It is clear that many such improvements might and should be made. There is no private institution of similar magnitude in which business is transacted now in the same way that it was thirty years ago. I have not during the last year been able to give this subject the slightest attention. The pressure of current business is constant and unremitting. In order to carry on the daily operations of the office it is not unfrequently necessary for the Register to sign his name at the rate of *ten or twelve times a minute during the entire day.* Under such circumstances no paper can be examined, and his whole reliance must be on the correctness and fidelity of his clerks, and the fact that the business of the past year has been done without error or mistake is the highest praise that could be awarded them. The Register cannot absent himself for an hour without causing

Ex. Doc. 1——10

serious inconvenience or delay to some branch of the public business. Daily and hourly, in sickness or health, this demand upon his attention and physical energies is incessant and continuous. Relaxation, the attention which such times as these require of every man to the comfort and interests of his fellow-citizens, private correspondence and business, all must give way before it. I have endured it as long as I can. The effect already produced upon myself admonishes that it is time to ask for some change.

The necessary relief, I think, may be given by the passage of an act of Congress giving to the Secretary of the Treasury authority to designate clerks in the office, or others, to sign warrants, certificates, bonds, &c., for the Register. The clerk recording drafts upon the Treasurer, or assistant treasurers, for example, might sign the certificate of record. The clerk recording the warrants might do the same, and thus the work be parcelled among three or four, which is now performed by the Register. I do not believe the slightest danger could result from this. The Register now is obliged to sign these certificates, without the slightest examination, for want of time, and to rely entirely upon the clerks. It would not be advisable that bonds or certificates of registered stock should be signed by any person other than the Register, so long as it can be avoided, because bankers, brokers, and other parties dealing in government securities are averse to the slightest change in their form or nature. But the time will soon come when the change in this respect must be made.

If such authority was conferred and exercised only in proper cases, I feel certain that the efficiency of this bureau would be greatly increased, its publications rendered infinitely more valuable to the country, the expenditures in the office greatly diminished, and the Register would be able to give the necessary supervision to the work of all his clerks, to introduce proper changes and improvements, and even to give that attention to public and social relations which may reasonably be demanded of every citizen, a pleasure which during the past year has been practically denied him. If it is not, only one result can be reasonably anticipated. The business of the office cannot be promptly done and must fall in arrear, and great inconvenience must ensue to the government and all parties doing business with it through the office of the Register.

While the increase of the business in nearly all the departments of the public service is a subject of notoriety, the increase in this bureau is far above the average proportion. This is because the business of many of them finally comes to the Register's office. If, for example, the number of accounts settled in the offices of the First and Fifth Auditor is increased in each twenty-five per cent. during the year, the increase in this office will be fifty per cent., for both series of accounts must be entered on the books of the Register. The same relation exists between this and many other departments of the government. It is no pleasure for me to urge the wants and claims of the office upon you, while so many urgent subjects are pressing upon your attention. I have deferred it as long as a proper regard to the interests of your department would permit me to do so.

Very respectfully, your obedient servant,

L. E. CHITTENDEN,
Register

Hon. S. P. CHASE,
   Secretary of the Treasury.

L.

TREASURY DEPARTMENT,
Office of Commissioner of Customs, October 20, 1862.

SIR: In compliance with your requisition of the 2d instant, I have the honor to submit a report of the operations of this office during the fiscal year ending June 30, 1862.

The number of accounts of collectors of the customs, and of surveyors designated as collectors, received and finally settled in this office during the year, amounts to one thousand eight hundred and twenty-eight.

Accounts relating to the superintendence and construction of light-houses, beacons, buoys, marine hospitals, and custom-houses, and for other miscellaneous purposes, amount to one thousand one hundred and seventy-one.

The number of bonds taken from collectors, naval officers, &c., and the notices issued thereon, amount to one hundred and fifty-four.

In disposing of this amount of business, with other matters referred by the department, four thousand four hundred and fifty-seven letters have been sent from, and two thousand and ninety-seven received at this office.

In making this, my annual report, I would respectfully remark that, in looking over the records of my office and the official correspondence of my predecessors, I cannot but observe that a much greater variety of business was formerly referred to or came, *as a matter of course,* to this bureau, than has of late years been referred to it. I have only to say that I shun neither labor nor responsibility, and am ready at all times to take upon myself any and all labor formerly performed by my predecessors.

I have the honor to be, with great respect, your obedient servant,

N. SARGENT,
Commissioner of Customs.

Hon. S. P. CHASE,
Secretary of the Treasury.

M.

LIGHT-HOUSE BOARD.

TREASURY DEPARTMENT,
Office Light-House Board, Washington City, November 1, 1862.

SIR: I have the honor respectfully to submit for your information, and for that of Congress, the report of the operations and condition of the light-house establishment for the fiscal year ending June 30, 1862.

In the first light-house district, embracing the coasts from the northeastern boundary of Maine to Hampton harbor, New Hampshire, the board has, through the exigencies of the military and naval branches of the public service, been deprived of both a naval officer as inspector and an officer of the army as engineer. It has therefore been compelled to rely upon such civil assistance as it could command; yet it is believed the service has been faithfully performed, and the condition of the various aids to navigation throughout the district is highly satisfactory.

Thorough inspections of the district have been made, and important repairs and renovations have been effected at Isle of Shoals, Whale's Back, Portsmouth, Boon Island, Cape Elizabeth, Dice's Head, Franklin Island, Hendrick's Head, Martinicus Rock, and Moose Peak light-houses, and those stations are now in good order. The buoy and beacon service has received due attention, and when, by casualties, these aids have been removed from their stations, they have been recovered and restationed as promptly as possible.

The second light-house district, embracing the coasts from Hampton harbor, New Hampshire, to Gooseberry Point, Massachusetts, has but recently had assigned to it an officer of the navy as inspector, previous to which assignment, and since the date of the last annual report, the duties have been discharged, under the immediate direction of the board, by civilians previously connected with the light-house establishment as light-house clerk and engineer's clerk.

Under this arrangement the various aids to navigation in the second district have been carefully looked after, and, it is believed, are now in a state of creditable efficiency.

Several of the light-vessels in this district have, during the past year, been driven, by stress of weather, from their stations. They have, however, been replaced as speedily as the delay necessary to make requisite repairs would permit. These accidents to light vessels and their replacement on their stations involve, in nearly every instance, an enormous expense, and this board makes it a part of its duty to cause careful investigations to elicit the facts of the accident, and in every instance where it is reasonable to believe that it is attributable to negligence or incompetence on the part of the keeper, the details of the case are promptly reported to the department, with a recommendation that the keeper be removed. Such precautions are taken to have the light-vessels securely moored that it is usually found that accidents of this character are mainly due to carelessness or inattention—sometimes to culpable timidity—on the part of keepers.

The buoyage and beaconage of this district have been well cared for. Extensive and thorough repairs, &c., have been made to the light stations at Ipswich, Straitsmouth, Bass harbor, Tarpaulin cove, Gay Head, Clarke's Point, Palmer's island, Ned's Point, Bird island, Long Point, Boston Narrows, Ten Pound island, Marblehead, Dumpling island, Newburyport, Annisquam, Egg Rock, Mayo's Beach, Long Island Head, and Hyannis. New beacons and daymarks, in place of others carried away by storm, have been erected at Monument Bar, Hardy's Rock, and Bowditch Ledge.

The third light-house district embraces the coasts from Gooseberry Point, Massachusetts, to Squam inlet, New Jersey, including Lake Champlain and Hudson river, and although for most of the time deprived, by the exigencies of the military department, of the services of a naval and army officer as inspector and engineer, yet the duties of the district have been carefully performed, and the various aids to navigation are in a state of high efficiency.

The two new towers at Navesink, which were under construction at the date of the last report, have been completed, and the lights exhibited on the 1st of May, 1862. This station now shows two fixed lights of the first order, and with a view to obviate an alleged tendency to confuse mariners by the risk of confounding the two fixed lights at this station with the two fixed lights on Sandy Hook light-vessel, one of the latter lanterns has been lowered some nine feet. This plan, it is hoped, will entirely remove the cause of complaint.

Extensive repairs to towers and keepers' dwellings have been made in this district, viz: at Juniper island, Burlington, Split Rock, Cumberland Head, Point au Roche, Windmill Point, Esopus Meadows, Rondout, Saugerties, Coxsakie, Stuyvesant, Stony Point, Sandy Hook, Robbins' Reef, Bergen Point, Passaic, Faulkner's island, Execution Rocks, and Elbow Beacon.

The light-vessel at Sandy Hook was found to require extensive repairs. These have been made, and the vessel replaced in complete condition on her station.

The buoyage of the district has received due attention, and has been maintained in a condition of great usefulness.

There are numerous other works of repair required in this district, which will be attended to during the next season as rapidly and completely as time and other circumstances will permit.

In the fourth district, embracing the coasts from Squam inlet, New Jersey, to Metomkin inlet, Virginia, including Delaware bay and tributaries, the light-house service has been maintained in an efficient condition, with but slight expense for repairs and renovations, the most important work being the rebuilding, on a proper site, of the light-house at Mahon's river, which change had been rendered necessary by reason of defective original location, and subsequent encroachment of the water, imperilling the structure. These dangers have been entirely removed by the new position.

At Cape Henlopen light-house it has been found necessary to take measures for building a new dwelling for the keeper, the old one at that place being threatened with speedy destruction by the steady progress in that direction of a remarkable sand hill, which has been moving inflexibly in a certain course at a constant rate of speed for many years, presenting in its existence and movement a most singular natural phenomenon. The new dwelling is in course of preparation.

The old light tower at Cape May, which, upon the completion of the new light-house, had been left standing, having been found to be productive of danger, by misleading mariners by day, has been thrown down, and steps taken to dispose of the old materials.

The light-vessels, buoys, and beacons in the district are in a state of efficiency.

In the fifth light-house district, embracing the coasts from Metomkin inlet, Virginia, to New River inlet, North Carolina, including Chesapeake bay and tributaries, Albermarle and Pamlico sounds, the service has been to some extent interrupted, the authority of the United States not yet having been re-established throughout the entire district.

Since the date of the last report strenuous efforts have been made to restore discontinued lights, and in view of the numerous grave difficulties to be encountered the board has reason to congratulate itself upon the success which has attended its exertions.

Immediately upon the restoration of the eastern shore of Virginia to governmental control by the military operations in that quarter, the lights at Cape Charles, Cherrystone, and Hog island were re-established, and have rendered assistance of no small importance to the immensely increased navigation of Chesapeake bay and tributaries. The lights, main and beacon, at Cape Hatteras have been restored and re-established. The light at Naval Hospital, near Norfolk, has been relighted. A temporary light has been exhibited from the ruins of the light-house at Craney island, and the work of permanently restoring that structure is in progress.

By authority of the department a vessel has been purchased and stationed off Smith's Point, in Chesapeake bay, to replace the light-vessel belonging to that station, which was removed and destroyed by the insurgents. Through the courtesy of the general commanding this department, a competent military guard for the protection of this vessel has been detailed for duty and is yet continued.

The light-vessel stations in the bounds of North Carolina have been marked by suitable vessels showing temporary lights, viz: Brant Island shoal, Royal shoal, Harbor island, Long shoal, and Roanoke river, and steps are now in progress for the early re-establishment of the light-house at Wade's Point, Croatan, Roanoke marshes, Pamlico Point, northwest point of Royal shoal, and Ocracoke.

The light-vessel which formerly marked Brant Island shoal, and which was recaptured on the taking, by the United States forces, of Forts Hatteras and Clark, at Hatteras inlet, was subsequently sunk by accident at that inlet. She has, however, been raised, and is now undergoing repairs to fit her for service as a light-vessel.

The light-house at the mouth of the Neuse river, which was under construction at the time of the breaking out of the rebellion, was necessarily abandoned. The work has been recommenced, and is rapidly approaching completion.

By act of Congress approved June 20, 1860, an appropriation of $5,000 was made for the erection of a beacon light at a suitable point at or near Cape Hatteras inlet. The requisite iron and wood work for this structure has been prepared at Wilmington, Delaware; a working party was sent to erect it; the materials were all safely landed at the site selected, and on the same night a storm of almost unparalleled severity swept them away, so that scarcely a vestige remained. Such of the materials as could be recovered (being such things as would be useful to the army) were sold to the quartermaster's department at Hatteras inlet, and the amount, together with the balance remaining of the appropriation, it is believed, will be sufficient to replace, in a measure, the lost structure.

Various and important repairs to light-vessels in the upper part of Chesapeake bay have been made, and are still in progress.

The buoyage and light-vessel service of the district, so far as it is practicable to attend to it, is in a condition of great efficiency. The light-vessel originally placed to mark the tail of the Horse Shoe, between Capes Charles and Henry, entrance to Chesapeake bay, was lost from her station during the storm in January last, and it was found necessary to place upon that station a vessel which the board had been refitting at Baltimore for another station. Measures have been taken to recover, with a view to future use, certain light-vessels which had been forcibly removed from their stations in this district, and sunk as obstructions to the channel in Elizabeth river, &c.

The lights on James river, at White shoal, Point of Shoals, and Deep Water shoal, were re-exhibited during the past summer; but, upon the withdrawal of the army from the peninsula, their services were no longer necessary, and the apparatus was taken down and stored at Fortress Monroe.

In the sixth light-house district, embracing the coasts from New River inlet, North Carolina, to Cape Cañaveral light-house, inclusive, Florida, but little has been done to replace lost or destroyed aids to navigation, in consequence of the larger portion of the district not yet having been brought under the control of the United States government. The care of this board will be to push forward such work of restoration parallel with the recovery of the territory.

The light-vessel stationed by the board off Port Royal entrance in place of the one destroyed by the insurgents, has been kept in position during the past year, and has proved of very material assistance to the numerous vessels bound into Port Royal and along that portion of the coast.

The seventh light-house district embraces the coast of Florida from St. Augustine to Egmont key. The lights in this district, with the exception of those at Jupiter inlet and Cape Florida, have been kept in useful operation during the past year, and the buoys have been carefully attended to.

Steps have been taken to have the light at Cape Florida relighted at the earliest practicable day.

The eighth light-house district, embracing the coast from St. Mark's, Florida, to the western extremity of Lake Pontchartrain, has not received so much attention from the board in the way of re-establishing lights and other aids to navigation (all of them having been removed or discontinued by the rebels) as had been desired, for the reason that the authority of the United States over that locality had not until recently been sufficiently established to warrant such action.

Steps have been taken to repair damage done to the lights at Ship island,

Cat island, St. Joseph's, Pleasanton head, Proctorsville, Rigolets, Bon Tonca, Port Pontchartrain, Bayou St. John, New Canal, Tchefuncti river, and Pass Manchac, and it is hoped and expected that by the 1st of January, 1863, all of these lights will be re-exhibited. The other lights and the buoys in this district will be restored as rapidly as circumstances shall warrant.

The ninth district, embracing the coast from the mouth of the Mississippi river to Rio Grande, inclusive, lying nearly entirely beyond the present control of the United States, has had but little done in the way of restoring aids to navigation. Chandeleur Island light has been kept in operation during the year.

The important light at South Pass has been repaired and relighted, and the no less important lights at Southwest Pass, Pass à l'Outre, and head of the passes, (mouths of the Mississippi river,) are in course of repair, preparatory to their immediate re-establishment.

In the tenth district, embracing all lights on the lakes Erie and Ontario, and rivers St. Lawrence and Niagara, the general routine duties have been performed with commendable zeal and fidelity, and the various aids to navigation are in a state of efficiency. Important repairs and renovations have been made, or are now making, at nearly all the light stations in the district requiring them, and the buoys and other day-marks have been the object of assiduous attention.

In the eleventh light-house district, embracing lakes St. Clair, Huron, Michigan, and Green Bay and tributaries. several important works of construction and repair have been in progress during the past year.

Under instructions from the honorable Secretary of the Treasury, the necessary steps have been taken for the immediate erection of the light-house at Green Bay, Wisconsin, authorized by Congress, March 3, 1859.

The light-house at Raspberry island, Lake Superior, for which an appropriation of $6,000 was made March 3, 1859, has been pushed nearly to completion, and will be exhibited on the opening of navigation next spring.

The work of constructing light-house piers at Milwaukie and Racine has been delayed by reason of the failure on the part of the contractor for timber to make deliveries in such quantities as would warrant the commencement of the framing at either locality. The engineer in charge has, however, been directed to transfer the timber delivered at Milwaukie to the Racine structure, which will insure an energetic prosecution of the work upon that pier, preparatory to the erection of the beacon light.

The necessary surveys and examinations in advance of the commencement of works on other light-houses in this district, for which appropriations have been made by Congress, have been in progress.

The buoyage of the district has been well attended to, and has been of material assistance to the navigating interests of the locality.

In the twelfth light-house district, embracing the entire Pacific coast of the United States, the various aids to navigation have received careful attention, and have been maintained in an efficient condition.

The want of an appropriation for the expenses of the steamer provided for that district, for attending buoys, transportation of supplies, &c., has obliged this board to lay this vessel up, and her services being urgently desired by the revenue marine on that coast, by authority of the honorable Secretary of the Treasury she has been temporarily loaned to that bureau. The withdrawal of this vessel from light-house duty has occasioned serious embarrassment to this board on account of the great difficulty experienced in having the buoyage of the district properly attended to; but Congress at its last session having made an adequate appropriation for her support, it is expected that this branch of the service will be more thoroughly and completely controlled.

The difficulty attending the collection of reliable and detailed information concerning the status of the light-house establishment on the coasts of seceded

States over which the control of the United States has not been yet thoroughly re-established renders it impossible to submit an exact statement of damages done and repairs required, but the following list, as derived from all sources, official and unofficial, that appeared to be worthy of attention, will be found to be approximately correct:

Cape Henry, Virginia, tower standing, lantern destroyed.

Craney island, iron pile structure, destroyed, except foundation piles.

Naval Hospital, lens removed, light re-exhibited.

White shoals, Point of Shoals, Deep Water shoals, James river, lenses, &c., removed.

Body island, tower standing, lens, &c., removed.

Ocracoke, tower standing, lens, &c., removed.

Cape Lookout, tower damaged, lens, &c., removed.

Bogue Bank and beacon, blown up.

Cape Romain, lens and lantern destroyed.

Cape Hatteras, lens and lantern destroyed, light re-exhibited.

Bull's bay, lens and lantern destroyed.

Charleston, lens and lantern destroyed.   ⋅ ⁄

Hunting island, tower blown up.

Tybee, interior of tower and lantern destroyed by fire, lens, &c., removed.

St. Simon, tower and lantern destroyed.

Jupiter inlet, tower and lantern destroyed.

Cape Florida, tower and lantern destroyed.

All of the light vessels from Cape Henry southward, including the two in the Potomac river and those in Chesapeake bay, (except Hooper's straits and Jane's island,) have been removed and sunk or destroyed by the insurgents.

The buoys on the southern coast have, as far as learned, been nearly all removed from or sunk at their stations. Under the authority of the department, the necessary illuminating apparatus to replace that removed or destroyed as above has, with the approbation of the Secretary of the Treasury, been ordered from France, and upon receipt will be kept on hand for re-establishing the lights as possession of the coast is regained.

In view of the pressing need of re-establishing the light vessel stations discontinued by the insurgents, this board asked and obtained permission from the department to construct under contract, after due public advertisement, two first class light-vessels designed for Fryingpan shoals, coast of North Carolina, and Rattlesnake shoal, South Carolina, and three second class light-vessels intended for service at positions of less exposure, which are all under contract and in progress of construction.

The necessary illuminating apparatus and lanterns for these vessels have been ordered, and it is hoped and expected that the spring of 1863 will see them completed and on their proper stations.

The board takes this occasion to acknowledge valuable assistance rendered by officers of the Coast Survey, under instructions from the superintendent, in replacing certain buoys on the coasts contiguous to the operations of their own regular service, viz: entrance to Metompkin inlet, New Jersey; Oregon inlet, North Carolina; entrance to Neuse river, North Carolina; entrance to Charleston harbor, South Carolina; Stono inlet, South Carolina; North Edisto bar, South Carolina; St. Helena sound, South Carolina; Port Royal, South Carolina; Tybee roads, Georgia; Wassaw sound, Georgia; St. Simon's sound, Georgia; Southwest Pass of the Mississippi river, Louisiana, and Mare Island straits, California.

It is respectfully submitted that since July, 1861, this board has been without the services of an engineer secretary, and since the 7th June without those of a naval secretary.

The patriotic impulse which calls every true man to serve the country in her hour of trial, and the field opened for distinction in the two branches of the military service, from which the law establishing the board directs that these officers shall be taken, has made it difficult, if not impossible, to withhold from the more exciting and imposing scenes of the camp or the ship young officers eligible and qualified for the useful but less brilliant duties of the desk.

Under these circumstances the chairman of the board, with the assistance of an executive committee, sanctioned by the president of the board, has, in addition to his own proper duties, discharged those appertaining to the naval secretary, and the member from "the corps of topographical engineers of the army" has been charged with the engineering duties.

It will be the endeavor of the board that the public service shall not suffer in consequence of this reduction of the force deemed proper by Congress for the due performance of the duties of the light-house establishment.

All of which is respectfully submitted.

Very respectfully,

U. K. STRIBLING,
For Chairman.

Hon. S. P. Chase,
Secretary of the Treasury.

N.

COAST SURVEY.

Station near West Cheshire, Connecticut,
November 5, 1862.

Sir: I have the honor to submit for your examination the estimates for the work of the Coast Survey for 1863–'64, and to request that, if approved, they may be inserted in your estimates of appropriations. They are adapted to the plan of working approved by you, by which all the aid possible is rendered by our organization to the operations of the army and navy, and the regular progress of the survey is carried on wherever protection can be had for them, or is not needed.

The amount of the estimates is but little more than half that of 1860–'61, and is much diminished from that of 1861–'62, as will be seen by the comparative table at the close of this letter. The items are the same as, or less than, those approved last year by the Executive and by Congress, with the addition of one for the pay of engineers of the Coast Survey steamers, not now provided, as formerly, by the Navy Department. The surplus of the year before last, from which these officers were paid in 1862–'63, will be exhausted during this fiscal year.

These estimates will enable us to continue the regular work of the survey wherever our parties can move freely; to continue steadily all the office-work, on, however, a reduced scale, so as to work up all the information already collected, and to place it in appropriate and simple form in possession of the officers of our government, civil, military, and naval; to give important aid, by charts and by the personal experience of our officers, to the fleets and expeditions upon the coast; to revise the surveys in localities known to be changeable; to collect new information by reconnaissance on shore or afloat, and to keep up the essential organization of the survey, which has, by the testimony of the most enterprising naval and military officers, proved itself so valuable. The statements of the use made of the Coast Survey parties in different important military and naval expeditions will be given in my annual report, with the acknowledgments made by their chiefs. The services at Port Royal and in the lower Mississippi were only a fractional part of those rendered.

In the directions of the Treasury Department for the year I was instructed to continue, as far as practicable, the operations heretofore ordered, and have succeeded as far as the limited means permitted. The means, and not the opportunities of working, have, as was intended, limited the work executed, while, by an economical administration of the appropriation, no considerable opportunity, it is believed, of usefulness was lost for want of means.

Three Coast Survey steamers have been kept at work during nearly the whole season—the Corwin, the Bibb, and the Vixen; being, when not actually employed by the survey, used by the Navy Department. The services of the Bibb, under command of Assistant C. O. Boutelle, were acknowledged by Admiral DuPont in his official report of the action at Port Royal. The familiarity of her commander with that part of the coast made his personal services of the greatest importance. The Sachem, loaned to the Coast Survey by the Navy Department, in place of the Hetzel, was also officered and manned by the Coast Survey, and accompanied the expedition to the lower Mississippi, rendering services warmly acknowledged by Commander (now Acting Rear Admiral) David D. Porter. The Corwin, when not engaged in her regular work at Hatteras and in the Potomac, was under the orders of Admiral Goldsborough, and performed good service in the York river and its tributaries, the Pamunkey and Mattapony. The details of these and other matters of the kind belong to my annual report; but I would remark here that no opportunity was lost to furnish officers familiar with the parts of the coast visited by our fleets and armies, as will appear from the tables in my annual report, showing the employment of the assistants and other officers of the survey, and from the particulars of their work, under the head of the different sections.

The operations generally have been executed by the civilians attached to the survey—all the army officers, and all but two of the naval officers, having been returned to their respective services. One of the two officers of the navy attached to the survey, Captain B. F. Sands, has been recently detached. We have lost, by death, the gallant Lieutenant Colonel W. R. Palmer, who had remained most acceptably in charge of the Coast Survey office, though serving as aide-de-camp to General McClellan, until the army of the Potomac moved forward to Manassas. Six of the assistants, sub-assistants, and aids have, under your authority, received leave of absence, without pay, to join the volunteer or regular service, and have shown great capacity in their several positions. Their services will elsewhere be particularly referred to.

No losses of vessels or other property have been incurred during the year; but the three vessels seized at Charleston and in Texas the year before have not been restored. Four sailing vessels have been loaned to the Navy Department and three to the revenue service, during the year, at times when there was great exigency for the use of light-draught vessels.

Sixteen officers of the survey, of different grades, have been detailed for service, chiefly topographical, with the army of the Potomac, near Washington, on the peninsula and on the upper Potomac; with the army of the Rappahannock, near Fredericksburg and at Manassas; with the army of Maryland and Virginia, on the eastern shore and at Norfolk; with the army of North Carolina at Hatteras, Roanoke island, Newbern, Beaufort, N. C., &c.

The regular work has gone on upon the Florida reefs, and parties were at and near Key West, ready to co-operate with the army had active operations been undertaken on the western coast of the peninsula.

The regular work upon the Pacific coast has gone steadily forward.

Of 17 assistants, 14 sub-assistants, and 18 aids serving in the field or afloat, 15 assistants, 11 sub-assistants, and 15 aids have devoted the whole or a part of the year to the regular progress of the survey, and 8 assistants, 10 sub-assistants, and 14 aids (32 officers) have rendered service in connexion with the operations of the army and navy, generally in addition to their regular duties.

Of course, this latter-named service was not without its special dangers. Sub-Assistant Dorr narrowly escaped accident when the lamented Wagner was mortally wounded, and one of the soldiers of Mr. Dorr's plane-table party was killed in front of Yorktown. The plane-table which Mr. Dorr was using was shattered to pieces.

Sub-Assistant Oltmanns was badly wounded in the reconnaissance of Pearl river, and while attached to the steamer Sachem, under command of Assistant F. H. Gerdes, and to the flotilla of Commander (now Rear Admiral) D. D. Porter.

The bravery of Mr. J. S. Bradford, Mr. C. H. Boyd, and their comrades, alone saved them from capture on James's island, putting several prisoners into their hands. Of the officers who have thus served, the chiefs of parties, Assistant Charles O. Boutelle, under Admiral DuPont, and Assistant F. H. Gerdes, under Admiral Porter, have made themselves especially useful, and have won the special commendations of the gallant officers under whom they served.

During the past season more than the usual number of parties have been at work in Maine, Massachusetts, Rhode Island, Connecticut, New York, New Jersey, Pennsylvania, Maryland, and Virginia, pushing the work on that part of the coast to completion.

In my letter of last year I stated that, under favorable circumstances, surveys could be made by parties accompanying the fleets. Such circumstances occurring with Admiral DuPont's command, enabling us to survey the Stono river and entrance; Skull creek, connecting Port Royal harbor with Savannah river and Calibogue sound; to resurvey the bar of Fernandina or St. Mary's. The party connected with Admiral Farragut and Admiral D. D. Porter were enabled to resurvey and mark the bars at the entrance of the passes of the Mississippi, and to make some minor surveys. Buoys were placed promptly for the use of the vessels of the fleets and of the transport vessels.

I have taken the opportunity presented by the visits of inspection of the chief engineer, General Joseph G. Totten, to inform myself personally, through the kindly official and personal relations between us, of the progress and direction of the plans of defence of the coast, with a view to special reference thereto in the progress of the surveys. I was much gratified to find that, as far as we had advanced, the progress was in the right direction, though I could not but recognize that the information obtained would enable me in future to make the connexion more intimate than in the past, where no such exigencies as are now probable seemed to be among the possibilities of the times. I should be only too glad to make rapid provision for these exigencies could adequate means be furnished. Perhaps some opportunity may yet occur to carry out such a purpose. It is certain that accurate maps must form the basis of well conducted military operations, and that the best time to procure them is not when an attack is impending, or the army waits, but when there is no hindrance to or pressure upon the surveyor. That no coast can be effectively attacked, defended, or blockaded without accurate maps and charts, has been fully proved by the events of the last two years, if, indeed, such a proposition required practical proof. The persons employed upon the various coasts being in the service of the government, their personal experience has been available in the various and complicated duties of pilotage, for lighting beacons, buoys, &c., in times of exigency, and during the derangement of regular modes of supply, inspection, &c.

The Hon. Secretary of the Navy acknowledges, in his report, the services of the Superintendent of the Coast Survey as a member of a commission in reference to places of blockade, &c., and has since, with your approval, placed him on an important commission for selecting a site for a navy yard "for iron-clads and iron vessels, to lay the foundation of an iron navy." The indispensable usefulness of the Coast Survey results to these two commissions was generously acknowledged by votes of each, without dissent. The acknowledgments of the hydrographical and topographical notes, prepared by the Coast Survey, lithographed, and with the maps and charts illustrating them, furnished to the principal military and naval officers, have been numerous and very complimentary. During the year (November to November) 25,434 copies of the Coast Survey maps and charts have been furnished for distribution by the active chief of the hydrographic office to the naval vessels, and 1,476 have been delivered to captains and pilots in the government transport service. Maps compiled from the surveys of the coast, and from other authorities, have been published by the process of color printing, and have been so popular as, at the low prices for which they have been issued, more than to pay for themselves.

The estimates now submitted are intended to provide for the usual progress on the coast from Passamaquoddy to the capes of Virginia, and the progress which seems most probable from thence to the Rio Grande. They also provide for parties to aid the fleets and armies operating on the coast, in pursuance of the plan which you have fully approved, and which has, under your direction, proved so useful. Flexibility, in a work like this, is a most important feature, and that you have successfully impressed upon it. If I have erred in the estimates, it is in restricting them too much, the safest side upon which to err under the circumstances.

I suppose that one more appropriation, of about the amount now asked, will enable us to complete the survey of the Florida reefs and keys. There is now a gap in the hydrography of this dangerous part of the coast, which I expect to be able to have completed this season. It may require the application of the small appropriation for the triangulation across the peninsula, which cannot be used, under present circumstances, for completing the work for which it was designed, for this purpose. All these matters of detail will be set forth in my annual report.

The estimates include, as usual, separate items for the Atlantic and Gulf coast, Florida reefs, and western coast of the United States, without, however, the facilities formerly extended by the War and Navy Departments by the detail of officers.

Amount asked for, $306,000.

Estimates for the fiscal year 1063–'64, and appropriations for the present year and 1861–'62.

Object.	Estimates for fiscal year 1863–'64.	Estimated for fiscal year 1862–'63.	Appropriated for fiscal year 1861–'62.
For survey of the Atlantic and Gulf coasts of the United States, including compensation of civilians engaged in the work, per act of March 3, 1843....	$178,000	$178,000	$230,000
For continuing the survey of the western coast of the United States, including compensation of civilians engaged in the work, per act of September 30, 1850.	100,000	100,000	110,000
For continuing the survey of the Florida reefs and keys, including compensation of civilians engaged in the work, per act of March 3, 1849............	11,000	11,000	25,000
For completing the line to connect the triangulation on the Atlantic coast with that on the Gulf of Mexico, across the Florida peninsula, including compensation of civilians engaged in the work, per act of March 3, 1843	----------	----------	5,000
For publishing the observations made in the progress of the survey of the coast of the United States, including compensation of civilians engaged in the work, per act of March 3, 1843..................	4,000	5,000	5,000
For repairs of steamers and sailing schooners used in the survey, per act of March 2, 1853.............	4,000	5,000	10,000
For fuel and quarters, and for mileage or transportation, for officers or enlisted soldiers of the army serving in the coast survey, in cases no longer provided for by the quartermaster's department, per act of August 31, 1852...........................	----------	----------	*5,000
For pay and rations of engineers for seven steamers used in the hydrography of the Coast Survey, no longer supplied by the Navy Department.........	†9,000	----------	†12,800
Total.......................................	306,000	299,000	402,800

* Formerly included in estimates of War Department.
† Formerly included in estimates of Navy Department.

Very respectfully, yours,

A. D. BACHE,
Superintendent United States Coast Survey.

Hon. S. P. CHASE, *Secretary of the Treasury.*

O.

ANNUAL REPORT OF THE BOARD OF SUPERVISING INSPECTORS.

SIR: The board of supervising inspectors of steamboats having met in Philadelphia on the 16th day of October, 1862, pursuant to adjournment of their last annual meeting, have the honor of submitting to you their tenth annual report.

From year to year in the annual reports of the board we have expressed the opinion, based upon our observation and experience, while endeavoring within our respective districts to secure a strict obedience of its requirements, that the steamboat law under which we act has, through observance of its humane provisions, been highly instrumental in lessening the number of accidents to steam vessels, and is of incalculable benefit and value to the thousands who travel daily on our passenger steamers. We are still fully of this opinion, which the operations and incidents of the year just past have only served to strengthen.

Accidents from various causes yet occasionally occur; but judging by comparison with former years previous to the passage of this act by Congress, undoubtedly many have been prevented, and many lives and much property have been saved through the enforcement and observance of its provisions.

Aware of the many risks incident to steam navigation, it does not idly enter into our expectations that through the provisions of any law, however well devised or strict its enforcement, all accidents can be entirely prevented. Such results, however, as may be reasonably looked for as following a faithful compliance with the provisions of this law, have been, to a great extent, realized. The systematic habits of management which have been induced in those entrusted with the navigation of steamers, by its wholesome regulations, have not been without their effect; and many owners of steam vessels, instead of exhibiting, as at first, opposition to its enforcement, now make frequent offers of cooperation with inspectors to attain in the highest degree possible the benefits which they feel assured must follow a faithful compliance with its requirements, both in additional safety to their property as well as to passengers travelling on their vessels.

A general admission of the great utility of the laws and expressions of satisfaction at the results which have followed its observance, which to those interested in such property is now fully apparent, has now taken the place of the original opposition with which the inspectors were met in many instances ; and incomplete as this law may be in some respects, the cause of almost every accident to passenger steamers which now occur can be readily traced to a violation of its provisions, or of the regulations of this board made pursuant thereto.

The system of licensing pilots and engineers has produced a marked improvement in those officers in many parts of the country, both socially and professionally, and will do much to secure in a greater degree the objects of the law in years to come. We regret to have to recall in this report the occurrence during the past year of two very serious disasters, from which great loss of life has resulted—the burning of the steamship Golden Gate, on the Pacific coast, and the collision of the steamers George Peabody and West Point, on the Potomac river; but as these cases are very fully described in their appropriate place in this report, we will merely mention them here as the most prominent amongst the accidents which we have to report, and also in some respects of a most unusual and extraordinary character, and especially do we refer to the loss of the Golden Gate by fire.

FIRST SUPERVISING DISTRICT.

There have been inspected by the local board at San Francisco during the past year fifty steam vessels, to which certificates have been granted. Some of these have been rebuilt or repaired at great cost. The Uncle Sam and Brother Jonathan have been rebuilt at a cost of $60,000 and $100,000, respectively; and the steamers Sierra Nevada, Peteluma, and Senator have been very extensively repaired; the three last named and the Brother Jonathan having been also supplied with new boilers. Five boilers have given away under the hydrostatic test, and nine have been condemned from further use.

There have been granted by this board forty-eight licenses to pilots, and one hundred and thirty-one licenses to engineers, all of whom, in addition to the usual oath required by the steamboat law, have been required to record in this office their allegiance to the Constitution and government of the United States.

Three investigations have been held by the board under the 9th section of the steamboat act, and they have suspended or revoked the licenses of three engineers, and have refused license to five engineers, and four have been refused change of grade.

LOSS OF THE STEAMER NEVADA.

February 7, 1862.—The steamer Nevada, on her trip from Sacramento to San Francisco, struck a sunken snag in the Sacramento slue, about forty miles below Sacramento; she continued on her course for about nine miles, when the captain ordered the pilot to run her ashore for the purpose of making an effort to stop the leak, as it was evident she could not be kept free. She was accordingly run into the bank and lines made fast to the shore from the bow, which was now within fifteen or twenty feet. The current swung her stern into the bank, when lines were also employed aft to secure her to the shore. The pumps and buckets were resorted to without success, and she gradually sunk— her stern in thirty-two feet of water and her bow in three feet. No loss of life occurred, the passengers having been all previously taken off by the steamer Chrysopolis. She has not as yet been raised, although several ineffectual attempts have been made, and but little hope is left of being able to save her. Her machinery will be saved with but little trouble. No blame was attached to the officers of the vessel under the circumstances.

LOSS OF THE STEAMSHIP GOLDEN GATE.

As soon as the first of the passengers and crew arrived from the scene of this frightful disaster, an investigation of the case was commenced, and there have been examined, in all, twenty-seven witnesses, embracing passengers, officers, and crew.

The Golden Gate was a first-class steamship of 2,029 tons, belonging to the Pacific Mail Steamship Company of New York, and was engaged in the passenger carrying trade between San Francisco and Panama. She sailed from San Francisco July 21, and had on board 236 passengers and 102 officers and crew; total 338. Of this number, 138 passengers and 37 crew were lost; total 175. The ship took fire on the afternoon of July 27, about 5 o'clock p. m., when about fourteen miles to the northward of Manzanillo, Mexico, and about three and one-half or four miles from the shore. The sea was perfectly calm.

The Golden Gate was inspected by the board at San Francisco on the 28th day of April, 1862, and was found, as regards machinery and hull, to be sound, substantial, and sea-worthy, and well supplied with all the equipments required by law for the prevention of accident, and for saving life in case of accident. She was furnished with two oscillating engines, nine feet stroke and eighty-six inches diameter of cylinder, placed side by side directly under the paddle wheel shaft; four return tubular boilers, fired athwart ship, two being placed forward and two abaft of the engines, each pair having an independent smoke stack amidship. The vessel was about 265 feet in length, 40 feet beam, and 22 feet depth of hold. She was provided with three permanent decks, and a spar deck running the whole length of the vessel. The houses on the main deck extended forward within about seventy feet of the head of the vessel, and aft within about four feet of the stern, and as far aft as the after part of the wheel houses were in general width about eighteen feet, and situated centrally in the ship. Between these houses just described and the starboard wheel house were situated the after galley and cabin pantry; the former being abreast of the forward smoke stack, the pipes from the stoves of this galley leading into this stack, and the pantry, which was situated immediately behind the galley, occupied the entire space between the central deck houses and the starboard wheel house, leaving a gangway fore and aft on the main deck only on the port side of the ship. On the port side of the ship, abreast of the smoke stacks and engine room hatch, were situated the porters' room, chief engineer's room, assistant engineers' rooms, and bar room; the gangway above mentioned being between these rooms and the engine room hatch, and was in width about seven feet. The saloon, which occupied the after part of the main deck, was, including the state-rooms, about fifty feet in width, narrowing toward the after part of the ship. This vessel was furnished with a fantail, and had guards running from the extreme after part of the ship as far forward as the fore rigging; these guards furnishing a gangway and promenade in front of the saloon state-rooms, a part of which were entered from the guard, and others from the saloon. There was a gangway athwart ship from one after guard to the other; immediately forward of the saloon from this cross gangway two doors entered into the saloon. On the deck next below the main deck the central portion of the ship was occupied by the machinery and the firemen's and water tenders' rooms. On the after part of this deck was the second cabin, and the forward part of the ship on this deck was occupied by the steerage passengers. The central part of the lower deck was also occupied by the machinery; the after part was divided into freight rooms, store room, baggage room, and special room; the forward part was used as a freight room, and below this deck were coal bunkers. The upper or spar deck was clear fore and aft, except the engine hatch, smoke stacks, and watch officers' rooms.

The equipment provided to meet accidents by fire were as follows, viz: Four fire pumps—two worked by hand and two by steam, and all were double acting pumps. The forward hand fire-pump was five inches diameter and twelve inches stroke, and was worked upon the main deck; the after pump was four inches diameter, eight inches stroke, and worked upon the spar deck. The steam-pumps were situated on the working floor of the engine room (lower deck,) one on the starboard and the other on the port side, both fitted with copper pipes leading up to the main deck, with nozzles for attaching hose on each deck. The main deck nozzles from the starboard and port steam-pumps were situated respectively alongside of the forward and after smoke stacks in the port gangway. These steam-pumps were each twelve inches stroke and ten inches diameter; and the ship was provided with 650 feet of hose, 24 axes, 80 buckets, 1,000 life-preservers, seven metallic life-boats, and one wooden boat. She had six sets of boat cranes, three on each side of the ship; one set in each case being forward of the paddle wheels and two sets aft; and had two gangway steps, one on each side abaft the wheels. Each boat was provided with life lines and all other necessary equipments, and all were substantial and in good order.

When fire was first discovered the chief officer of the ship, who was on duty, ordered the forward and after pumps to be put to work on the fire. The hose was not attached at this time. The hose of the forward pumps, 200 feet in length, was kept on a reel directly over the pumps, and the pipe or nozzle was always kept attached thereto, but the hose was not kept attached to the pumps except at night. This hose, which was two inches in diameter, was first stretched aft on the spar deck, but was finally ordered to be taken below to the main deck, and was stretched along on the port side of the ship, and from this time, until within a few moments of the ship striking the ground, was kept to work upon the fire.

The after fire-pump, as was shown by the evidence, had to be primed with water before it would draw, and it does not appear that this pump was got in condition to work. The hose to this pump was kept in a hose-tub outside the rail, opposite the pump; it was about 150 feet in length, and was not attached in the daytime. 200 feet of hose belonging to the steam-pumps were kept on a reel just inside the firemen's room, which entered off the engine room on the second deck; 100 feet more hung in the engine room, and 50 feet were kept in the port gangway on the main deck, for attaching to the starboard steam-pump. Both these steam-pumps were set to work with as little delay as possible. The starboard steam-pump was of little service, as the flames enveloped the copper pipe leading from this pump to the main deck, where the hose had been attached; and the branch pipe leading to the hose, being attached to the main with a soft soldered joint, melted at this point, cutting off the supply of water from the hose. The hose was attached to port steam-pumps on the same deck where the pump was situated, (lower deck,) and carried up into the crank room and used upon the fire until the persons using it were driven from the engine room by the flames. The hose was connected to both deck pumps and one steam-pump every night, by order of the officers of the ship. The hose of the fire-pumps was not kept attached in the daytime, and from one and a half to two minutes was lost in consequence. The general practice of these ships has been to attach the hose to the fire-pumps at sundown and remove them at sunrise. It is believed all the officers of the ship did their best to save life in the trying circumstances under which they were called to act. By the orders of Captain Hudson, the chief engineer kept the engines going until the ship struck. The steam fire-pumps were worked as long as could be done amidst the flame and smoke, and every precaution was taken to prevent explosion. By orders of the captain, the chief officer launched as many of the boats as possible with the ship under way, and the flames spreading aft with such fearful rapidity; and when he finally left the ship, there remained on her after decks only three persons—the man at the wheel, and a man and his wife who could not be induced to get into the boats. After getting clear of the ship, he still followed in her wake, picking up those whom he found struggling in the water. After picking up all he could find, he brought the boats together, properly distributing the crew and passengers amongst the several boats, and having arranged as far as was possible for the comfort of the persons under his care, made for the harbor of Manzanillo. It is believed that Captain Hudson did what he thought best to save life. He issued his orders promptly, and was cool, calm, and without fear under the most trying circumstances. He assisted the passengers forward, entreating them not to get excited, but to stay on the ship until she struck. Cut off from the after part of the ship by the fire, and from the assistance of his officers and most of the crew, he also did all that he could have done to save life after the ship struck.

It is the opinion of the inspector who examined this case that the fire originated from the baker's oven in the forward part of the cabin galley. The floor under the oven was of brick work, laid in cement two layers thick, and the bulkhead back of the oven and stoves made of iron plates, so that the nearest wood work to the baker's oven was the deck upon which the brick floor was laid. The cooking stoves and oven were raised at least three inches from the brick floor, leaving a space for air to pass under them. The fire first made its appearance behind the stoves and under this oven. The carlines or deck beams under this galley were cased in to make a snug finish to the upper engine room. On the day of the fire, from ten o'clock in the forenoon until half-past four in the afternoon, the heat in the galley had been so great that the cooks complained to the head steward that they could not stand it, and said it was caused by the having so much fire on. It is believed that the bottom of the bake-oven was burned through, letting the fire down in the ash pan on the brick work, as the most probable way the fire originated; and there is no doubt that the carlines spoken of (cased in) and deck had been on fire for some time and to a considerable extent, before it had burned through the casing into the engine room and water tender's room. This alone can account for the rapidity with which the fire spread after it was discovered, and the then impossibility of getting it under. Her boats were ample, and more than the law required, but were not in that state of readiness to lower away promptly that they should have been; they were, however, secured as sea steamers usually have them.

The supervising inspector of the district makes a report to the board of his doings during the past season, which is as follows:

To the Board of Supervising Inspectors, &c.:

GENTLEMEN: Having been, at the last annual meeting of the board, held in Washington city December 16, 1861, assigned the supervision of the Pacific coast of the United States as an independent district, under a new division of the supervising districts, I proceeded to that coast at as early a date after the adjournment as the circumstances of the case would allow, consistent with making the necessary arrangements for my departure, and providing myself, by the approval of the department, with proper instruments with which to make inspections; being aware that steamers navigating the northern waters of my district would necessarily come under my own personal examination.

I left New York March 11 in the steamship Northern Light for Aspinwall, and arrived in San Francisco April 6, in the steamship St. Louis, belonging to the Pacific Mail Steamship Company, in which I took passage at Panama.

On my arrival in San Francisco, I found that of the local inspectors who had until recently administered the duties of the office at San Francisco, the inspector of hulls had died about the end of the last year, and the inspector of boilers had been removed from office, but was still contending that his successor had not been duly appointed, and was not, therefore, entitled to receive the records of the office. This caused the new incumbents considerable embarrassment in the discharge of their duties, not having in their possession the instruments for testing boilers, the records of their office, or any of the forms or regulations adopted by this board for the guidance of local inspectors.

Having satisfied myself that the new inspectors had been duly commissioned, I addressed a communication to the inspector who had been removed, stating this fact, and requesting that the books, records, instruments, and other property pertaining to the office be delivered over to the new incumbents. Thus advised, this request was cheerfully complied with. I found, upon examination of the records, that many errors have crept into the practice of the old board, probably the result of having been left to carry out the laws after their own construction, without the advantage of communication with other inspectors; and the interpretation put on certain of its requirements, and the manner of its enforcement in many particulars, were unwarrantably liberal, and certainly at great variance with the usual construction and the practices of inspectors in other parts of the country. Observance of the rules for the government of pilots has never been enforced on the Pacific coast until the present season; no colored signal lights have been used except upon the ocean steamers, nor have whistle signals been employed, and life-preservers have not been demanded as a necessary part of the equipment of river steamers.

The new inspectors entered into their duties at the end of last year, and, being without the records of their office and the regulations of this board, although aiming to perform their duty in the most faithful manner, fell into many of the easy constructions of the old board of inspectors, who had established a precedent which, in the hurry of the transaction of a large amount of business, was difficult to contend with in the absence of a knowledge of the most strict enforcement of the law in other districts; and many certificates were at first issued entailing the old errors of construction and administration.

But this state of things is now happily at an end. I do not in the remotest degree intend to impugn the motives of the inspectors who inaugurated these practices, but attribute their existence to the fact that these inspectors were far removed from communication with other boards, which otherwise, by an interchange of views and opinions, would have led to a true understanding of their duties under the law, and a more particular and strict enforcement of its provisions.

Under these circumstances, and having a large number of steamers in Oregon and Washington Territory to inspect personally during the summer, I issued from my office, under date of May 28, a circular addressed to the owners, masters, engineers, and pilots of passenger steamers navigating the waters of the first district, setting forth, in as concise terms as possible, the provisions of the law in its application to the several classes of steamers employed upon these waters, together with the regulations of this board as affecting the construction to be put upon these provisions to meet the inspection to which these vessels would be hereafter subjected. These instructions were furnished to the local inspectors, who were charged with their distribution, and were issued as the readiest means at my command through which a better state of things might be inaugurated with the least possible delay.

After visiting almost every steamer in this district, and aiding the local inspectors in making inspections of several ocean and other steamers, and imparting to them all the information in regard to their duties which the circumstances seemed to suggest, I took passage for Portland, Oregon, on the 3d day of June, arriving at that port on the 7th.

On the Columbia and Willamette rivers I inspected, in all, twenty-five steamers, having an aggregate tonnage of 2,823 tons, licensed 49 pilots and 30 engineers, and refused license to three engineers and one pilot; nine boilers were found defective upon inspection, and five gave way under the hydrostatic test. These were repaired and retested. Some of these steamers are very fine vessels of their class, and are especially adapted to the navigation in which they are employed; are well found in many respects, and are generally staunch and well-built steamers. I was much pleased with the arrangement and management of many of these vessels; and, notwithstanding previous reports, I was unprepared to find upon these waters so fine a class of river steamers.

The steamboat law has not, however, been observed to any great extent on these rivers up to the present time; not that the owners have any disinclination to comply with the provisions of the law, but, on the contrary, are ready and desirous to do so, but have awaited as to what would be considered by the proper officer of the law a suitable compliance with its provisions by steamers of the class employed in this navigation. I found no life-preservers or water-gauges on any of the steamers running on any of these rivers, with one exception; and for this and other reasons, which it is unnecessary to mention here, the certificates of inspection were withheld for the present, and will not be issued until early in next season. I found on board some of these steamers a certificate licensing them to carry gunpowder, &c., but found none equipped for this purpose. All such licenses were recalled. Soon after my return to San Francisco the news reached me of the destruction of the steamship Golden Gate by fire, and the loss of many lives. I immediately gave directions for the investigation of the case by the local inspectors at that port, and aided them in the examination of witnesses up to the day of my departure for the east, at which time they had concluded their investigation. All the owners and officers of the vessels on the Pacific coast express a readiness to comply with the laws to the fullest extent, and I am satisfied it is from no lack of this disposition that the law has not been as fully observed in this as in other parts of the country.

In the district of San Francisco the law is now fully complied with in most particulars, and a little time is only needed to secure the full benefit of its humane provisions; and I would add that I hope to be able to report to the board, at its next annual meeting, that a full compliance with the law has been secured throughout my entire district.

Your obedient servant,

WM. BURNETT,
Supervising Inspector, &c.

SECOND SUPERVISING DISTRICT.

In this district, although one of very large extent, we feel happy to be able to state that very few casualties have occurred, and but a small sacrifice of life on the part of the vast public travel by steam navigation during the past year.

The steamer Francis Skiddy, plying between New York and Troy, on her upward trip, when about two miles below Poughkeepsie, on the night of November 28, 1861, came into collision with the sloop W. W. Reynolds. Upon investigation, it appeared that the Francis Skiddy was stopped: that is, that her engine was stopped at the time, the night being dark and rainy, with no wind, and that the sloop showed no light. Also that the end of the boom of of the sloop penetrated the forward end of the Skiddy's forward starboard boiler, and that the sloop was seen too late to avoid a collision. Nine persons were scalded by the escaping steam, three of whom died from their injuries, viz: two firemen and the cook's mate. In this case all was done that could be by the licensed officers.

At the New London district no accident has occurred involving loss of life or injury to the person of either passengers or crew. On the 3d of May the steamer City of New York came in collision with the schooner Mary Mankin, in a fog, at the entrance of this harbor. The schooner was a coasting vessel, with cargo, and was not seen until too late to avoid a collision. She filled with water and sunk. Loss unknown.

On the 27th of March the steamer Bay State, of Fall River, while entering New York harbor, came in contact with a ship attached to a steam tug, by which the ship's boom entered the steam chimney of one of her boilers, which detained the steamer twenty-four hours. No injury occurred to any of the passengers or crew.

On the morning of August 1 the steamer Meneman Sanford, on her passage from Bangor to Boston, during a thick fog, ran on to a ledge of rocks near Cape Ann, called the Salvages, and bilged. All the passengers, with their baggage, were taken off the steamer and forwarded to Boston. Upon investigation into the cause of this accident, it was ascertained that the pilots of the steamer had made use of the usual precautions in running their courses. The steamer was ultimately floated off and repaired. Loss on the vessel estimated at $40,000.

Many of our steamers from this district have been called off from their usual routes, and employed as transports in the government service.

We feel pleased further to state that the owners and officers of all steamers in our district continue to manifest their confidence in the wise and humane provisions of the steamboat law.

From the local board at Philadelphia we learn that for the past year there has been no casualty by which life has been lost or property destroyed; nor has there been any explosion or collision, or a report of the loss of life on steamers under the law.

Everything, so far as the workings of law have been concerned, has been harmonious; nor has there been a single complaint made, by reason of any jar or conflict, during the past year.

Under this view of things, we are happy to report the benefits that are constantly showing themselves by the act of Congress of 1852 relating to the duties and obligations of steam vessels navigating our waters.

THIRD SUPERVISING DISTRICT.

On the 18th of January, 1862, the steamer Pocahontas was lost in a gale of wind at Cape Hatteras inlet. This boat had been chartered by the United States government to carry horses to North Carolina for the Burnside expedition. She had proceeded on her voyage beyond Cape Henry, when she encountered a severe gale from the northeast. In the gale her boiler, which was old and much worn, by reason of the rolling of the vessel, fell off its legs, and completely disabled the steamer from going on her voyage. The captain immediately ordered the vessel to be run on the beach, to save the lives of those on board, which was done; but all the horses were drowned. The vessel a total wreck.

This vessel should have had a new boiler before going on this voyage; and such was the verdict rendered by the local board.

On the 13th of August, 1862, the steamers George Peabody and West Point collided on the Potomac river near Ragged Point, about 8½ o'clock in the evening. Both these vessels were in the employ of the government at the time. The testimony went to show that the George Peabody was on her way down the Potomac to Fortress Monroe, and that the West Point was on her way up to Aquia creek. When meeting in the vicinity of Ragged Point, the pilot of the George Peabody, steering at the time S.SE., about eight o'clock in the evening, gave one blast of the whistle, as a signal to the coming vessel that the George Peabody would keep to the right, in accordance with the law.

The pilot of the West Point answered promptly, with one blast of his whistle, that he also would keep to the right, then steering, as he states, west half south. At the same time the captain was at the wheel, and states that the pilot told him to starboard his wheel, and he replied to the pilot, " You don't mean that, you mean port." He answered, " Yes, port; hard a port." But as the course of the vessel was thus shifted, this was undoubtedly the cause of the collision, as she continued with *force* and *headway* until she came in contact with the larboard guard and water wheel of the George Peabody, breaking in some twelve feet of the deck and guard work in front of the wheel. The bow of the West Point was stove in some ten feet, when it was directly ascertained that she was in a sinking condition. As soon as extricated from the Peabody, she made for the Maryland side of the Potomac, and sunk in four fathoms water. She went down, having on board two hundred and seventy-nine souls, three of whom were ladies. Every exertion was made by Captain Doyle, of the West Point, to save the lives of his passengers; also a gunboat, which was near, hearing the cries of distress, gave relief. The machinery of the Peabody was seriously crippled from the collision, preventing her from giving aid to those on board of the sinking vessel for some time after, but drifted down the river until she could get her engine in working order, when she put out both boats in pursuit of those floating on the broken fragments of the sunken vessel. By this sad disaster seventy-six persons have been drowned.

On the 21st of August, 1862, a collision took place between the steamers Belvidere and Elm City on the Potomac, both employed at the time as transports for the government. The circumstances and testimony concerning this case have not yet been fully obtained. Happily, by this disaster no lives were lost. The supervising inspector of this district and the local inspectors at Baltimore have also been engaged during the past season in directing and superintending repairs of steamers which have been employed as war transports and have been brought to this port for repairs.

The district of Norfolk has been represented by Mr. G. V. Davids, boiler inspector, whose residence and station has been at Old Point. He has visited, examined, and inspected over one hundred steamers employed by the United States government as transports, and also in the United States navy; recorded defects and gave orders for their repair while engaged by the government, and lying off Old Point. He has licensed seven engineers at the fortress, besides attending and giving his services to a great deal of public work of this character. No reports from Charleston, Savannah, or Mobile.

FOURTH SUPERVISING DISTRICT.

During the year ending October 1, 1862, only one life was lost by steamboat accidents in this district; the person was intoxicated, and sleeping on board the steamboat Jeannie Deans, when the steam-pipe exploded, causing his death by inhaling the escaping steam. The cause of the explosion was a defect in the copper of which the pipe was made.

The steamers Callie and Skylark were captured and burned by the rebels on the Tennessee river. Both were laden with government stores. The amount of the loss could not be ascertained.

A collision took place between the steamers Rowena and Estelle near Cape Girardeau, on the Mississippi. No lives lost. The case is still undergoing an investigation.

The steamer John D. Perry snagged in the Mississippi river. No lives lost, and damage trifling.

The steamers Alex. Smith and Choctaw have left the passenger trade, and are being turned into government rams.

On the 20th day of August last the steamer Acacia, on her voyage from Memphis to Helena, Arkansas, struck a snag about twenty-five miles above Helena, and sunk in a few minutes in twenty feet water. By this disaster over a hundred human beings found a watery grave. The supervising inspector, in investigating the case, found that the Acacia was an old worn-out boat that had been condemned several years ago. She was navigating without a license, and under a *military permit.* Except the captain and pilot, the whole crew consisted of negroes. The pilot employed never had been licensed, and is unknown to the Mississippi pilots. Although he escaped unhurt, he could not be found afterwards. The escaped passengers and the inhabitants of Helena having threatened him with summary justice, he left for parts unknown. No inspection took place south and west of White river, Arkansas, this season, this portion of the fourth district being still in open rebellion.

FIFTH SUPERVISING DISTRICT.

The supervising inspector of this district reports as follows: In this district but three accidents have occurred, none of which have involved the loss of life or injury to the person of either passengers or crew.

In the month of August, 1862, on the Minnesota river, the steamer New Ulm Belle, a small freight and passenger boat, ran on a snag and sunk. No lives lost. Loss, $1,000.

In the month of September, 1862, the steamer Hannibal City, a large and powerful boat, owned and inspected in St. Louis, but running into the fifth district, while on her passage from St. Louis to Keokuk, just below Louisiana, Missouri, ran on to a sunken log raft, and immediately sunk in seven or eight feet of water. No lives lost; upper works and machinery all saved. Loss, $12,000.

On the night of September 18, 1862, the steamer Arizona, while on her passage from Keokuk to Quincy, when about two miles below Lagrange, Missouri, ran into the steamer Eagle, and sunk the latter in five or six feet of water, within thirty yards of the shore. No lives lost. Loss, $1,000. Upon examination into the facts of the case, I found both pilots to blame, though I consider the pilot of the' Arizona much more to blame than the pilot of the Eagle, but for carelessness and inattention to duty I suspended the licenses of both pilots. In another case I refused to renew, for a time, the license of a pilot who ran a heavily laden steamer on shore at the imminent risk of instant destruction to the boat and great damage to the lives of passengers.

There have been inspected in this district twenty-nine steamboats, with an aggregate tonnage of 4,424 tons.

There have been carried by the different lines of steamers in this district ·54,000 passengers, without the loss of a single life.

The operation of the law in this district has been very harmonious, the owners and officers being desirous to conform to the requirements of the law, and to aid in making the same effective.

SIXTH SUPERVISING DISTRICT.

In this district we have to report but few casualties of a serious character. The Monongahela, a small towboat belonging the canal to company, (and not inspected under the act of 1852,) exploded a boiler on the 20th of February last, about twelve miles below Louisville, Kentucky, while under way towing a flatboat; the captain of the boat and three of the crew were killed. The boiler of this boat had been in use for a long time, and, from the examination made soon after the explosion occurred, the boiler was considered very defective and unfit for use; and had this boiler been inspected under the act of 1852, it would have been condemned.

On the 2d of August last one of the boilers of the steamer Commodore Perry, while lying at the wharf at Louisville, Kentucky, exploded, by which one life was lost, (a fireman.) After a careful examination of the persons who witnessed this disaster, and also a careful inspection of the exploded boiler, no doubt was entertained that the explosion was caused by the negligence and inattention of the engineer having charge of the engines at the time in the performance of his duties, and for which his license was revoked; and all the evidence taken in the case was handed to the United States attorney for the prosecution of the delinquent engineer.

On the 5th of October, 1861, the steamer Curlew struck on a sunken flatboat four miles above Golconda, Illinois ,on the Ohio river, and sunk. The boat and cargo were nearly a total loss.

The steamer Arizona, on the 10th of January last, while passing out of the mouth of the canal between Portland and Louisville, Kentucky, swung round on the head of the pier and sunk, which caused considerable loss to the boat and cargo; the boat, however, was subsequently raised and repaired.

It will be observed, by reference to the tabular report, that the number of steamers inspected in this district, when compared with former years, has been much reduced. This is owing to the derangement in our navigation growing out of the rebellion and not to any actual reduction in the number and tonnage of the steamers in this district; and from the same cause no reports have been obtained from either Nashville or New Orleans.

SEVENTH SUPERVISING DISTRICT.

Within the year there have been inspected in this district one hundred and thirty-eight steamers, amounting to thirty thousand three hundred and twenty-seven (30,327) tons. Licenses have been granted to four hundred and ninety-two pilots and five hundred and forty-seven engineers.

The local boards find a ready acquiescence in the requirements of the law by owners and officers of boats, and the diminution of accidents attests the advantage of its workings alike to commerce and the safety of human lives.

In making a synopsis of the several reports of the local boards of inspection of the seventh district, the following casualties have occurred :

The steamer Igo exploded, killing one person and wounding two. At the time and prior to the explosion she was navigating and carrying passengers without having undergone an inspection, either under the law of 1838 or that of 1852. This case was placed in the hands of the United States district attorney at Cincinnati, who is prosecuting the same. Loss, $2,000.

The towboat Advance exploded, killing three and wounding ten. From this explosion the boat caught fire, and was a total loss; she was running under the law of 1838. The engineer in charge was licensed under the law of 1852; his license was revoked. Loss, $8,000.

The General Meigs, a steamer built by order of government and not inspected, collapsed a flue, the machinery being in charge of a licensed engineer, who, when the case was examined by the local board, was exonerated from blame, a defective connexion of steam-pipe with the steam-drum being the cause of the disaster. No lives lost. Damage, $500.

Steamer Bostona, inspected under the law of 1852, burst her mud drum. Engineer on watch, through fright, leaped overboard and was lost. Loss of property trifling.

Collision occurred between the steamer Freestone and Belle Creole, whereby the latter was sunk. No lives lost. License of pilot of Freestone revoked. Loss, $4,000.

Steamers Emma Graham and Leonora, both boats ascending the river, came in collision; damage unimportant. Pilot of Leonora suspended for sixty days.

Steamers Bay City and St. Louis came in collision while running in fog, the latter boat injured in hull to the amount of $500. Pilots of both boats suspended for thirty days.

Steamer Eunice, a government boat, came in collision with the Commodore Perry ; the Eunice was sunk and a total loss. No lives lost. Loss, $3,000. License of the pilot of the Eunice revoked.

Steamers Echo and Home came in collison on the Alleghany river. A loss of $3,000 occurred from the sinking of a bulk oil boat in tow of the Home. No lives lost. License of pilot of Echo revoked.

In the investigation of these several cases of collision by the local boards, it was shown that in every case the rules for the government of pilots had been neglected.

EIGHTH SUPERVISING DISTRICT.

There have been inspected in this district during the past year fifty-seven steam vessels, with an aggregate tonnage of twenty-two thousand six hundred and forty-six (22,646) tons.

There have been transported by these steamers one hundred and forty-five thousand five hundred (145,500) passengers, not one of whom has received the slightest injury.

No collisions have occurred between licensed steamers running in this district, nor has there been any accident of a serious character to any such vessel; but there have been several collisions between inspected steamers and sail vessels, which in one instance occasioned the loss of twelve persons, who were on board the sail vessel. With this exception no loss of life has occurred; but still the other collisions mentioned have placed in immediate danger the lives of a large number of passengers, whose escape may be attributed in a great measure to the good conduct of the officers and crews of the steamers.

These frequent collisions upon the northern and western lakes between steam and sailing vessels are a source of constant anxiety and alarm with all persons called to travel on the water. It is, indeed, fraught with much danger, and until Congress shall make some provisions further regulating the carrying of signal lights and the management of vessels in passing steamers, these serious and often fatal disasters will surely continue.

There have been some few accidents by derangement of machinery, but none producing serious results. There have been one hundred and fifty-five pilots licensed during the year, and one hundred and sixty-one engineers, all of whom have, so far as known, discharged their duties with care and fidelity, and all of whom have taken the oath to support the Constitution and government of the United States.

The propeller Kenosha, early in April, while entering the harbor at Milwaukie, ran upon an unknown sunken obstruction, which broke through her bottom. She had to go into dry dock for repairs. No lives lost.

Propellers Rocket and the Chicago, about the first of May, ran into the sunken wreck of the tug Zouave in the Detroit river, and were placed in dry dock for repairs. No lives lost.

Steamer Ariel, Saginaw river, bulged the crown sheet of her boiler, supposed by the hydrostatic pressure; subsequently repaired by the introduction of a new crown sheet. No lives lost or persons injured.

The steamer Planet collided with sail vessel on Lake Erie in the night, on the 22d of August, between Cleveland and Detroit, receiving serious damage, which occasioned loss of her trip, and required her to go in dry dock for repairs. Though no lives were lost or persons injured, yet the damage was so serious that it was with great difficulty she was kept from sinking with a large number of passengers on board. No blame was attached to any of the officers of the steamer, the collision being entirely attributed to the mismangement of the sail vessel.

The May Queen, about the first of September, was run into by a sailing vessel between Cleveland and Detroit, doing some injury, but not of a serious character The two vessels, after laying by until they ascertained that no serious injury had occurred to either continued on their course.

The propeller Allegheny, about the last of September, on Lake Huron, in a fog, collided with a sailing vessel, and was seriously damaged, requiring a large amount of freight to be thrown overboard. Being in a sinking condition, by sounding signals of distress she brought to her aid the steamer Illinois, which happened to be passing at the time, and by which she was undoubtedly saved from going down.

The propeller Michigan, about the last of September, grounded on a reef while attempting, in a storm, to make a harbor at St. Helena island, Lake Michigan, having been deceived in her position by some Indian camp-fire on the shore. No loss of life, but vessel and freight much damaged.

The steamer Illinois, on the night of the 9th of August, off the Pictured Rocks, Lake Superior, in a fog, collided with the schooner Oriole, loaded with iron, on her passage down the lake, by which the Oriole went down almost instantly, with thirteen persons on board, all of whom, with one exception, were drowned. The Illinois has been on fire upon one occasion, owing to the water being deficient in the water-jasket, the heat passing through three sheets of iron and three open spaces to the upper deck, where the fire occurred. It was extinguished without difficulty.

There have been several explosions of boilers in this district upon uninspected steamers and tug-boats, in every instance accompanied by the loss of life, showing conclusively the great value of inspections and licensing of engineers. We will mention the following examples, which have come to our knowledge:

The tug Zouave, engaged in towing vessels on the Detroit river, some time about the first of May last exploded her boiler, while under way, about ten miles above Detroit, and sunk immediately, killing the captain, engineer, and one hand. The cause, so far as ascertained, was want of water in the boilers. It was stated that, while passing Detroit, the force-pump had failed to work, and the water in the boiler was low; but expecting to be able to get it to work, the boat continued on her course until the explosion took place.

The tug Union, plying upon the Chicago river, in August, while towing a vessel out into the lake, exploded her boiler and instantly sunk, killing four or five persons, mostly citizens, who went on board for an excursion.

The Little Nellie, running from Saginaw to Saint Charles, in Michigan, exploded her boiler at the dock at Saginaw City. It appears, from what is known, that the engineer on duty had been temporarily employed for a trip or two in consequence of the sickness of the regular engineer, and that he had fastened down the safety valve and left the boat to go on the dock, and that, during his absence, the boiler exploded, killing four passengers who were on board. This man is in jail for trial. The captain of the boat had made application for her inspection, but it had not been done. It may be proper to say that this boat was of a class of small boats now coming into much use in some localities in this and other districts, fitted with screw propellers, and running up the various small rivers emptying into the lakes. They are from thirty to forty feet in length, and from six to eight feet beam, covered with light decks or awnings; their engines and boilers light, and of a very simple construction, requiring but a small amount of fuel, and running with considerable speed. They, in many instances, are almost an indispensable necessity in the new and sparsely settled district.

As these boats are of quite recent introduction, it is hardly probable that Congress intended to legislate for them. They are too small to carry a life-boat, a fire-pump, hose, life-preservers, or floats, to any amount, and yet some of them are carrying a very large number of passengers, but on very short routes. The owners, and those in charge of these boats, are generally willing and anxious to have them inspected and the engineers and pilots licensed, and many have been so inspected.

NINTH SUPERVISING DISTRICT.

Eighty-two steamers, carrying passengers, have been inspected in this district since the date of the last annual report, the aggregate tonnage amounting to 46,142 tons. In making the above inspection one boiler gave way, (at Buffalo, New York,) under the hydrostatic test. Upon examination, several stay-braces were found broken, which, on being replaced, the boiler stood the required test.

Forty-seven original licenses and two hundred and thirty-two renewals of licenses of pilots; also twenty-five original licenses and one hundred and ninety-two renewals of licenses to engineers, have been issued by the various local boards of inspectors in this district since the date of the last report.

Several collisions have occurred, during the time referred to, to licensed steamers belonging in this district, and sail vessels navigating the lakes; in no instance, however, of a serious character, no loss of life nor bodily injury having been sustained, by either passengers or crew, upon the steamers and vessels so colliding.

The screw steamer Jefferson, bound from Cleveland, Ohio, to Ogdensburg, New York, in April last, stranded upon the rocks near Port Colburn, Canada West, during a fog, and was obliged to throw overboard a portion of the cargo in order to save the vessel. The value of property lost in this instance was $4,945. No loss of life, nor injury to passengers or crew, attended this disaster.

Three steamers licensed to carry passengers, and belonging in this district, have been totally lost since the date of last report, one of which, the steamer

North Star, was burned by incendiary, in February, 1862, while lying up for the winter. The value of property lost was $40,000. The others were the screw steamers Pocahontas and Euphrates—both ships wrecked—the former upon Long Point, Canada West, and the latter upon the bar at the entrance to Sandusky bay. The loss of property in these instances was about $50,000; no loss of life nor injury to passengers or crew, in either case, attending these disasters.

The above constitute the only casualties that have come to the knowledge of the several local boards in this district, or to the supervising inspector.

In addition to the loss of the steamers above named, the steamers Western Metropolis and City of Buffalo, heretofore inspected in this district, and operated in connexion with the railroads, have been withdrawn from service, their machinery and equipments taken out, and the hulls converted into barges for the lumber trade.

Nine new screw steamers, (one of iron,) constructed with reference to carrying passengers and freight, have been inspected in this district, and put in commission since the date of last report. The iron steamer Merchant, among the number above referred to, is worthy of special notice as inaugurating a new era in the ship-building for merchant service upon the northern and western lakes.

With this report will be found the usual statement, exhibiting, in a tabular form, the duty performed by the local and other inspectors during the past year, together with causes of the various disasters to steam vessels within the several districts, and which is of usual interest.

Very respectfully,

JOHN SHALLCROSS,
President of the Board.
JAMES N. MULLER, Sr.,
Secretary.

Hon. SALMON P. CHASE,
Secretary of the Treasury.

No. 6.—*Statement showing the present liabilities of the United States to Indian tribes, under stipulations of treaties, &c.*

Names of tribes.	Descriptions of annuities, stipulations, &c.	References to laws; Statutes at Large.	Number of instalments yet unappropriated, explanations, remarks, &c.	Annual amount necessary to meet stipulations, indefinite as to time, now allowed, but liable to be discontinued.	Aggregate of future appropriations that will be required during a limited number of years to pay limited annuities that may expire; amount incidentally necessary to effect the payment.	Amount of annual liabilities of a permanent character.	Am't held in trust by the U. S. on which five per cent. is annually paid; said amounts which, invested at five per cent., annually produce the principal sum annexed.
Blackfoot nation......	Purchase of goods, provisions, and other useful articles, &c.; 9th article treaty October 17, 1855.	Vol. 11, page 659....	Ten instalments of $20,000, three instalments to be appropriated.	....	$60,000 00	....	....
Comanches, Kinways, and Apaches of the Arkansas river.	For purchase of goods, provisions, and agricultural implements; 6th article treaty July 27, 1853.	Vol. 10, page 1014....	Ten instalments of $18,000, one unappropriated.	....	18,000 00	....	....
Do......	For transportation of goods, &c.......	.......do.	Transportation for one year at $7,000...	....	7,000 00	....	....
Chippewas of Lake Superior.	For money, goods, support of schools, provisions, two carpenters, and tobacco; compare 4th article treaty October 4, 1842, and 8th article treaty September 30, 1854.	Vol. 7, page 592, and vol. 10, page 1111.	Twenty-five instalments, four yet to be appropriated.	....	75,040 34	....	....
Do.............	Twenty instalments in coin, goods, implements, &c., and for education; 4th article treaty September 30, 1854.	Vol. 10, page 11.....	Twenty instalments of $19,000 each, twelve yet unappropriated.	....	228,000 00	....	....
Do.............	Twenty instalments for six smiths and assistants and for iron and steel; 2d and 5th articles treaty Sept. 30, 1854.	Vol. 10, page 1109, and vol. 10, page 1111.	Twenty instalments, estimated at $6,300 each, twelve yet unpaid.	....	75,600 00	....	....
Do............	Twenty instalments for the seventh smith, &c.	.......do.	Twenty instalments, estimated at $1,060 each, fourteen yet unappropriated.	....	14,840 00	....	....
Do.............	For support of a smith, assistant, and shop, and pay of two farmers during the pleasure of the President; 12th article treaty.	Vol. 10, page 1119....	Estimated at $2,960 per annum	$2,960 00	....	....	....
Chippewas of the Mississippi.	Money, goods, support of schools, provisions, and tobacco; compare 4th article treaty October 4, 1842, and 8th article treaty October 4, 1842, and 8th article treaty September 30, 1854.	Vol. 7, page 592, and vol. 10, page 1111.	Twenty-five instalments, four unexpended.	....	36,000 00	....	....
Do.............	Two farmers, two carpenters, and smiths and assistants, iron and steel; 4th article treaty October 4, 1842, and September 30, 1854.	.......do.	Twenty-five instalments, four unexpended, one-third payable to these Indians ($1,400) for four years.	....	5,600 00	....	....

......	Twenty instalments in money, $20,000 each.	Vol. 10, page 1167....	3d article treaty February 22, 1855, twelve unexpended.		240,000 00	
ewns, Pillagers, Lake Winnebaish.	Money, $10,666 67; goods, $8,000; and purposes of utility, $4,000; 3d article treaty February 22, 1855.	Vol. 10, page 1168....	Thirty instalments, twenty-two unappropriated.		498,666 74	
o............	For purposes of education; same article and treaty.	......do...........	Twenty instalments of $3,000 each, twelve unappropriated.		36,000 00	
o............	For support of smiths' shop; same article and treaty.	......do...........	Fifteen instalm'ts estimated at $2,120 each; seven unappropriated.		14,840 00	
aanws	Permanent annuity in goods..........	Vol. 1, page 619......	Act February 26, 1790, $3,000 per year.			$3,000 00	$60,000 00
wns, Menomo- Winnebagoes, New York Indi-a.	Education during the pleasure of Congress.	Vol. 7, page 304......	5th article treaty August 11, 1827....	1,500 00		
awas of Saginaw, n creek, and ck river.	Ten instalments in coin of $10,000 each; and for the support of smiths' shops ten years, $1,040 per year; same article, &c.	Vol. 11, page 634......	Three instalments yet to be appropriated, and two subsequent instalments of $18,000.		69,720 00	
aws............	Permanent annuities..............	Vol. 7, pages 99, 213, and 236.	2d article treaty Nov. 16, 1805, $3,000; 13th article treaty Oct 18, 1820; $800; 2d article treaty Jan. 20, 1825, $6,000.		9,600 00	192,000 00
o............	Provisions for smith, &c..........	Vol. 7, pages 219 and 236.	6th article treaty October 18, 1820, and 9th article treaty January 20, 1825, say $920.		920 00	18,400 00
o............	Interest on $500,000; articles 10 and 13 treaty June 22, 1855.	Vol. 11, pages 612 and 614.	Five per cent. for educational purposes		25,000 00	500,000 00
o............	Permanent annuities..............	Vol. 7, pages 36, 60, and 287.	4th article treaty August, 1790, $1,500; 2d article treaty June 16, 1803, $3,000; 4th article treaty January 24, 1826, $20,000.		24,500 00	490,000 00
o............	Smiths' shops, &c..............	Vol. 7, page 287......	8th article treaty January 24, 1826, say $1,110.		1,110 00	22,200 00
o............	Smiths, &c., two for twenty-seven years; treaties March 24, 1832, and August 7, 1856.	Vol. 7, page 368, &c..	One of twenty-seven instalments to be appropriated.		2,200 00	
o............	Wheelwright, permanent.	Vol. 7, page 287.....	8th article treaty January, 1826, $600..		600 00	12,000 00
o............	Thirty-three instalments for education; 13th article treaty March, 1832, and 4th article treaty January, 1845.	Vol. 7, page 368, and vol. 9, page 852.	Thirty-three instalments of $3,000 each; one yet unappropriated.		3,000 00	
o............	Twenty instalments for education; 4th article treaty January, 1845.	Vol. 9, page 852......	Twenty instalments of $3,000 each; one unappropriated.		3,000 00	
o............	Allowance during the pleasure of the President.	Vol. 7, pages 287 and 419.	5th article treaty February 14, 1833, and 8th article treaty January 24, 1826.	4,710 00		
o............	Interest on $200,000 held in trust; 6th article treaty August 7, 1856.	Vol. 11, pages 701 and 702.	Five per cent. for education		10,000 00	200,000 00
ares..........	Life annuities, &c., two chiefs........	Vol. 7, page 399.....	Treaties of 1818, 1829, and 1832........	200 00		
o............	Interest on $46,080, at five per centum	Vol. 7, page 327......	Resolution of the Senate January 19, 1838.		2,304 00	46,080 00
oles, (Florida In-s.)	Ten instalments for support of schools; 6th article treaty August 7, 1856.	Vol. 11, page 702	Five payments of $3,000 each..........		15,000 00	
o............	Ten instalments for agricultural assistance; same article and treaty.	...... do	Five payments of $2,000 each..........		10,000 00	

No. 6.—*Statement showing the present liabilities of the United States to Indian tribes, &c.*—Continued

Names of tribes.	Descriptions of annuities, stipulations, &c.	References to laws; Statutes at Large.	Number of instalments yet unappropriated, explanations, remarks, &c.	Amount necessary to meet stipulations, indefinite as to time, now allowed, but liable to be discontinued.	Aggregate of future appropriations that will be required during a limited number of years to pay limited annuities till they expire; amount incidentally necessary to effect the payment.	Amount of annual liabilities of a permanent character.	Am't held in trust by the U. S. on which five per cent. is annually paid, and amounts which, invested at five per cent., would produce the permanent annuities.
Seminoles, (Florida Indians.)	Ten instalments for support of smiths' and shops; same article and treaty.	Vol. 11, page 702.....	Five payments of $2,200.........		$11,000 00		
Do..............	Interest on $500,000, per 8th article treaty August 7, 1856.	......do	$25,000 annuities.............			$25,000 00	$500,000 00
Ioways..............	Interest on $57,000, being the balance of $157,500.	Vol. 7, page 558, and vol. 10, page 1071.	2d article treaty October 19, 1838, and 9th article treaty May 17, 1854.			2,875 00	57,000 00
Do..............	Interest on $200,000.., ...	Vol. 9, page 842.....	2d article treaty January 14, 1846.			10,000 00	200,000 00
Kickapoos..........	Interest on $100,000.........	Vol. 10, page 1079....	2d article treaty May 18, 1854....			5,000 00	100,000 00
Do..............	Graduated payments on $300,000..	......do	2d article treaty May 18, 1854, $129,000 heretofore appropriated. Due.		71,000 00		
Menomonees	Pay of miller for fifteen years	Vol. 9, page 953, and vol. 10, page 1065.	3d article treaty May 12, 1854, $9,000; $4,200 heretofore appropriated. Due.		4,800 00		
Do.............	Support of smiths' shops twelve years..	......do	Five instalments of $915 66 unappropriated.		4,583 30		
Do..............	Ten instalments of $20,000 each.....	Vol. 9, page 953....	4th article treaty 1848, three unappropriated.		60,000 00		
Do..............	Fifteen equal instalments, to pay $242,686; to commence in 1867.	Vol. 10, page 1065...	4th article treaty May 12, 1854, and Senate's amendment thereto.		242,686 00		
Miamies..............	Permanent provisions for smith's shop, &c., and miller.	Vol. 7, pages 191 and 464; and vol. 10, page 1093.	5th article treaty October 6, 1818; 5th article treaty October 23, 1834; and 4th article treaty June 5, 1854—say, $940 for shop and $600 for miller.			1,540 00	30,800 00
Do..............	Twenty instalments upon $200,000...	Vol. 10, page 1094...	$150,000 of said sum payable in twenty instalments of $7,500 each, seventeen unappropriated.		127,500 00		
Do..............	Interest on $50,000, at 5 per centum..	......do	3d article treaty June 5, 1854			2,500 00	50,000 00
Do..............	Interest on $221,257 86, in trust	......do	Senate's amendment to 4th article treaty of 1854.			11,062 89	221,257 86
Eel River Miamies....	Permanent annuities	Vol. 7, pages 51, 91, 114, and 116.	4th article treaty 1795; 3d article treaty 1805; and 3d article treaty September, 1809, aggregate.			1,100 00	22,000 00

tians ...... Puyallup, r tribes and Indians.	Presents to Indians	Vol. 9, page 975	10th article treaty September 9, 1849..	$5,000 00	....	....	....
	For payment of $30,000 in graduated payments.	Vol. 10, page 1133...	4th article treaty December 26, 1854 ; still unappropriated.	....	12,750 00	....	....
....	Pay of instructor, smith, physician, carpenter, &c., twenty years.	Vol. 10, page 1134...	10th article treaty December 26, 1854, estimated at $6,700 per year ; (twelve instalments yet to be appropriated.	....	80,400 00	....	....
....	Forty instalm'ts graduated, ($840,000,) extending for forty years.	Vol. 10, page 1044...	Eight instalments paid, (see 4th arti- cle treaty March 16, 1854,) to be appropriated.	....	570,000 00	....	....
....	Support of smiths' shops, miller, and farmer, ten years.	Vol. 10, page 1045....	8th article treaty, estimated $9,140 per year ; two years to be provided for.	....	4,280 00	....	....
Miscourins.	Forty instalm'ts graduated, ($385,000,) extending through forty years.	Vol. 10, page 1039....	4th article treaty March 15, 1854, esti- mated at $6,500 per year ; two years to be appropriated hereafter.	....	260,000 00	....	....
....	Support of smiths' shops, miller, and farmer, ten years.	Vol. 10, page 1040....	7th article treaty March 15, 1854, esti- mated at $3,940 per year, eight ap- propriated.	....	7,880 00	....	....
....	Interest on $69,120, at 5 per cent.....	Pamphlet copy Laws 1st session 36th Congress, page 51.	For educational purposes, (Senate's resolution of January 19, 1833.)	....	....	3,456 00	69,120 00
r Kansas....	Permanent annuities, their proportion of.	Vol. 7, pages 54, 105, 178, and 220.	4th article of treaty August 13, 1795 ; 4th and 5th articles of treaty September 17, 1818 ; 4th article treaty August 29, 1821 ; and 2d article treaty No- vember 17, 1807.	....	....	2,600 00	52,000 00
nd Chippe- ichigan.	Interest on $940,000, at 5 per cent.....	Vol. 7, page 497....	Resolution of Senate May 19, 1836, per year.	....	12,000 00	240,000 00
....	Education, $5,000; missions, $3,000; medicines, $300, during the pleasure of Congress.	Vol. 7, page 492....	See 4th article treaty March 28, 1836.	8,300 00	....	....	....
....	Three blacksmiths, &c.; one gun- smith, &c.; two farmers and assist- ants, during the pleasure of the Pre- sident.	Vol. 7, page 493...	See 7th article treaty of March 28, 1836, annually allowed since the expira- tion of the number of years named in treaty. Aggregate $6,440.	6,440 00	....	....	....
....	Ten equal instalments for education, $8,000 each.	Vol. 11, page 623...	2d article treaty July 31, 1855 ; three instalments yet unappropriated.	....	24,000 00	....	....
....	Support of four smiths' shops for ten years.	......do............	2d article treaty July 31, 1855 ; three instalments yet unappropriated of $4,250 each.	....	12,750 00	....	....
....	In part payment of $306,000, ...	...........'.......	Same article and treaty ; $10,000 for ten years; three appropriations yet to be made.	....	-30,000 00	....	....
....	$206,000 to be paid after ten years	Vol. 11, page 624...	Treaty July 31, 1855	....	206,000 00	....	....
....	Interest on $936,000 three years, being the principal sum remaining of the $306,000.	......do............	Interest on unpaid consideration to be paid as annuity, per 2d article treaty July 31, 1855.	....	33,400 00	....	....
....	Ten instalments of $3,500 each to be paid to the Grand River Ottowas.	......do.....	To be paid as per capita ; three instal- ments yet to be appropriated.	....	10,500 00	....	....
....	Agricultural implements, during the pleasure of the President.	Vol. 7, page 486.....	See 4th article treaty October 9, 1833..	1,000 00	....	....	....

Names of tribes.	Descriptions of annuities, stipulations, &c.	References to laws; Statutes at Large.	Number of instalments yet unappropriated, explanations, remarks, &c.	Annual amount necessary to meet stipulation- inerefinite as to time, now allowed, but liable to be discontinued.	Aggregate of future appropriations that will be required during a limited number of years to pay limited annuities till they expire; amounts which surely necessary to effect the payment.	Amount of annual liability of a permanent character.	Am't held in trust by the U. S. on which five per cent. is annually paid; and amount which invested at five per cent. would produce the permanent annuities.
Pawnees	Five instalments in goods, and such articles as may be necessary for them.	Vol. 11, page 729....	See 2d article treaty September 24, 1857; first payment of annuities of a permanent character, (being the second series.)			$30,000 00	
Do	For the support of two manual labor schools.	....do............	3d article treaty; annually. during the pleasure of the President.	$10,000 00			
Do	For pay of two teachers	..... do............	Same article and treaty; annual appropriation required.	1,200 00			
Do	For purchase of iron and steel, and other necessaries for same, during the pleasure of the President.		4th article treaty; annual appropriation.	500 00			
Do	For pay of two blacksmiths, one of whom to be a gunsmith and tinsmith.	......do......	4th article treaty; annual appropriation required.	1,200 00			
Do	For compensation of two strikers and apprentices.	......do....	.....do.............do..........	480 00			
Do	Ten instalments for farming utensils and stock.	......do............	4th article treaty; five appropriations remaining unpaid, at the pleasure of the President.		$6,000 00		
Do	For pay of farmer............	....do............	4th article treaty; annual appropriations required.	600 00			
Do	Ten instalments for pay of miller	......do	4th article treaty; five appropriations remaining at the discretion of the President.		3,600 00		
Do	Ten instalments for pay of an engineer	......do	Five appropriations yet required, at the discretion of the President, $1,200.		6,000 00		
Do	For compensation to apprentices to assist in working the mill.	......do	4th article treaty; annual appropriations required.		500 00		
Pottawatomies	Permanent annuity in money.	Vol. 7, pages 51, 114, 185, 317, 320, and vol. 9, page 855.	4th article treaty 1795, $1,000; 3d article treaty 1809, $500; 3d article treaty 1818, $2,500; 3d article treaty 1828, $2,000; 3d article treaty July, 1829, $16,000; 10th article treaty June, 1846, $300.			22,300 00	$446,000

o, ...	Life annuities to surviving chiefs	Vol. 7, page 379	3d article treaty October 16, 1832, $200; 3d article treaty September 26, 1833, $700.	900 00	....	....
Jo, ...	Education during the pleasure of Congress.	Vol. 7, pages 296, 318, 401.	3d article treaty October 16, 1826, 2d article treaty September 20, 1828, and 4th article treaty October 27, 1832, $5,000.	5,000 00	....	....
Jo, ...	Permanent provisions for three smiths.	Vol. 7, pages 318, 296, 321.	2d article treaty September 20, 1828; 3d article treaty October 16, 1826; 2d article treaty July 29, 1829; three shops, at $940 each per year, $2,820	....	....	2,820 00	56,400 00
o, ...	Permanent provisions for furnishing salt.	Vol. 7, pages 75, 296, 330.	3d article treaty 1803, 3d article treaty October, 1826, and 2d article treaty July 29, 1829—estimated, $500.	....	500 00	10,000 00
Jo, ...	Interest on $643,000, at 5 per cent....	Vol. 9, page 854	7th article treaty June, 1846, annual interest, $32,150.	....	32,150 00	643,000 00
awatomies of Huron	Permanent annuities	Vol. 7, page 106	2d article treaty Nov'ber 17, 1807, $400.	....	400 00	8,000 00
aws..........	Provisions for education, $1,000 per year, and for smith and farmer and smith shop during the pleasure of the President.	Vol. 7, page 625	3d article treaty May 13, 1833, $1,000 per year for education, and $1,660 for smith, farmer, &c., $2,660.	2,600 00	....	....
e River	Sixteen instalments of $2,500 each....	Vol. 10, page 1019...	3d article treaty September 10, 1853, seven instalments unappropriated.	....	17,500 00	....
a, Scoton, and ppua Indians.	$2,000 annually for fifteen years	Vol. 10, page 1122 ...	3d article treaty November 18, 1854, seven instalments yet to be appropriated.	....	14,000 00	....
Do, ...	Support of schools and farmers fifteen years.	Vol. 10, page 1193...	Same treaty, 5th article, estimated for schools, $1,000; farmers, $1,000; seven appropriations due.	....	15,400 00	... ..
Do, ...	Support of physicians, medicines, &c., ten instalments.	Vol. 10, page 1123...	Two instalments yet due of $1,500 each.	....	3,000 00	... ...
Do, ...	Interest on $157,400..............	Vol. 10, page 544...	2d article treaty October 21, 1837......	....	7,870 00	157,400 00
and Foxes of Missri.	Permanent annuity	Vol. 7, page 85, ...	3d article treaty November, 1804	....	1,000 00	20,000 00
and Foxes of Missippi.						
Do, ...	Interest on $200,000, at 5 per cent....	Vol. 7, page 541	2d article treaty October, 1837.........	....	10,000 00	200,000 00
Do, ...	Interest on $800,000, at 5 per cent....	Vol. 7, page 596	2d article treaty October 11, 1842	....	40,000 00	800,000 00
oas	Permanent annuities.	Vol. 7, pages 161 and 170.	4th article treaty September 29, 1817, $500; 4th article treaty September 17, 1817, $500.	....	1,000 00	20,000 00
Do, ...	Provisions for smith and millers during the pleasure of the President.	Vol 7, page 349........	4th article treaty February 28, 1831—say $1,660.	1,660 00	.	.
cas of New York.	Permanent annuity	Vol. 4, page 442	Act February 19, 1831 ..... $6,000 00			
Do, ...	Interest on $7,500	Vol. 9, page 35	Act June 27, 1846 ...... 2,789 00			
Do, ...	Interest on $43,050, transferred from the Ontario Bank to the treasury of the United States.	.......do..........	Act June 27, 1846 ...... 2,152 50	....	11,902 50	238,050 00
eas and Shawnees	Permanent annuity	Vol. 7, page 179	4th article treaty September 17, 1818	....	1,000 00	20,000 00
Do, ...	Provisions for support of smith and smiths' shops during the pleasure of the President.	Vol. 7, page 353	4th article treaty July 20, 1831........	1,660 00		

Names of tribes	Descriptions of annuities, stipulations, &c.	References to laws; Statutes at Large.	Number of instalments yet unappropriated, explanations, remarks, &c.	Amount necessary to meet stipulations, indefinite as to time, now allowed, but liable to be discontinued.	Aggregate of future appropriations that will be required during a limited number of years to pay limited annuities—till the expiration whereof periodically necessary to effect the payment.	Amount of annual liabilities of a permanent character.	Am't held in trust by the U.S. on which five per cent. is annually paid; and amount which, invested at five per cent., would produce the permanent annuities.
Shawnees	Permanent annuities for education	Vol. 7, pages 51 and 161, and vol. 10, page 1065.	4th article treaty August 3, 1795; 4th article treaty September 29, 1817; and 3d article treaty May 10, 1854.			$5,000 00	$100,000 00
Do	Interest on $40,000	do	3d article treaty May 10, 1854			2,000 00	40,000 00
Six Nations of New York.	Permanent annuity in clothing, &c	Vol. 7, page 46	6th article treaty November 11, 1794, $4,500.			4,500 00	90,000 00
Sioux of the Mississippi.	Interest on $300,000	Vol. 7, page 539	2d article treaty September 29, 1837			15,000 00	300,000 00
Do	Fifty instalments of interest on $112,000, being ten cents per acre for reservation	Vol. 10, page 951	Senate's amendment to 3d article; thirty-eight instalments to be provided for, of $5,600 each.		$212,800 00		
Do	Fifty instalments of interest on $1,360,000, at 5 per centum.	Vol. 10, page 950	4th article treaty July 23, 1851, $68,000 per annum; thirty-eight instalments to be provided for.		2,584,000 00		
Do	Fifty instalments of interest on $1,100,000.	Vol. 10, page 955	4th article treaty August 5, 1851, $58,000 per annum; thirty-eight instalments yet to be appropriated.		2,204,000 00		
Do	Fifty instalments of interest on $59,000.	do	Treaty August 5, 1851; thirty-eight in-		131,100 00		

	Support of physician, fifteen years...	...do...	6th article treaty, estimated at $2,000 per year; seven instalments yet to be appropriated.		14,000 00		
	Support of smith and shop, and farmer, ten years.		6th article treaty, estimated at $1,500 per year; two instalments yet unappropriated.		3,000 00		
nette Valley s.	Twenty instalments, graduated payments.	Vol. 10, page 1144....	2d article treaty January 22, 1855; twelve instalments yet to be appropriated under the direction of the President.		76,000 00		
ibagoes	Interest on $1,100,000	Vol. 7, page 546....	4th article treaty November, 1837			25,000 00	1,100,000 00
o...........	Thirty instalments of interest on $85,000.	Vol. 9, page 879....	4th article treaty October 13, 1838, $4,250 per year; fourteen instalments to be provided for.		59,500 00		
s..............	Five instalments of $12,000 each for beneficial objects.	Pamphlet copy Laws 1st session 36th Congress, page 67.	Two instalments to be appropriated..		24,000 00		
o..............	Ten instalments for manual labor schools.	......do...........	Seven instalments of $5,000 each to be provided for.		35,000 00		
o..............	Ten instalments, during the pleasure of the President, for aid in agricultural and mechanical pursuits.	......do...........	Seven instalments of 7,500 each to be provided.		52,500 00		
ish and other d tribes in Washon Territory.	Por $150,000 in graduated payments, under the direction of the President, in twenty instalments.	Pamphlet copy Laws 1st session 36th Congress, page 3.	Seventeen instalments to be provided for.		111,000 00		
o..............	Twenty instalments for an agricultural school and teachers.	Pamphlet copy Laws 1st session 36th Congress, page 3.	Seventeen instalments yet to be provided for, estimated at $3,000 a year.		51,000 00		
o..............	Twenty instalments for smith and carpenter shop, and tools.	......do...........	Seventeen instalments yet to be provided for, estimated at $500 per year.		8,500 00		
o..............	Twenty instalments, blacksmith, carpenter, farmer, and physician.	......do...........	Seventeen instalments yet to be appropriated, estimated at $4,600 each year.		78,200 00		
h tribe.	For beneficial objects $30,000, under the direction of the President.	Pamphlet copy Laws 1st session 39th Congress, page 14.	Seventeen instalments yet to be appropriated, in graduated payments, per 5th article treaty.		22,000 00		
o.	Twenty instalments for an agricultural and industrial school and teachers.	Pamphlet copy Laws 1st session 36th Congress, page 15.	Seventeen instalments yet unappropriated, estimated at $2,500 per year.		42,500 00		
o.	Twenty instalments for smith, carpenter, shop and tools.	......do...........	Seventeen instalments yet unappropriated, estimated at $500 each year.		8,500 00		
o.	Twenty instalments for blacksmith, carpenter, farmer, and physician.	......do...........	Seventeen instalments yet unappropriated, estimated amount necessary each year $4,600.		78,200 00		
Walla, Cayuse, & Umatilla tribes.	For beneficial objects $100,000, to be expended under the direction of the President.	Pamphlet copy Laws 1st session 36th Congress, page 20.	Seventeen instalments in graduated payments.		76,000 00		
o.	For two millers, one farmer, one superintendent of farming operations, two school teachers, one blacksmith, one wagon and plough maker, and one carpenter and joiner.	......do...........	Seventeen instalments to be provided for, estimated at $11,200 each year.		190,400 00		

Names of tribes.	Descriptions of annuities, stipulations, &c.	References to laws; Statutes at Large.	Number of instalments yet unappropriated, explanations, remarks, &c.	Annual amount necessary to meet stipulations, indefinite as to time, now allowed, but liable to be discontinued.	Aggregate of future appropriations that will be required during a limited number of years to pay limited annuities till they expire, amounts incidentally necessary to effect the payment.	Amount of annual liabilities of a permanent character.	Am't held in trust by the U. S. on which five per cent. is annually paid; and amounts which, at five per cent., would produce the permanent annuities.
Walla-Walla, Cayuse, and Umatilla tribes.	Twenty instalments for mill fixtures, tools, medicines, books, stationery, furniture, &c.	Pamphlet copy Laws, 1st session 36th Congress, page 21.	Seventeen instalments of appropriations yet due of $3,000 each.	....	$51,000 00	....	....
Do..............	Twenty instalments of $500, for each of the head chiefs of these bands.	......do.............	Seventeen instalments yet due.......	....	25,500 00	....	....
Do..............	Twenty instalments for salary of son of Piu-piu-mox-mox.	......do.............	Seventeen instalments yet due of $100 each.	....	1,700 00	....	....
Yakama nation	For $200,000 for beneficial objects, under direction of the President, in twenty-one instalments, in graduated payments.	Pamphlet copy Laws, 1st session 36th Congress, page 27.	Seventeen instalments to be provided for.	....	110,000 00	....	....
Do..............	Support of two schools, one of which to be an agricultural and industrial school, keeping them in repair, and providing furniture, books, and stationery.	......do........	Twenty instalments, three appropriated, seventeen yet to be provided, estimated at $500.	....	8,500 00	....	....
Do..............	For one superintendent of teaching and two teachers twenty years.	.....do.............	Seventeen instalments yet to be appropriated, estimated at $3,200.	....	54,400 00	....	....
Do..............	For one superintendent of farming and two farmers, two millers, two blacksmiths, one tinner, one gunsmith, one carpenter, and one wagon and plough maker, for twenty years.	......do............	Seventeen instalments yet to be appropriated, estimated at $9,400.	....	159,800 00	....	....
Do..............	Twenty instalments keeping in repair grist and saw mill, and furnishing the necessary tools therefor.	......do............	Seventeen instalments yet to be provided for, estimated at $500 each.	....	8,500 00	....	....
Do..............	Twenty instalments for keeping in repair hospital and furnishing medicines, &c.	......do............	Seventeen instalments yet unappropriated, estimated at $300 each.	....	5,100 00	....	....
Do..............	Twenty instalments for pay of physician.	......do............	Seventeen instalments yet to be appropriated, estimated at $1,400.	....	23,800 00	....	....
Do..............	Twenty instalments for keeping in repair buildings for employés.	......do............	Seventeen instalments yet due of $300.	....	5,100 00	....	....

....	For salary of head chief for twenty years.	......do............	Seventeen instalments unappropriated of $500 each.	....	8,500 00
ds.....,......	For beneficial objects $900,000, under the direction of the President, in graduated payments, extending for twenty-one years.	Pamphlet copy Laws, 1st session 36th Congress, page 38.	Seventeen instalments yet to be appropriated.	....	110,000 00
....	For support of two schools, one of which to be an agricultural and industrial school, keeping them in repair, and providing furniture, books, and stationery.	......do............	Seventeen instalments yet to be appropriated, estimated at $500 each year.	....	8,500 00
,.............	Twenty instalments for one superintendent of teaching and two teachers.	......do............	Seventeen instalments to be appropriated, estimated at $3,200 each.	....	54,400 00
....	Twenty instalments for one superintendent of farming and two farmers, two millers, two blacksmiths, one tinner, one gunsmith, one carpenter, and one wagon and plough maker.	Pamphlet copy Laws 1st session 36th Congress, page 39.	Seventeen instalments yet to be appropriated, estimated at $9,400 each year.	....	159,800 00
....	Twenty instalments for keeping in repair grist and saw mill, and furnishing the necessary tools therefor.	......do............	Seventeen instalments yet to be appropriated, estimated at $500 each year.	....	8,500 00
,.............	Twenty instalments for keeping in repair hospital and furnishing necessary medicines, &c.	......do............	Seventeen instalments yet unappropriated, estimated at $300 each year.	....	5,100 00
....	Twenty instalments for pay of physician.	......do..........	Seventeen instalments yet due, estimated at $1,400 each.	....	26,800 00
....	Twenty instalments for keeping in repair buildings for employés.	......do............	Seventeen instalments yet due, estimated at $300 each.	....	5,100 00
,.............	Twenty instalments for salary of head chief.	......do............	Seventeen instalments yet to be appropriated, of $500.	....	8,500 00
and other rated tribes.	Twenty instalments for beneficial objects, under the direction of the President, $100,000.	Pamphlet copy Laws 1st session 36th Congress, page 50.	Sixteen instalments yet to be appropriated, in graduated payments.	....	66,000 00
,.............	For the support of an agricultural and industrial school, providing necessary furniture, books, stationery, &c.	Pamphlet copy Laws 1st session 36th Congress, page 51.	Seventeen instalments yet to be appropriated, estimated at $300.	....	5,100 00
....	For employment of suitable instructors therefor.	......do............	Seventeen instalments yet to be appropriated, $1,300.	....	23,800 00
....	For keeping in repair blacksmith shop, one carpenter's shop, one wagon and plough maker's shop, and furnishing tools therefor.	......do............	Seventeen instalments yet to be appropriated, $500.	....	8,500 00
,....	For two farmers, two millers, one blacksmith, one gunsmith, one tinner, one carpenter and joiner, and one wagon and plough maker.	......do............	Seventeen appropriations yet due, of $7,400 each.	....	125,800 00
....	For keeping in repair flouring and saw mill, and supplying the necessary fixtures.	......do............	Seventeen appropriations yet to be made, estimated at $500 each year.	....	8,500 00
....	For keeping in repair hospital, and furnishing the necessary medicines, &c.	......do............	Seventeen instalments yet to be appropriated, estimated value each year $300.	....	5,100 00

Names of tribes.	Descriptions of annuities, stipulations, &c.	References to laws; Statutes at Large.	Number of instalments yet unappropriated, explanations, remarks, &c.	Amount amount necessary to meet stipulations, indefinite as to time, now allowed, but liable to be discontinued.	Aggregate of future appropriations that will be required during a limited number of years to pay limited annuities till they expire, amounts incidentally necessary to effect the payment.	Amount of annual liabilities of a permanent character.	Am't held in trust by the U.S. on which five per cent. is annually paid, and amounts which, invested at five per cent., would produce the...
Flathead and other confederated tribes.	For pay of physician twenty years....	Pamphlet copy Laws 1st session 36th Congress, page 51.	Seventeen instalments yet due, estimated at $1,400.	....	$23,800 00	....	....
Do.............	For keeping in repair the buildings of employes, &c., for twenty years.	......do..............	Seventeen instalments yet to be made, of $300 each.	....	5,100 00	....	....
Do.............	For $500 per annum for twenty years for each of the head chiefs.	......do.	Seventeen instalments yet to be appropriated, estima'd at $1,500 each year.	....	25,500 00	....	....
Confederated tribes and bands of Indians in Middle Oregon.	For beneficial objects, under the direction of the President, $100,000 in graduated payments.	Pamphlet copy Laws 1st session 36th Congress, page 39.	Seventeen instalments yet to be appropriated.	....	66,000 00	....	....
Do.............	For farmer, blacksmith, and wagon and plough maker, for the term of fifteen years.	......do.	Twelve instalments yet to be appropriated, estimated at $3,500 each year.	....	42,000 00	....	....
Do.............	For physician, sawyer, miller, superintendent of farming, and school teacher, fifteen years.	......do.	Twelve instalments yet to be appropriated, estimated at $5,600 each year.	....	67,200 00	....	....
Do.............	Salary of the head chief of the confederated band, twenty years.	......do.	Seventeen instalments yet to be appropriated.	....	8,500 00	....	....
Moici Indians	For keeping in repair saw and flouring mills and furnishing suitable persons to attend the same, for a period of ten years.	Pamphlet copy Laws 1st session 36th Congress, page 55.	Seven instalments yet due, estimated at $1,500 each.	....	10,500 00	....	....
Do.............	For iron and steel and other materials for the smith shop and the shop provided for in treaty of November 29, 1854, and for the pay of the services of the necessary mechanics, for five years.	......do.	Two instalm'ts yet to be appropriated, estimated at $1,800 each year.	....	3,600 00	....	....
Do.............	For pay of teacher to manual labor school, and for subsistence of pupils and necessary supplies.	......do.	Amount necessary during the pleasure of the President.	$3,000 00	....	....	....
Do.............	For carpenter and joiner to aid in erecting buildings, making furniture, &c.	......do.	Seven instalments yet to be appropriated, estimated at $2,000 each year.	....	14,000 00	....	....

Do............	For pay of an additional farmer, five years.	......do.............	Two instalments, of $800 each, yet to be appropriated.	....	1,600 00	....	....
al and Quil-leh-ndians.	For $35,000 to be expended for beneficial objects, under the direction of the President.	Pamphlet copy Laws 1st session 36th Congress, page 46.	Seventeen instalments in graduated payments yet to be provided for, amounting to.	....	18,500 00	....	....
Do......	For support of an agricultural and industrial school, and for the employment of suitable instruction, for the term of twenty years.	Pamphlet copy Laws 1st session 36th Congress, page 47.	Seventeen instalments yet to be appropriated, estimated at $2,500 each year.	....	42,500 00	....	....
Do.......	For twenty instalments for the support of a smith and carpenter's shop and tools.	......do.............	Seventeen instalments yet to be appropriated, estimated at $500 each year.	....	8,500 00	....	....
Do.............	For the employment of blacksmith, carpenter, farmer, and physician, for twenty years.	......do.............	Seventeen instalments yet to be appropriated, estimated at $4,600 each year.	....	78,200 00	....	....
ams	Twenty instalments in graduated payments, under the direction of the President, for $60,000.	Pamphlet copy Laws 1st session 36th Congress, page 8.	Seventeen payments yet to be provided for.	....	44,000 00	....	....
Do.............	Twenty instalments for support of an agricultural and industrial school and for teachers.	Pamphlet copy Laws 1st session 36th Congress, page 9.	Seventeen instalments yet to be appropriated, estimated at $2,500 each.	....	42,500 00	....	....
Do.............	Twenty years employment of blacksmith, carpenter, farmer, and physician.	......do.............	Seventeen instalments yet to be appropriated, estimated at $4,600 each.	....	78,200 00	....	....
toes and Che-e Indians of Jpper Arkansas	For $450,000 in fifteen equal annual instalments, under the direction of the Secretary of the Interior, of $30,000 each.	Pamphlet copy Laws 2d session 37th Congress, page 229.	Thirteen instalments yet to be appropriated of $30,000 each.	....	390,000 00	....	....
Do.............	For five instalments providing for sawing timber and grinding grain, mechanics' shops and tools, and building purposes for interpreter, engineer, miller, farmer, &c.	......do.............	Five instalments to be provided for, estimated at $5,000.	....	25,000 00	....	....
Do.............	For transportation and necessary expenses of the delivery of annuity goods and provisions.	......do.............	5th article treaty February 18, 1861; thirteen instalments yet to be appropriated, estimated at $5,000 each.	....	65,000 00	....	....
a Indians of chard's Fork Roche de Bœuf.	The sum of $18,000, to be paid in 1862, and in four equal annual instalments thereafter, as near as may be, all the money which the United States holds or may hold for them, with accruing interest on all moneys remaining within two years.	......do.............	Treaty June 24, 1862, 4th article, providing for the payment of $18,000 in 1862; same treaty, June 24, 1862, the latter clause of the 4th article, providing for the remaining four payments, being indefinite as to amount.		18,000 00	....	....
Do.............	For $15,000, providing for the debts of the tribes, to be approved by the Secretary of the Interior.	......do.............	Treaty June 24, 1862, 5th article; this amount to be appropriated.	....	15,000 00	....	....
Do.........?..	Providing for claims already approved by the Secretary of the Interior, $13,005 95, and also for other claims for damages within two years, such claims not to exceed $3,500.	......do.............	10th article treaty June 24, 1862; the sum required, in compliance with the treaty, to be provided within two years.	57,670 00	16,505 95		
				57,670 00	11,870,891 23	$366,510 39	$7,331,707 86

REPORT ON THE FINANCES.

No. 7.

Gold and silver coinage at the mint of the United States in the several years from its establishment, in 1792, and including the coinage of the branch mints and the assay office, (New York,) from their organization to June 30, 1861.

Years.	Gold.	Silver.	Aggregate.
1793 to 1795	$71,485 00	$370,683 80	$444,168 80
1796	102,727 50	79,077 50	181,805 00
1797	103,422 50	12,591 45	116,013 95
1798	205,610 00	330,291 00	535,901 00
1799	213,285 00	423,515 00	636,800 00
1800	317,760 00	224,296 00	542,056 00
1801	422,570 00	74,758 00	497,328 00
1802	423,310 00	58,343 00	481,653 00
1803	258,377 50	87,118 00	345,495 50
1804	258,642 50	100,340 50	358,983 00
1805	170,367 50	149,368 50	319,736 00
1806	324,505 00	471,319 00	795,824 00
1807	437,495 00	597,448 75	1,034,943 75
1808	284,665 00	684,300 00	968,965 00
1809	169,375 00	707,376 00	876,751 00
1810	501,435 00	638,773 50	1,140,208 50
1811	497,905 00	608,340 00	1,106,245 00
1812	290,435 00	814,029 50	1,104,464 50
1813	477,140 00	620,951 50	1,098,091 50
1814	77,270 00	561,687 50	638,957 50
1815	3,175 00	17,308 00	20,483 00
1816	....	28,575 75	28,575 75
1817	....	607,783 50	607,783 50
1818	242,940 00	1,070,454 50	1,313,394 50
1819	258,615 00	1,140,000 00	1,398,615 00
1820	1,319,030 00	501,680 70	1,820,710 70
1821	189,325 00	825,762 45	1,015,087 45
1822	88,980 00	805,806 50	894,786 50
1823	72,425 00	895,550 00	967,975 00
1824	93,200 00	1,752,477 00	1,845,677 00
1825	156,385 00	1,564,583 00	1,720,968 00
1826	92,245 00	2,002,090 00	2,094,335 00
1827	131,565 00	2,869,200 00	3,000,765 00
1828	140,145 00	1,575,600 00	1,715,745 00
1829	295,717 50	1,994,578 00	2,290,295 50
1830	643,105 00	2,495,400 00	3,138,505 00
1831	714,270 00	3,175,600 00	3,889,870 00
1832	798,435 00	2,579,000 00	3,377,435 00
1833	978,550 00	2,769,000 00	3,737,550 00
1834	3,954,270 00	3,415,002 00	7,369,272 00
1835	2,186,175 00	3,443,003 00	5,629,178 00
1836	4,135,700 00	3,606,100 00	7,741,800 00
1837	1,148,305 00	2,096,010 00	3,244,315 00
1838	1,809,595 00	2,315,250 00	4,124,845 00
1839	1,375,700 00	2,098,636 00	3,474,396 00
1840	1,690,802 00	1,712,178 00	3,402,980 00
1841	1,102,007 50	1,115,875 00	2,217,972 50
1842	1,883,170 50	2,325,750 00	4,158,920 50
1843	8,302,787 50	3,722,250 00	12,025,037 50
1844	5,428,230 00	2,235,550 00	7,663,780 00
1845	3,756,447 50	1,873,200 00	5,629,647 50
1846	4,034,177 50	2,558,580 00	6,592,757 50
1847	20,221,385 00	2,374,450 00	22,595,835 00

Gold and silver coinage at the mint of the United States, &c.—Continued.

Years.	Gold.	Silver.	Aggregate.
1848	$3,775,512 50	$2,040,050 00	$5,815,562 50
1849	9,007,761 50	2,114,950 00	11,122,711 50
1850	31,981,738 50	1,866,100 00	33,847,838 50
1851	62,614,492 50	774,397 00	63,388,889 50
1852	56,846,187 50	999,410 00	57,845,597 50
1853	55,213,906 94	9,077,571 00	64,291,477 94
1854	52,094,595 47	8,619,270 00	60,713,865 47
1855 (to September 30) ..	41,166,557 03	2,893,745 00	44,060,302 03
1856 (to September 30) ..	58,936,893 41	5,347,070 49	64,283,963 90
1857 (to September 30) ..	48,437,964 31	3,375,608 01	51,813,572 32
1858 (to September 30) ..	51,841,433 91	9,028,531 44	60,869,965 35
1859 (to June 30)	19,777,418 70	4,699,223 95	24,476,642 65
1860 (to June 30)	23,447,283 35	3,250,636 26	26,697,919 61
1861 (to June 30)	80,708,400 64	2,883,706 94	83,592,107 58
1862 (to June 30)	61,676,576 55	3,231,081 51	64,907,658 06
Total.............	730,331,516 21	131,368,263 50	861,699,779 71

General result of all receipts and disposal of merchandise within the United States during the fiscal year ending June 30, 1862.

| | 1861. | | | | | | | |
| | July. | | August. | | September. | | October. | |
	Amount.	Duty.	'Amount.	Duty.	Amount.	Duty.	Amount.	Duty.
1. Value of merchandise in warehouse on the first of each month	*$31,769,579 89	*$7,275,630 89	$23,860,834 80	$5,822,077 26	$23,453,392 66	$5,891,597 80	$21,271,782 83	$5,521,708 41
2. Value of merchandise received in warehouse from foreign ports during each month	2,493,669 61	698,723 16	3,234,230 32	946,402 54	1,974,649 33	693,073 54	2,666,366 65	921,062 82
3. Value of merchandise received in warehouse transported from other ports during each month	139,863 00	40,893 20	134,605 40	33,198 44	221,954 00	76,200 71	248,350 60	76,498 39
4. Value of dutiable merchandise entered for consumption from foreign ports during each month	3,937,387 59	625,358 70	4,107,108 51	1,113,814 85	3,769,482 96	1,094,920 15	4,592,967 18	1,299,857 26
5. Value of free merchandise entered for consumption from foreign ports during each month	13,099,446 55	....	4,732,465 52	....	4,362,255 58	....	8,373,866 94	....
6. Value of merchandise entered for consumption from warehouse during each month	9,934,649 10	2,053,850 90	3,176,796 22	760,829 31	3,635,733 08	894,201 31	3,211,638 77	790,502 98
7. Value of merchandise entered for transportation to other ports during each month	186,378 15	52,072 66	279,660 00	82,777 68	247,380 03	78,865 21	285,900 65	81,139 06
8. Value of merchandise entered for exportation from warehouse during each month	421,290 45	87,446 45	319,821 64	88,473 45	505,417 07	166,189 22	584,649 26	174,290 15
9. Value of merchandise in warehouse at the close of each month	23,860,834 80	5,822,077 26	23,453,392 66	5,891,597 80	21,271,782 83	5,521,708 41	20,104,300 40	5,467,277 43
10. Value of merchandise in transitu at the close of each month	754,996 00	237,906 36	839,067 00	267,908 73	945,980 00	307,321 52	797,455 00	359,484 16

* Returns from insurrectionary ports not included, as in report of June, 1861.

| | 1861. | | | | 1862. | | | |
| | November. | | December. | | January. | | February. | |
	Amount.	Duty.	Amount.	Duty.	Amount.	Duty.	Amount.	Duty.
Value of merchandise in warehouse on the first of each month	$20,104,300 40	$5,467,277 43	$19,902,959 09	$5,809,709 63	$16,944,250 71	$5,103,739 46	$14,800,907 67	$4,946,700 25
Value of merchandise received in warehouse from foreign ports during each month	2,915,464 78	1,209,644 70	2,864,366 49	1,085,264 96	3,681,399 62	1,606,436 53	4,356,045 00	1,906,827 69
Value of merchandise received in warehouse transported from other ports during each month	318,238 57	85,313 28	203,689 00	53,951 27	155,877 00	56,960 76	357,877 15	110,793 13
Value of dutiable merchandise entered for consumption from foreign ports during each month	5,600,858 70	1,614,300 77	5,961,356 21	1,704,119 75	8,078,966 10	2,390,345 06	8,978,550 80	2,922,943 55
Value of free merchandise entered for consumption from foreign ports during each month	4,321,481 04	....	4,854,301 01	....	4,149,006 53	....	5,908,501 00	....
Value of merchandise entered for consumption during each month	2,696,122 14	732,048 28	5,333,775 27	1,542,742 51	5,454,991 21	1,637,363 21	4,451,415 05	1,605,391 60
Value of merchandise entered for transportation to other ports during each month	239,887 95	79,553 90	295,397 30	74,781 68	195,853 62	67,276 18	313,580 00	104,852 95
Value of merchandise entered for exportation from warehouse during each month	499,054 57	148,113 60	397,388 21	136,968 19	330,774 82	115,017 15	404,625 00	156,438 53
Value of merchandise in warehouse at the close of each month	19,909,959 09	5,809,709 63	16,944,250 71	5,103,709 48	14,800,907 67	4,946,700 25	14,345,300 77	5,187,737 99
Value of merchandise in transitu at the close of each month	750,374 13	253,191 36	751,243 14	259,468 07	763,603 00	272,169 39	874,850 95	302,415 11

No. 7½.—*General result of all receipts and disposal of merchandise within the United States, &c.*—Continued.

	1862.							
	March.		April.		May.		June.	
	Amount.	Duty.	Amount.	Duty.	Amount.	Duty.	Amount.	Duty.
1. Value of merchandise in warehouse on the first of each month	$14,346,309 77	$5,187,737 99	$15,958,117 56	$5,735,977 66	$15,859,472 35	$5,702,768 57	$14,971,653 05	$6,039,318
2. Value of merchandise received in warehouse from foreign ports during each month	6,356,243 38	2,512,616 62	5,445,020 49	2,681,481 38	6,236,939 78	3,657,366 96	5,436,262 15	·2,776,754
3. Value of merchandise received in warehouse transported from other ports during each month	170,251 70	60,355 89	318,013 40	136,992 72	336,425 21	168,763 54	353,593 00	203,883
4. Value of dutiable merchandise entered for consumption from foreign ports during each month	12,198,353 63	4,063,577 47	6,390,828 78	2,835,022 23	10,917,663 98	3,550,368 57	9,186,683 64	3,008,18
5. Value of free merchandise entered for consumption from foreign ports during each month	4,973,418 00	....	5,079,041 30	....	4,357,395 99	....	2,833,821 60	....
6. Value of merchandise entered for consumption from warehouse during each month	3,987,871 77	1,691,723 03	5,380,183 60	2,517,369 24	5,271,476 75	2,842,899 82	6,686,138 97	3,164,88
7. Value of merchandise entered for transportation to other ports during each month	209,418 19	93,060 66	204,238 50	83,725 83	271,693 78	143,162 20	185,794 25	83,736
8. Value of merchandise entered for exportation from warehouse during each month	667,647 33	309,049 15	1,067,857 00	449,856 12	1,130,013 76	503,518 61	912,102 00	424,906
9. Value of merchandise in warehouse at the close of each month	15,958,117 56	5,735,977 66	15,859,472 35	5,702,768 57	14,971,653 05	6,039,318 44	12,977,473 68	5,348,426
10. Value of merchandise in *transitu* at the close of each month	811,010 00	268,387 08	687,597 00	250,800 44	665,309 00	265,971 56	547,976 00	·227,483

No. 8.

SYNOPSIS

OF

THE RETURNS OF THE BANKS

IN THE

DIFFERENT STATES AT THE DATES ANNEXED.

Synopsis of the returns of the banks in the different States at the dates annexed.

State.	Date.	Number of banks and branches.	Capital.	Loans and discounts.	Stocks.	Real estate.	Other investments.	Due by other banks.	Notes of other banks.	Cash items.	Specie.	Circulation.	Deposits.	Due to other banks.	Other liabilities.
Maine............	Dec., 1854	71	$7,361,950	$13,181,908	$6,850	$119,694	....	$1,781,065	$539,974	....	$1,025,908	$5,891,815	$9,914,601	$172,628	$10,559
	Dec., 1855	75	7,399,793	13,060,956	....	113,679	....	1,396,430	464,561	....	753,085	5,077,948	2,011,038	218,978	104,173
	Jan., 1857	76	8,133,735	13,277,620	....	135,251	....	1,158,978	375,916	....	703,143	4,641,646	1,994,789	145,083	101,743
	Jan., 1858	70	7,614,200	11,910,945	....	135,363	....	875,709	945,191	....	615,441	3,964,397	1,742,959	139,204	76,069
	Jan., 1859	68	7,408,945	11,815,127	....	145,583	....	1,478,896	373,303	....	653,754	3,986,509	2,369,810	89,271	90,082
	Jan., 1860	68	7,505,890	12,654,794	..h.	161,199	....	1,019,909	290,204	....	670,979	4,140,718	2,411,092	103,309	87,165
	Jan., 1861	71	7,655,250	13,408,594	....	235,531	....	993,550	208,709	....	653,534	4,313,065	2,864,871	151,437	*606,951
	Jun., 1862	71	7,970,650	12,879,244	....	935,060	....	9,084,553	219,370	....	710,392	4,047,780	3,307,626	65,601	*639,918
New Hampshire ..	Dec., 1854	36	3,925,000	6,891,831	....	52,343	....	603,447	194,800	....	176,434	3,079,548	775,410	....	....
	Dec., 1855	46	4,419,300	8,037,427	....	56,519	....	789,963	241,383	....	226,411	3,589,482	958,474	....	....
	Dec., 1856	49	4,831,000	8,846,421	....	75,893	....	741,473	136,609	....	236,013	3,677,029	1,056,803	....	....
	Dec., 1857	52	5,041,000	7,389,813	....	82,000	....	625,169	156,132	....	275,933	9,086,939	875,789	....	....
	Dec., 1858	52	5,041,000	8,250,754	....	66,085	....	860,330	170,994	....	294,433	3,115,643	1,069,920	....	....
	Dec., 1859	52	5,016,000	8,591,688	....	72,919	....	776,173	161,994	....	255,978	3,271,183	1,187,991	....	....
	Dec., 1860	51	4,981,000	8,794,948	....	75,645	....	756,200	157,366	....	243,790	3,339,010	1,034,628	....	....
	Dec., 1861	59	5,031,000	8,368,941	....	76,253	....	907,440	203,822	....	318,196	2,994,408	1,376,853	....	....
Vermont........	Aug., 1854	40	3,975,856	5,579,951	140,884	136,115	$65,132	1,079,686	195,909	$34,677	195,680	3,079,709	745,170	15,715	979
	Aug., 1855	42	3,603,480	6,710,929	151,875	192,977	49,428	1,150,362	54,556	33,845	201,548	3,704,341	801,039	4,786	7,617
	Aug., 1856	41	3,856,946	7,302,951	114,589	135,966	52,681	1,145,104	43,146	28,440	208,858	3,970,790	797,535	7,946	....
	Aug., 1857	41	4,026,749	7,905,711	30,591	136,582	17,185	996,206	122,923	36,351	185,586	4,275,517	746,557	1,539	....
	Aug., 1858	41	4,082,415	6,592,992	108,500	202,360	70,954	701,545	41,780	209,605	178,556	3,691,147	615,674	5,441	1,443
	July, 1859	46	4,029,240	6,945,593	176,400	100,565	176,419	1,167,009	69,435	69,867	198,406	3,862,083	767,634	19,130	3,780
	Aug., 1860	43	3,873,643	6,748,500	190,372	174,730	168,662	1,499,535	58,558	105,577	185,870	3,784,678	814,693	15,049	....
	Aug., 1861	40	3,916,000	6,913,730	89,741	157,380	....	753,235	....	136,550	173,332	2,592,687	715,997	....	61,177
Massachusetts....	Aug., 1854	143	54,439,050	93,361,953	....	1,186,509	.....	8,325,662	5,325,594	....	3,826,493	24,803,788	18,783,410	6,930,098	563,313
	Aug., 1855	169	56,632,350	99,806,711	....	1,281,691	....	7,016,393	4,547,710	....	4,408,459	23,118,024	21,478,717	5,947,635	494,540
	Oct., 1856	172	58,908,800	101,132,792	....	1,436,392	....	7,574,791	5,248,319	....	4,555,571	26,364,313	23,437,358	4,807,801	931,888
	Oct., 1857	173	60,319,720	92,458,572	....	1,506,613	....	5,509,068	4,385,650	....	3,611,097	18,104,897	17,531,196	4,106,594	1,343,918
	Oct., 1858	174	61,819,625	101,502,947	....	1,584,584	....	9,187,945	4,993,491	....	11,119,715	20,639,438	30,538,153	7,654,204	1,527,853
	Oct., 1859	174	64,519,990	107,417,323	....	1,601,079	....	7,919,519	5,183,456	....	7,520,647	22,066,920	27,804,809	6,937,043	444,528
	Oct., 1860	176	64,519,990	107,417,323	....	1,601,072	....	7,919,531	5,128,549	....	7,539,647	20,945,820	27,804,609	6,937,040	441,388
	Oct., 1861	183	67,344,200	111,938,626	....	1,626,494	....	9,197,986	4,050,935	....	8,777,193	18,517,306	33,395,711	8,000,529	933,598

e Island	Sept.,	1854	87	17,511,189	25,239,304	111,988	262,164	35,409	933,619	880,794	....	312,608	5,035,073	2,772,367	1,046,658	329,495
	Sept.,	1855	92	18,683,892	26,365,458	131,079	353,092	70,285	1,949,302	1,157,251	....	385,767	5,404,104	2,914,598	1,192,449	357,530
	Dec.,	1856	98	20,275,898	28,679,343	108,539	478,652	70,133	1,935,322	1,281,756	....	548,348	5,501,900	3,141,657	1,475,921	659,703
	Dec.,	1857	93	20,334,777	28,823,152	148,129	527,787	50,760	1,410,675	860,778	....	570,650	3,192,661	2,510,108	1,861,204	381,402
	May,	1858	83	20,070,741	24,905,894	161,309	536,403	93,365	1,700,185	755,049	....	723,629	2,544,195	2,624,295	1,150,667	296,689
	Jan.,	1859	90	20,391,069	25,131,156	161,309	536,403	93,365	1,491,502	802,660	....	608,853	3,316,681	3,130,475	936,081	296,889
	Jan.,	1860	91	20,865,569	26,719,877	214,100	504,015	100,293	1,143,501	974,620	....	450,939	3,558,998	3,553,104	1,029,377	....
	Nov.,	1860	74	21,151,879	27,980,855	276,425	613,747	140,548	846,333	966,080	....	471,581	3,772,942	3,717,234	1,796,183	1,285,338
	Nov.,	1861	90	21,234,529	26,360,718	496,638	683,188	195,100	1,041,048	867,274	....	606,977	3,306,530	3,742,171	965,906	1,344,883
ecticut	April,	1854	63	15,597,892	28,999,201	1,298,877	386,210	584,592	2,905,068	459,502	996,991	1,397,361	11,219,866	3,910,160	1,008,855	1,022,940
	April,	1855	68	17,147,385	23,704,456	1,591,918	375,612	673,037	3,372,566	341,754	281,993	810,101	6,871,102	3,433,081	945,844	482,975
	April,	1856	71	18,913,378	28,511,149	1,916,630	433,132	488,138	3,434,975	367,310	945,949	1,006,493	9,197,762	4,690,535	875,987	911,456
	April,	1857	74	19,933,553	33,108,527	945,749	820,241	614,763	3,551,143	443,500	270,733	1,159,708	10,590,421	4,685,643	1,090,711	503,135
	April,	1858	78	20,917,164	26,789,430	938,755	1,085,179	877,000	2,584,819	273,281	262,595	915,544	5,360,947	4,184,910	814,910	893,155
	May,	1859	74	21,519,176	27,686,785	1,867,406	1,915,047	795,244	2,994,938	308,617	255,844	980,990	7,561,819	5,574,000	926,308	5,806
	April,	1860	74	21,606,997	30,518,090	1,104,343	929,817	832,928	9,904,963	373,853	262,065	950,753	7,702,436	5,506,507	1,166,728	153,916
	Jan.,	1862	73	21,794,937	27,086,326	2,828,612	1,331,519	123,261	4,359,577	404,953	433,322	1,329,855	6,918,616	6,142,754	964,752	296,434
York	Sept.,	1854	329	83,773,288	163,916,390	120,890,653	5,178,831	767,642	12,478,599	3,655,334	16,453,339	13,561,565	311,507,786	84,970,840	21,081,436	6,731,884
	Sept.,	1855	338	85,589,598	192,161,111	120,890,150	5,357,637	....	12,666,517	2,998,036	16,098,545	12,310,330	31,346,903	88,852,395	26,945,439	3,615,560
	Sept.,	1856	311	96,381,301	203,693,499	124,027,533	6,868,945	....	12,179,169	9,935,305	22,575,628	12,898,771	34,019,633	96,907,970	29,014,125	6,761,333
	Dec.,	1857	294	107,449,143	193,807,376	122,923,785	7,423,614	467,855	11,795,973	1,857,658	14,130,573	79,313,421	33,899,964	93,043,353	21,968,569	9,299,656
	March,	1858	296	109,587,702	170,438,240	122,894,677	7,681,994	....	10,803,512	1,705,537	16,152,746	35,071,074	29,710,158	93,738,858	27,718,077	5,993,940
	June,	1858	297	109,340,541	187,488,810	123,307,661	7,896,958	331,509	13,589,231	1,914,051	15,019,241	33,587,211	24,979,193	100,762,969	34,290,768	2,442,619
	Sept.,	1858	300	109,995,550	194,794,990	125,031,416	6,189,992	350,155	12,860,855	2,106,653	13,740,731	29,905,296	36,605,407	103,481,745	31,610,449	2,539,639
	Dec.,	1858	300	110,288,480	200,577,198	125,268,694	6,264,425	397,330	15,189,559	2,044,765	18,436,967	36,335,884	28,507,899	110,465,798	35,134,049	2,894,418
	Dec.,	1859	303	111,441,320	200,351,330	96,807,674	6,793,826	....	14,181,749	2,951,767	17,376,730	20,931,545	29,959,369	104,070,272	38,807,492	3,059,277
	Dec.,	1860	306	111,801,957	209,791,880	108,605,318	6,827,331	....	12,932,095	2,987,843	16,044,320	26,497,334	26,939,950	114,845,379	29,492,676	6,572,786
	Dec.,	1861	302	109,403,379	198,058,968	150,278,038	9,219,978	9,179,913	18,798,700	2,921,735	18,965,778	29,102,715	30,553,020	146,215,486	34,431,615	14,153,658
ersey	Jan.,	1855	32	5,314,885	9,177,334	891,954	240,292	158,396	1,810,707	418,349	....	836,452	3,552,585	3,290,464	483,875	....
	Jan.,	1856	35	5,682,989	10,999,919	760,697	255,296	71,587	1,536,949	502,949	....	782,659	4,285,979	3,494,541	616,301	....
	Jan.,	1857	46	5,580,770	13,380,085	581,773	234,711	288,295	2,237,924	710,079	....	849,958	4,759,855	4,891,970	636,658	....
	Jan.,	1858	47	7,494,919	11,364,319	721,098	344,045	288,609	1,605,817	494,197	....	1,308,851	3,995,936	3,696,600	507,077	80,763
	Jan.,	1859	46	7,354,122	12,449,460	785,393	421,793	391,194	2,223,925	576,006	....	952,331	4,054,779	4,239,235	770,935	....
	Jan.,	1860	49	7,844,412	14,928,174	963,911	448,303	599,884	2,295,028	663,196	....	946,709	4,811,832	5,741,465	1,141,664	....
	Jan.,	1861	50	8,046,944	13,884,045	890,831	461,724	2,363,059	1,853,151	533,699	....	1,049,099	4,164,799	5,117,817	559,579	....
	Jan.,	1862	51	8,358,919	12,796,026	1,502,518	465,057	96,524	2,793,284	549,792	....	1,493,103	3,937,535	5,687,903	450,572	1,552,760
ylvania	Nov.,	1854	64	19,864,825	48,541,393	2,133,400	1,159,740	509,662	4,840,118	3,769,420	3,927,949	3,944,600	10,739,069	21,076,464	3,930,663	3,718,873
	Nov.,	1856	71	23,408,596	52,949,199	2,714,933	1,198,574	678,018	5,847,643	4,460,673	135,378	6,736,653	18,983,199	25,340,814	4,955,485	96,792
	Nov.,	1856	77	23,609,344	55,987,934	2,301,638	1,906,569	303,730	5,143,330	5,719,334	1,893,695	5,173,198	17,368,086	37,493,534	6,913,515	127,659
	Nov.,	1857	76	25,691,430	49,149,333	3,689,119	1,353,985	244,120	3,773,397	4,814,977	75,429	4,560,528	11,610,438	18,924,113	5,847,970	80,706
	Nov.,	1858	87	24,555,605	48,815,959	2,954,443	1,493,953	253,591	4,418,436	634,194	3,349,621	4,345,538	11,980,486	26,054,566	4,569,625	429,167
	Nov.,	1859	90	25,565,569	50,337,157	2,813,674	1,719,138	568,561	3,073,910	4,977,999	....	5,378,474	13,132,809	26,167,843	3,837,554	975,192
	Nov.,	1860	89	25,808,553	51,997,479	2,377,774	1,765,255	1,045,641	4,548,829	....	4,919,286	7,818,789	13,630,033	27,092,104	4,118,993	073,159
	Nov.,	1861	111	26,135,530	46,747,190	10,231,700	1,958,300	2,102,185	4,700,260	3,666,130	446,166	11,464,600	16,364,643	28,986,370	3,979,826	707,008
vare	Jan.,	1855	10	1,393,175	3,048,141	37,465	194,356	29,140	409,562	39,051	287,215	90,149	1,386,991	850,010	127,516	....
	Jan.,	1856	11	1,493,185	2,906,958	44,085	137,524	9,814	387,079	39,630	155,055	180,651	1,199,204	886,164	125,303	8,000

* Profits.

State.	Date.	Number of banks and branches.	Capital.	Loans and discounts.	Stocks.	Real estate.	Other investments.	Due by other banks.	Notes of other banks.	Cash items.	Specie.	Circulation.	Deposits.	Due to other banks.	Other liabilities.
Delaware—Cont'd.	Jan., 1857	11	$1,408,185	$3,001,378	$23,076	$130,800	$1,065	$506,514	$40,636	$195,691	$146,367	$1,394,094	$868,414	$147,250	....
	Jan., 1838	11	1,355,010	2,544,212	18,610	57,655	934	507,955	58,639	108,516	203,928	1,340,370	609,179	72,297	....
	Jan., 1838	12	1,638,185	3,009,285	22,610	41,499	.....	308,222	61,446	116,819	217,342	968,846	832,657	86,180	....
	Jan., 1860	12	1,640,778	3,160,915	4,750	83,182	.....	411,989	122,195	103,862	208,924	1,135,772	976,226	102,166	....
	Jan., '60–'61	12	1,640,785	3,014,655	3,950	83,983	.....	336,787	130,422	104,025	187,263	1,080,892	818,201	105,948	....
	Jan., 1808	6	409,865	1,604,088	4,550	49,268	3,604	159,128	27,136	17,238	195,723	445,819	465,282	53,009	$147,582
Maryland	Jan., 1855	29	10,411,874	17,368,718	616,295	333,930	295,293	1,490,659	1,566,361	96,518	2,967,095	4,118,107	7,968,888	1,511,970	891,030
	Jan., 1856	31	11,908,806	20,615,005	644,250	318,896	698,890	1,849,166	1,482,744	89,961	3,398,101	5,297,983	8,370,345	1,924,786	938,108
	Jan., 1857	31	12,597,276	22,993,534	758,379	402,217	93,898	1,894,791	1,666,653	9,188	3,824,561	5,158,098	9,811,324	1,895,284	879,701
	Jan., 1858	31	12,451,545	21,804,111	641,318	417,925	14,741	3,926,119	1,473,413	3,164	2,614,729	4,041,051	7,541,186	4,194,677	549,933
	Jan., 1859	32	12,560,530	21,854,934	692,265	484,625	67,574	1,017,641	69,863	1,521,653	3,190,011	5,977,971	9,098,684	1,725,807	417,667
	Jan., 1860	31	12,568,962	20,896,769	848,983	505,179	41,500	1,657,016	1,897,918	....	2,779,416	4,106,809	8,874,160	1,324,740	357,195
	Jan., 1, 1861	31	12,867,791	20,299,928	635,825	535,329	.....	1,874,430	1,824,998	....	2,367,153	3,558,947	9,086,160	2,108,990	408,434
	Jan., 1863	28	19,155,979	17,440,111	856,425	545,089	6,420	1,337,068	1,489,799	120,478	3,689,471	3,794,290	7,637,092	1,167,555	1,631,140
Virginia	Jan., 1855	58	14,033,838	23,331,920	3,127,300	786,952	75,309	1,596,434	1,925,106	947,909	2,726,462	10,634,963	5,615,666	815,830	51,546
	Jan., 1856	57	13,606,118	23,319,948	2,647,365	807,951	114,433	2,186,725	999,764	25,999	3,151,105	13,014,926	6,304,340	663,968	36,609
	Jan., 1857	57	13,863,000	24,809,875	3,184,966	879,368	494,682	2,405,211	1,509,089	13,492	3,092,741	19,685,637	7,397,474	729,507	98,935
	Jan., 1858	62	14,851,800	23,326,411	2,591,564	910,394	381,987	2,085,494	1,874,733	6,287	2,710,777	10,347,874	6,971,325	899,796	87,210
	Jan., 1859	63	14,646,270	26,419,812	3,569,437	954,629	413,675	2,557,182	814,060	495,663	3,677,686	10,345,342	7,401,701	962,351	58,780
	Jan., 1860	65	16,005,150	24,975,799	3,584,078	1,019,932	433,423	2,755,047	1,294,092	29,836	3,943,657	9,819,197	7,729,650	1,136,397	34,600
	Jan., 1, 1861	66	18,486,210	23,866,869	3,685,125	1,070,869	340,791	1,893,416	2,003,703	32,209	3,017,389	19,817,148	7,157,270	1,310,888	317,405
North Carolina....	Nov., 1854	26	5,205,073	11,468,597	193,275	145,033	12,769	672,991	409,764	39,236	1,291,439	6,667,762	1,130,329	234,632	16,907
	Nov. & Dec., 1855.	28	6,031,945	11,558,430	123,985	171,037	4,087	785,852	376,690	....	1,360,995	5,750,092	1,101,113	224,821	10,710
	Nov., Dec., 1856, Jan., 1857.	28	6,485,950	10,636,891	94,118	199,475	7,913	846,416	386,076	1,378	1,153,993	6,301,262	1,179,090	119,847	6,645
	Dec., 1857, Jan., 1858.	28	6,505,100	11,967,733	180,270	196,671	14,275	700,630	363,018	....	1,035,869	5,699,497	1,037,457	62,347	66
	Jan., 1859	28	6,505,800	13,247,300	198,951	210,347	45,696	1,291,343	317,369	51,649	1,248,505	6,209,695	1,502,312	184,356	7,766
	Jan., 1860	30	6,629,478	15,211,272	363,898	188,568	68,009	1,081,463	601,115	54,254	1,617,687	5,594,057	1,487,373	100,139	196,478
	Jan., 1, 1861	31	7,863,466	14,080,746	537,714	230,456	26,912	630,355	513,183	45,620	1,059,715	5,218,598	2,034,391	105,631	291,466
South Carolina....	Sept., 1854	19	16,663,953	23,149,098	1,670,305	510,565	571,049	1,198,421	441,864	....	1,923,284	6,739,033	9,871,095	1,197,949	53,936

Sept., 1855	20	17,516,000	22,938,900	3,483,011	600,880	951,832	1,057,478	424,135	....	1,228,221	6,504,679	3,068,188	1,100,299	46,539
Jan., 1857	20	14,837,649	26,927,310	3,258,876	631,273	698,663	1,180,938	539,497	....	1,187,774	10,634,652	3,502,723	3,318,963	353,119
Dec., 1857	20	14,885,631	22,036,561	3,223,887	698,688	1,065,448	1,631,109	669,729	....	1,104,126	6,185,895	2,556,854	3,074,740	700,612
Dec., 1858	20	14,688,451	24,446,944	3,721,966	677,641	2,904,540	2,200,450	605,299	....	2,601,414	9,170,333	3,897,840	3,746,604	214,920
Dec., 1859	20	14,962,062	27,801,912	2,994,688	681,945	1,455,486	1,699,644	443,478	....	2,324,121	11,475,634	4,165,615	1,490,918	1,417,837
Sept., 1860	20	14,932,458	22,930,759	2,965,872	684,144	2,384,994	587,645	277,549	....	1,698,336	6,089,030	3,334,037	1,315,659	658,100
Aug., 1855	Mar., 1856.	24	11,508,717	16,758,403	1,671,934	4,853,503	135,298	1,985,694	846,675	513,697	1,955,956	10,092,809	2,525,256	1,334,009	623,918
Oct., Nov., Dec., 1856, Jan., 1857.		23	15,498,690	16,649,201	2,948,063	8,368,280	534,619	1,368,971	1,480,570	31,398	1,702,108	9,147,011	3,196,530	1,663,429	879,644
Sept. & Oct., 1857.		30	16,015,256	19,677,863	2,358,584	8,470,709	549,639	1,194,465	454,156	259,576	1,417,545	5,518,425	9,915,853	533,819	689,662
Ap'l, 1858, to Jan., 1859.		28	19,479,111	17,929,066	1,805,127	4,791,022	676,274	4,073,665	720,592	409,481	3,751,988	11,687,582	5,317,993	1,727,925	552,954
Oct., 1859		29	16,679,560	16,776,282	2,583,158	6,424,463	1,110,377	9,005,768	1,063,710	101,939	3,211,974	8,796,100	4,738,980	1,987,268	787,733
Oct., 1859, Jan., 1861.		28	16,555,480	16,680,261	2,529,706	6,565,261	689,791	1,987,125	970,050	100,447	2,358,555	8,311,728	3,846,176	1,389,011	657,800
Jan., 1860	2	300,000	464,630	100,002	....	....	26,853	94,580	....	33,876	183,640	109,518	5,144	....
Jan., 1861	2	425,000	424,382	125,000	....	19,362	40,118	16,419	774	33,071	116,250	108,806	....	....
Jan., 1855	4	2,296,400	4,307,026	768,650	53,568	....	371,801	57,061	45,647	1,125,490	9,389,178	1,276,092	181,558	15,000
Jan., 1856	4	2,297,800	5,117,427	713,026	80,648	....	1,421,445	561,489	....	1,274,944	3,467,240	9,837,556	481,989	10,000
Jan., 1857	4	2,937,800	6,545,209	142,201	78,148	1,250	685,302	504,987	....	1,139,312	3,177,224	2,493,209	703,443	5,000
Jan., 1858	6	3,935,550	5,585,424	146,539	150,141	24,506	1,163,973	181,706	....	1,302,312	2,581,791	1,408,837	571,556	....
Jan., 1859	6	3,603,400	9,058,370	160,919	160,410	....	3,192,019	879,748	....	3,371,956	6,051,117	3,830,607	1,005,839	9,131
Jan., 1860	8	4,901,000	13,570,007	524,512	171,300	28,298	1,308,805	643,657	20,800	2,747,174	7,477,970	4,851,153	874,800	103,049
Jan. 1, 1860, and 1861.	8	4,975,000	10,934,060	565,829	171,300	28,555	1,131,530	684,601	105,786	2,715,119	5,059,292	3,435,685	2,230,855	160,982
Jan., 1855	19	20,179,107	27,149,907	4,187,180	3,317,492	1,985,373	3,154,497	....	....	6,570,568	6,885,601	11,688,998	1,154,536	9,370,973
Dec., 1855	19	19,097,798	27,500,348	2,591,400	2,341,335	2,933,419	6,699,855	....	....	8,191,625	7,092,614	14,747,470	1,687,531	2,301,747
Dec., 1856	19	21,730,400	31,900,996	4,794,885	2,470,683	1,493,965	6,416,798	....	....	6,811,160	9,191,139	13,478,729	955,555	9,907,583
Dec. 26, 1857	15	23,800,830	23,929,096	5,318,418	2,493,494	1,147,287	3,951,905	....	....	10,370,701	4,336,694	11,636,100	1,940,619	....
Dec., 1858	12	24,215,829	29,424,278	5,564,590	2,398,500	873,471	4,368,984	....	....	16,918,027	9,064,089	21,802,538	2,198,989	1,781,058
Dec., 1859	13	24,498,860	35,401,609	5,849,095	2,141,681	1,082,041	7,305,115	....	6,073,419	19,115,431	11,578,313	19,777,812	1,165,679	2,201,138
Jan. 1, 1861	13	21,634,844	26,364,513	5,783,687	2,126,413	1,093,540	....	....	....	13,556,058	6,181,374	17,056,860	753,359	1,012,115
Jan., 1855	1	240,163	352,739	5,914	11,904	50,000	60,710	5,450	....	8,063	231,760	49,738	....	....
Jan., 1856	1	240,185	488,411	4,894	19,613	....	81,152	7,740	....	7,744	324,080	35,800	....	....
Jan., 1857	1	336,000	657,026	519	11,413	....	257,505	96,563	....	7,918	556,345	83,435	....	....
Jan., 1858	2	1,110,500	593,316	1,007	780,767	30,209	219,086	973	47,254	591	105,400	49,781	31,799	60
Jan., 1855	30	6,717,848	11,755,729	871,076	486,455	166,395	1,057,140	491,600	68,909	1,473,040	5,850,582	2,413,418	211,581	85,501
Jan., 1856	45	8,593,693	14,880,609	1,486,453	541,771	143,686	2,617,686	859,936	16,037	2,231,418	8,518,545	3,740,101	467,070	664,910
Jan., 1857	40	8,454,423	16,892,390	2,450,306	590,715	94,109	3,280,700	1,069,406	69,767	2,994,532	8,401,848	4,875,346	944,917	951,262
July, 1857	45	9,083,069	13,194,992	3,317,060	583,406	116,363	3,307,332	969,317	....	2,670,751	6,026,582	4,545,104	1,617,519	768,141
Jan., 1858	39	8,381,357	13,962,766	1,577,578	486,602	8,238	2,375,465	581,793	1,287,077	2,863,018	6,479,892	4,659,809	1,073,369	441,165
Jan., 1860	34	8,067,027	11,751,019	1,933,432	595,759	84,355	9,613,910	493,362	932,092	2,957,710	5,636,378	4,324,799	364,627	462,490
Jan., 1861	33	8,466,543	11,942,988	464,372	577,514	1,163,498	655,679	422,969	1,221,480	1,341,269	4,285,174	3,998,063	355,924	1,501,922

State	Date	Number of banks and branches	Capital	Loans and discounts	Stocks	Real estate	Other investments	Due by other banks	Notes of other banks	Cash items	Specie	Circulation	Deposits	Due to other banks	Other liabilities
Kentucky	Jan., 1855	34	$10,369,717	$17,307,587	$743,035	$416,970	$216,505	$3,319,718	$586,370	....	$4,192,988	$8,628,946	$3,011,719	$2,577,684	$096
	Jan., 1856	33	10,454,572	21,132,519	678,389	488,504	535,730	3,731,463	965,878	....	4,611,786	12,634,533	3,508,757	2,505,953	532
	Jan., 1857	35	10,596,305	23,404,551	739,105	465,907	363,994	4,115,430	840,959	....	4,406,106	13,682,215	4,473,378	2,983,373	50
	Jan., 1858	37	10,789,522	17,681,983	735,705	500,202	2,611	4,431,131	725,450	$139	4,097,925	8,8±±,925	3,932,132	3,185,392	1
	Jan., 1859	37	12,216,795	24,404,942	793,641	508,502	144,075	6,535,915	1,017,580	199	4,984,141	14,345,696	5,114,879	4,338,384	
	Jan., 1860	45	12,835,870	25,394,869	851,562	477,971	188,391	5,099,678	779,565	90,909	4,502,950	13,520,907	5,662,892	3,259,717	
	Jan., 1861	43	13,709,725	22,455,175	467,357	593,382	308,147	4,314,209	763,683	149,167	4,466,996	10,873,620	3,725,828	3,073,919	
	Jan., 1862	44	13,453,306	15,391,868	2,343,360	589,974	....	3,659,482	700,553	....	5,991,915	7,465,613	4,369,218	1,352,737	9,085
Missouri	Nov., 1854	6	1,215,398	3,441,643	....	111,185	....	49,960	....	....	975,491	1,460,650	1,847,651	964,776	
	Dec., 1855	6	1,215,405	4,393,029	....	104,692	....	28,331	33,870	....	4,355,050	2,605,060	1,331,106	170,495	
	Dec., 1856	6	2,215,405	4,112,791	....	96,254	....	75,991	196,910	....	1,245,184	2,780,360	1,188,982	111,984	
	Jan., 1858	10	3,620,815	4,635,534	72,000	29,773	116,084	96,626	394,705	....	1,424,004	1,718,750	1,462,442	242,117	
	Jan., 1859	22	5,796,781	9,620,426	417,338	169,549	....	597,679	1,007,573	348,653	3,921,782	6,069,100	5,193,629	579,630	
	Jan., 1860	38	9,089,951	15,461,199	795,670	226,609	....	1,090,506	1,045,015	....	4,160,912	7,884,888	3,357,176	1,900,010	
	Jan., 1861	42	11,133,899	17,373,459	970,550	221,754	....	1,281,748	1,521,516	97,559	3,820,533	8,204,845	3,360,384	1,247,338	
	July, 1861	42	11,204,920	12,704,000	1,277,690	391,103	1,347,394	1,747,455	2,836,578	....	4,181,931	8,111,720	2,894,860	1,483,184	5,592
	Jan., 1862	42	11,249,990	11,243,088	1,285,965	628,965	1,562,395	2,047,551	3,160,120	....	2,987,108	6,511,851	2,968,473	1,450,793	15,025
Illinois	April, 1854	29	2,513,790	315,841	2,671,903	31,158	1,368,983	878,619	365,339	63,809	565,159	2,983,596	1,986,102	....	294
	Jan., 1856	36	3,840,948	337,675	3,777,676	79,940	1,108,148	2,354,571	517,066	27,165	759,474	3,420,985	1,267,934	....	241
	Oct., 1856	42	5,872,144	1,740,671	6,109,613	52,839	....	3,953,450	433,717	19,097	635,810	5,534,945	1,902,399	210,483	157
	Jan., 1858	45	4,679,325	1,146,770	6,164,017	59,567	4,757	3,813,578	965,034	6,433	333,539	5,936,930	658,521	19,669	131
	Oct., 1858	48	4,000,334	1,296,616	6,486,652	87,769	1,837	5,627,690	971,526	9,279	269,585	5,707,048	649,058	15,621	525
	Jan., 1860	74	5,251,925	487,929	9,526,691	96,429	1,679,277	5,291,416	343,269	39,397	933,814	8,981,703	697,037	28,533	552
	Oct., 1860	94	6,750,742	546,876	12,264,580	116,551	2,035,736	5,793,752	287,411	37,900	209,905	11,910,837	807,763	64,900	622
	Jan., 1862	19									1,413,076				
Indiana	Dec., 1853	44	5,554,552	7,247,366	3,257,054	289,673	127,236	1,985,114	715,305	108,860	1,890,760	7,116,827	1,764,747	445,350	100
	July & Oct., 1854	59	7,281,934	9,305,651	6,146,837	249,298	....	2,057,897	911,000	173,573	1,894,357	6,155,856	9,269,805	603,849	
	Oct., 1855, & Jan., 1856	45	4,045,325	6,986,990	1,705,070	231,929	139,946	1,274,992	595,262	369,600	1,599,014	4,516,422	1,957,097	379,804	161
	July & Oct., 1856	46	4,193,089	7,030,691	1,694,357	927,899	380,911	1,336,418	557,238	68,500	1,420,076	4,731,705	1,850,742	279,815	177
	Nov., 1857, & Jan., 1858	40	3,585,922	4,861,445	1,410,737	104,224	10,691	930,441	395,536	236,661	1,261,720	3,363,976	1,417,966	380,569	60

Nov., 1858, & Jan., 1859.	37	3,617,829	6,468,308	1,930,981	195,711	111,089	1,177,489	505,685	36,625	1,869,000	5,379,936	1,723,840	176,366	68,215
Jan., 1860	37	4,343,210	7,675,861	1,349,466	258,309	991,467	950,836	418,991	80,799	1,583,540	5,399,246	1,709,479	80,530	140,695
Jan. 1, 1861	39	4,744,570	8,158,036	1,297,628	316,004	77,293	1,198,961	355,095	105,875	2,290,648	5,755,401	1,841,051	117,868	152,650
Jan., 1862	37	4,519,985	6,949,043	1,358,002	354,799	...	2,012,966	445,144	67,975	4,577,259	6,844,700	2,076,548	160,890	1,400,385
Nov., 1854	66	7,166,581	13,576,339	2,466,347	298,229	1,006,525	2,751,312	905,555	158,310	1,690,105	8,074,132	5,450,566	049,727	411,592
Feb., 1855	65	6,491,421	14,921,998	2,476,751	350,708	1,195,047	3,177,178	1,639,965	105,559	2,096,809	9,080,589	7,101,328	1,712,040	290,902
Nov., 1856	61	6,742,431	15,223,541	2,749,866	310,145	687,337	2,749,558	1,199,863	34,007	2,016,814	9,153,529	6,543,400	1,292,961	392,758
Feb., 1856	49	6,550,770	9,358,927	2,062,778	592,041	010,436	3,199,364	768,243	191,354	1,734,693	6,991,266	3,915,781	260,786	263,071
Aug., 1856	53	6,675,428	10,549,574	2,015,597	604,000	749,681	2,347,041	796,999	195,517	1,935,025	7,588,291	3,780,514	305,783	195,164
Nov., 1858	53	5,707,151	11,171,349	2,059,769	596,670	711,157	2,613,615	1,192,439	150,741	1,845,441	8,040,304	4,368,831	488,878	206,925
Feb., 1860	59	6,890,639	11,100,462	1,153,552	718,919	961,720	2,667,763	698,377	157,378	1,826,640	7,983,860	4,039,516	790,568	144,781
Feb., 1861	55	7,151,039	10,913,007	2,089,819	671,590	849,325	3,206,580	841,682	110,987	2,377,456	8,143,611	4,046,811	3,206,580	101,698
Feb., 1862	55	5,685,850	10,475,082	2,677,853	703,637	...	2,828,357	1,426,066	144,845	3,655,944	9,217,520	5,762,353	450,035	2,418,043
Jan., 1855	6	980,416	1,900,942	565,431	146,035	15,345	392,550	118,764	6,160	143,123	509,942	1,170,974	95,597	187,522
Dec., 1855	4	730,436	1,988,067	517,945	124,486	21,347	402,590	97,285	6,432	152,080	573,440	1,366,768	53,425	198,916
Dec., 1856	4	841,489	1,903,603	586,384	60,110	11,145	945,061	159,489	9,141	90,762	679,549	1,347,856	115,962	53,646
Dec., 1857, & Jan., 1858	4	851,504	1,111,766	399,466	115,661	15,797	77,034	31,411	10,043	92,776	364,076	310,479	76,979	124,198
Dec., 1858	3	745,304	1,153,547	256,776	124,357	14,440	137,059	54,963	22,579	49,018	331,978	555,593	35,165	126,011
Dec., 1859	4	735,488	699,949	192,831	130,661	30,119	193,379	44,644	23,871	24,175	920,197	375,397	13,469	76,206
Dec., 1860	2	250,000	578,043	-79,973	39,200	...	133,768	52,379	1,879	98,399	47,510	436,437	4,777	139,878
Dec., 1861	4	413,030	788,024	233,613	96,440	19,349	968,679	65,500	17,903	37,996	190,194	749,628	125,693	117,800
Jan., 1855	23	1,400,000	1,861,043	1,044,021	94,390	8,791	305,980	341,174	103,164	334,383	740,764	1,469,053	...	456,739
Jan., 1856	39	1,970,000	3,906,079	1,230,083	94,961	1,501	363,181	603,848	57,216	531,713	1,068,165	2,806,341	...	1,073,874
Jan., 1857	49	2,955,000	5,280,834	2,025,180	160,315	1,890	453,791	701,161	73,999	542,938	1,709,570	3,305,569	...	1,290,486
Jan., 1858	56	5,515,000	6,930,851	3,626,466	929,936	45,986	498,794	457,411	67,429	576,543	2,913,671	5,077,862	...	1,278,672
Jan., 1859	98	7,095,000	9,962,457	5,114,415	304,149	...	892,775	892,983	83,893	706,069	4,695,170	3,929,384	...	573,604
Jan., 1860	108	7,530,000	7,592,361	5,031,504	368,461	1,392,668	890,454	925,110	64,430	419,947	4,499,855	3,935,813	...	1,493,529
Jan., 1861	110	6,769,000	7,793,387	4,949,886	...	1,720,779	745,063	1,162,936	...	372,518	4,310,175	4,083,141	...	1,632,201
Jan., 1862	60	3,907,000	4,573,512	1,830,316	317,880	550,108	484,054	693,246	61,442	304,478	1,419,422	2,341,112	...	1,257,718
Jan., 1859	9	50,000	5,185	50,000	...	1,250	30,808	4,223	512	15,279	48,643	13,131	...	...
Jan., 1861	3	155,000	123,163	71,987	...	1,804	18,285	9,803	14,671	9,926	8,702	54,065	10	36,902
Dec., 1861	4	155,000									81,329			
Dec., 1859	12	460,450	794,228	101,849	...	49,308	948,817	913,661	...	255,545	563,808	527,778	16,689	25,056
Jan., 1861	13	589,130	1,169,877	...	...	292,453	984,968	592,695	...	378,030	689,600	1,154,923	50,504	99,898
July, 1861	14	642,785	1,117,145	154,049	...	217,559	366,710	324,089	...	547,363	938,073	1,002,305	37,529	106,918
Jan., 1862	14	780,300	1,094,912	219,723	...	321,715	334,185	271,550	...	725,443	1,281,453	809,387	47,476	108,422
Jan., 1859	1	52,000	48,956	...	2,995	...	4,088	...	...	8,268	8,805	2,695	...	...
Jan., 1861	2	93,130	48,014	40,000	6,523	...	6,586	4,414	4,450	4,350	5,443	14,783	...	4,922
Jan., 1862	1	99,070	43,420	...	9,280	...	750	...	...	...	2,440	6,300	...	4,414
Jan., 1852	1	205,000	418,097	...	3,975	129,804	15,069	210	136,325	253,796	125,291	1,749	...
Jan., 1857	6	15,000	15,879	...	5,850	39,601	1,000	...	5,683	41,641	3,072	...	2,576
Nov., 1858	2	56,000	97,067	...	1,145	1,341	3,170	1,399	-26	6,629	23,346	23,748	4,418	...
Nov., 1860	1	80,000	72,406	...	7,685	404	4,443	2,209	...	5,627	16,007	10,717	...	5,530

No. 9.

Comparative view of the condition of the banks in different sections of the Union in 1857, 1858, 1859, 1860, 1861, and 1862.

Sections.	BANKS AND BRANCHES.						CAPITAL PAID IN.					
	1856-'57.	1857-'58.	1858-'59.	1859-'60.	1860-'61.	1861-'62.	1856-'57,	1857-'58,	1858-'59,	1859-'60,	1860-'61,	1861-'62,
Eastern States......	507	498	501	505	506	511	$114,611,759	$117,961,990	$119,590,423	$123,449,075	$123,706,708	$127,291,3
Middle States.......	478	459	477	485	488	498	140,998,676	154,449,049	156,369,297	159,091,051	160,085,360	156,363,7
Southern States.....	128	148	139	146	147	147	50,554,582	52,077,587	48,578,139	54,583,266	56,909,691	56,962,0
Southwestern States..	105	115	116	138	141	149	44,630,333	49,633,353	54,254,042	59,363,534	69,941,011	69,777,6
Western States......	206	210	243	288	319	194	50,739,143	21,597,821	93,171,418	95,373,189	98,577,013	15,494,3
Total United States..........	**1,416**	**1,429**	**1,476**	**1,562**	**1,601**	**1,492**	**370,834,898**	**394,699,799**	**401,976,942**	**431,880,095**	**499,599,713**	**416,139,74**

No. 9.—*Comparative view of the condition of the banks in different sections of the Union, &c.*—Continued.

Sections.	LOANS AND DISCOUNTS.						STOCKS.					
	1856-'57.	1857-'58.	1858-'59.	1859-'60.	1860-'61.	1861-'62.	1856-'57.	1857-'58.	1858-'59.	1859-'60.	1860-'61.	1861-'62.
Eastern States......	$187,750,278	$177,295,020	$179,992,400	$190,186,990	$194,866,619	$191,747,787	$1,459,756	$1,131,869	$1,206,564	$1,657,908	$1,489,949	$3,407,0
Middle States.......	299,874,750	217,669,341	224,716,143	289,636,046	304,217,593	276,046,381	27,703,286	26,578,900	26,994,425	31,297,492	33,581,858	68,873,2
Southern States.....	82,412,657	70,040,568	77,039,922	82,231,828	79,929,990	79,181,790	6,796,041	9,354,305	8,695,484	9,623,777	9,947,477	9,941,4
Southwestern States ..	82,813,957	64,633,845	85,980,791	101,468,716	89,089,505	75,875,815	7,127,639	9,523,729	8,515,363	9,177,273	8,951,799	10,443,2
Western States......	31,605,937	93,925,468	59,454,543	28,421,346	29,538,804	23,224,007	13,187,903	13,618,466	15,225,613	18,655,693	20,793,853	6,359,10
Total United States.....	**684,456,287**	**583,165,242**	**657,183,799**	**691,945,580**	**696,778,491**	**646,877,780**	**59,279,399**	**60,305,969**	**63,509,449**	**70,344,343**	**74,004,879**	**99,010,96**

Sections.	REAL ESTATE.						OTHER INVESTMENTS.					
	1856-'57.	1857-'58.	1858-'59.	1859-'60.	1860-'61.	1861-'62.	1856-'57.	1857-'58.	1858-'59.	1859-'60.	1860-'61.	1861-'62.
n States	$2,707,588	$3,310,426	$3,640,675	$3,844,810	$3,623,549	$4,461,804	$611,152	$683,708	$1,044,319	$1,075,879	$1,141,438	$318,361
States	8,632,442	9,598,594	10,675,795	11,481,225	11,685,602	12,127,993	616,619	1,015,722	1,309,819	1,319,363	3,829,149	3,392,547
rn States	10,064,396	10,276,482	6,639,639	10,313,308	10,552,530	10,559,530	1,725,876	1,951,349	4,109,195	3,067,297	3,469,790	5,460,780
estern States	3,715,190	4,537,783	3,720,584	3,613,520	3,722,463	3,696,266	1,552,250	1,438,020	1,025,804	1,383,083	3,393,320	4,577,568
n States	804,976	1,034,579	1,299,804	1,599,268	1,157,783	1,481,956	1,083,439	987,077	841,114	4,977,549	4,902,584	698,650
tal United States	26,124,592	28,755,834	25,976,497	30,782,131	30,748,927	32,326,549	5,980,336	6,075,906	8,323,041	11,123,171	16,657,511	13,648,006

No. 9.—*Comparative view of the condition of the banks in different sections of the Union, &c.*—Continued.

Sections.	DUE BY OTHER BANKS.						NOTES OF OTHER BANKS.					
	1856-'57.	1857-'58.	1858-'59.	1859-'60.	1860-'61.	1861-'62.	1856-'57.	1857-'58.	1858-'59.	1859-'60.	1860-'61.	1861-'62.
n States	$15,304,943	$12,915,423	$16,333,387	$14,310,756	$14,015,371	$18,073,564	$7,452,318	$6,916,504	$6,495,545	$7,026,319	$7,003,127	$5,765,319
States	21,961,908	20,843,384	23,137,793	20,061,485	22,835,292	28,941,119	11,071,854	6,898,885	3,548,204	9,220,561	4,476,153	7,834,522
rn States	5,801,536	5,320,828	10,192,640	7,461,775	5,138,659	5,138,659	3,885,232	3,401,609	2,459,404	3,446,976	3,762,597	5,762,997
estern States	13,911,656	13,188,355	21,168,632	17,317,715	7,623,183	7,694,299	2,638,057	2,901,763	3,479,694	2,964,599	3,463,069	4,968,245
n States	8,870,060	6,484,812	7,489,565	8,083,726	9,391,585	5,909,965	3,066,537	1,928,635	2,842,512	2,844,012	3,238,546	2,901,546
tal United States	65,849,205	58,052,802	78,944,987	57,235,457	58,793,990	65,256,596	28,124,008	29,447,436	18,858,989	25,509,567	21,903,909	25,253,589

Sections.	CASH ITEMS.						SPECIE.					
	1856-'57.	1857-'58.	1858-'59.	1859-'60.	1860-'61.	1861-'62.	1856-'57.	1857-'58.	1858-'59.	1859-'60.	1860-'61.	1861-'62.
Eastern States.............	$285,688	$307,073	$495,220	$325,511	$365,602	$571,772	$7,250,426	$6,391,617	$13,774,125	$10,098,162	$10,037,304	$12,115,855
Middle States.............	24,477,093	14,318,189	23,493,265	17,480,612	21,060,613	19,579,673	23,390,763	36,020,756	43,971,104	33,229,061	37,749,614	45,939,614
Southern States....	46,708	265,863	950,756	186,031	179,980	179,980	7,149,616	6,268,319	10,679,514	10,130,316	8,119,036	8,119,036
Southwestern States........	62,767	47,363	1,635,943	973,792	7,420,351	7,200,625	15,704,308	19,796,184	31,359,021	25,793,477	25,999,992	26,670,590
Western States.............	209,385	441,930	303,646	365,575	271,332	295,921	4,844,725	3,935,956	4,753,954	4,343,527	5,768,161	9,301,120
Total United States....	25,081,641	15,380,441	26,808,822	19,331,521	29,297,878	27,827,971	58,349,838	74,412,832	104,537,818	83,594,537	87,674,507	102,146,215

No. 9.—*Comparative view of the condition of the banks in different sections of the Union, &c.*—Continued.

Sections.	CIRCULATION.						DEPOSITS.					
	1856–'57.	1857–'58.	1858–'59.	1859–'60.	1860–'61.	1861–'62.	1856–'57.	1857–'58.	1858–'59.	1859–'60.	1860–'61.	1861–'62.
...ates	$53,554,041	$41,417,699	$39,564,689	$44,510,618	$44,991,285	$39,306,729	$34,520,868	$28,196,426	$41,877,420	$41,319,550	$40,622,523	$49,941,324
...tos	62,696,774	44,187,749	45,483,957	53,145,871	52,873,851	55,105,119	139,873,112	113,814,435	150,620,929	145,829,987	156,899,558	186,932,745
...States	38,798,582	27,751,551	37,400,983	35,863,618	39,552,760	39,558,760	15,196,763	13,160,489	18,119,776	16,250,347	16,480,480	16,460,480
...ern States	37,799,961	23,727,779	42,539,764	46,000,759	34,600,785	29,439,176	26,523,139	23,356,418	38,581,455	37,973,839	30,576,820	29,929,299
...States	22,147,194	18,123,580	24,226,425	27,580,611	29,987,086	20,382,302	14,237,370	5,384,282	10,368,705	10,428,413	12,450,063	11,745,560
United States	214,778,822	155,208,344	193,306,818	207,102,477	202,005,767	183,792,079	230,351,352	185,932,049	259,568,278	253,800,199	257,029,569	296,322,408

No. 9.—*Comparative view of the condition of the banks in different sections of the Union, &c.*—Continued.

Sections.	DUE TO OTHER BANKS.						OTHER LIABILITIES.					
	1856–'57.	1857–'58.	1858–'59.	1859–'60.	1860–'61.	1861–'62.	1856–'57.	1857–'58.	1858–'59.	1859–'60.	1860–'61.	1861–'62.
Eastern States............	$7,310,540	$6,909,559	$9,370,094	$8,987,151	$9,666,483	$10,014,087	$2,625,089	$3,304,554	$2,819,422	$1,541,091	$2,811,726	$10,144,
Middle States	36,710,539	31,890,583	42,286,596	35,913,553	36,386,050	40,082,375	7,574,093	3,541,956	3,731,452	4,391,664	11,072,379	24,191,
Southern States	6,136,719	4,590,702	6,641,306	4,636,006	4,117,389	4,117,389	4,332,643	2,670,550	3,823,790	3,436,648	4,135,271	4,135,
Southwestern States....	5,709,972	6,969,046	9,197,277	6,764,829	7,661,391	6,143,597	3,213,845	2,770,116	2,924,354	2,859,607	2,674,929	7,793,
Western States...........	1,806,970	759,999	720,448	937,289	3,443,963	786,494	2,071,080	1,880,435	2,499,499	2,452,905	2,863,697	5,306,
Total United States.....	57,674,333	51,159,875	68,215,051	55,932,918	61,275,256	61,144,059	19,816,850	14,166,713	15,048,497	14,661,815	23,058,004	51,573,

Eastern States.	*Middle States.*	*Southern States.*	*Southwestern States.*	*Western States.*
Maine.	New York.	Virginia.	Alabama.	Illinois.
New Hampshire.	New Jersey.	North Carolina.	Louisiana.	Indiana.
Vermont.	Pennsylvania.	South Carolina.	Mississippi.	Ohio.
Massachusetts.	Delaware.	Georgia.	Tennessee.	Michigan.
Rhode Island.	Maryland.	Florida.	Kentucky.	Wisconsin.
Connecticut.			Missouri.	Minnesota.
				Kansas.
				Nebraska Territory.

No. 10—*General view of the condition of the banks in the United States on or about January 1, 1851 to 1862, inclusive.*

	1851.	1854.	1855.	1856.	1857.	1858.	1859.	1860.	1861.	1862.
ber of banks	731	1,059	1,163	1,255	1,283	1,284	1,309	1,399	....	....
ber of branches	148	149	144	143	133	138	147	170	....	....
ber of banks and branches...	879	1,208	1,307	1,398	1,416	1,422	1,476	1,562	1,601	1,499
ual paid in	$227,807,553	$301,376,071	$332,177,288	$343,874,272	$370,834,686	$394,622,799	$401,976,242	$421,880,095	$429,592,713	$418,139,741
RESOURCES.										
ns and discounts	413,756,799	557,397,779	576,144,758	634,183,280	684,456,887	583,165,242	657,183,799	691,945,580	696,778,421	646,677,780
cks	22,388,389	44,350,330	52,727,062	49,485,215	59,279,329	60,305,260	63,502,449	70,344,343	74,604,879	99,010,987
estate....................	20,219,794	22,367,472	24,073,601	20,865,887	26,194,523	28,755,834	25,976,497	30,782,131	30,748,927	32,326,649
er investments.............	8,935,972	7,589,820	8,734,540	8,862,516	5,929,338	6,075,906	8,393,041	11,123,171	16,657,311	13,648,066
from other banks.........	50,718,015	55,516,065	55,758,735	62,639,725	55,849,903	58,053,802	78,944,987	67,233,457	58,793,996	65,256,596
s of other banks...........	17,195,062	22,559,066	23,429,518	24,779,049	25,121,008	23,447,436	18,858,289	25,502,567	21,903,902	25,263,589
items	15,241,196	25,579,253	21,935,738	19,937,710	25,081,541	15,380,441	25,808,822	19,331,521	22,297,878	27,827,971
ie	48,671,048	59,410,253	53,944,546	59,314,063	58,349,838	74,412,632	104,537,818	83,594,537	87,674,507	102,146,215
LIABILITIES.										
ulation	155,165,251	204,689,207	186,952,223	195,747,950	214,778,822	155,208,344	193,306,818	207,102,477	202,005,767	183,792,019
osits.....................	128,957,712	188,188,744	190,400,342	212,705,662	230,351,352	185,932,049	259,568,278	253,802,129	257,229,562	296,322,408
to other banks	46,416,928	50,394,162	45,156,697	52,719,956	57,674,333	51,169,875	58,215,651	55,932,818	61,275,256	51,144,052
r liabilities	6,426,327	13,429,276	15,599,683	13,227,807	19,816,850	14,166,713	15,048,427	14,661,615	23,258,004	51,573,590
egate of immediate liabilities, of circulation, deposits, and s to other banks	330,539,891	443,200,113	422,509,269	461,173,568	502,804,507	392,310,268	521,090,747	516,837,524	520,510,585	541,258,539
egate of immediate means, of specie, cash items, notes other banks, and dues from er banks...................	131,926,342	163,164,657	158,048,537	166,670,547	177,404,692	170,293,511	248,449,916	195,654,082	197,670,277	220,484,371
and silver in United States asury depositories	11,164,727	25,135,252	27,168,869	23,705,431	20,066,114	10,259,229	3,933,600	6,695,225	3,600,000	*3,400,000
f specie in banks and treas- depositories..............	59,835,775	84,546,505	81,133,435	82,020,494	78,415,952	84,642,061	107,571,418	90,289,762	91,274,507	105,546,215

* February 8, 1862.

Note.—The amount of specie in the United States depositories does not include the amount to the credit of disbursing officers.

REPORT ON THE FINANCES.

No. 11.—*Condensed statement of the condition of the banks*

STATES.	No. of banks and branches.	Date of report.	LIABILITIES.				
			Capital.	Circulation.	Deposits.	Due to other banks.	Other liabilities.
Maine	71	Jan. 1862	$7,970,650	$4,047,780	$3,307,608	$63,601	$638,916
New Hampshire	59	Dec. 1861	5,031,000	2,994,408	1,376,853		
Vermont	40	Aug. 1861	3,916,000	2,592,687	715,907		61,177
Massachusetts	183	Oct. 1861	67,344,200	19,317,306	33,926,711	8,000,595	5,902,598
Rhode Island	90	Nov. 1861	21,524,509	3,396,530	2,749,171	965,396	1,244,863
Connecticut	75	Jan. 1862	21,794,937	6,918,018	6,140,784	964,789	2,996,634
Six Eastern States	511		127,591,316	39,306,729	49,241,394	10,014,087	10,144,408
New York	302	Dec. 1861	109,403,376	30,553,090	146,215,488	34,431,615	14,150,658
New Jersey	51	Jan. 1862	8,358,912	3,927,535	5,687,923	450,572	1,552,760
Pennsylvania	111	Nov. 1861	26,135,630	16,384,643	28,986,370	3,979,824	6,707,008
Delaware*	6	Jan. 1862	409,865	445,619	405,362	53,009	147,582
Maryland*	98	Jan. 1862	12,155,970	3,794,925	7,677,602	1,167,555	1,631,140
Five Middle States	408		156,363,765	55,105,119	188,932,745	40,082,575	24,191,148
Virginia†	66	Jan. 1861	16,466,910	19,817,148	7,157,970	1,310,068	317,905
North Carolina†	31	do.	7,963,466	5,918,598	9,034,391	105,631	291,466
South Carolina†	20	Sept. 1860	14,952,436	6,089,010	3,334,6..	1,318,684	2,868,100
Georgia†	28	Jan. 1861	16,555,466	8,317,728	3,848,176	1,389,011	657,800
Florida†	2	do.	425,000	116,250	108,505		
Five Southern States	147		56,962,692	39,556,760	15,480,480	4,117,369	4,135,271
Alabama†	8	Jan. 1861	4,976,000	5,035,222	3,435,685	2,250,855	166,890
Louisiana†	13	Dec. 1860	24,631,844	5,181,374	17,050,660	753,359	1,012,115
Tennessee†	35	Jan. 1851	8,460,543	4,265,714	2,996,063	335,923	1,501,922
Kentucky†	44	Jan. 1862	12,453,306	7,465,015	4,369,218	1,302,737	2,095,774
Missouri	49	do.	11,949,990	6,511,851	2,068,473	1,450,723	3,025,278
Five Southwestern States	149		62,777,683	29,439,176	29,929,299	6,143,597	7,795,981
Illinois	19	Jan. 1862		1,415,076			
Indiana	37	do.	4,579,985	6,844,700	3,076,548	168,890	1,400,385
Ohio	55	Feb. 1862	5,665,950	9,417,690	5,763,355	450,025	2,418,043
Michigan	4	Dec. 1861	413,945	190,124	749,898	125,623	117,860
Wisconsin	60	Jan. 1862	3,807,000	1,419,493	2,341,112		1,257,716
Iowa	14	do.	720,390	1,281,453	605,387	47,876	108,422
Minnesota*	4	Dec. 1861	155,000	61,236			
Kansas	1	Jan. 1862	55,000	9,710	6,530		4,414
Nebraska							
Nine Northwestern States	194		15,424,355	90,362,202	11,745,560	786,424	5,306,780
RECAPITULATION.							
Six Eastern States	511		127,591,316	39,306,729	49,241,394	10,014,087	10,144,408
Five Middle States	408		156,363,765	55,105,119	188,932,745	40,082,575	24,191,148
Five Southern States	147		56,962,692	39,556,760	16,480,480	4,117,369	4,135,271
Five Southwestern States	149		62,777,683	29,439,176	29,929,299	6,143,597	7,795,981
Nine Northwestern States	194		15,424,355	90,382,302	11,745,560	786,424	5,306,780
Totals	1,409		418,139,741	153,799,079	296,329,408	61,144,059	51,573,590

* The returns from these States are slightly incomplete.
† No later returns have been received from these States.

of the United States on or about the 1st of January, 1862.

RESOURCES.

Loans.	Stocks.	Real estate.	Other investments.	Due from other banks.	Notes of other banks.	Cash items.	Specie.
$12,679,244	....	$255,060	....	$2,084,263	$219,370	....	$710,392
8,358,941	....	78,253	....	907,440	903,822	....	318,106
6,013,730	$82,741	167,380	....	753,350	....	$136,550	173,332
111,038,898	....	1,626,464	....	9,137,983	4,030,830	....	8,773,193
26,560,718	490,638	653,188	$195,100	1,941,048	887,274	....	606,977
27,056,326	2,828,612	1,351,519	123,261	4,369,577	404,923	433,222	1,529,855
191,747,787	3,407,991	4,161,804	318,361	18,273,564	5,786,319	571,772	12,115,855
196,058,966	56,278,059	9,319,278	2,179,913	16,796,709	2,121,735	16,995,773	29,102,715
12,796,096	1,562,518	468,057	96,504	2,750,954	549,792	....	1,493,393
46,749,190	10,231,700	1,858,200	2,102,166	4,700,260	3,666,130	446,186	11,464,600
1,904,068	4,550	42,269	3,604	152,128	27,136	177,238	196,725
17,440,111	856,425	540,089	6,420	1,837,068	1,469,799	190,476	3,682,471
275,048,381	68,873,252	12,127,963	4,392,647	26,241,119	7,834,532	19,579,673	45,909,614
25,666,962	3,585,135	1,070,569	340,791	1,893,416	2,003,703	59,939	3,017,359
14,080,746	537,714	230,456	96,919	630,355	543,183	45,620	1,059,715
22,730,259	2,969,872	684,144	2,386,994	587,645	277,649	....	1,692,336
16,680,261	2,623,706	8,563,261	669,781	1,987,125	970,050	100,447	2,366,555
424,522	235,000	....	19,302	40,118	18,412	774	55,071
79,781,750	9,947,427	10,559,530	3,468,750	5,138,659	3,782,997	178,960	8,119,036
10,934,060	565,826	171,300	96,835	1,131,530	684,601	105,786	2,715,120
26,364,513	5,783,087	2,198,413	1,203,840	....	....	6,073,419	13,656,568
11,942,268	464,372	577,614	1,592,498	855,576	422,969	1,021,430	1,041,289
15,391,566	2,343,320	569,974	....	3,659,482	700,353	....	5,991,015
11,243,288	1,285,955	598,955	1,563,395	2,047,551	3,160,122	....	2,967,108
75,875,815	10,443,210	3,966,266	4,577,568	7,694,239	4,968,245	7,200,625	26,670,500
6,949,043	1,358,002	354,769	....	2,012,986	445,144	67,275	4,577,259
10,475,062	2,577,253	702,557	....	2,828,357	1,425,056	144,845	3,655,944
768,028	233,613	96,440	19,249	268,672	65,500	17,503	37,936
4,572,512	1,250,516	317,880	550,106	464,064	693,946	61,448	304,478
1,594,912	219,723	....	321,715	334,186	271,850	....	725,443
43,450	....	9,280	7,580	750	....	4,450	....
23,324,007	6,339,107	1,481,056	898,650	5,909,015	2,901,506	295,921	9,301,120
191,747,787	3,407,991	4,161,804	318,361	18,273,564	5,786,319	571,772	12,115,855
275,048,381	68,873,252	12,127,963	4,392,647	26,241,119	7,834,529	19,579,673	45,909,614
79,781,750	9,947,427	10,559,530	3,468,780	5,138,659	3,782,997	178,960	8,119,036
75,875,815	10,443,210	3,966,266	4,577,568	7,694,239	4,968,245	7,200,625	26,670,500
23,324,007	6,339,107	1,481,056	898,650	5,909,015	2,901,506	295,921	9,301,120
646,577,780	99,010,987	32,396,649	13,648,006	65,256,596	25,253,589	27,827,971	102,146,215

No. 12.

Statement in relation to the deposit accounts, receipts and payments, and outstanding drafts, condensed from the Treasurer's weekly exhibits rendered during the year ending June 30, 1862.

Period.	Am't of deposits.	Outstanding drafts.	Subject to draft.	Am't of receipts.	Amount of drafts paid.
1861.					
July 8	$4,016,766 15	$1,426,440 32	$2,590,325 83	$663,574 42	$2,156,394 05
15	7,495,746 05	1,552,135 65	5,943,610 40	5,430,590 49	1,953,713 59
22	5,781,471 39	1,800,943 97	3,980,598 05	348,960 81	2,063,955 34
29	9,155,943 43	4,872,468 92	7,253,475 91	6,573,977 91	3,189,505 10
August 5	6,844,493 27	1,950,271 63	4,885,221 64	1,406,197 20	3,717,647 46
12	5,740,590 54	1,849,014 03	3,891,596 51	806,561 79	1,912,534 52
19	4,150,599 49	1,976,897 56	2,873,602 93	607,268 17	2,177,198 92
26	7,615,612 83	3,040,709 33	4,574,903 50	5,636,182 76	2,173,160 42
September 2	9,871,768 18	5,416,841 94	4,452,946 24	6,437,859 41	4,181,794 06
9	10,891,102 55	4,432,376 39	7,458,726 16	10,866,866 68	7,847,579 31
16	15,719,173 72	8,245,378 15	7,473,795 57	15,406,176 70	19,576,105 53
23	10,756,119 20	5,512,574 71	14,944,044 59	14,068,444 33	3,972,498 75
30	15,640,109 08	5,276,388 87	10,363,712 91	4,563,373 59	9,079,346 81
October 14	14,012,864 39	10,971,248 94	3,041,615 45	16,452,847 90	18,080,025 59
26	16,485,915 07	10,826,397 50	5,668,817 57	27,556,995 94	25,254,574 56
November 2	15,804,431 68	7,931,045 50	8,850,875 16	13,995,991 91	13,766,065 30
9	15,190,081 38	6,630,992 15	8,874,062 23	11,052,971 83	19,939,319 13
16	15,933,357 46	11,814,471 10	4,117,886 36	11,324,396 59	16,497,190 51
23	13,566,330 53	9,494,516 33	4,071,814 50	13,556,916 69	15,979,243 39
30	....	....	....	9,865,332 46	9,568,700 63
December 9	15,346,787 76	12,295,828 75	3,050,959 03	19,116,538 43	10,653,413 31
16	13,894,499 39	5,970,081 29	5,954,418 10	9,369,661 33	11,091,949 72
23	11,961,613 89	9,080,392 98	2,881,921 01	8,145,709 18	9,708,594 58
31	9,705,364 14	6,147,227 10	3,559,137 04	17,263,348 08	19,518,597 93
1862.					
January 20	9,539,691 05	7,155,192 24	*77,917 92	13,230,450 42	10,359,200 77
27	9,671,046 39	6,534,815 57	569,284 88	9,995,543 21	9,178,347 08
February 3	9,979,131 59	5,916,711 34	1,303,638 74	8,587,934 86	9,178,975 93
10	7,178,953 92	5,084,226 88	*43,421 19	9,448,379 08	10,997,916 47
17	5,851,917 52	6,460,740 18	*250,412 59	5,391,321 60	4,261,799 79
24	7,096,661 49	7,454,441 43	*1,469,660 92	6,079,293 31	6,063,859 99
March 3	7,493,500 54	7,373,410 77	*1,157,511 49	6,109,190 67	5,989,093 00
10	8,315,804 85	3,487,983 67	4,829,541 18	8,970,978 06	6,790,049 49
17	10,583,950 87	7,346,548 48	3,163,029 97	6,058,681 84	3,846,508 24
24	11,242,812 18	6,601,514 10	1,136,116 85	4,718,611 08	5,476,857 08
31	10,366,681 20	10,812,542 65	*27,279,101 77	9,947,744 99	30,471,935 66
April 12	10,397,610 43	4,366,553 85	*11,492,766 90	44,829,557 82	35,358,865 75
26	16,603,931 88	15,765,984 37	816,575 65	61,997,911 92	37,580,444 15
May 12	26,940,879 80	9,634,893 16	17,305,986 34	51,304,171 54	40,944,050 06
19	26,875,133 76	11,065,374 94	15,866,759 56	13,364,752 09	13,433,497 83
26	20,994,001 33	16,628,471 66	15,729,673 11	14,386,057 81	14,809,046 80
31	23,957,265 31	8,901,134 55	15,056,130 96	10,848,289 15	13,240,168 61
June 9	27,818,750 76	9,945,556 00	17,923,194 76	10,350,728 19	6,449,253 74
16	28,313,487 85	7,342,445 76	21,571,449 09	9,997,115 72	9,051,978 63
23	30,175,946 73	6,351,557 49	23,845,389 24	9,793,035 17	8,429,976 29
30	29,534,699 98	10,984,204 59	18,369,904 01	12,827,058 01	14,349,896 14

*Over.

No. 13.

NATIONAL LOAN—SEVEN-THIRTY BONDS.

Proposals will be received at the Treasury Department until 12 o'clock of Monday, the 17th instant, and then opened for thirteen millions four hundred and twenty thousand five hundred and fifty dollars, ($13,420,550,) being the whole amount of 7.30 three years bonds authorized by law and remaining .undisposed of. These bonds will be of the issue of October 1, 1861, and will have the coupon due April 1, 1863, attached. The accrued interest from October 1, 1862, to date of payment will be required to be paid in gold coin or in United States legal tender notes.· Offers for any amount not less than one bond of fifty dollars will be considered, but the department will be at liberty to decline all proposals not regarded as advantageous to the government.

Ten per cent. of each amount offered must be deposited with an assistant treasurer, and will be forfeited in case of acceptance of proposal and non-payment of the balance within ten days from date of notice of acceptance.

All deposits on account of proposal not accepted will be immediately returned to the offerers. On receiving deposits the assistant treasurers will, when any deposit may be made, issue duplicate certificates—the original of which he will deliver to the offerer, by whom it must be sent, with his proposal, to the Secretary of the Treasury. No proposal will be considered in absence of such a certificate; nor will any proposal be received after 12 o'clock of the day fixed for the opening.

                                         S. P. CHASE,
                                    Secretary of the Treasury.

No. 13.

Schedule of bids for $13,613,450 three years' 7.30 bonds, under act of July 17, 1861, with the per centum amount accepted, and amount rejected, (notice November 10, 1862.)

No.	Name.	Residence.	Amount bid.	Rate.	Amount accepted.	Amount declined.
				Per cent.		
1	G. F. Work & Co	Philadelphia	$5,000	4.19½	$5,000	
			6,000	4.00	6,000	
			10,000	3.75	10,000	
			5,000	3.87½	5,000	
			13,000	3.06	13,000	
			6,000	3.37½	6,000	
			5,000	3.00		$5,000
2	Jay, Cooke & Co	Washington, D. C.	200,000	4.00	200,000	
			200,000	3.76	200,000	
			200,000	3.62½	200,000	
			100,000	3.50	100,000	
			50,000	3.30	50,000	
			50,000	3.25	50,000	
			50,000	3.12½	50,000	
			250,000	3.05	148,500	101,400
			150,000	3.00		150,000
			250,000	2.75		250,000
3	Gebhard Fire Insurance Comp'y	do	5,000	4.05	5,000	
			5,000	3.87½	5,000	
			5,000	3.62½	5,000	
			5,000	3.37½	5,000	
			5,000	3.12½	5,000	
4	Florence & Conant	Washington, D. C.	1,000	4.50	1,000	
5	G. D. Rosengarten	Philadelphia	5,000	4.00	5,000	
6	Jacob L. Smith	do	750	4.00	750	
7	C. S. Darrow	Boston	1,000	4.00	1,000	
8	Vermilye & Co	New York	10,000	4.00	10,000	
			50,000	3.80	50,000	
			20,000	3.75	20,000	
			25,000	3.60	20,000	
			50,000	3.55	50,000	
			20,000	3.50	20,000	
			100,000	3.31	100,000	
			20,000	3.10	20,000	
			50,000	3.05	29,700	20,300
			10,000	3.00		10,000
			20,000	2.90		20,000
			50,000	2.81		50,000
			50,000	2.61		50,000
			20,000	2.55		20,000
			10,000	2.50		10,000
9	Richard Vallant	do	7,500	4.00	7,500	
10	Farmers and Mechanics' Bank	Philadelphia	50,000	3.85	50,000	
			100,000	3.65	100,000	
			100,000	3.35	100,000	
			250,000	3.85		250,000
11	E. W. Clark & Co	do	25,000	3.79	25,000	
			50,000	3.57	50,000	
			50,000	3.29	50,000	
			50,000	3.06	50,000	
12	John Gardner	Boston	2,000	3.76	2,000	
			3,000	3.50	3,000	
13	Brewster, Sweet & Co	do	15,000	3.75	15,000	
			100,000	3.50	100,000	
			100,000	3.25	100,000	
			100,000	3.19½	100,000	
			10,000	3.19½	10,000	
14	G. S. Robbins & Sons, agents	New York	20,000	3.75	20,000	
15	Roosevelt & Son	do	20,000	3.50	20,000	
			100,000	3.75	100,000	
			100,000	3.50	100,000	
			100,000	3.25	100,000	
16	Jeremiah Pangburn	do	5,000	3.70	5,000	
17	Benjamin Tomes	do	5,550	3.60	5,550	
			5,000	3.49	5,000	
18	Daniel Le Roy	do	5,000	3.55	5,000	
			5,000	3.40	5,000	
19	Thomas V. C. Morgan	Philadelphia	1,500	3.60	1,500	
20	Edward Haight, president	New York	150,000	3.55	150,000	
			150,000	3.30	150,000	
			150,000	3.05	69,200	80,800
21	James A. Cowing	do	25,000	3.55	25,000	

No. 13.—*Schedule of bids, &c.*—Continued.

No.	Name.	Residence.	Amount bid.	Rate.	Amount accepted.	Amount declined.
				Per cent.		
22	Samuel A. Way	Boston	$10,000	3.50	$10,000	
			10,000	3.00		$10,000
			20,000	2.50		20,000
			10,000	1.50		10,000
23	Cambridge City Bank	Cambridgeport, Mass.	10,000	3.50	10,000	
24	Henry P. Ketcham	New York	10,000	3.50	10,000	
25	Read, Drexel & Co.	...do	21,000	3.50	21,000	
			56,000	3.00		56,000
			754,000	2.85		754,000
			50,000	2.10		50,000
			75,000	2.00		75,000
			50,000	1.00		50,000
26	J. De Ricqles	Cincinnati	250	3.50	250	
27	Benkard & Hutton	New York	250,000	3.50	250,000	
			250,000	3.37½	250,000	
			250,000	3.25	250,000	
			250,000	3.12½	250,000	
28	T. D. Armstrong	Mount Holly, N. J.	5,000	3.50	5,000	
			5,000	3.00		5,000
29	H. C. Young, cashier	Philadelphia	25,000	3.50	25,000	
			25,000	3.00		25,000
			25,000	2.50		25,000
			25,000	2.00		25,000
30	Wm. Amer	...do	5,000	3.50	5,000	
			5,000	3.25	5,000	
31	P. Tomes, jr	New York	5,000	3.50	5,000	
32	George W. Welsh	...do	10,000	3.50	10,000	
33	Jay, Cooke & Co	Washington, D. C.	25,000	3.50	25,000	
			25,000	3.25	25,000	
			25,000	3.12½	25,000	
			25,000	3.00		25,000
34	Clarke, Dodge & Co	New York	50,000	3.50	50,000	
			100,000	3.37½	100,000	
			100,000	3.25	100,000	
			100,000	3.12½	100,000	
35	Judd Linseed and Sperm Oil Co.	...do	50,000	3.50	50,000	
36	Geo. and Samuel Brown	...do	25,000	3.50	25,000	
			25,000	3.25	25,000	
			25,000	3.00		25,000
			25,000	2.75		25,000
37	John De Voe, executor	...do	3,400	3.50	3,400	
38	Clarkson Brothers	...do	10,000	3.41	10,000	
			10,000	3.17	10,000	
			10,000	3.15	10,000	
			10,000	3.10	10,000	
39	James H. Banker	...do	20,000	3.40	20,000	
			20,000	3.37½	20,000	
			20,000	3.33½	20,000	
			20,000	3.10	20,000	
			20,000	3.00		20,000
40	Stuart & Brother	Philadelphia	25,000	3.38	25,000	
			25,000	3.02		25,000
			25,000	2.90		25,000
			25,000	2.80		25,000
41	Corn Exchange Bank	...do	20,000	3.37½	20,000	
			20,000	3.25	20,000	
			20,000	3.12½	20,000	
			20,000	3.00		20,000
			20,000	2.75		20,000
42	Robert Stuyvesant	New York	500	3.37½	500	
			500	2.60½		500
43	Drexel & Co.	Philadelphia	150,000	3.37½	150,000	
			250,000	3.02		250,000
			150,000	2.91		150,000
			150,000	2.80		150,000
44	Livermore, Clews & Co.	New York	5,000	3.37½	5,000	
			10,000	3.25	10,000	
			20,000	3.12½	20,000	
			30,000	3.10	30,000	
			30,000	3.05	17,800	12,200
			50,000	3.01		50,000
			50,000	3.00		50,000
45	E. D. Stanton	...do	100,000	3.36	100,000	
			100,000	3.30	100,000	
			100,000	3.25	100,000	
46	James F. Penniman	...do	3,000	3.38	3,000	
47	Merchants' Bank	...do	50,000	3.35	50,000	
			50,000	3.25	50,000	
			50,000	2.90		50,000
			50,000	2.75		53,000

No. 13.—*Schedule of bids, &c.*—Continued.

No.	Name.	Residence.	Amount bid.	Rate. *Per cent.*	Amount accepted.	Amount declined.
47	Merchants' Bank	New York	$100,000	2.50	......	$100,000
48	E. L. Boies	...do	5,000	3.33	$5,000	......
49	J. Van Duzer, president	...do	20,000	3.31	20,000	......
			20,000	3.26	20,000	......
			20,000	3 13	20,000	......
			20,000	2.96	......	20,000
			60,000	2.76	......	20,000
50	G. S. Robbins & Son	...do	157,000	3.30	157,000	......
51	John P. Yelverton, cashier	...do	150,000	3.70	150,000	......
			250,000	3.27	250,000	......
52	Rittenhouse, Fant & Co	Washington, D. C.	250,000	3.93	250,000	......
			20,000	3.25	20,000	......
			20,080		20,000	......
			160,000	3.05	107,100	72,900
			30,000	2.52	......	30,000
53	O. H. Schreiner, cashier	New York	25,000	3.06	25,000	......
			25,000	3.06	25,000	......
			25,000	2.76	......	25,000
			25,000	2.56	......	25,000
54	E. W. Tallman, cashier	...do	60,000	3.26	60,000	......
			50,000	3.20	50,000	......
			50,000	3.10	50,000	......
			50,000	3.05	22,700	90,300
55	Ward, Campbell & Co	...do	60,000	3.05	60,000	......
			490,000	3.05	248,700	170,300
			10,000	3.00	......	10,000
			250,000	2.75	......	250,000
			510,000	2.50	......	510,000
56	B. M. Freleigh	Saugerties, N. Y.	10,000	3.35	10,000	......
			5,000	3.19½	......	5,000
57	John Gulliver	Philadelphia	5,000	3.75	......	5,000
58	D. C. Spooner	...do	2,000	3.25	2,000	......
59	De Coursey, Lafourcade & Co	...do	10,000	3.25	10,000	......
60	E. Whitehouse, Son & Morrison	New York	5,000	3.25	5,000	......
			75,000	3.25	75,000	......
			90,000	3.00	......	90,000
61	Benj. H. Field	...do	10,000	3.25	10,000	......
			10,000	3.00	......	10,000
			90,000	1.00	......	90,000
62	Charles P. Gulick	...do	2,500	3.25	2,500	......
63	Mutual Life Insurance Comp'y	...do	100,000	3.25	100,000	......
			100,000	3.00	......	100,000
			100,000	2.75	......	100,000
			100,000	2.50	......	100,000
			100,000	2.00	......	100,000
64	G. S. Robbins & Sons, trustees	...do	40,000	3.25	40,000	......
			40,000	2.90	......	40,000
65	John Ponder	Washington, D. C.	25,000	3.25	25,000	......
66	Thompson Brothers	New York	500,000	3.21	500,000	......
			300,000	3.17	300,000	......
			200,000	3.07	200,000	......
67	Livermore, Clews & Co	...do	50,000	3.17	50,000	......
			150,000	3.13	150,000	......
68	E. W. Dunham	...do	55,000	3.07	55,000	......
			50,000	3.17	50,000	......
			60,000	3.01	......	50,000
			50,000	2.70	......	50,000
69	Edward J. King	...do	5,000	3.16	5,000	......
			5,000	2.83	......	5,000
			5,000	2.27	......	5,000
70	Livermore, Clews & Co	...do	100,000	3.15	100,000	......
			300,000	3.13	300,000	......
			100,000	3.11	100,000	......
71	John Olmstead	Yonkers, N. Y.	10,000	3.15	10,000	......
			10,000	2.80	......	10,000
			10,000	2.15	......	10,000
72	Samuel F. Ashton	Philadelphia	10,000	3.12½	10,000	......
73	Manhattan Savings Institution	New York	125,000	3.12½	125,000	......
74	Henry F. Vail, cashier	...do	650,000	3.10	650,000	......
			650,000	3.00	......	650,000
			600,000	2.75	......	600,000
			500,000	2.50	......	500,000
75	Wm. Burton	Brooklyn, N. Y.	5,000	3.10*	5,000	......
			5,000	3.10*	......	5,000
76	W. H. Cox, cashier	New York	25,000	3.10	25,000	......
			297,500	3.00	......	297,500
			210,000	2.50	......	210,000
			10,000	1.50	......	10,000
77	Joseph Jones	Philadelphia	25,000	3.10	25,000	......

No. 13.—*Schedule of bids, &c.*—Continued.

No.	Name.	Residence.	Amount bid.	Rate.	Amount accepted.	Amount declined.
				Per cent.		
77	Joseph Jones	Philadelphia..........	$2,000	3.00	....	$2,000
78	Winslow, Lanier & Co., and C. P. Culver.	New York.............	250,000	3.10	$250,000	....
			350,000	3.00	....	350,000
			200,000	2.90	....	200,000
			100,000	2.50	....	100,000
			100,000	2.25	....	100,000
79	Underhill & Haven	......do	5,000	3.07	....	....
			5,000	2.97	5,000	5,000
			5,000	2.77	....	5,000
			5,000	2.67	....	5,000
			5,000	2.57	....	5,000
			5,000	2.47	....	5,000
			5,000	2.37	....	5,000
			5,000	2.27	....	5,000
			5,000	2.17	....	5,000
			5,000	1.97	....	5,000
			5,000	1.77	....	5,000
			5,000	1.57	....	5,000
80	American Exchange Bank	...do	750,000	3.05	445,500	304,100
81	W. H. Cox, cashier..........	...do	25,000	3.05	14,900	10,100
82	Fearing & Dalton	...do	25,000	3.05	14,000	10,100
			25,000	3.00	....	25,000
			25,000	2.95	....	25,000
83	Ketchum, Son & Co., for themselves and others.	...do	4,642,500	3.05	2,760,300	1,882,200
			107,500	3.05	63,900	43,600
			50,000	3.05	29,700	20,300
			25,000	2.40	....	25,000
			15,000	1.01	....	15,000
			100,000	2.07	....	100,000
84	Anthony Halsey, cashier	......do	130,000	3.05	77,300	52,700
			25,000	2.76	....	25,000
			25,000	2.26	....	25,000
			20,000	1.76	....	20,000
85	Ward & Co	......do	50,000	3.05	20,700	20,300
			50,000	2.85	....	50,000
			50,000	2.65	....	50,000
			50,000	2.15	....	50,000
86	Franklin Haven	Boston	500,000	3.05½	....	500,000
			500,000	2.77½	....	500,000
87	Samuel Hoo	....do	200	3.00	....	200
88	Ira Steward	.....do	100	3.00	....	100
89	Naumkeag Bank	Salem, Mass	100,000	3.00	....	100,000
90	W. Ropes & Co	Boston	10,000	3.00	....	10,000
			10,000	2.50	....	10,000
			10,000	2.00	....	10,000
			10,000	1.00	....	10,000
			10,000	Par.	....	10,000
91	John E. Kendall	Washington, D. C ...	4,000	3.00	....	4,000
92	M. A. Falkenburgh	Jersey City	500	3.00	....	500
93	J. C. Lewis.................	Washington, D. C....	100	3.00	....	100
			200	2.00	....	200
			100	1.09	....	100
94	Christopher Becker	New York............	5,000	3.00	....	5,000
95	J. B. Orton...	.....do	2,500	3.00	....	2,500
			2,500	2.75	....	2,500
96	C. S. Underwood	Washington, D. C...	400	3.00	....	400
97	Riggs & Co.................	...do	100,000	3.00	....	100,000
98	Wm. P. Dole	...do	400	3.00	....	400
99	Anna G. Dudley	...do	150	3.00	....	150
100	Boylston Bank	Boston.............	40,000	3.00	....	40,000
101	Jas. E. Southworth, president...	New York...........	25,000	3.00	....	25,000
			25,000	2.86	....	25,000
102	Daicr & Timpson	....do	20,000	3.00	....	20,000
103	Metacomet Bank	Fall River, Mass....	15,000	3.00	....	15,000
			15,000	2.75	....	15,000
			15,000	2.50	....	15,000
			15,000	2.25	....	15,000
104	Henry W. Shaw	New York...........	1,000	3.00	....	1,000
105	Allen Danforth, treasurer.....	Boston..............	10,000	3.00	....	10,000
			10,000	2.50	....	10,000
			10,000	2.00	....	10,000
106	Rebecca Nathans	Philadelphia	3,000	3.00	....	3,000
107	John L. Rogers	New York............	20,000	3.00	....	20,000
108	Thomas Lamb...............	Boston..............	25,000	3.00	....	25,000
			25,000	2.75	....	25,000
109	Charles H. Delavan	New York............	15,000	3.00	....	15,000
			15,000	2.75	....	15,000
			20,000	2.50	....	20,000
			30,000	2.25	....	30,000

No. 13.—*Schedule of bids, &c.*—Continued.

No.	Name.	Residence.	Amount bid.	Rate.	Amount accepted.	Amount declined.
				Per cent.		
110	J. M. Goddard	New York	$1,500	3.00	....	$1,500
111	Otis Daniel, for estate of M. Grant.	do	10,000	3.00	....	10,000
			10,000	3.00	....	10,000
112	E. L. Kelsey	do	250	3.00	....	250
113	Alfonso Deschovitz	do	10,000	3.00	....	10,000
114	John Wadsworth	do	10,000	3.00	....	10,000
			10,000	2.75	....	10,000
115	J. F. De Lanier	do	100,000	3.00	....	100,000
			100,000	2.90	....	100,000
116	F. M. Harris, cashier	do	25,000	3.00	....	25,000
			25,000	2.75	....	25,000
			25,000	2.50	....	25,000
			25,000	2.25	....	25,000
			25,000	2.00	....	25,000
117	East River Savings Institution	do	25,000	3.00	....	25,000
			25,000	2.60	....	25,000
118	Lewis Johnson & Co	Washington, D. C.	200,000	2.95	....	200,000
			50,000	2.70	....	50,000
			100,000	2.60½	....	100,000
119	Livermore, Clews & Co	New York	5,000	2.90	....	5,000
			5,000	2.87½	....	5,000
			5,000	2.75	....	5,000
			5,000	2.62½	....	5,000
			5,000	2.60	....	5,000
			5,000	2.55	....	5,000
			84,000	2.50	....	84,000
			40,000	2.40	....	40,000
			5,000	2.37½	....	5,000
			40,000	1.90	....	40,000
120	J. E. Park	Downington, Pa.	5,000	2.87½	....	5,000
121	Philip Speyer & Co	New York	5,000	2.77	....	5,000
			5,000	2.76	....	5,000
			5,000	2.75	....	5,000
			5,000	2.73	....	5,000
			5,000	2.71	....	5,000
			5,000	2.68	....	5,000
			10,000	2.64	....	10,000
			10,000	2.62	....	10,000
			10,000	2.59	....	10,000
			10,000	2.56	....	10,000
			10,000	2.52	....	10,000
			20,000	2.51	....	20,000
122	Webster Bank	Boston	75,000	2.75	....	75,000
			75,000	2.62½	....	75,000
			75,000	2.50	....	75,000
			75,000	2.37½	....	75,000
			100,000	2.25	....	100,000
123	Maria McGregor	New York	7,000	2.75	....	7,000
124	Home Insurance Company	do	25,000	2.75	....	25,000
			25,000	2.55	....	25,000
			25,000	2.30	....	25,000
			25,000	2.00	....	25,000
125	Augustus A. L. Chase, cashier		3,000	2.50	....	3,000
126	John F. Elton	Waterbury, Conn.	10,000	2.60	....	10,000
			15,000	2.50	....	15,000
127	S. & W. Welsh	Philadelphia	100,000	2.50	....	100,000
128	New England Bank	do	40,000	2.50	....	40,000
			40,000	2.00	....	40,000
			80,000	1.50	....	80,000
			80,000	1.00	....	80,000
			10,000	.50	....	10,000
129	Miners' Bank	Pottsville, Pa.	50,000	2.50	....	50,000
130	G. W. Berrien	Jersey City	8,000	2.50	....	8,000
131	Josiah T. Cook	Boston	10,000	2.50	....	10,000
132	E. L. Bushnell	New York	5,000	2.50	....	5,000
			5,000	2.00	....	5,000
			5,000	1.50	....	5,000
			5,000	1.00	....	5,000
133	Nathan Nathans	Philadelphia	1,000	2.50	....	1,000
134	J. Amory Davis	Boston	25,000	2.50	....	25,000
135	Otis Daniel	do	10,000	2.50	....	10,000
			10,000	2.00	....	10,000
			10,000	1.10	....	10,000
136	James W. Harris	do	1,000	2.50	....	1,000
137	Samuel F. Ashton	Philadelphia	10,000	2.50	....	10,000
138	John T. Vincent	Washington, D. C.	1,000	2.50	....	1,000
139	John Binke	New York	1,000	2.50	....	1,000
140	Joseph M. Price, cashier	do	50,000	2.50	....	50,000
141	Geo. S. Robbins & Sons, trustees	do	40,000	2.50	....	40,000

No. 13.—*Schedule of bids, &c.*—Continued.

No.	Name.	Residence.	Amount bid.	Rate.	Amount accepted.	Amount declined.
				Per cent.		
142	James Gallatin, president	New York	$50,000	2.50	....	$50,000
143	W. H. Slocum	....do	10,000	2.50	....	10,000
144	Bliss, Williams & Co	....do	25,000	2.30	....	25,000
			25,000	2.25	....	25,000
			50,000	2.05	....	50,000
			25,000	1.90	....	25,000
			25,000	1.75	....	25,000
145	Charles Stoddard	Boston	6,000	2.25	....	6,000
146	F. S. Bayley, cashier	Springfield, Mass	5,000	2.25	....	5,000
			5,000	2.00	....	5,000
			5,000	1.75	....	5,000
			5,000	1.50	....	5,000
			5,000	1.25	....	5,000
147	B. F. Mansfield	New York	5,000	2.30	....	5,000
			5,000	1.50	....	5,000
148	Underhill & Haven	....do	20,000	2.00	....	20,000
149	Hamilton Fire Insurance Co	....do	25,000	2.10	....	25,000
150	National Bank	Boston	70,000	2.00	....	70,000
151	Bank of America	New York	500,000	2.00	....	500,000
			10,000	2.00	....	10,000
152	George A. Black	....do	1,000	2.03	....	1,000
153	A. E. Giles	Boston	1,000	2.00	....	1,000
154	William Wright	Philadelphia	15,000	2.00	....	15,000
155	Joseph Hutchinson	Washington, D. C.	2,000	2.00	....	2,000
			2,000	1.30	....	2,000
			2,000	1.00	....	2,000
			2,000	Par.	....	2,000
156	Leaman Thompson	Albany, N. Y.	5,000	2.00	....	5,000
157	Albany Exchange Bank	....do	90,000	2.00	....	90,000
			20,000	1.50	....	20,000
			20,000	1.00	....	20,000
158	Robert White	Boston	3,000	2.00	....	3,000
159	Thomas Trueman	New York	500	2.00	....	500
160	Amanda Mebean	Washington, D. C.	1,000	2.00	....	1,000
161	Isaac Sweetser	Boston	1,000	2.00	....	1,000
162	John Slattery	New York	10,000	2.00	....	10,000
			10,000	Par.	....	10,000
163	Jefferson Branch State Bank of Ohio		31,000	2.00	....	31,000
164	Charles W. Swartz	Washington, D. C.	500	1.75	....	500
165	Isaac W. Blain, for himself and others	New York	4,500	1.50	....	4,500
166	Hostetter & Smith	Pittsburg	10,000	1.25	....	10,000
167	Clarkson & Co	New York	5,000	1.01	....	5,000
			10,000	.01	....	10,000
168	J. Kendall	Boston	2,000	1.00	....	2,000
169	John H. Robinson	Paterson, N. J	300	1.00	....	300
170	A. B. Johnson	Utica, N. Y.	10,000	1.00	....	10,000
171	Francis Jagn	Philadelphia	4,000	1.00	....	4,000
172	George B. Milton	Boston	1,000	1.00	....	1,000
173	V. de Amerilla	Philadelphia	300	1.00	....	300
174	Seth Caldwell	Worcester, Mass	1,000	1.00	....	1,000
175	Drevoort Fire Insurance Co	New York	10,000	1.00	....	10,000
			10,000	.50	....	10,000
			10,000	Par.	....	10,000
176	C. T. Willard	Philadelphia	50	1.00	....	50
177	Albany Exchange Bank	Albany, N. Y.	90,000	.75	....	90,000
			20,000	.50	....	20,000
178	George W. Uternehle	Washington, D. C.	6,000	Par.	....	6,000
179	S. J. Coss	....do	750	Par.	....	750
180	Henry H. Bownell	New Haven, Conn	3,000	Par.	....	3,000
181	White & Hill	Nashua, N. H.	5,000	Par.	....	5,000
182	Henry S. Milton	Boston	1,000	Par.	....	1,000
183	Pemberton Smith	Philadelphia	3,000	Par.	....	3,000
184	G. P. Hunting	Boston	400	Par.	....	400
185	W. M. Webster	Philadelphia	2,500	Par.	....	2,500
186	J. M. Dalisse	New York	1,000	Par.	....	1,000
187	J. M. Hines	Shippensburg, Pa	1,000	Par.	....	1,000
188	Mrs. S. E. Edwards	Philadelphia	2,000	Par.	....	2,000
	Total		29,994,350	......	$13,613,450	16,380,900

No. 14.

Statement of the public debt on the 1st day of January in each of the year from 1791 to 1842, inclusive, and at various dates in subsequent years, to July 1, 1862.

On the 1st day of January..	1791	$75, 463, 476 52
	1792	77, 227, 924 66
	1793	80, 352, 634 04
	1794	78, 427, 404 77
	1795	80, 747, 587 38
	1796	83, 762, 172 07
	1797	82, 064, 479 33
	1798	79, 228, 529 12
	1799	78, 408, 669 77
	1800	82, 976, 294 35
	1801	83, 038, 050 80
	1802	80, 712, 632 25
	1803	77, 054, 686 30
	1804	86, 427, 120 88
	1805	82, 312, 150 50
	1806	75, 723, 270 66
	1807	69, 218, 398 64
	1808	65, 196, 317 97
	1809	57, 023, 192 09
	1810	53, 173, 217 52
	1811	48, 005, 587 76
	1812	45, 209, 737 90
	1813	55, 962, 827 57
	1814	81, 487, 846 24
	1815	99, 833, 660 15
	1816	127, 334, 933 74
	1817	123, 491, 965 16
	1818	103, 466, 633 83
	1819	95, 529, 648 28
	1820	91, 015, 566 15
	1821	89, 987, 427 66
	1822	93, 546, 676 98
	1823	90, 875, 877 28
	1824	90, 269, 777 77
	1825	83, 788, 432 71
	1826	81, 054, 059 99
	1827	73, 987, 357 20
	1828	67, 475, 043 87
	1829	58, 421, 413 67
	1830	48, 565, 406 50
	1831	39, 123; 191 68
	1832	24, 322, 235 18
	1833	7, 001; 032 88
	1834	4, 760, 082 08
	1835	351, 289 05
	1836	291, 089 05
	1837	1, 878, 223 55
	1838	4, 857, 660 46

No. 14.—*Statement of the public debt, &c.*—Continued.

On the 1st day of January..1839	$11,983,737	53
1840	5,125,077	63
1841	6,737,398	00
1842	15,028,486	37
On the 1st day of July......1843	27,203,450	69
1844	24,748,188	23
1845	17,093,794	80
1846	16,750,926	33
1847	38,956,623	38
1848	48,526,379	37
On the 1st day of December..1849	64,704,693	71
1850	64,228,238	37
On the 20th day of November..1851	62,560,395	26
On the 30th day of December..1852	65,131,692	13
On the 1st day of July......1853	67,340,628	78
1854	47,242,206	05
On the 17th day of November..1855	39,969,731	05
On the 15th day of November..1856	30,963,909	64
On the 1st day of July......1857	29,060,386	90
1858	44,910,777	66
1859	58,754,699	33
1860	64,769,703	08
1861	90,867,828	68
1862	514,211,371	92

L. E. CHITTENDEN, *Register.*

TREASURY DEPARTMENT,
    Register's Office, November 29, 1862.

No. 15.

Statement showing the payments made annually on account of the interest and reimbursement of the domestic debt, interest on the public debt, and redemption of the public debt, from March 4, 1789, to June 30, 1862.

	Interest and re-imbursement of domestic debt.	Interest on the public debt.	Redemption of the public debt.
From Mar. 4, 1789, to Dec. 31, 1791	$1,140,177 20	$37,685 83	$699,984 23
Year ending 1792	2,373,611 28	....	4,711,405 04
1793	2,079,105 76	13,753 41	2,672,048 54
1794	2,455,856 60	296,666 44	2,874,356 39
1795	2,727,959 07	219,099 99	2,985,742 55
1796	2,914,847 68	324,500 00	2,685,658 33
1797	2,879,976 73	292,540 00	2,708,682 55
1798	3,726,238 40	229,637 50	1,004,518 97
1799	2,599,351 41	216,400 00	1,706,578 84
1800	3,186,201 04	216,400 00	1,138,563 11
1801	4,213,430 06	198,400 00	2,879,876 98
1802	4,077,147 16	162,025 00	5,293,235 24
1803	3,949,462 36	82,000 00	3,224,697 07
1804	3,977,206 07	592,031 03	3,593,017 66
1805	3,318,141 48	751,707 41	3,171,225 96
1806	5,572,018 64	485,216 12	2,883,753 14
1807	4,183,990 40	509,098 74	1,614,730 96
1808	7,701,288 96	600,633 28	1,956,440 95
1809	3,859,596 27	688,923 42	1,910,734 47
1810	4,835,241 12	844,674 35	2,318,996 74
1811	2,010,656 49	654,802 94	5,334,540 57
1812	1,098,488 49	627,051 64	2,724,082 32
1813	1,948,639 73	806,740 74	8,352,742 97
1814	1,712,897 50	216,835 31	5,970,811 13
1815	3,343,263 09	793,366 18	8,492,293 08
1816	4,537,779 77	699,730 83	19,643,552 33
1817	5,442,503 62	344,019 85	19,636,512 65
1818	5,506,814 60	190,743 82	2,005,367 27
1819	7,355,167 52	46,720 04	13,894,314 06
1820	5,465,998 95	188,133 87	2,974,364 46
1821	5,623,331 38	36,56.0 88	2,707,211 56
1822	5,730,760 62	....	2,109,188 50
1823	5,524,034 37	....	5,982 04
1824	5,301,104 19	....	11,267,289 57
1825	....	4,366,757 40	7,728,578 38
1826	....	3,975,542 95	7,065,539 24
1827	....	3,486,071 51	6,517,506 80
1828	....	3,098,800 60	9,064,637 49
1829	....	2,542,843 23	9,841,024 55
1830	....	1,912,574 93	9,443,175 01
1831	....	1,373,748 74	14,800,629 48
1832	....	772,561 50	17,067,747 79
1833	....	303,796 87	1,239,746 51
1834	50 00	202,152 98	5,974,362 21
1835	....	57,863 08	390 37
1836	....	....	....
1837	27 76	....	21,824 03
1838	2,000 75	14,997 54	5,588,711 98
1839	3,000 00	399,834 23	10,715,153 19
1840	2,000 00	174,635 77	3,909,977 93
1841	2,261 13	288,063 45	5,310,365 16

No. 15.—*Statement showing the payments made annually, &c.*—Continued.

Year ending	Interest and reimbursement of domestic debt.	Interest on the public debt.	Redemption of the public debt.
1842	$5,000 00	$773,550 06	$7,896,989 88
1843	5,000 00	523,584 57	333,011 98
1844	44,548 16	1,833,484 37	11,113,870 31
1845	26,031 95	1,040,953 09	7,509,822 63
1846	22,649 35	843,228 77	347,945 19
1847	6,956 74	1,119,246 86	5,593,078 77
1848	4,767 38	2,391,652 17	13,031,268 87
1849	4,500 00	3,565,835 32	12,729,679 00
1850	2,000 00	3,782,406 74	3,654,321 43
1851	2,338 49	3,701,979 60	652,123 55
1852	1,359 78	4,000,654 35	2,150,576 72
1853	....	3,665,551 08	6,412,855 67
1854	....	3,066,646 51	18,269,718 40
1855	....	2,314,464 99	6,665,165 86
1856	23 50	1,954,708 84	10,052,099 88
1857	3 21	1,593,765 23	4,284,686 78
1858	....	1,652,055 67	7,544,568 29
1859	....	2,637,664 39	14,713,572 81
1860	....	3,144,620 94	13,900,392 13
1861	....	4,000,173 76	18,221,707 27
1862	3 06	13,190,324 45	96,096,919 03
Total	131,498,896 27	95,107,895 21	532,688,184 38

L. E. CRITTENDEN, *Register.*

TREASURY DEPARTMENT,
Register's Office, November 29, 1862.

No. 16.

Summary statement of the value of the exports of the growth, produce, and manufacture of the United States during the year commencing July 1, 1861, and ending June 30, 1862.

PRODUCT OF THE SEA.			
Fisheries—			
Oil, spermaceti		$962,603	
Oil, whale and other fish		1,286,329	
Whalebone		556,795	
Spermaceti and sperm candles		64,481	
Fish, dried or smoked		714,582	
Fish, pickled		328,687	
			$3,913,477
PRODUCT OF THE FOREST.			
Wood—			
Staves and headings	$2,590,649		
Shingles	67,356		
Boards, plank, and scantling	2,015,982		
Hewn timber	138,521		
Other lumber	1,178,753		
Oak-bark and other dye	186,363		
All manufactures of	1,753,259		
Naval stores—			
Tar and pitch	55,884		
Rosin and turpentine	293,400		
Ashes, pot and pearl	451,047		
Ginseng	406,590		
Skins and furs	794,407		
			9,934,211
PRODUCT OF AGRICULTURE.			
Animals—			
Beef	2,017,077		
Tallow	4,026,113		
Hides	518,687		
Horned cattle	193,019		
Butter	4,114,057		
Cheese	2,712,899		
Pork, pickled	3,980,003		
Hams and bacon	10,290,572		
Lard	10,004,521		
Wool	296,225		
Hogs	23,562		
Horses	157,442		
Mules	212,187		
Sheep	34,600		
		38,580,964	
Vegetable food—			
Wheat	42,568,790		
Flour	27,513,196		
Indian corn	10,387,651		
Indian meal	778,076		
Rye meal	54,488		
Rye, oats, and other small grain and pulse	2,364,625		
Biscuit or ship-bread	490,942		
Potatoes	300,599		
Apples	219,528		

No. 16.—*Summary statement of the value of exports, &c.*—Continued.

PRODUCT OF AGRICULTURE—Continued.			
Vegetable food—			
Onions	$90,412		
Rice	156,899		
		$84,925,206	
Cotton	....	1,180,113	
Tobacco	....	12,325,356	
Hemp	....	8,960	
Other agricultural products—			
Clover-seed	295,255		
Flaxseed	59		
Brown sugar	90,022		
Hops	681,308		
		1,046,644	$138,066,583
MANUFACTURES.			
Refined sugar	147,397		
Wax	47,383		
Chocolate	4,288		
Spirits from grain	328,414		
Spirits from molasses	715,702		
Spirits from other materials	1,577,861		
Molasses	21,914		
Vinegar	29,701		
Beer, ale, porter, and cider, (in casks)	45,464		
Beer, ale, porter, and cider, (in bottles)	9,232		
Linseed oil	20,928		
Spirits of turpentine	54,731		
Household furniture	939,168		
Carriages and parts, and railroad cars and parts.	517,175		
Hats of fur or silk	77,281		
Hats of palm leaf	55,446		
Saddlery	67,759		
Trunks and valises	50,771		
Adamantine and other candles	836,849		
Soap	636,049		
Snuff	7,914		
Tobacco, manufactured	1,068,080		
Gunpowder	101,803		
Leather	389,037		
Leather boots and shoes	721,206		
Cables and cordage	199,669		
Salt	228,109		
Lead	7,334		
Iron—			
Pig	38,412		
Bar	45,584		
Nails	175,656		
Castings	54,761		
All manufactures	4,312,448		
		13,433,636	
Copper and brass, and manufactures of	....	1,088,021	
Drugs and medicines	....	1,490,376	
Cotton piece goods—			
Printed or colored	587,500		
White, other than duck	508,004		
Duck	221,685		
All manufactures of	1,629,275		
		2,946,464	

No. 16.—*Summary statement of the value of exports, &c.*—Continued.

MANUFACTURES—Continued.			
Hemp—			
Thread	$253		
Bags	2,106		
Cloth	1,140		
Other manufactures	28,441		
		$31,940	
Wearing apparel	472,924		
Earthen and stone ware	31,158		
Combs	12,994		
Buttons	1,227		
Brooms and brushes of all kinds	99,166		
Billiard-tables and apparatus	19,884		
Umbrellas, parasols, and sunshades	553		
Morocco and other leather not sold by the pound	13,049		
Fire-engines	34,930		
Printing presses and type	168,647		
Musical instruments	147,826		
Books and maps	214,231		
Paper and stationery	398,546		
Paints and varnish	259,064		
Jewelry, real and imitation	67,750		
Other manufactures of gold and silver, and gold leaf	63,078		
Glass	522,606		
Tin	62,286		
Pewter and lead	31,366		
Marble and stone	190,067		
Bricks, lime, and cement	83,385		
India-rubber shoes	35,903		
India-rubber, other than shoes	107,953		
Lard oil	148,026		
Oil-cake	875,841		
Artificial flowers	130		
		4,062,590	
			$23,053,027
Coal		837,117	
Ice		162,667	
Gold and silver coin		17,776,912	
Gold and silver bullion		13,267,739	
Quicksilver		1,237,643	
Articles not enumerated—			
Manufactured		2,880,347	
Raw produce		1,770,916	
			37,953,341
Total			212,920 639

L. E. CHITTENDEN, *Register.*

TREASURY DEPARTMENT,
   Register's Office, December 26, 1862.

ment showing the revenue collected from the beginning of the government to June 30, 1862, under the several heads of customs, direct tax, public lands, and miscellaneous sources, including loans and treasury notes; also the expenditures during the same period, and the particular tariff, and the price of lands under which the revenue from those sources was collected.

Years.	From customs.	Date of tariff.	Direct tax.	From public lands.	Price per acre.	From miscellan's sources, including loans and treasury notes.	That portion of miscell's arising from loans and treasury notes.	Total receipts.	Total expenditures.
March 4, to Dec. 91.	$4,399,473 09	July 4, 1789, general; Aug. 10, 1790, general; Mar. 3, 1791, general.			$1, by act of May 20, 1785.	$5,810,559 66	$5,791,112 56	$10,210,025 75	$7,207,539 02
1792	3,433,070 85	May 9, general.				5,297,695 92	5,070,806 46	8,740,766 77	9,141,569 67
1793	4,255,306 56					1,465,317 72	1,067,701 14	5,720,624 28	7,529,575 55
1794	4,801,065 28	June 5, spe'l; June 7, general.				5,240,036 37	4,609,196 78	10,041,101 65	9,302,124 74
1795	5,588,461 26	Jan. 29, general.				3,831,341 53	3,305,968 20	9,419,802 79	10,435,069 85
1796	6,567,987 94			$4,836 13	$2, by act of May 18, 1796.	2,167,505 56	368,800 60	8,740,329 63	8,367,776 84
1797	7,549,649 65	March 3, general; July 8, special.		83,540 60		1,125,726 15	70,135 41	8,758,916 40	8,626,012 78
1798	7,106,061 93			11,963 11		1,001,046 03	308,574 27	8,209,070 07	8,613,517 68
1799	6,610,449 31					6,011,010 53	5,074,646 53	12,621,459 84	11,077,043 50
1800	9,080,932 73	May 13, special.		443 75		5,369,807 66	1,602,435 04	12,451,184 14	11,989,739 92
1801	10,750,778 93			167,726 06		3,026,950 96	10,125 00	13,943,455 95	12,273,376 94
1802	12,438,235 74			188,628 02		3,374,597 55	5,597 36	15,001,391 31	13,276,084 67
1803	10,479,417 61			165,675 69		419,004 33		11,064,097 63	11,258,983 57
1804	11,098,565 33	March 26, special; Mar. 27, special.		497,536 79		249,747 90	9,532 64	11,835,840 02	12,624,646 36
1805	12,935,487 04			540,193 80		219,627 30	128,814 94	13,689,508 14	13,727,124 41
1806	14,667,698 17			765,245 73		175,684 68	48,897 71	15,608,828 78	15,070,093 97
1807	15,845,521 61			466,163 27		86,534 38		16,398,019 26	11,292,292 99
1808	16,363,550 58			647,939 06		51,034 45	1,862 16	17,062,544 09	16,764,584 20
1809	7,296,020 58			442,252 33		35,289 21		7,773,473 12	13,867,226 30
1810	8,583,309 31			696,548 80		2,664,348 40	2,759,992 25	12,144,206 53	13,319,986 74
1811	13,313,222 73			1,040,237 53		78,377 88	8,309 05	14,431,823 14	13,601,808 91
1812	8,958,777 53	July 1, special.		710,427 78		12,969,827 45	12,837,900 00	22,639,032 76	22,279,121 15
1813	13,224,623 25	July 29, special.		835,655 14		26,464,566 56	26,184,435 00	40,524,844 95	39,190,520 36
1814	5,998,772 08			1,135,971 09		27,424,793 78	23,377,911 79	34,559,536 95	38,028,230 32
1815	7,282,942 22			1,287,959 28		42,290,336 10	35,264,320 78	50,961,237 60	39,582,493 35
1816	36,306,874 88	Feb. 5, spe'l; Apr. 27, general.		1,717,985 03		19,146,561 91	9,484,436 16	57,171,421 82	48,244,495 51
1817	26,283,348 49			1,991,226 06		5,559,017 78	734,543 39	33,833,592 33	40,877,646 04

No. 17.—*Statement showing the revenue collected from the beginning of the government to June 30, 1862, &c.*—Continued.

Years.	From customs.	Date of tariff.	Direct tax.	From public lands.	Price per acre.	From miscellan's sources, including loans and treasury notes.	That portion of miscell'h arising from loans and treasury notes.	Total receipts.	Total expenditures.
1818	$17,176,385 00	April 20, special ...	....	$2,606,564 77	.........1.....	$1,810,986 89	$8,765 62	$21,593,936 66	$35,104,875 40
1819	20,283,608 76	March 3, special ...	....	3,274,492 78	....	1,047,633 83	2,291 00	24,605,665 37	24,004,199 73
1820	15,005,612 15	....	....	1,635,871 61	....	4,040,609 93	3,040,824 13	20,881,493 69	21,763,024 85
1821	13,004,447 15	....	....	1,212,966 46	....	3,305,990 11	3,000,824 00	19,573,703 72	19,090,572 69
1822	17,589,761 94	....	....	1,803,581 54	....	859,084 46	....	20,232,427 94	17,676,592 63
1823	19,088,433 44	....	....	916,523 10	....	535,709 79	....	20,541,646 26	15,314,171 00
1824	17,878,325 71	May 22, general...	....	984,418 15	....	5,918,488 93	5,000,000 00	24,381,212 79	31,898,538 47
1825	20,098,713 45	....	....	1,216,090 56	....	5,506,054 01	5,000,000 00	26,840,858 02	23,585,804 72
1826	23,341,331 77	....	....	1,393,785 09	....	525,317 25	....	25,260,434 21	24,103,398 46
1827	19,712,283 29	....	....	1,495,845 26	....	1,759,535 41	....	22,966,363 96	22,656,764 04
1828	23,005,523 64	May 19, gen'l; May 24, special.	....	1,018,308 75	....	530,795 84	....	24,763,629 03	25,459,479 52
1829	22,681,965 91	....	....	1,517,175 13	....	628,486 34	....	24,827,627 28	25,044,358 40
1830	21,922,391 39	May 20, spe'l; May 29, special.	....	2,329,356 14	....	592,368 98	....	24,844,116 51	24,585,281 55
1831	24,224,441 77	....	....	3,210,815 48	....	1,291,563 87	....	28,526,820 82	30,038,446 12
1832	28,465,237 24	July 13, spe'l; July 14, general.	....	2,623,381 03	....	776,942 89	....	31,865,561 16	34,356,698 06
1833	29,032,508 91	Mar. 2, spe'l; Mar. 2, compromise.	....	3,967,682 55	....	948,924 79	....	33,948,426 25	24,257,298 49
1834	16,214,957 15	....	....	4,857,600 69	....	718,377 71	....	21,791,935 55	24,601,982 44
To Dec. 31, 1835	19,391,310 59	....	....	14,757,600 75	....	1,381,175 76	....	35,430,087 10	17,573,141 56
1836	23,409,940 53	....	....	24,877,179 86	....	2,558,675 69	....	50,826,796 08	30,868,164 04
1837	11,169,290 39	....	....	6,776,236 59	....	9,926,326 93	2,992,989 15	27,983,852 64	37,265,037 15
1838	16,158,800 36	....	....	3,081,939 47	....	19,778,649 77	12,716,820 86	39,019,382 90	39,455,438 35
1839	23,137,924 81	....	....	7,076,447 35	....	5,195,653 66	3,857,276 21	35,340,025 82	37,614,936 15
1840	13,499,502 17	....	....	3,292,285 58	....	8,940,495 84	5,589,547 51	25,072,182 59	28,226,533 81
1841	14,487,216 74	Sept. 11, general ..	....	1,365,627 42	....	14,666,633 49	13,659,317 38	30,519,477 65	31,797,530 03
1842	18,187,908 76	Aug. 30, general ..	....	1,335,797 52	....	15,950,038 61	14,808,735 84	34,793,744 89	32,936,876 53
To June 30, 1843	7,046,843 91	....	....	897,818 11	....	19,837,748 43	18,581,409 19	20,782,410 45	19,148,195 15
1843-'44	26,183,570 94	....	....	2,059,939 80	....	1,935,044 89	1,877,847 95	31,198,555 73	32,842,070 85
1844-'45	27,528,119 70	....	....	2,077,022 30	....	388,719 90	....	29,941,853 90	30,490,408 71
1845-'46	26,712,667 87	....	....	2,694,452 48	....	222,947 39	....	29,629,167 74	27,632,282 90
1846-'47	23,747,864 66	July 30, 1846, gen'l.	....	2,498,355 20	....	28,001,948 66	28,900,763 36	55,336,198 52	60,520,851 74
1847-'48	31,757,070 96	Mar. 29, 1846, spe'l.	....	3,328,642 56	....	21,908,765 69	21,903,380 00	56,992,479 21	60,685,143 19
1848-'49	28,346,738 82	Aug. 19, 1848, spe'l; Jan. 26, 1849, sp'l.	....	1,688,959 55	....	29,761,194 61	29,075,815 48	59,796,893 98	56,386,422 74
1849-'50	39,668,686 42	....	....	1,859,894 25	....	6,190,808 21	4,066,500 00	47,649,383 88	44,604,718 96
1850-'51	49,017,567 92	....	....	2,350,305 30	....	1,399,831 03	207,664 92	52,762,704 25	48,476,104 31
1851-'52	47,339,326 62	....	....	2,043,239 58	....	516,549 40	46,300 00	49,893,115 60	46,712,608 83

654-'55	53,025,794 21	....	....	11,497,049 07	....	898,531 40	800 00	65,351,374 68	66,164,775 96
655-'56	64,022,863 50	....	....	8,917,644 93	....	1,116,391 81	200 00	74,056,699 24	72,726,341 57
656-'57	63,875,905 05	....	....	3,889,488 64	....	1,263,890 88	3,900 00	68,969,212 57	71,274,587 37
657-'58	41,789,620 98	Mar. 3, 1857, gen'l.	....	3,513,715 87	....	25,069,329 13	23,717,300 00	70,372,665 98	82,062,186 74
658-'59	49,565,824 38	....	....	1,795,687 30	....	30,451,453 96	28,287,500 00	81,773,965 64	83,678,642 92
659-'60	53,187,511 87	Mar. 2, 1861, gen'l.	....	1,778,557 71	....	21,875,338 95	20,776,800 00	76,841,407 83	77,055,125 65
660-'61	39,582,125 64	Mar. 2, 1861, gen'l;	....	870,658 54	....	49,753,909 38	41,861,709 74	83,206,693 56	84,578,834 47
661-'62	49,056,397 62	Aug. 5 and Dec. 24, 1861, special.	$1,795,331 73	159,203 77	....	530,624,946 14	529,692,460 50	581,625,181 26	570,841,700 25
	1,694,208,977 54	....	1,795,331 73	175,979,164 97	....	1,046,412,450 75	952,175,340 96	2,850,366,924 99	2,606,518,861 86

L. E. CHITTENDEN, *Register.*

Statement exhibiting the quantity and value of cotton exported annually from 1821 to 1862, inclusive, and the average price per pound.

| Years. | COTTON. | | | | Value. | Average cost per pound. |
| | Bales. | Sea Island. | Other. | Total. | | |
	Number of.	Pounds.			Dollars.	Cents.
1821		11,344,066	113,549,339	124,893,405	20,157,484	16.2
1822		11,250,635	133,424,460	144,675,095	24,035,058	16.6
1823		12,136,688	161,586,582	173,723,270	20,445,520	11.8
1824		9,525,722	132,843,941	142,369,663	21,947,401	15.4
1825		9,665,278	166,784,629	176,449,907	36,846,649	20.9
1826		5,972,852	198,562,563	204,535,415	25,025,214	12.2
1827		15,140,798	279,169,317	294,310,115	29,359,545	10
1828		11,288,419	199,302,044	210,590,463	22,487,229	10.7
1829		12,833,307	252,003,879	264,837,186	26,575,311	10
1830		8,147,165	290,311,937	298,459,102	29,674,883	9.9
1831		8,311,762	268,668,022	276,979,784	25,289,492	9.1
1832		8,743,373	313,451,749	322,215,122	31,724,682	9.8
1833		11,142,987	313,535,617	324,698,604	36,191,105	11.1
1834		8,085,937	376,601,970	384,717,907	49,448,402	12.8
1835		7,752,736	379,686,256	387,358,992	64,961,302	16.8
1836		7,849,597	415,721,710	423,631,307	71,284,925	16.8
1837		5,286,971	438,964,566	444,211,537	63,240,102	14.2
1838		7,286,340	588,615,957	595,952,297	61,566,811	10.3
1839		5,107,404	408,566,808	413,624,212	61,238,982	14.8
1840		8,779,669	735,161,392	743,941,061	63,870,307	8.5
1841		6,237,424	523,966,676	530,204,100	54,330,341	10.2
1842		7,254,099	577,462,918	584,717,017	47,593,464	8.1
1843		7,515,079	784,782,027	792,297,106	49,119,806	6.2

....	....	9,380 625	863,516,371	872,905,996	51,739,643	5.92
....	....	9,386,533	538,169,522	547,558,055	42,767,341	7.81
....	....	6,293,973	520,925,985	527,219,958	53,415,846	10.34
....	....	7,724,148	806,550,283	814,274,431*	61,998,294	7.61
....	....	11,969,259	1,014,633,010	1,026,602,269	66,396,967	6.4
....	....	8,236,463	627,145,141	635,381,604	71,984,616	11.3
....	....	8,299,656	918,937,433	927,237,089	112,315,317	12.11
....	....	11,738,075	1,081,492,564	1,093,230,639	87,965,732	8.05
....	....	11,165,165	1,100,405,205	1,111,570,370	109,455,404	9.85
....	....	10,486,423	977,346,683	987,833,106	93,595,220	9.47
....	2,303,403	13,058,590	995,366,011	1,008,424,601	88,143,844	8.74
....	2,991,175	12,797,225	1,338,634,476	1,351,431,701	128,382,351	9.49
....	2,265,588	12,940,735	1,035,341,750	1,048,282,475	361,575,859	12.55
....	2,454,529	12,101,058	1,106,522,954	1,118,624,012	131,386,661	11.72
....	3,006,536	13,713,556	1,372,755,000	1,386,468,556	161,434,923	12.72
....	3,812,345	15,598,698	1,752,087,640	1,767,686,338	191,806,555	10.85
....	671,403	6,170,321	301,345,778	307,516,099	34,051,483	11.07
....	11,890	66,443	4,998,121	5,064,564	1,180,113	23.30
otal..........................	17,522,869	393,895,320	25,066,509,114	25,460,404,434	2,600,065,687	......

L. E. CHITTENDEN, *Register.*

ASURY DEPARTMENT, *Register's Office, December 26, 1862.*

Statement exhibiting the quantity and value of tobacco and rice exported annually, from 1821 to 1862.

Years.	TOBACCO.				RICE.		
	Bales.	Cases.	Hogsheads.	Value.	Barrels.	Tierces.	Value.
1821			66,858	$5,648,962		88,221	$1,494,
1822			83,169	6,222,838		87,089	1,553,
1823			99,009	6,282,672		101,365	1,820,
1824			77,883	4,855,566		113,229	1,882,
1825			75,984	6,115,623		97,015	1,925,
1826			64,098	5,347,208		111,063	1,917,
1827			100,025	6,577,123		113,528	2,343,
1828			96,278	5,269,960		175,019	2,620,
1829			77,131	4,982,974		132,923	2,514,
1830			83,810	5,586,365		130,697	1,986,
1831			86,718	4,892,388		116,517	2,016,
1832			106,806	5,999,769		120,327	2,152,
1833			83,153	5,755,968		144,163	2,744,
1834			87,979	6,595,305		121,886	2,122,
1835			94,353	8,250,577		119,861	2,210,
1836			109,042	10,058,640		212,983	2,548,

....	....	....	130,665	7,551,122	....	100,403	2,331,524
....	....	....	101,521	5,804,207	....	128,861	2,569,362
....	....	....	145,729	9,951,023	....	127,069	2,631,557
....	....	....	95,945	9,219,251	....	105,590	2,170,927
....	....	....	137,097	10,031,283	....	119,733	2,470,029
....	....	....	159,853	11,319,319	....	67,707	1,657,658
....	12,913	13,366	126,107	10,016,046	....	105,121	2,534,127
....	17,772	9,384	150,213	14,712,468	19,774	52,520	1,717,953
....	14,432	5,631	116,962	12,221,843	51,038	58,668	2,390,233
....	12,640	4,841	156,848	20,662,772	74,309	64,332	2,290,400
....	19,651	7,188	127,670	17,009,767	49,283	64,015	1,870,578
....	17,817	15,035	198,846	21,074,038	69,946	81,820	2,207,148
....	19,450	18,815	167,274	15,906,547	77,837	84,163	2,567,390
....	15,489	31,972	160,816	13,784,710	50,038	39,162	1,382,178
			107,229	12,325,356	7,335	2,146	156,899
Total.....................	130,164	106,232	4,869,337	381,291,133	429,560	4,415,058	89,393,588

L. E. CHITTENDEN, *Register.*

TREASURY DEPARTMENT, *Register's Office, December 26, 1862.*

No. 20.

Statement showing the imports and exports of specie and bullion, the imports entered for consumption, and specie and bullion, the domestic exports and specie and bullion, the excess of specie and bullion exports over specie and bullion imports, and the excess of specie and bullion imports over specie and bullion exports.

	Imports of specie and bullion.	Imports for consumption, and specie and bullion imports.	Exports of specie and bullion.	Domestic exports and specie and bullion exp'ts.	Excess of specie and bullion exports over specie and bullion imports.	Excess of specie and bullion imports over specie and bullion exports.
1848	$6,360,224	$147,012,126	$15,841,616	$154,032,131	$9,481,392	
1849	6,651,240	139,216,408	5,404,648	145,755,820		$1,246,592
1850	4,628,792	168,660,625	7,522,994	151,898,720	2,894,202	
1851	5,453,592	205,929,811	29,472,252	218,387,511	24,018,660	
1852	5,505,044	200,577,739	42,674,135	208,658,366	37,169,091	
1853	4,201,382	255,272,740	27,486,875	230,976,157	23,285,493	
1854	6,958,184	282,914,077	41,436,456	278,241,064	34,478,272	
1855	3,659,812	235,310,152	56,247,343	275,156,846	52,587,531	
1856	4,207,632	299,858,570	45,745,485	326,964,908	41,537,853	
1857	12,461,799	345,973,724	69,136,922	362,960,682	56,675,123	
1858	19,274,496	261,952,909	52,633,147	324,644,421	33,358,651	
1859	7,434,789	324,258,421	63,887,411	342,279,491	56,452,622	
1860	8,550,135	335,230,919	66,546,239	382,788,662	57,996,104	
1861	46,339,611	320,995,936	29,791,080	234,690,696		16,548,531
1862	16,415,052	198,673,052	36,886,956	218,762,944	20,471,904	
Total	158,101,784	3,721,836,209	590,713,559	3,857,198,419	450,406,898	17,795,123

TREASURY DEPARTMENT, *Register's Office, December 26, 1862.*

L. E. CHITTENDEN, *Register.*

No. 21.

Statement exhibiting the amount of coin and bullion imported and exported annually from 1821 to 1862, inclusive, and also the amount of importation over exportation, and exportation over importation, during the same years.

Year ending—	Coin and bullion.			
	Imported.	Exported.	Excess of importation over exportation.	Excess of exportation over importation.
September 30.........1821	$8,064,890	$10,477,969	....	$2,413,079
1822	3,369,846	10,810,180	....	7,440,334
1823	5,097,896	6,372,987	....	1,275,091
1824	8,379,835	7,014,552	$1,365,283	....
1825	6,150,765	8,787,659	....	2,636,894
1826	6,880,966	4,704,533	2,176,433	....
1827	8,151,130	8,014,880	136,250	....
1828	7,489,741	8,243,476	....	753,735
1829	7,403,612	4,924,020	2,479,592	....
1830	8,155,964	2,178,773	5,977,191	....
1831	7,305,945	9,014,931	....	1,708,986
1832	5,907,504	5,656,340	251,164	....
1833	7,070,368	2,611,701	4,458,667	....
1834	17,911,632	2,076,758	15,834,874	....
1835	13,131,447	6,477,775	6,653,662	....
1836	13,400,881	4,324,336	9,076,545	....
1837	10,516,414	5,976,249	4,540,165	....
1838	17,747,116	3,508,046	14,239,070	....
1839	5,595,176	8,776,743	....	3,181,567
1840	8,882,813	8,417,014	465,799	....
1841	4,988,633	10,034,332	....	5,045,699
1842	4,987,016	4,813,539	....	726,523
9 months, to June 30, 1843	22,390,559	1,520,791	20,869,768	....
Year ending June 30, 1844	5,830,429	5,454,214	376,215	....
1845	4,070,242	8,606,495	....	4,536,253
1846	3,777,732	3,905,268	....	127,536
1847	24,121,289	1,907,024	22,214,265	....
1848	6,360,224	15,841,616	....	9,481,392
1849	6,651,240	5,404,648	1,246,592	....
1850	4,628,792	7,522,994	....	2,894,202
1851	5,453,592	29,472,752	....	24,019,160
1852	5,505,044	42,674,135	....	37,169,091
1853	4,201,382	27,486,875	....	23,285,493
1854	6,958,184	41,436,456	....	34,478,272
1855	3,659,812	56,247,343	....	52,587,531
1856	4,207,632	45,745,485	....	41,537,853
1857	12,461,799	69,136,922	....	56,675,123
1858	19,274,496	52,633,147	....	33,358,651
1859	6,369,703	63,887,411	....	57,517,708
1860	8,550,135	66,546,239	....	57,996,104
1861	46,339,611	29,791,080	16,548,531	....
1862	16,415,052	36,886,956	....	20,471,904
Total...............	402,916,539	755,324,644	128,910,076	481,318,181

L. E. CHITTENDEN, *Register.*

TREASURY DEPARTMENT,
Register's Office, December 26, 1862.

No. 22.

Statement exhibiting the gross value of exports and imports from the beginning of the government to the 30th June, 1862.

Year ending—	Exports.			Imports—total.
	Domestic produce.	Foreign merchandise.	Total.	
September 30....1790	$19,666,000	$539,156	$20,205,156	$23,000,000
1791	18,500,000	512,041	19,012,041	29,200,000
1792	19,000,000	1,753,098	20,753,098	31,500,000
1793	24,000,000	2,109,572	26,109,572	31,100,000
1794	26,500,000	6,526,233	33,026,233	34,600,000
1795	39,500,000	8,489,472	47,989,472	69,756,268
1796	40,764,097	26,300,000	67,064,097	81,436,164
1897	29,850,206	27,000,000	56,850,206	75,379,400
1798	28,527,097	33,000,000	61,527,097	68,551,700
1799	33,142,522	45,523,000	78,665,522	79,069,148
1800	31,840,903	39,130,877	70,971,780	91,252,768
1801	47,473,204	46,642,721	94,115,925	111,363,511
1802	36,708,189	35,774,971	72,483,160	76,333,333
1803	42,205,961	13,594,072	55,800,033	64,666,666
1804	41,467,477	36,231,597	77,699,074	85,000,000
1805	42,387,002	53,179,019	95,566,021	120,600,000
1806	41,253,727	60,283,236	101,536,963	129,410.000
1807	48,699,592	59,643,558	108,343,150	138,500,000
1808	9,433,546	12,997,414	22,430.960	56,990,000
1809	31,405,702	20,797,531	52,203,233	59,400,000
1810	42,366,675	24,391,295	66,657,970	85,400,000
1811	45,294,043	16,022,790	61,316,833	53,400,000
1812	30,032,109	8,495,127	38,527,236	77,030,000
1813	25,008,132	2,847,865	27,855,997	22,005,000
1814	6,782.272	145,169	6,927,441	12,965,000
1815	45,974,403	6,583,350	52,557,753	113,041,274
1816	64,781,896	17,138,156	81,920,462	147,103.000
1817	68,313,500	19,358,069	87,671,560	99,250.000
1818	73,854,437	19,426,696	93,281,133	121,750.000
1819	50,976,838	19,165,683	70,142,521	87,125,000
1820	51,683,640	18,008,029	69,691,669	74,450,000
1821	43,671,894	21,302,488	64,974,382	62,585,724
1822	49,874,079	22,286,202	72,160,281	83,241,541
1823	47,155,408	27,543,622	74,699,030	77,579,267
1824	50,649,500	25,337,157	75,986,657	80,549,007
1825	66,944,745	32,590,643	99,535,388	96.340,075
1826	53,055,710	24,530,612	77,595,322	84,974,477
1827	58,921,691	23,403,136	82,324,727	79,484,068
1828	50,669,669	21,595,017	72,264,686	88,509,824
1829	55,700,193	16,658,478	72,358,671	74,492,527
1830	59,462.029	14,387,479	73,849,508	70,876,920
1831	61,277,057	20,033,526	81,310,583	103,191,124
1832	63,137,470	24,039,473	87,176,943	101,029,266
1833	70,317,698	19,822,735	90,140,443	108,118,311
1834	81,024,162	23,312,811	104,336,973	126,521,332
1835	101,189,082	20,504,495	121,693,577	149,895,742
1836	106,916,680	21,746,360	128,663,040	189,980,035
1837	95,564,414	21,854,962	117,419,376	140,989,217
1838	96,033,821	12,452,795	108,486,616	113,717,404
1839	103,533,891	17,494,525	121,028,416	162,092,132

No. 22.—*Statement exhibiting the gross value of exports, &c.*—Continued.

Year ending—	Exports.			Imports—total.
	Domestic produce.	Foreign merchandise.	Total.	
September 30....1840	$113,895,634	$18,190,312	$132,085,936	$107,141,519
1841	106,382,722	15,469,081	121,851,803	127,946,177
1842	92,969,996	11,721,538	104,691,534	100,162,087
Nov. 9 to June 30, 1843	77,793,783	6,552,697	84,346,480	64,753,799
1844	99,715,179	11,484,867	111,200,046	108,435,035
1845	99,299,776	15,346,830	114,646,606	117,254,564
1846	102,141,893	11,346,623	113,488,516	121,691,797
1847	150,637,464	8,011,158	158,648,622	146,545,638
1848	132,904,121	21,128,010	154,032,131	154,998,928
1849	132,666,955	13,088,865	145,755,820	147,851,439
1850	135,946,912	14,951,808	151,898,720	178,138,318
1851	196,689,718	21,698,293	218,388,011	216,224,932
1852	192,368,984	17,289,382	209,658,366	212,945,442
1853	213,417,697	17,558,460	230,976,157	167,978,647
1854	253,390,870	24,850,194	278,241,064	304,562,381
1855	246,708,553	28,448,293	275,156,846	261,468,520
1856	310,586,330	16,378,578	326,964,908	314,639,942
1857	338,985,065	23,975,617	362,960,682	360,890,141
1858	293,758,279	30,886,142	324,644,421	282,613,150
1859	335,894,385	20,895,077	356,789,462	338,765,130
1860	373,189,274	26,933,022	400,122,296	362,163,941
1861	228,699,486	20,645,427	249,344,913	335,650,153
1862	212,920,639	16,869,641	229,790,280	205,819,823
Total..........	6,914,456,078	1,506,235,628	8,420,691,706	9,183,446,734

NOTE.—Prior to 1821 the treasury reports did not give the value of imports. To that period their value, and also the value of domestic and foreign exports, have been estimated from sources believed to be authentic. From 1821 to 1862, inclusive, their value has been taken from official documents.

L. E. CHITTENDEN, *Register.*

TREASURY DEPARTMENT,
Register's Office, December 26, 1862.

No. 23.

Statement exhibiting the amount of the tonnage of the United States annually from 1789 to 1862, inclusive; also the registered and enrolled and licensed tonnage employed in steam navigation in each year.

Year ending—	Registered sail tonnage.	Registered steam tonnage.	Enrolled and licensed sail tonnage.	Enrolled and licensed steam tonnage.	Total tonnage.
	Tons.	*Tons.*	*Tons.*	*Tons.*	*Tons.*
Dec. 31, 1789....	123,893	....	77,669	....	201,562
1790....	346,254	....	132,123	....	274,377
1791....	362,110	....	139,036	....	502,146
1792....	411,438	....	153,019	....	564,457
1793....	367,734	....	153,030	....	520,764
1794....	438,863	....	189,755	....	628,618
1795....	529,471	....	218,494	....	747,965
1796....	575,733	....	255,166	....	831,899
1797....	597,777	....	279,136	....	876,913
1798....	603,376	....	294,952	....	898,328
1799....	662,197	....	277,212	....	939,409
1800....	559,921	....	302,571	....	972,492
1801....	632,907	....	314,670	....	947,577
1802....	560,380	....	331,724	....	892,104
1803....	597,157	....	352,015	....	949,172
1804....	672,530	....	369,874	..........-v.	1,042,404
1805....	749,341	....	391,027	....	1,140,368
1806....	808,265	....	400,451	....	1,208,716
1807....	848,307	....	420,241	....	1,268,548
1808....	769,054	....	473,542	....	1,242,596
1809....	910,059	....	440,222	....	1,350,281
1810....	984,269	....	440,515	....	1,424,784
1811....	768,852	....	463,650	....	1,232,502
1812....	760,624	....	509,373	....	1,269,997
1813....	674,853	....	491,776	....	1,166,629
1814....	674,633	....	484,577	....	1,159,210
1815....	854,295	....	513,833	....	1,368,128
1816 ...	800,760	....	571,459	....	1,372,219
1817....	800,725	....	590,187	....	1,399,912
1818....	606,089	....	619,096	....	1,225,185
1819....	612,930	....	647,821	........-.....	1,260,751
1820....	619,048	....	661,119	....	1,280,167
1821....	619,896	....	679,062	....	1,298,958
1822....	628,150	....	696,549	....	1,324,699
1823....	639,921	....	671,766	24,879	1,336,566
1824....	669,973	....	697,680	21,610	1,389,163
1825....	700,788	....	699,263	23,061	1,423,112
1826....	737,978	....	762,154	34,059	1,534,191
1827....	747,170	....	833,240	40,198	1,620,608
1828....	812,619	....	889,355	39,418	1,741,392
1829....	650,143	....	556,618	54,037	1,260,798
1830....	575,056	1,419	552,248	63,053	1,191,776
1831....	610,575	877	613,827	33,568	1,267,847
1832....	686,809	181	661,827	90,633	1,439,450
1833....	749,482	545	754,819	101,305	1,606,151
1834	857,098	340	778,995	122,474	1,758,907
Sept. 30, 1835....	885,481	340	816,645	122,474	1,824,940
1836....	897,321	454	839,226	145,102	1,822,103
1837....	809,343	1,104	932,576	153,561	1,896,684
1838....	819,801	2,791	982,416	190,632	1,995,640

No. 23.—*Statement exhibiting the amount of tonnage, &c.*—Continued.

Year ending—	Registered sail tonnage.	Registered steam tonnage.	Enrolled and licensed sail tonnage.	Enrolled and licensed steam tonnage.	Total tonnage.
	Tons.	*Tons.*	*Tons.*	*Tons.*	*Tons.*
Sept. 30, 1839	829,096	5,149	1,062,445	199,789	2,096,479
1840	895,610	4,155	1,082,815	198,184	2,180,764
1841	945,057	746	1,010,599	174,342	2,130,744
1842	970,658	4,701	892,072	224,960	2,092,391
June 30, 1843	1,003,932	5,373	917,804	231,494	2,158,603
1844	1,061,856	6,909	946,060	265,270	2,280,095
1845	1,088,680	6,492	1,002,303	319,527	2,417,002
1846	1,123,999	6,287	1,090,192	341,606	2,562,084
1847	1,235,682	5,631	1,198,523	399,310	2,839,046
1848	1,364,819	16,068	1,381,332	411,823	3,154,042
1849	1,418,072	20,870	1,453,459	441,525	3,334,016
1850	1,540,769	44,429	1,468,738	481,005	3,535,454
1851	1,663,917	62,390	1,524,915	521,217	3,772,439
1852	1,819,744	79,704	1,675,456	563,536	4,138,440
1853	2,013,154	90,520	1,789,238	514,098	4,407,010
1854	2,238,783	95,036	1,887,512	581,571	4,802,902
1855	2,440,091	115,045	2,021,625	655,240	5,212,001
1856	2,401,087	89,715	1,796,888	583,362	4,871,652
1857	2,377,094	86,873	1,857,964	618,911	4,940,842
1858	2,499,742	78,027	2,050,067	651,363	5,049,808
1859	2,414,654	92,748	1,961,631	676,005	5,145,038
1860	2,448,941	97,296	2,036,990	770,641	5,353,868
1861	2,540,020	102,608	2,122,589	774,596	5,539,813
1862	2,177,253	113,998	2,224,449	596,465	5,112,165

L. E. CHITTENDEN, *Register.*

TREASURY DEPARTMENT, *Register's Office, December* 26, 1862.

Statement exhibiting the value of manufactured articles of domestic produce exported to foreign countries from June 30, 1846, to June 30, 1862.

Articles.	1847.	1848.	1849.	1850.	1851.	1852.	1853.	1854.
Wax	$181,577	$134,577	$121,790	$118,055	$122,835	$91,499	$113,509	$87,140
Refined sugar	124,824	253,960	129,001	265,936	219,568	149,991	375,780	270,488
Chocolate	1,053	9,907	1,941	9,260	3,955	3,967	10,930	130,237
Spirits from grain	67,781	90,957	67,199	46,314	36,094	48,737	141,173	282,919
Spirits from molasses	593,609	269,467	288,452	268,290	289,622	393,941	569,381	809,965
Spirits from other materials								
Molasses	20,859	5,563	7,442	14,127	16,870	13,163	17,582	131,048
Vinegar	6,598	13,490	14,036	11,182	16,015	13,290	20,443	16,945
Beer, ale, porter, and cider	68,114	78,071	81,290	23,531	57,375	43,053	54,077	35,503
Linseed oil and spirits of turpentine	496,116	331,404	148,058	229,741	145,410	183,827	363,080	1,084,209
Lard oil								
Household furniture	295,700	297,353	337,343	278,025	363,830	430,182	714,556	763,157
Coaches and other carriages	75,369	59,953	95,933	95,729	196,491	179,445	184,497	944,638
Hats	59,506	55,493	64,967	66,671	103,768	83,452	91,961	178,404
Saddlery	13,102	27,436	37,376	96,093	30,100	47,937	48,909	53,311
Tallow candles and soap, and other candles	605,794	676,293	637,280	664,965	609,739	660,054	681,183	691,565
Snuff and tobacco	658,980	568,435	613,044	648,632	1,143,547	1,316,522	1,071,300	1,551,471
Leather, boots, and shoes	242,816	194,095	151,774	193,398	458,838	498,708	673,708	896,555
Cordage	27,054	29,911	41,636	51,357	52,054	62,903	103,916	194,070
Gunpowder	88,397	195,962	131,597	190,352	154,257	121,560	181,048	212,700
Salt	45,333	73,274	87,970	76,103	64,424	89,316	119,709	158,026
Lead	194,981	84,318	90,198	19,797	11,774	33,796	5,540	90,874
Iron—								
Pig, bar, and nails	166,817	154,036	140,358	154,910	215,652	118,624	181,098	306,127
Castings	68,889	83,188	60,175	79,318	164,405	191,868	290,490	459,775
All manufactures of	939,776	1,509,408	586,639	1,677,792	1,675,691	1,993,807	2,007,234	3,473,467
Copper and brass, manufactures of	64,940	61,468	66,903	105,000	91,871	163,039	108,905	99,108
Medicinal drugs	165,793	210,581	299,894	334,780	351,585	263,852	337,073	454,789
Cotton piece goods—								
Printed or colored	290,114	393,534	469,777	606,631	1,006,561	936,404	1,066,167	1,147,789
Uncolored	3,345,992	4,996,559	3,955,117	3,774,407	5,571,576	6,139,391	6,928,485	4,130,149
Twist, yarn, and thread	108,122	170,633	93,555	17,403	37,960	34,718	93,594	49,315
Other manufactures of	336,373	327,479	415,680	335,981	625,608	571,636	733,048	463,985
Hemp and flax—								
Cloth and thread	477	495	1,609	1,183	1,647	5,468	9,994	24,456
Bags and all manufactures of	5,305	6,918	4,849	16,593	6,376	8,154	13,890	55,361
Wearing apparel	47,101	574,464	78,945	207,632	1,911,694	950,998	859,733	934,368
Earthen and stone ware	4,758	8,819	10,632	15,844	23,096	16,310	54,685	34,555
Combs and buttons	17,096	16,461	36,135	23,987	27,304	28,633	31,395	37,684

lables and apparatus................	815	12	701	2,295	1,798	1,088	1,673	3,204
las, parasols, and sunshades..........	2,150	2,916	800	3,305	12,060	8,340	6,183	11,656
ctures of India-rubber...............	20,836	16,480	9,427	9,800	13,309	16,617	6,448	17,018
r and morocco, (not sold per pound)....	2,443	7,686	548	3,140	9,468	16,784	9,652	6,597
gines and apparatus..................	17,431	30,403	28,031	30,942	71,401	47,781	38,050	33,019
presses and types...................	16,097	38,508	23,713	21,634	55,700	67,732	50,397	120,108
instruments........................	44,751	75,193	94,427	110,475	153,919	917,829	142,604	187,335
nd maps...........................	86,731	78,307	86,827	99,696	155,864	119,825	129,212	192,339
nd stationery.......................	54,115	50,739	55,145	67,807	109,834	85,360	83,020	121,823
and varnish........................	71,155	76,007	101,419	136,682	185,435	194,634	170,551	280,476
ctures of glass.....................	6,303	10,353	13,143	13,590	27,893	23,420	23,988	30,750
ctures of tin.......................	13,694	7,729	13,196	23,682	16,496	18,460	14,054	16,478
ctures of pewter and lead............	11,320	22,466	20,982	34,510	41,449	57,240	47,638	89,327
ctures of marble and stone..........	4,968	6,241	4,502	4,583	68,039	20,032	11,673	1,311,513
ctures of gold and silver, and gold leaf....								442,383
silver.............................								
al flowers and jewelry...............	3,126	11,217	8,557	45,283	121,013	114,738	66,397	80,471
and valises.......................	5,970	6,196	5,069	19,370	12,207	13,035	27,148	23,673
and line..........................	17,623	24,174	8,671	16,348	22,045	13,839	32,625	303,314
e								
s not enumerated...................	1,108,964	1,127,826	1,408,276	3,869,071	3,703,341	2,877,650	3,788,700	4,972,064
Total.........	10,476,345	12,838,758	11,980,075	15,106,451	20,150,967	18,863,931	23,590,930	25,849,411
Gold and silver coin and bullion	62,320	2,700,412	956,874	2,045,679	18,064,580	37,437,857	23,548,533	38,234,566
	10,538,965	15,539,170	12,936,949	17,943,130	38,206,547	56,300,708	46,148,465	65,083,977

No. 24.—*Statement exhibiting the value of manufactured articles of domestic produce exported, &c.*—Continued.

Articles.	1855.	1856.	1857.	1858.	1859.	1860.	1861.	1862.
Wax	$69,905	$74,005	$91,983	$65,936	$94,850	$131,803	$94,495	$47,383
Refined sugar	536,453	360,444	368,206	900,734	377,944	301,674	287,681	147,397
Chocolate	9,771	1,476	1,932	2,304	9,444	2,563	2,157	4,388
Spirits from grain	384,144	500,945	1,248,234	476,723	273,576	311,595	867,954	308,414
Spirits from molasses	1,446,280	1,329,151	1,216,635	1,267,691	780,889	830,644	850,546	715,732
Spirits from other materials	101,836	95,484	120,011	249,432	188,746	219,199	593,185	1,577,861
Molasses	189,849	154,639	108,063	115,893	75,690	35,299	39,134	91,914
Vinegar	17,221	26,604	36,788	24,336	35,156	41,368	38,262	20,701
Beer, ale, porter, and cider	45,069	45,086	43,732	55,532	78,226	53,573	39,480	54,698
Linseed oil and spirits of turpentine	1,186,732	896,238	795,490	1,137,507	1,340,229	1,043,088	1,920,709	78,650
Lard oil	89,945	161,232	92,499	60,958	50,793	55,783	87,783	148,026
Household furniture	803,969	982,049	879,448	930,499	1,067,107	1,079,114	838,049	930,168
Coaches and other carriages	290,525	370,959	476,394	777,921	655,000	818,973	473,080	517,175
Hats	177,914	326,082	254,908	198,525	918,704	211,602	156,956	132,737
Saddlery	64,886	31,249	45,222	55,280	56,870	71,333	81,460	67,759
Tallow candles and soap, and other candles	1,311,349	1,206,764	1,242,604	934,303	1,137,965	1,203,104	1,136,696	1,472,898
Snuff and tobacco	1,506,113	1,829,907	1,458,553	2,410,994	3,409,491	3,383,488	2,760,531	1,075,994
Leather, boots, and shoes	1,053,406	1,912,311	1,311,709	1,969,494	1,319,893	1,435,834	1,335,078	1,110,243
Cordage	315,267	367,182	296,163	212,640	320,435	945,579	255,274	199,669
Gunpowder	356,051	844,974	398,244	385,173	371,603	467,772	347,103	101,833
Salt	156,879	311,495	190,699	162,650	212,710	129,717	144,046	228,109
Lead	14,198	27,512	58,684	48,119	28,575	50,446	6,241	7,334
Iron—								
Pig, bar, and nails	288,437	286,960	397,313	205,931	257,662	945,154	311,321	259,852
Castings	306,439	288,315	289,967	484,415	128,659	282,848	76,750	54,671
All manufactures of	3,156,596	3,585,712	4,197,087	4,059,598	5,117,346	5,174,049	5,536,576	4,912,448
Copper and brass, manufactures of	690,766	534,846	607,054	1,985,223	1,048,246	1,664,122	2,375,020	1,068,021
Medicinal drugs	786,114	1,066,294	886,909	846,278	798,908	1,115,455	1,149,433	1,490,376
Cotton piece goods—								
Printed or colored	2,613,655	1,966,845	1,785,685	2,069,194	2,320,890	3,358,449	2,215,039	587,500
Uncolored	2,907,276	4,616,364	3,715,329	1,782,025	1,518,236	1,785,595	1,377,627	508,004
Twist, yarn, and thread								

es and apparatus	14,829	29,088	21,524	7,290	3,013	9,048	7,940	34,030
resses and types	36,405	67,517	52,747	105,498	68,868	157,124	106,562	168,047
struments	106,857	135,517	107,748	97,775	155,101	129,653	150,974	147,805
maps	207,918	209,502	277,047	209,774	3·0,080	278,064	250,365	214,221
stationery	185,837	203,013	224,767	299,961	209,457	285,708	347,915	398,546
varnish	163,096	217,179	223,320	131,217	165,068	223,809	246,923	258,064
ure of glass	204,079	216,439	170,900	214,608	252,316	277,948	394,731	522,606
ures of tin	14,279	13,610	5,682	24,166	39,269	39,464	70,929	62,995
ures of pewter and lead	5,233	5,698	4,818	27,327	23,782	46,081	30,534	31,366
ures of marble and stone	108,546	103,376	111,403	138,590	113,014	176,239*	185,307	190,067
ures of gold and silver, and gold leaf	9,051	6,116	15,477	95,266	35,947	140,187	53,272	63,078
er,	806,119	631,724	665,480	199,184		238,882	631,450	1,937,643
flowers and jewelry	22,043	26,386	26,970	25,901	58,570	24,966	50,199	67,669
nd values	35,903	32,457	37,748	59,441	42,153	50,184	40,622	50,771
d lime	57,360	64,997	68,000	103,821	160,611	154,045	93,092	83,385
ot enumerated				1,435,691	1,198,581	1,609,328	1,385,691	875,841
	4,014,432	3,559,613	3,293,722	3,001,788	3,374,652	3,397,445	2,530,689	2,885,347
Total	28,833,299	30,970,999	29,653,967	36,372,180	33,853,660	39,803,080	36,418,954	27,171,317
Gold and silver coin and bullion	53,957,418	44,148,979	60,078,352	42,407,246	57,502,305	56,946,851	23,799,870	31,044,651
	82,790,717	75,119,971	89,731,619	78,779,426	91,355,965	96,749,931	60,218,194	58,215,088

TREASURY DEPARTMENT,
Register's Office, December 26, 1862.

L. E. CHITTENDEN,
Register.

No. 25.

Statement exhibiting the value of foreign merchandise imported, re-exported, and consumed, annually, from 1821 to 1862, inclusive; and also the estimated population and rate of consumption per capita during the same period.

Years ending—	Value of foreign merchandise.			Population.	Consumption per capita.
	Imported.	Re-exported.	Consumed and on hand.		
September 30, 1821	$62,585,724	$21,302,488	$41,283,236	9,960,974	$4 14
1822	83,241,541	22,286,202	60,955,339	10,283.757	5 92
1823	77,579,267	27,543,622	50,035,645	10,606,540	4 71
1824	80,549,007	25,337,157	55,211,850	10,929,323	5 05
1825	96,340,075	32,590,643	63,749,432	11,252,106	5 66
1826	84,974,477	24,539,612	60,434,865	11,574,889	5 22
1827	79,484,068	23,403,136	56,030,932	11,897,672	4 71
1828	88,509,824	21,595,017	66,914,807	12,220,455	5 47
1829	74,492,527	16,658,478	57,834,049	12,243.238	4 61
1830	70,876,920	14,387,479	56,489,441	12,866,020	4 31
1831	103,191,124	20,033.526	83,157,598	13,286.364	6 25
1832	101,029,266	24,039,473	76,989,793	13,706,707	5 61
1833	108,118,311	19,822,735	88,295,576	14,127,050	6 25
1834	126,521,332	23,312,811	103,208,521	14,547,393	7 09
1835	149,895,742	20,504,495	129,391,247	14,967,736	8 64
1836	189,980,035	21,746,360	168,233,675	15,388,079	10 93
1837	140,989,217	21,854,962	119,134,255	15,808,422	7 53
1838	113,717,604	12,452,795	101,264,609	16,228,765	6 23
1839	162,092,132	17,494,525	144,597,607	16,649,108	8 68
1840	107,141,519	18,190,312	88,951,207	17,069,453	5 21
1841	127,946,177	15,469,081	112,477,096	17,612,507	6 38
1842	100,162,087	11,721,538	88,440,549	18,155,561	4 87
9 months to June 30, 1843	64,753,799	6,552,697	58,201,102	18,698,615	4 15
Year to June 30, 1844	108,435,035	11,464,867	96,950,168	19,241,670	5 03
1845	117,254,564	15,346,830	101,907,734	19,784,725	5 15
1846	121,691,797	11,346,623	110,345,174	20,327,780	5 42
1847	146,545,638	8,011,158	138,534,480	20,780,835	6 60
1848	154,998,928	21,128,010	133,870,918	21,413,890	6 25
1849	147,857,439	13,088,865	134,768,574	21,956,945	6 13
1850	178,138,318	14,951,808	163,186,510	23,191,676	7 03
1851	216,224,932	21,698,293	194,526,530	23,887,632	8 14
1852	212,945,442	17,289,382	195,656,060	24,604,361	7 95
1853	267,978,647	17,558,460	250,420,187	25,342,388	9 88
1854	304,562,381	24,850,194	279,712,187	26,102,659	10 71
1855	261,468,520	28,448,293	233,020,227	26,885,738	8 67
1856	314,639,942	16,378,578	298,261,304	27,692,310	10 77
1857	360,890,141	23,975,617	336,914,524	28,523,079	11 81
1858	282,613,150	30,886,142	251,727,008	29,378,771	8 57
1859	338,768,130	20,895,077	317,873,053	30,260,134	10 50
1860	362,163,941	26,933,022	335,230,919	31,429,891	10 66
1861	335,650,153	20,645,425	315,004,728	32,373,388	9 73
1862	205,819,823	16,869,641	188,950,182	33,344,589	5 67
Total	6,832,818,496	824,755,788	6,008,193,067	....	......

L. E. CHITTENDEN, *Register.*

TREASURY DEPARTMENT, *Register's Office, December 26,* 1862.

...ment exhibiting the total value of imports, and imports consumed in the United States, exclusive of specie, during each fiscal year from 1821 to 1862, inclusive; showing also the value of foreign and domestic exports, exclusive of specie; the aggregate exports, including specie, and the tonnage employed during the same period.

Years.	Total imports, including specie.	Imports entered for consumption, exclusive of specie.	Domestic produce exported, exclusive of specie.	Foreign merchandise exported, exclusive of specie.	Total exports, including specie.	Tonnage.
1821	$62,585,724	$43,696,405	$43,671,894	$10,824,519	$64,974,382	1,298,958
1822	83,241,541	68,367,425	49,874,079	11,476,022	72,160,281	1,324,799
1823	77,579,267	51,308,936	47,155,408	21,170,635	74,699,030	1,336,566
1824	80,549,007	53,846,567	50,649,500	18,322,605	75,986,657	1,389,163
1825	96,340,075	66,375,722	66,944,745	23,802,984	99,535,388	1,423,112
1826	84,974,477	57,653,577	52,449,855	20,440,934	77,595,322	1,534,191
1827	79,484,068	54,901,108	57,878,117	16,431,830	82,324,827	1,620,608
1828	88,509,824	66,975,475	49,976,632	14,044,578	72,264,686	1,741,392
1829	74,492,527	54,741,571	55,087,307	12,347,544	72,358,871	1,260,798
1830	70,876,920	49,575,000	58,524,878	13,145,857	73,849,508	1,191,776
1831	103,191,124	82,808,110	59,218,583	13,077,069	81,310,583	1,267,847
1832	101,029,266	75,327,688	61,726,529	19,794,074	87,176,943	1,439,450
1833	108,118,311	83,470,067	69,950,856	17,577,876	90,140,433	1,606,151
1834	126,521,332	86,973,147	80,623,662	21,636,553	104,336,973	1,758,907
1835	149,895,742	122,007,974	100,459,481	14,756,321	121,693,577	1,824,940
1836	189,980,035	158,811,392	106,570,942	17,767,762	128,663,040	1,882,103
1837	140,989,217	113,310,571	94,280,895	17,162,232	117,419,376	1,896,686
1838	113,717,404	86,552,598	95,560,880	9,417,690	108,486,616	1,994,640
1839	162,092,132	145,870,816	101,625,533	10,626,140	121,028,416	2,096,380
1840	107,141,519	86,250,335	111,660,561	12,088,371	132,085,946	2,180,764
1841	127,946,177	114,776,309	103,636,236	8,181,235	121,851,803	2,130,744
1842	100,162,087	87,996,318	91,798,242	8,078,753	104,690,531	2,092,391
nths to June 30 1843	64,753,799	37,294,129	77,686,354	5,139,335	84,346,480	2,158,603
ending June 30 1844	108,435,035	98,390,548	99,531,774	6,214,058	111,200,046	2,280,095
1845	117,254,564	105,599,541	98,455,330	7,584,781	114,646,606	2,417,002
1846	121,691,797	110,048,859	101,718,042	7,865,206	113,488,516	2,562,085

No. 26.—*Statement exhibiting the total value of imports, &c.*—Continued.

Years.	Total imports, including specie.	Imports entered for consumption, exclusive of specie.	Domestic produce exported, exclusive of specie.	Foreign merchandise exported, exclusive of specie.	Total exports, including specie.	Tonnage.
Year ending June 30......1847	$146,545,638	$116,257,595	$150,574,844	$6,166,754	$158,648,622	2,839,046
1848	154,998,928	140,651,902	130,203,709	7,986,806	154,032,131	3,154,042
1849	147,857,439	132,565,108	131,710,081	8,641,091	145,755,820	3,334,015
1850	178,138,318	164,032,033	134,900,233	9,475,493	151,698,720	3,535,454
1851	216,224,932	200,476,219	178,620,138	10,295,121	218,388,011	3,772,439
1852	212,945,442	195,072,695	154,931,147	12,053,084	209,658,366	4,138,441
1853	267,978,647	251,071,358	189,869,162	13,620,120	230,976,157	4,407,010
1854	304,562,381	275,955,893	215,156,304	21,648,304	278,241,064	4,802,903
1855	261,468,520	231,650,340	192,751,135	26,158,368	275,156,846	5,212,001
1856	314,639,942	295,650,938	266,438,051	14,781,372	326,904,908	4,871,652
1857	360,890,141	333,511,295	278,906,713	14,917,047	362,960,682	4,940,843
1858	282,613,150	242,678,413	251,351,033	20,660,241	324,644,421	5,049,808
1859	338,768,130	317,888,456	278,392,080	14,509,971	356,789,462	5,145,037
1860	362,163,941	336,280,172	316,242,423	17,333,634	400,122,296	5,353,868
1861	335,650,153	274,656,325	204,899,616	14,654,217	240,344,913	....
1862	205,819,823	178,377,435	181,875,968	11,027,336	229,790,280	5,112,165
Total................	6,832,818,496	5,847,705,428	5,243,538,972	582,823,723	6,581,687,539	....

TREASURY DEPARTMENT, *Register's Office, December 26, 1862.*

L. E. CHITTENDEN, *Register.*

ment exhibiting a summary view of the exports of domestic produce, &c., of the United States during the years ending on June 30, 1847, 1848, 1849, 1850, 1851, 1852, 1853, 1854, 1855, 1856, 1857, 1858, 1859, 1860, 1861, and 1862.

Years ending—	Product of—						Raw produce.	Specie and bullion.	Total value.
	The sea.	The forest.	Agriculture.	Tobacco.	Cotton.	Manufactures.			
30, 1847	$3,468,033	$5,996,073	$66,450,383	$7,242,086	$53,415,848	$10,476,345	$1,800,076	$62,620	$150,637,464
1848	1,980,963	7,059,084	37,781,446	7,551,122	61,998,294	12,856,758	974,842	2,700,412	132,904,191
1849	2,517,654	5,017,994	38,155,204	5,804,207	66,396,967	11,260,075	904,980	955,874	133,686,905
1850	2,604,518	7,442,503	26,547,158	9,951,023	71,984,616	15,196,451	953,854	2,046,679	136,946,912
1851	3,294,091	7,847,099	24,368,910	9,219,251	112,315,317	22,105,987	1,437,680	18,069,580	106,689,718
1852	2,282,349	7,864,920	26,378,272	10,031,283	87,965,732	18,263,931	1,545,787	37,437,827	192,368,184
1853	3,279,413	7,915,259	32,453,373	11,319,319	109,456,404	22,589,030	1,735,284	23,548,535	213,417,697
1854	3,054,069	11,761,185	67,104,592	10,016,046	93,596,920	26,849,411	2,764,781	38,234,566	253,390,870
1855	3,516,894	12,603,857	49,567,476	14,714,458	88,143,844	28,853,999	2,373,317	53,957,418	246,708,553
1856	3,336,797	10,694,164	77,686,455	12,991,843	128,382,351	30,976,999	3,125,429	44,148,979	310,586,330
1857	3,704,323	14,690,711	75,722,098	20,260,772	131,575,858	29,653,687	3,290,485	60,078,352	338,985,065
1858	3,550,995	13,478,671	53,233,920	17,009,767	131,386,661	30,372,180	3,390,479	42,407,246	293,758,279
1859	4,402,914	14,489,406	40,400,757	21,074,038	161,434,923	33,853,660	2,676,322	57,502,305	355,894,365
1860	4,156,426	13,738,559	48,451,894	15,906,547	191,806,555	39,803,020	2,279,308	56,946,851	373,183,274
1861	4,451,515	10,350,609	101,655,833	13,784,710	34,051,483	36,416,954	3,543,695	23,799,870	227,966,169
1862	3,913,477	9,934,211	124,561,114	12,395,336	1,180,113	27,171,017	9,190,700	31,044,651	219,920,639
Total	53,854,936	161,696,708	867,935,043	198,429,838	1,525,091,187	395,336,617	34,441,989	492,942,075	3,740,031,415

TREASURY DEPARTMENT, *Register's Office, December 26, 1862.*

L. E. CHITTENDEN, *Register.*

Statement exhibiting the value of foreign merchandise and domestic produce exported annually, from 1821 to 1862.

Year ending—	VALUE OF EXPORTS, EXCLUSIVE OF SPECIE.					Specie and bullion.
	Foreign merchandise.			Domestic produce.	Aggregate value of exports.	
	Free of duty.	Paying duty.	Total.			
September 30........1821......	$286,788	$10,537,731	$10,824,519	$43,671,894	$54,496,413	$10,477,969
1822......	374,716	11,101,306	11,476,022	49,874,079	61,350,101	10,810,180
1823......	1,323,762	19,846,873	21,170,635	47,155,408	68,326,043	6,372,987
1824......	1,100,630	17,222,075	18,322,605	50,649,500	68,972,105	7,014,552
1825......	1,098,181	22,704,803	23,802,984	66,944,745	90,747,729	8,787,659
1826......	1,036,430	19,404,504	20,440,934	52,449,855	72,890,789	4,704,533
1827......	813,844	15,617,986	16,431,830	57,878,117	74,309,947	8,014,880
1828......	877,239	13,167,339	14,044,578	49,976,632	64,021,210	8,243,476
1829......	919,943	11,427,401	12,347,344	55,087,307	67,434,651	4,924,020
1830......	1,078,895	12,067,162	13,146,057	58,524,878	71,670,735	2,178,773
1831......	642,585	12,434,483	13,077,069	59,218,583	72,295,652	9,014,931
1832......	1,345,217	18,448,857	19,794,074	61,726,529	81,520,603	5,656,340
1833......	5,165,907	12,411,969	17,577,875	69,950,856	87,528,732	2,611,701
1834......	10,757,033	10,879,520	21,636,553	80,623,662	102,260,215	2,076,758
1835......	7,012,666	7,743,655	14,756,321	100,459,481	115,215,802	6,477,775
1836......	8,584,895	9,232,867	17,767,762	106,570,942	124,338,704	4,324,336
1837......	7,756,189	9,406,043	17,162,232	94,280,895	111,443,727	5,976,249
1838......	4,951,306	4,466,384	9,417,690	95,560,880	104,978,570	3,508,046
1839......	5,618,442	5,007,698	10,626,140	101,625,533	112,261,673	8,776,743
1840......	6,202,562	5,805,809	12,008,371	111,660,561	123,668,932	8,417,014
1841......	3,953,054	4,228,181	8,181,235	103,636,236	111,817,471	10,034,332
1842......	3,194,299	4,884,454	8,078,753	91,798,242	99,876,995	4,813,539
9 months to June 30, 1843......	1,682,763	3,456,572	5,139,335	77,686,354	82,825,689	1,520,791

1845......	2,413,050	5,171,731	7,584,781	98,455,330	106,040,111	8,606,495
1846......	2,342,629	5,522,577	7,865,206	101,718,042	109,583,248	3,905,268
1847......	1,512,847	4,353,907	6,166,754	150,574,844	156,741,598	1,907,024
1848......	1,410,307	6,576,499	7,986,806	130,203,709	138,190,515	15,841,616
1849......	2,015,815	6,625,276	8,641,091	131,510,081	140,351,172	5,404,648
1850......	2,099,132	7,376,361	9,475,493	134,900,233	144,375,726	7,522,994
1851......	1,742,154	8,552,967	10,295,121	178,620,138	188,915,259	29,472,252
1852......	2,538,159	9,514,925	12,053,084	164,931,147	166,984,231	42,674,135
1853......	2,449,539	11,170,571	13,620,120	189,869,162	203,489,282	27,486,875
1854......	3,210,907	18,437,397	21,648,304	215,156,304	236,804,608	41,436,456
1855......	6,516,550	19,641,818	26,158,368	192,751,135	218,909,503	56,247,343
1856......	3,144,604	11,636,768	14,781,372	266,438,051	281,219,423	45,745,485
1857......	4,325,400	10,591,647	14,917,047	278,906,713	293,823,760	69,136,922
1858......	6,751,850	14,908,391	20,660,241	251,351,033	272,011,274	52,633,147
1859......	5,429,921	9,080,050	14,509,971	278,392,080	292,902,051	63,887,411
1860......	5,350,441	11,983,193	17,333,634	316,242,423	333,576,057	66,546,239
1861......	3,709,329	10,944,888	14,654,217	204,899,616	219,553,833	29,791,080
1862......	2,879,565	8,147,771	11,027,336	181,875,988	192,903,324	36,886,956
Total......	137,120,796	445,702,927	582,823,723	5,243,538,972	5,826,362,695	755,324,644

TREASURY DEPARTMENT, *Register's Office, December 26, 1862.*

L. E CHITTENDEN, *Register.*

No. 29.

Statement exhibiting the value of imports, annually, from 1821 to 1862.

Year ending.	Value of merchandise imported.			
	Specie and bullion.	Free of duty.	Paying duty.	Total.
September 30;..... 1821	$8,064,890	$2,017,423	$52,503,411	$62,585,724
1822	3,369,846	3,928,862	75,942,833	83,241,541
1823	5,097,896	3,950,392	68,530,979	77,579,267
1824	8,379,835	4,183,938	67,985,234	80,549,007
1825	6,150,765	4,796,745	85,392,565	96,340,075
1826	6,880,966	5,686,803	72,406,708	84,974,477
1827	8,151,130	3,703,974	67,628,964	79,484,068
1828	7,489,741	4,889,435	76,130,648	88,509,824
1829	7,403,612	4,401,889	62,657,026	74,462,527
1830	8,155,964	4,590,281	58,130,675	70,876,920
1831	7,305,945	6,150,680	89,734,499	103,191,124
1832	5,907,504	8,341,949	86,779,813	101,029,266
1833	7,070,368	25,377,582	75,670,361	108,118,311
1834	17,911,632	50,481,548	58,128,152	126,521,332
1835	13,131,447	64,809,046	71,955,249	149,895,742
1836	13,400,881	78,655,600	97,923,554	189,980,035
1837	10,516,414	58,733,617	71,739,186	140,989,217
1838	17,747,116	43,112,889	52,857,399	113,717,404
1839	5,595,176	70,806,616	85,690,340	162,092,132
1840	8,882,813	48,313,391	49,945,315	107,141,519
1841	4,988,633	61,031,098	61,926,446	127,946,177
1842	4,087,016	26,540,470	69,535,601	100,152,087
9 months to June 30, 1843	22,390,559	13,184,025	29,179,215	64,753,799
Year to June 30...1844	5,830,429	18,936,452	83,668,154	108,435,035
1845	4,070,242	18,077,598	95,106,724	117,254,564
1846	3,777,732	20,990,007	96,924,058	121,691,797
1847	24,121,289	17,651,347	104,773,002	146,545,638
1848	6,360,224	16,356,379	132,282,325	154,998,928
1849	6,651,240	15,726,425	125,479,774	147,857,439
1850	4,628,792	18,081,590	155,427,936	178,138,318
1851	5,453,592	19,652,995	191,118,345	216,224,932
1852	5,505,044	24,187,890	183,252,508	212,945,442
1853	4,201,382	27,182,152	236,595,113	267,978,647
1854	6,958,184	26,327,637	371,276,560	304,562,381
1855	3,659,812	36,430,524	221,378,184	261,468,520
1856	4,207,632	52,748,074	257,684,236	314,639,942
1857	12,461,799	64,267,507	294,160,835	360,890,141
1858	19,274,496	61,044,779	202,293,875	282,613,150
1859	7,434,789	72,286,327	259,047,014	336,768,130
1860	8,550,135	73,741,479	279,874,640	362,166,254
1861	46,339,611	71,130,351	218,180,191	335,650,153
1862	16,415,052	52,721,648	136,683,123	205,819,823
Total..........	403,981,625	1,295,229,414	5,133,609,770	6,832,820,808

L. E. CHITTENDEN, *Register.*

TREASURY DEPARTMENT, *Register's Office, December* 26, 1862.

No. 30.

Statement exhibiting the aggregate value of breadstuffs and provisions exported,
annually, from 1821 to 1862.

Year ending—		Amount.
September 30	1821	$12,341,901
	1822	13,886,856
	1823	13,767,847
	1824	16,059,484
	1825	11,634,449
	1826	11,303,496
	1827	11,685,556
	1828	11,461,144
	1829	13,131,858
	1830	12,075,430
	1831	17,538,227
	1832	12,424,703
	1833	14,209,128
	1834	11,524,024
	1835	12,009,399
	1836	10,614,130
	1837	9,588,359
	1838	9,636,650
	1839	14,147,779
	1840	19,067,535
	1841	17,196,102
	1842	16,902,876
Nine months ending June 30	1843	11,204,123
Year ending June 30	1844	17,970,135
	1845	16,743,421
	1846	27,701,921
	1847	68,701,121
	1848	37,472,751
	1849	38,155,507
	1850	26,051,373
	1851	21,948,651
	1852	25,857,027
	1853	32,935,322
	1854	65,941,323
	1855	38,895,348
	1856	77,187,301
	1857	74,667,852
	1858	50,683,285
	1859	38,305,991
	1860	45,271,850
	1861	94,866,735
	1862	119,338,785
Total		1,221,156,755

L. E. CHITTENDEN, *Register.*
TREASURY DEPARTMENT, *Register's Office, December 26, 1862.*

No. 31.

Statement of the expenditures and receipts of the Marine Hospital Fund for the relief of sick and disabled seamen in the ports of the United States for the fiscal year ending June 30, 1862.

Districts and agents.	Seamen admitted.	Seamen discharged.	Mode of accommodation.	Rate per week.	Board and nursing.	Medical services.	Medicines.	Travelling expenses.	Clothing.	Other charges.	Funeral expenses.	Number of deaths.	Total expenditures	Hospital money collected.
MAINE.														
Passamaquoddy, Washington Long.	99	99	Private	$3 00	$1,049 16	$618 00	$318 35			$19 94	$6 00	1	$2,012 45	$634 76
Machias, William B. Smith............	36	36	....do	$2 to $2 50	981 37	929 50	249 10	$13 50		11 84	19 00	2	1,097 31	429 97
Frenchman's Bay, Isaac H. Thomas....	35	35	....do	2 50 to $3	363 00	146 35	73 15	3 00		5 85			591 35	402 72
Penobscot, no returns................														311 86
Waldoborough, Davis Tillson........	58	50	Private		1,059 10	287 55	45 10			13 90			1,405 65	1,016 49
Wiscasset, Erastus Foote	2	2	Hospital...............	$3 50	39 00	14 00	11 70			64			65 34	26 90
Bath, Roland Fisher................	52	55	....do	3 50	2,0-3 63	899 60	10 87			99 35	12 00	2	2,965 95	290 08
Portland and Falmouth, Jedediah Jewell.	48	43	....do	3 50	3,123 47	749 99	97 83	8 00		36 95	17 00	4	4,035 64	1,943 97
Saco, Thomas K. Lane......	2	2	....do	3 50	91 00	14 00	10 50			1 15			116 65	45 95
Kennebunk, John Cousens;					12 99					19			13 19	5 36
Kennebunk, N. K. Sargent..........	3	3	....		68 90					69			69 59	49 14
York, Jeremiah S. Putnam...........	8	8	Private	2 00	144 35	46 95	23 70			9 13			216 43	24 50
Belfast, T. Harmon	62	61	Hospital...............	3 50	1,077 75	469 50	134 00			16 93	6 00	4	1,705 71	425 62
Bangor, W. P. Wingate..............	96	96	....do	3 00	1,300 97	561 60				19 96	12 00	2	1,918 53	551 27
	501	510	....		11,009 69	4,087 34	973 70	24 50		162 47	65 00	15	16,913 04	6,317 91
NEW HAMPSHIRE.														
Portsmouth, J. B. Upham	33	33	Hospital...............	3 00	690 91	132 80	70 30			8 90			901 89	250 22
VERMONT.														
Burlington, William C. Clapp............	8	8	Private	2 50	72 15	42 75	7 50			1 16			117 56	262 00

ester, John S. Webber			do	3 00	15 00		6 25			all		21 46	422 67
and Beverly, no returns													554 77
head, no returns													94 84
a and Charlestown, J. Z. Goodrich	768	774	Hospital		20,942 73	2,309 80	749 22			240 08	7 00	29 24,248 53	11,515 73
uib, no returns													63 38
iver, Charles Almy	1	1	Private		46 00	9 30	5 54			61		61 65	616 12
uble, J. M. Day	33	33	Hospital	3 50	710 00	210 50	213 15			11 34		1,144 99	219 84
able, Charles F. Swift	187	191	do	3 50	3,416 50	949 30	1,024 95			54 03	12 00	2 5,456 78	935 52
edford, Lawrence Grinnell	15	15	do		292 20	84 45	56 90			3 73	12 00	2 376 69	456 65
own, John Vinson	29	28	Hospital and private		770 00					7 80	12 00	3 789 80	595 91
cket, no returns													301 82
	1,055	1,044			26,388 45	3,577 25	2,088 66	5 00		319 41	43 00	36 32,954 18	15,878 20
RHODE ISLAND.													
dence, Charles Anthony	68	68	Hospital	3 50 & 3 75	1,991 79	371 50	557 90	3 50		29 37	12 00	2 2,965 37	644 02
d and Warren, W. H. S. Bayley	1	1	Private	3 50	78 00	15 00	9 00			1 01		103 01	65 37
d & Warren, W. R. Taylor	1	2	Hospital	3 50	87 50	12 50	7 50			1 57		108 57	
ort, Seth W. Macy	9	12	Private	3 50	386 00	80 25	115 80	6 50		5 00	12 00	2 605 55	360 70
	73	77			2,543 29	479 25	689 50	10 00		36 45	24 00	4 3,782 50	1,078 29
CONNECTICUT.													
stown, Origen Utley	28	28	Hospital and private	3 00	308 15	122 35	2 02			4 44	12 00	2 448 96	715 30
London, Edward Prentis	3	3	Hospital	3 50	142 50	52 25	46 95			15 53	12 00	2 256 13	630 92
Haven, James F. Babcock	33	40	do		773 00			6 50		7 82	6 00	1 791 32	681 10
ld, S. C. Boothe	5	5	Private	3 & 3 50	135 50	31 75	37 20			2 10	6 00	1 212 55	490 09
gton, no returns													157 37
	69	76			1,359 15	206 35	86 17	6 50		16 89	36 00	6 1,708 96	2,674 78
NEW YORK.													
tt's Harbor, C. W. Inglehart	2	2			10 00	5 00				15		15 15	35 37
ee, P. M. Crandall	4	4	Hospital		140 00	10 00				1 50		151 50	63 53
go, John B. Higgins	46	48	do	5 00	2,626 25					26 28		2,053 88	489 92
o, C. A. Perkins	1	33	do	4 50	4,393 28					44 04	12 50	2 4,449 32	671 55
ra, no returns													98 03
u Creek, Christian Metz, Jr	294	309	Hospital	2 50	3,480 91			1 80		34 98	18 00	3 3,533 19	2,994 60
gzichie, David M. Chapin	1	3	Private	2 50	35 28	10 00				47		47 55	141 91
arbor, John Sherry	2	2	do	3 50	49 00	12 00				52		53 62	430 39
York City, Hiram Barney	2,346	2,194	Hospitals	4 00 & 4 50	55,109 70	1,250 00				569 34	574 00	92 57,503 04	45,490 40
plain, George W. Goff	14	12	Private	3 00	920 08	58 25	23 30			3 15	12 00	2 316 78	555 90
Vincent, no returns													362 03
rk, George M. Abell	1	1	Private, x		39 00	16 70				56		56 26	238 43
	2,711	2,606			66,095 60	1,361 95	25 10			680 99	616 00	99 58,179 69	51,691 63
NEW JERSEY.													
stown, William S. Bowen	19	20	Private	3 00	395 91	134 30				5 40	12 00	2 547 61	1,137 54
gton, no returns													134 00
Amboy, J. Lawrence Boggs	2	2	Hospital	3 00 & 3 50	59 50	5 00	1 00	1 50		97		67 67	980 65
Egg Harbor, J. S. Adams	6	6	Private	3 00	144 00	70 90	10 00			2 30	6 00	1 230 30	680 53

Districts and agents.	Seamen admitted.	Seamen discharged.	Mode of accommodation	Rate per week.	Board and nursing.	Medical services.	Medicines.	Travelling expenses.	Clothing.	Other charges.	Funeral expenses.	Number of deaths.
NEW JERSEY—Continued.												
Little Egg Harbor, no returns.....	....	....	....	....	....	....	....	....	....	....	....	....
Newark, no returns...............	....	....	....	....	....	....	....	....	....	....	....	....
Camden, S. Birdsell...............	6	6	Private	$3 50	$216 25	$60 85	$31 55	....	....	$3 09	....	....
	33	34	....	....	·815 66	270 15	42 55	$1 50	....	11 40	$18 00	3
PENNSYLVANIA.												
Philadelphia, William B. Thomas......	170	228	Hospitals.............	2 50 & 5 25	8,866 00	....	....	44 75	$165 10	92 10	135 00	21
Presque Isle, Thomas Wilkins	10	10	Ho-pital and private....	2 50	134 82	62 75	24 55	50	....	2 13	....	....
Pittsburg, Charles W. Batchelor......	72	77	Hospital..............	....	3,921 98	1,000 00	196 23	13 00	36 00	53 17	95 00	11
	252	315	....	....	12,922 80	1,062 75	220 78	58 25	201 10	147 40	230 00	32
DELAWARE.												
No returns	....	....	....	....	....	....	....	....	....	....	....	....
MARYLAND.												
Baltimore, H. W. Hoffman............	201	176	Hospital.............	3 00	3,112 97	....	....	....	....	31 39	40 00	8
Annapolis, no returns	....	....	....	....	....	....	....	....	....	....	....	....
Oxford, no returns	....	....	....	....	....	....	....	....	....	....	....	....
Vienna, no returns...............	....	....	....	....	....	....	....	....	....	....	....	....
Havre de Grace, no returns.	....	....	....	....	....	....	....	....	....	....	....	....
Town Creek, no returns	....	....	....	....	....	....	....	....	....	....	....	....
	201	176	....	....	3,112 97	....	....	....	....	31 39	40 00	8
DISTRICT OF COLUMBIA.												
Georgetown, Judson Mitchell...........	9	9	Hospital.............	3 00	242 20	....	....	....	....	2 62	18 00	3

ystone, Edw'd S. Bailey, no returns.																
her ports have made returns.	6	5			108 80	56 75	4 88			1 79			180 57	1,327 10	

NORTH CAROLINA.

fort, no returns															2 48

SOUTH CAROLINA.

fort, no returns															61 30

GEORGIA.

swick, (no others,) Woodford Mabry	10	10	Hospital	3 50	47 00	23 50	14 10			84			85 44	

FLORIDA.

West, Charles Howe	212	188	Hospital		3,706 04		240 51			40 11	48 08	5	4,026 78	730 49
her ports returned														
	212	188			3,706 04		240 51			40 11	48 00	5	4,026 78	730 49

ALABAMA.

turns														

MISSISSIPPI.

turns														

LOUISIANA.

turns														

TEXAS.

turns														

OHIO.

ni, Emery D. Potter	32	32	Sisters of Charity	4 50	882 64					8 81			891 45	291 35
ni, Andrew Stephan	7	6	do do	4 50	1,068 78		17 61	9 85		19 80	19 00	2	1,293 58	551 22
usky, John Younge	6	6	Private	3 00	31 90					51			32 30	534 22
hoga, Chas. J. Ballard	78	71	Hospital		5,715 16	1,950 00	582 30		78 99	86 48	24 00	5	8,736 93	2,092 22
nnati, Enoch T. Carson	254	384	do		12,372 97					124 69	96 00	16	12,594 66	1,689 98
	377	499			21,272 45	1,957 01	585 15		78 99	233 29	139 00	23	23,568 92	4,537 77

MICHIGAN.

ni, N. G. Isbell	141	222	Hospital		4,174 02	1,500 00	464 43	104 00		63 24	84 00	15	6,389 69	2,602 38
lmackinac, J. W. McMath	12	12	do	3 00	41 88	22 00	9 00	7 00		79			80 67	242 34
	153	234			4,215 90	1,522 00	473 43	111 00		64 03	84 00	15	6,470 36	2,684 72

Districts and agents.	Seamen admitted.	Seamen discharged.	Mode of accommodation.	Rate per week.	Board and nursing.	Medical services.	Medicines.	Travelling expenses.	Clothing.	Other charges.	Funeral expenses.	Number of deaths.
ILLINOIS.												
Chicago, Julius White............	....	....	Hospital.....	....	$1,665 83	$250 03	$181 26	....	....	$21 10	$12 00	2
Chicago, Luther Haven...........	174	171	...do........	....	4,584 96	750 00	514 89	....	....	58 65	18 00	3
Alton, no returns	....	....	....	....	......	......	......	....	....	......	......	...
Galena, Daniel Wann.............	8	8	Hospital.....	..n...	1,693 92	800 00	9 75	....	....	25 04	......	...
Quincy, no returns.............	....	......	....	......	......	......	......	....	....	......	... ..	...
	182	179	... .	....	7,944 71	1,800 03	705 99	....	....	104 79	30 00	5
INDIANA.												
Evansville, A. L. Robinson	72	72	Hospital...............	....	2,876 55	638 89	264 37	....	....	37 80	......	....
New Albany, no returns.............	....	......	....	....	......	......	......	....	....	......	......	...
	72	72	....	......	2,876 55	638 89	264 37	....	....	37 80	... ...	....
IOWA.												
Burlington, Philip Harvey	......	......	Hospital...............	......	1,567 90	......	......	......		15 56	......	....
Burlington, Clark Dunham.............	......	......	...do.....	......	787 17	905 56	34 90	......	......	17 23	......	....
Keokuk, no returns......	......	......	....	......	......	......	......	......	......	......	......	....
	......	......	....	......	2,355 07	905 56	34 90	......	......	32 79	......	....
WISCONSIN.												
Milwaukie, Edwin Palmer	96	116	Hospital...............	$3 50	1,760 83	1,072 00	34 11	....	....	26 73	6 00	1
MINNESOTA.												

MISSOURI.

...uls, R. J. Howard...............	343	385	Hospital..........	....	9,711 06	968 88	873 89	...../....	....	115 64	15 00	3	11,583 48	4,344 30
...hal, no returns.................	.....	......	....	....	....	....	......	......	....	......	......	....	....	....
	343	385	....	....	9,711 06	968 88	873 89	....	....	115 64	15 00	3	11,683 48	4,344 30

KENTUCKY.

...ville, Charles B. Colton..........	......	.....	Hospital..........	....	4,159 35	1,185 00	169 42	......	.....	54 77	24 00	3	5,532 54	760 64
...ah, Warren Thornton	......	.....	....	....	3,251 72	1,114 79	316 22	.....	.....	47 12	30 00	5	4,759 85	
	......	.....	....	....	7,411 07	2,299 79	485 64	....	....	101 89	54 00	8	10,292 39	760 64

TENNESSEE.

...turns	.....	.....	....	....	....	....	......	......	......	.....	....	....	....	....

WASHINGTON TERRITORY.

...'s Sound, Morris H. Frost	.....	......			4,854 00	....	....	....	......	48 54	....	...	4,902 54	56 78

OREGON.

...n, Wm. L. Adams	1	1	Private...............	6 00	20 60	13 00	4 80			37	....	...	37 77	169 88
...Perpetua, no returns.............	......	......	....	....	....	....	....	....	....	......	....	....	....	....
...Orford, no returns..............	......	......												44 30
	1	1	....	....	20 60	13 00	4 80	....	....	37	....	..	37 77	234 18

CALIFORNIA.

...rancisco, Ira P. Rankin	584	548	Hospital	....	26,260 05	3,610 04	1,686 18	....	....	320 17	462 00	66	32,338 45	10,639 65
...na, no returns*...............	......	......	....	....	....	....	....	....	....	......	....	...	....	147 27
...osquia, no returns............	......	......	....	....	....	....	....	....	....	......	....	...	....	95 52
...mento, no returns............	......	......	....	....	....	....	....	....	....	......	....	...	....	....
...)iego, no returns.............	......	......	....	....	....	....	....	....	....	......	....	...	....	2 40
...erey, no returns..............	......	......	....	....	....	....	....	....	....	......	....	...	....	24 49
...edro, no returns..............	.....	......	....	....	....	....	....	....	....	......	....	..	....	48 65
	584	548	....	....	26,260 05	3,610 04	1,686 18	....	....	320 17	462 00	66	32,338 45	10,957 89

Many of the marine hospital reports are so given as to make it impossible to classify the accounts.
* No marine hospital reports.

L. E. CHITTENDEN, *Register.*

TREASURY DEPARTMENT, *Register's Office, December 8, 1862.*

No. 32.

Statement showing the amount of moneys expended at each custom-house in the United States during the fiscal year ending June 30, 1862, per act of March 3, 1849.

Districts.	Present collectors.	Amount.
Passamaquoddy, Maine	Washington Long	$17,150 58
Machias, Maine (a)	William B. Smith	1,707 37
Frenchman's Bay, Maine	Isaac H. Thomas	4,931 60
Penobscot, Maine	Seth K. Devereux	4,472 74
Waldoborough, Maine	Davis Tillson	7,166 47
Wiscasset	Erastus Foote	6,723 01
Bath, Maine	Roland Fisher	7,652 89
Portland and Falmouth, Maine (b)	J. Jewett	2,025 02
Saco, Maine	O. B. Chadbourne	1,648 00
Kennebunk, Maine	Nathaniel K. Sargent	742 77
York, Maine	J. S Putnam	620 00
Belfast, Maine	Truman Harmon	6,651 70
Bangor, Maine	William P. Wingate	6,368 20
Portsmouth, New Hampshire	Joseph B. Upham	6,377 81
Vermont, Vermont	William Clapp	13,980 62
Newburyport, Massachusetts	Enoch G. Currier	5,080 35
Gloucester, Massachusetts (a)	John S Webber	4,551 46
Salem and Beverly, Massachusetts	Willard P. Phillips	13,334 81
Marblehead, Massachusetts	William Standley	3,077 73
Boston and Charlestown, Massachusetts (d)	John Z. Goodrich	295,494 32
Plymouth, Massachusetts	Thomas Loring	3,441 69
Fall River, Massachusetts	Charles Almy	3,166 74
Barnstable, Massachusetts	Joseph M. Day	6,582 34
New Bedford, Massachusetts	Laurence Grinnell	22,989 17
Edgartown, Massachusetts	John Vinson	2,837 66
Nantucket, Massachusetts	Alfred Macy	2,144 24
Providence, Rhode Island	Charles Anthony	10,219 70
Bristol and Warren, Rhode Island	William R. Taylor	2,540 35
Newport, Rhode Island	Seth W. Macy	5,379 23
Middletown, Connecticut	Origen Utley	2,277 80
New London, Connecticut	Edward Prentis	4,975 12
New Haven, Connecticut	James F. Babcock	16,016 50
Fairfield, Connecticut	Silas C. Booth	2,144 54
Stonington, Connecticut	Franklin A. Palmer	1,346 08
Sackett's Harbor, New York	Cornelius W. Iglehart	2,678 57
Genesee, New York	P. M. Crandall	5,749 70
Oswego, New York	Charles A. Perkins	14,331 23
Niagara, New York	Franklin Spalding	12,073 78
Buffalo Creek, New York	Christian Metz, jr	15,472 43
Oswegatchie, New York	David M. Chapin	6,757 81
Sag Harbor, New York	John Sherry	3,326 59
New York, New York	Hiram Barney	1,488,727 18
Champlain, New York	George W. Goff	8,791 34
Cape Vincent, New York	John W. Ingalls	6,050 21
Dunkirk, New York	George M. Abell	1,134 60
Bridgetown, New Jersey	J. H. Elmer	362 47
Burlington, New Jersey	W. L. Ashmore	152 90
Perth Amboy, New Jersey	John L. Boggs	3,956 81
Great Egg Harbor, New Jersey	J. S. Adams	723 71
Little Egg Harbor, New Jersey	Jarvis H. Bartlett	1,720 42
Newark, New Jersey	Peter W. Martin	1,920 99
Camden, New Jersey	Sylvester Birdsell	297 14
Philadelphia, Pennsylvania	William B. Thomas	258,437 25

No. 32.—*Statement showing the amount of moneys expended, &c.*—Continued.

Districts.	Present collectors.	Amount.
Presque Isle, Pennsylvania	Thomas Wilkins	$1,962 12
Pittsburg, Pennsylvania	C. W. Batchelor	5,713 12
Delaware, Delaware	Thomas M. Rodney	12,513 94
Baltimore, Maryland	Henry W. Hoffman	214,871 13
Annapolis, Maryland	John E. Stalker	915 17
Oxford, Maryland	William H. Valliant	259 30
Vienna, Maryland	D. J. Waddell	1,482 51
Town Creek, Maryland	James Jones	150 84
Havre de Grace, Maryland	Levi Kline	154 41
Georgetown, District of Columbia	Judson Mitchell	4,428 02
Richmond, Virginia	(No returns)	
Norfolk and Portsmouth, Virginia	do	
Tappahannock, Virginia	do	
Cherrystone, Virginia	E. L. Bayly	42 85
Yorktown, Virginia	(No returns)	
Petersburg, Virginia	do	
Alexandria, Virginia	Andrew Jamieson	3,962 75
Wheeling, Virginia	Thomas Hornbrook	2,747 73
Yeocomico, Virginia	(No returns)	
Camden, North Carolina	do	
Edenton, North Carolina	do	
Plymouth, North Carolina	do	
Washington, North Carolina	do	
Newbern, North Carolina	do	
Ocracoke, North Carolina	do	
Beaufort, North Carolina	J. D. Hedrick	45 29
Wilmington, North Carolina	(No returns)	
Charleston, South Carolina	do	
Georgetown, South Carolina	do	
Beaufort, South Carolina	T. C. Severance	874 45
Savannah, Georgia	(No returns)	
Saint Mary's, Georgia	do	
Brunswick, Georgia	do	
Augusta, Georgia	do	
Pensacola, Florida	do	
Saint Augustine, Florida	do	
Saint Mark's, Florida	do	
Key West, Florida	Charles Howe	4,955 39
Saint John's, Florida	(No returns)	
Apalachicola, Florida	do	
Fernandina, Florida	do	
Bayport, Florida	do	
Palatka, Florida	do	
Mobile, Alabama	do	
Tuscumbia, Alabama	do	
Pearl River, Mississippi	do	
Natchez, Mississippi	do	
Vicksburg, Mississippi	do	
New Orleans, Louisiana	do	
Teche, Louisiana	do	
Shreveport, Louisiana	do	
Texas, Texas	do	
Brazos de Santiago, Texas	do	
Saluria, Texas	do	
Paso del Norte, New Mexico	Samuel N. Wood, (no returns)	
Nashville, Tennessee	(No returns)	
Memphis, Tennessee	do	
Knoxville, Tennessee	do	
Chattanooga, Tennessee	do	

No. 32.—*Statement showing the amount of moneys expended, &c.*—Continued.

Districts.	Present collectors.	Amount.
Louisville, Kentucky (g)	C. B. Cotton	$458 12
Paducah, Kentucky	W. Thornberry	966 31
Hickman, Kentucky	(No returns)	
Columbus, Kentucky	...do...	
Miami, Ohio	Andrew Stephan	3,916 42
Sandusky, Ohio	John Youngs	4,042 38
Cuyahoga, Ohio	Charles J. Ballard	7,630 30
Cincinnati, Ohio	Enoch T. Carson	8,734 91
Detroit, Michigan	Nelson G. Isbell	18,280 60
Michilimackinac, Michigan	John W. McMath	5,621 78
Evansville, Indiana	A. L. Robinson	3,645 31
Madison, Indiana	Robert P. Jones	533 00
New Albany, Indiana	Jacob Anthony	1,468 65
Chicago, Illinois	Luther Haven	12,880 30
Alton, Illinois	John H. Yager	597 40
Galena, Illinois	Daniel Wann	416 45
Quincy, Illinois	J. J. Langden	518 00
Cairo, Illinois	Daniel Arter	3,474 69
Peoria, Illinois	L. K. Webb, (no returns)	
Saint Louis, Missouri	R. J. Howard	6,074 71
Hannibal, Missouri	N. O. Archer	1,170 00
Burlington, Iowa	C. Dunham	350 00
Keokuk, Iowa	John Stannus	1,358 07
Dubuque, Iowa	John B. Heniou	705 13
Milwaukie, Wisconsin	Edwin Palmer	6,560 42
Minnesota, Minnesota	Joseph Lemay	2,143 07
Puget's Sound, Washington Territory (e)	Victor Smith	529 07
Oregon, Oregon	William L. Adams	5,174 43
Cape Perpetua, Oregon	E. R. Drew	2,218 71
Port Orford, Oregon	William Tichner	2,750 00
San Francisco, California (f)	Ira P. Rankin	201,534 26
Sonoma, California	Seth M. Swain	3,002 30
San Joaquin, California	S. W. Sperry	3,540 00
Sacramento, California (a)	L. H. Foote	2,452 87
San Diego, California	Joshua Sloane	3,000 55
Monterey, California	J. T. Porter	5,289 82
San Pedro, California	Oscar Macy	5,330 55
Total		2,907,327 34

L. E. CHITTENDEN, *Register.*

TREASURY DEPARTMENT, *Register's Office, November* 19, 1862.

NOTES.

(a.) To the 31st of March, 1862.
(b.) To the 6th of August, 1861.
(g.) To the 30th of October, 1861.
(e.) To the 2d of August, 1861.
(f.) To the 30th of April, 1862.

No. 33.

Statement of the number of persons employed in each district of the United States, for the collection of customs, during the fiscal year ending June 30, 1862, with their occupation and compensation, per act of March 3, 1849.

Districts.	No. of persons employed.	Occupation.	Compensation to each person.
Passamaquoddy, Me...	1	Collector..........................	$3,000 00
	1	Surveyor	1,193 00
	7	Inspectors	1,095 00
	3	....do	842 00
	1	....do	730 00
	1	Deputy collector..................	730 00
	1	Aid to the revenue	825 00
	1	....do	730 00
	1	Weigher, measurer, and aid	1,083 00
	1	Weigher and measurer.............	218 00
	1	Boatman	360 00
	1	....do	240 00
Machias, Me..........	1	Collector	1,660 40
	1	Inspector and deputy collector....	500 00
	1	....do	500 00
	1	....do	365 00
	1	....do	250 00
Frenchman's Bay, Me.	1	Collector	1,751 70
	1	Deputy collector and inspector....	1,095 00
	1	....do.......do	1,000 00
	2	....do.......do	300 00
	1	Inspector	730 00
	1	Boatman	360 00
	1	....do	240 00
	1	Measurer	91 46
	1	Aid to the revenue	359 00
Penobscot, Me........	1	Collector	1,500 00
	2	Deputy collectors.................	750 00
	1	....do	780 00
	1	....do	600 00
	1	....do	1,000 00
Waldoborough, Me ...	1	Collector	1,800 00
	2	Inspectors	1,095 00
	2	....do	936 00
	2	....do	300 00
	1	....do	600 00
	1	....do	730 00
Wiscasset, Me	1	Collector	909 43
	1	Inspector	1,095 00
	1	....do	912 50
	1	....do	800 00
	1	....do	730 00
	2	....do	700 00
Bath, Me	1	Collector	1,236 47
	1	Inspector, weigher, gauger, and measurer..	1,491 24
	1	....do.......do	1,450 06
	1	Inspector	1,095 00
	1	....do	650 00
	1	....do	600 00

No. 33.—*Statement*—Continued.

Districts.	No. of persons employed.	Occupation.	Compensation to each person.
Bath, Me.—Continued	2	Inspectors	$396 00
	1	....do	350 00
	1	....do	230 00
Portland and Falmouth, Me.	1	Collector	3,000 00
	1	Weigher, gauger, measurer, and deputy collector	1,500 00
	1	Superintendent	1,500 00
	1	Clerk	1,500 00
	1	Storekeeper	1,095 00
	1	Surveyor	2,000 00
	2	Weighers, gaugers, and measurers	1,500 00
	7	Inspectors	1,095 00
	4	Occasional inspectors	1,095 00
	2	Night watchmen	730 00
	2	Aids to revenue	626 00
	2	Boatmen	365 00
	1	....do	456 25
	1	Occasional weigher, &c., at $3 per day, when employed	....
Saco, Me.	1	Collector	329 42
	1	Inspector	500 00
	1	....do	450 00
	1	Aid to revenue	100 00
Kennebunk, Me	1	Collector	100 39
	1	Deputy collector	600 00
	2	Inspectors	56 00
York, Me	1	Collector	264 78
	1	Inspector	200 00
	1	....do	120 00
Bangor, Me	1	Collector	2,042 00
	2	Deputy collectors	1,095 00
	1	Deputy collector and gauger, &c	1,124 00
	1	....do..........do	893 00
	1	Weigher, gauger, and measurer	1,078 00
	1	Aid to revenue	200 00
Belfast, Me.	1	Collector	1,375 76
	2	Deputy collectors of customs	1,095 00
	1	Inspector, weigher, gauger, and measurer	865 17
	1	Deputy collector, inspector, weigher, &c	1,186 66
	1	....do..........do	934 10
	1	Aid to revenue	200 00
	1	Seaman employed in revenue boat	300 00
Portsmouth, N. H	1	Collector	439 78
	1	Naval officer	397 90
	1	Surveyor	329 84
	1	Deputy collector and inspector	1,000 00
	1	....do	119 75
	1	Inspector, weigher, and measurer	1,108 37
	1	Inspector	1,095 00
	1	....do	1,028 00
	1	....do	500 00
	1	Inspector, discontinued August 10, 1861	55 36
Vermont, Vt	1	Collector	1,090 84
	2	Deputy collectors and inspectors	1,000 00
	3	....do..........do	912 50

No. 33.—*Statement*—Continued.

Districts.	No. of persons employed.	Occupation.	Compensation to each person.
Vermont -Continued..	1	Deputy collector and inspector...................	$600 00
	6	....do ....do	500 00
	7	....do ....do	360 00
	1	Deputy collector................................	750 00
	1	Deputy inspector	360 00
	1	....do	240 00
	3	Revenue boatmen	240 00
Newburyport, Mass ...	1	Collector	323 05
	1	Surveyor	362 91
	1	Naval officer	363 53
	1	Deputy collector and inspector.................	1,095 00
	1	Inspector, weigher, measurer, and gauger...	1,095 00
	1	Inspector	1,095 00
	1	Surveyor	250 00
Gloucester, Mass......	1	Collector	1,438 21
	1	Surveyor	595 08
	1	Deputy collector	850 00
	2	Inspectors	1,095 00
	1	....do	300 00
	1	....do	112 50
	1	Weigher, gauger, and measurer	375 00
	1	....do	715 20
	1	Boatman	262 50
	1	Keeper of custom-house	150 00
Salem and Beverly, Mass.	1	Collector.....................................	1,025 38
	1	Surveyor	497 09
	1	Surveyor, Beverly	175 41
	1	Naval officer..................................	712 77
	1	Weigher and gauger	985 42
	1	....do	838 23
	1	Clerk	1,000 00
	1	Inspector and deputy collector	1,095 00
	1	Inspector and storekeeper	1,095 00
	1	Inspector	633 00
	1	....do	630 00
	1	....do	540 00
	1	....do	402 00
	1	....do	282 00
	1	....do	252 00
	1	....do	315 00
	1	....do	306 00
	1	Inspector, Danvers	204 00
	1	Inspector, Beverly...........................	249 00
	1	Aid to revenue...............................	730 00
	1	....do	75 00
	1	....do	42 00
	1	....do	57 00
	2	....do	81 00
	1	....do	78 00
	1	Measurer	400 00
	1	Boatman	300 00
	1	Porter and messenger.......................	300 00
Marblehead, Mass.....	1	Collector	344 30
	2	Deputy collectors and inspectors	547 50
	1	Surveyor......................................	142 36

No. 33.—*Statement*—Continued.

Districts.	No. of persons employed.	Occupation.	Compensation to each person.
Marblehead, Mass.— Continued.	1	Boatman	$150 00
	1	Deputy collector and inspector..........	365 00
	1	Inspector and Swampscot................	.182 50
	1	Boatman	100 00
Boston and Charlestown, Mass.	......	No returns........................	....
Plymouth, Mass	1	Collector	328 00
	1	Deputy collector and inspector..........	1,092 00
	1	...do.........do	400 00
	1	...do.........do	300 00
	1	...do.........do	300 00
Fall River, Mass	1	Collector	1,126 37
	1	Inspector, weigher, measurer, and gauger..	885 81
	1	...do.........do	731 96
	1	...do.........do	638 00
	1	Revenue boatman	300 00
Barnstable, Mass......	1	Collector	1,700 00
	1	Deputy collector and inspector...........	900 00
	1	Deputy collector and inspector, Provincetown	750 00
	2	Deputies, Wellfleet and Chatham	569 33
	1	Deputy collector and inspector, South Danvers	500 00
	1	Deputy collector and inspector, Falmouth..	274 00
	1	Deputy collector and inspector, Sandwich...	112 00
	1	Deputy collector and inspector, Hyannis...	450 00
	1	Aid to the revenue, Harwich	150 00
	1	Aid to the revenue, Chatham...........	148 00
	1	Aid to the revenue, Wellfleet............	148 00
	1	Aid to the revenue, Provincetown	148 00
	1	Revenue boatman, Provincetown..........	150 00
	1	Revenue boatman, Barnstable,...........	112 50
	1	Revenue boatman, Hyannis..............	93 75
	1	Keeper of custom-house.................	350 00
	1	Inspector, Barnstable	550 00
New Bedford, Mass ...	1	Collector, disbursing agent, marine hospital,&c	2,173 46
	2	Inspectors	1,095 00
	1	Inspector, weigher, and measurer	1,365 74
	1	Inspector	300 00
	1	...do	125 00
	2	...do	80 00
	1	...do	500 00
	1	Clerk............................	800 00
	1	Boatman	420 00
	1	Aid to revenue	....
Edgartown, Mass	1	Collector	1,010 63
	1	Deputy collector ,...................	1,095 00
	1	...do	600 00
	1	Occasional inspector	372 00
	2	Special aids to revenue.................	52 50
	1	Boatman	240 00
Nantucket, Mass......	1	Collector	350 85
	1	Deputy collector and inspector..........	1,000 00
	1	Inspector, weigher, and measurer	600 00
Providence, R. I......	1	Collector	710 38
	1	Deputy collector	1,000 00
	1	Clerk............................	900 00

No. 33.—*Statement*—Continued.

Districts.	No. of persons employed.	Occupation.	Compensation to each person.
Providence, R. I.—	1	Naval officer	$678 45
Continued.	1	Surveyor, Providence	574 11
	1	Surveyor, E. Greenwich........................	251 69
	1	Surveyor, Pawtuxet	200 00
	2	Coastwise inspectors	547 50
	6	Foreign inspectors...............................	556 00
	1	Inspector, Pawtuxet.	450 00
	1	Inspector, E. Greenwich	300 00
	1	Weigher...	675 03
	1	Gauger	35 16
	1	Measurer	1,500 00
	1	Boatman, Pawtuxet.	420 00
	1	Messenger, Providence........................	400 00
Bristol and Warren, R. I.	1	Collector	419 04
	2	Inspectors	549 00
	3	Inspectors, $123, $72, $24	219 00
	2	Gaugers	151 32
	1	Boatman	216 00
	1	Surveyor	327 72
	½	....do	261 83
Newport, R. I	1	Collector, superintendent of lights	1,108 88
	1	Naval officer	413 23
	1	Surveyor, Newport	390 68
	1	Surveyor, Tiverton	200 00
	1	Surveyor, North Kingston	250 00
	1	Deputy collector and inspector, Newport...	1,000 00
	2	Inspectors, Newport	274 00
	1	Inspector, Nottingham.........................	222 00
	1	Inspector, New Shoreham	200 00
	1	Occasional inspector	201 00
	1	....do	213 00
	1	....do	147 00
	1	....do	75 00
	1	Gauger...	170 52
	1	Weigher..	167 88
	1	Measurer	54 63
	1	Boatman	450 00
Middletown, Conn	1	Collector	696 56
	3	Surveyors..	836 22
	3	Inspectors, $650, $350, $300	1,300 00
New London, Conn ...	1	Collector and superintendent of lights.....	2,363 84
	1	Inspector, weigher, gauger, &c.............	793 82
	1	....do..............do	972 51
	1	....do..............do	450 00
	1	....do..............do	66 67
	1	Surveyor	370 91
New Haven, Conn	1	Collector	3,000 00
	1	Deputy collector	1,500 00
	1	Surveyor	660 00
	2	Weighers, measurers, and gaugers	1,500 00
	4	Inspectors	1,095 00
	3	Inspectors, $730, $72, $60	862 00
	2	Aids to revenue, $730, $48	778 00
	1	Watchman and porter.	450 00
	1	Messenger and porter	500 00
	2	Boatmen and aids to revenue	400 00

No. 33.—*Statement*—Continued.

Districts.	No. of persons employed.	Occupation.	Compensation to each person.
Fairfield, Conn	1	Collector	$912 36
	1	Inspector	1,283 45
	1	....do	256 00
	1	....do	143 50
	1	Deputy collector................	150 00
Stonington, Conn.....	1	Collector	650 00
	2	Inspectors	450 00
	1	Surveyor	150 00
	1	Boat keeper.....................	144 00
Sackett's Harbor, N. Y.	1	Collector	717 80
	1	Deputy collector	730 00
	1	....do	365 00
	1	....do	300 00
	1	....do	250 00
	1	Night watch	275 00
Genesee, N. Y.........	1	Collector.......................	784 24
	1	Deputy collector...............	900 00
	1	....do	800 00
	1	....do	730 00
	2	Aids and inspectors	730 00
	1	Clerk and inspector............	730 00
Oswego, N. Y	1	Collector	961 84
	1	Deputy collector	1,000 00
	1	....do	500 00
	1	....do	410 62
	1	....do	366 00
	1	....do	300 00
	2	Clerks........................	730 00
	1	....do	470 00
	1	....do	382 87
	1	....do	500 00
	2	Inspectors	730 00
	1	....do	32 00
	1	Revenue aid	488 00
	3	....do	306 00
	1	....do	382 50
	1	Night watch	366 00
	2	....do	365 00
	1	....do	183 00
	2	....do	153 00
	1	Porter and boatman	263 00
Niagara, N. Y.........	1	Collector	1,410 79
	2	Deputy collectors..............	900 00
	1	....do.............	730 00
	2	Deputy collectors and aid	730 00
	1	....do.........do.....	608 00
	1	Deputy collector and inspector..	730 00
	1	....do.........do.....	400 00
	3	....do.........do.....	365 00
	2	Inspectors....................	730 00
	1	Clerk........................	730 00
	2	Watchmen....................	547 50
	2	Night watch..................	304 00
Buffalo Creek, N. Y...,	1	Collector.....................	1,954 23
	1	Deputy collector..............	1,000 00

No. 33.—*Statement*—Continued.

Districts.	No. of persons employed.	Occupation.	Compensation to each person.
Buffalo Creek, N. Y.—Continued.	1	Deputy collector	$900 00
	1	....do......	730 00
	1	Inspector	1,000 00
	1	....do......	900 00
	1	....do......	600 00
	2	Inspectors during navigation	822 00
	2	Clerks	912 00
	5	Night watch	730 00
Oswegatchie, N. Y....	1	Collector	1,466 10
	1	Deputy collector and inspector	900 00
	1	Aid to revenue	900 00
	1	Inspector	730 00
	2	Deputy collectors and inspectors	468 75
	1	....do.........do....	450 00
	1	....do.........do....	300 00
	1	....do.........do....	402 70
	1	Night watch	240 00
Sag Harbor, N. Y.....	1	Collector	688 22
	1	Inspector	98 00
	1	....do......	39 00
	1	....do......	89 60
New York city, N. Y..	1	Collector	6,340 00
	1	Auditor	4,000 00
	1	Cashier	3,000 00
	1	Assistant auditor	3,000 00
	1	Assistant cashier	2,000 00
	7	Deputy collectors	2,500 00
	1	Clerk	2,400 00
	1	....do......	2,000 00
	1	....do......	1,800 00
	4	....do......	1,600 00
	21	....do......	1,500 00
	11	....do......	1,400 00
	8	....do......	1,300 00
	42	....do......	1,200 00
	43	....do......	1,100 00
	16	....do......	1,000 00
	13	....do......	800 00
	1	....do......	750 00
	4	....do......	700 00
	2	....do......	650 00
	2	....do......	600 00
	1	Keeper of custom-house	1,200 00
	2	Messengers	800 00
	1	....do......	700 00
	7	....do......	650 00
	13	....do......	600 00
	2	....do......	400 00
	3	Porters	480 00
	2	....do......	420 00
	1	Fireman	547 50
	2	Watchmen	625 50
	4	....do......	547 50
	2	....do......	45 00
	1	Warehouse superintendent	2,000 00
	1	Storekeeper	1,200 00

No. 33.—*Statement*—Continued.

District.	No. of persons employed.	Occupation.	Compensation to each person.
New York city, N. Y.—Continued.	69	Storekeepers	$1,095 00
	1	Clerk	780 00
	2	Assistant storekeepers	600 00
	19	Weighers	1,485 00
	8	Gaugers	1,485 00
	6	Measurers	1,485 00
	193	Inspectors	1,095 00
	4	....do	195 00
	1	Inspector at Albany	1,095 00
	3	Temporary aids	1,095 00
	2	....do	550 00
	75	Night inspectors	547 50
	50	Night watchmen	547 50
	4	Measurers of vessels	1,095 00
	1	Measurer of marble	1,000 00
	9	Debenture clerks	1,000 00
	1	Captain of the night watch	800 00
	3	Lieutenants of the night watch	650 00
	1	Superintendent of marine hospital	1,000 00
	1	Examiner of drugs	2,000 00
	1	Clerk and examiner of drugs	1,000 00
	1	Clerk, cotton agency	2,400 00
	1	....do.......do	1,500 00
	1	....do.......do	900 00
	18	Bargemen	600 00
	1	Surveyor at Troy	250 00
	1	Surveyor at Albany	150 00
	1	Surveyor at Cold Spring	Fees.
		Appraiser's department.	
	1	General appraiser	2,500 00
	3	Appraisers	2,500 00
	5	Assistant appraisers	2,000 00
	1	Examiner of damages	2,000 00
	10	Appraiser's clerks	1,500 00
	6	......do	1,400 00
	2	......do	1,300 00
	10	......do	1,200 00
	1	......do	1,150 00
	4	......do	1,000 00
	3	......do	800 00
	21	......do	650 00
	1	Messenger	600 00
	1	Storekeeper, appraiser of stores	1,400 00
	1	Clerk, appraiser of stores	1,300 00
	5	....do.........do	1,100 00
	1	....do.........do	1,000 00
	5	....do.........do	800 00
	2	Messengers, appraisers of stores	600 00
		Naval office.	
	1	Naval officer	4,950 00
	3	Deputies	2,000 00
	2	Clerks	1,500 00

No. 33.—*Statement*—Continued.

Districts.	No. of persons employed.	Occupation.	Compensation to each person.
New York city, N. Y.—Continued.	8	Clerks....................................	$1,400 00
	6	....do...................................	1,200 00
	29	....do...................................	1,000 00
	3	....do...................................	900 00
	1	....do...................................	600 00
	8	....do...................................	500 00
	2	Porters..................................	500 00
		Surveyor's office.	
	1	Surveyor and inspector....................	4,559 13
	2	Deputy surveyors.........................	2,000 00
	1	....do...................................	1,612 00
	1	Clerk....................................	1,200 00
	4	....do...................................	1,100 00
	1	....do...................................	1,095 00
	5	....do...................................	1,000 00
	1	....do...................................	700 00
	4	Messengers...............................	650 00
	1	....do...................................	77 97
	1	Porter...................................	480 00
Champlain, N. Y......	1	Collector................................	1,050 71
	1	Deputy collector and inspector............	1,000 00
	1	Deputy collector and clerk,...............	800 00
	1	....do.............do....................	600 00
	1	Deputy collector and aid.................	600 00
	1	Deputy collector and inspector...........	600 00
	2	Deputy collectors and aids...............	500 00
	1	Deputy collector and inspector...........	500 00
	4	....do.....;......do....................	400 00
	1	Boatman..................................	180 00
Cape Vincent, N. Y....	1	Collector................................	1,014 00
	4	Deputy collectors and inspectors..........	730 00
	1	....do.............do....................	365 00
	2	....do.............do....................	245 00
	1	....do.............do....................	160 00
	1	Aid of revenue...........................	547 50
	1	Boatman..................................	200 00
Dunkirk, N. Y........	1	Collector................................	500 00
	1	Deputy collector.........................	187 50
Bridgetown, N. J......	1	Collector................................	250 00
Burlington. N. J......	1	....do...................................	174 00
Perth Amboy, N. J....	1	....do...................................	2,041 20
	1	Deputy collector.........................	600 00
	1	Surveyor.................................	150 00
	3	Inspectors...............................	600 00
	1	....do...................................	500 00
	1	....do...................................	400 00
	4	Bargemen.................................	223 00
Great Egg Harbor, N.J.	1	Collector................................	564 33
	1	Inspector................................	345 00
	1	....do...................................	51 00
	2	Boatman..................................	12 00
Little Egg Harbor, N.J.	1	Inspector................................	552 00
	7	Temporary inspectors, at $3 per day.......	....

No. 33.—*Statement*—Continued.

Districts.	No. of persons employed.	Occupation.	Compensation to each person.
Little Egg Harbor, N. J.—Continued.	2	Temporary appraisers, at $5 per day	
	2	Revenue boat hands, at $3 per day	
Newark, N. J.	1	Collector	$464 72
	1	Deputy collector	730 00
	1	Temporary inspector	586 00
	1	Messenger	550 00
Camden, N. J.	1	Surveyor	687 46
Philadelphia, Pa.	1	Collector	6,400 00
	2	Deputy collectors	2,500 00
	1	Cashier	1,500 00
	1	Clerk	1,400 00
	1	Clerk for 8 months	929 44
	2	Clerks	1,200 00
	1	....do	1,188 30
	3	....do	1,100 00
	1	Clerk for 8 months	733 33
	11	Clerks	1,000 00
	1	Keeper	800 00
	1	Messenger	600 00
	1	Porter	547 50
	2	Watchmen	547 50
	1	Naval officer	5,000 00
	1	Deputy naval officer	2,000 00
	2	Clerks	1,200 00
	6	....do	1,000 00
	1	Messenger	600 00
	1	Surveyor	4,654 37
	1	Deputy surveyor	2,000 00
	1	Clerk	1,200 00
	1	....do	1,100 00
	1	Messenger	600 00
	1	General appraiser	2,500 00
	1	Messenger to general appraiser	547 50
	1	Principal appraiser	2,500 00
	2	Assistant appraisers	2,000 00
	4	Examiners	1,095 00
	1	Examiner for nine months and one-half	864 00
	6	Packers	730 00
	4	Clerks	1,000 00
	1	Messenger	600 00
	1	Clerk of appraiser's stores	1,000 00
	2	Foremen of appraiser's stores	638 75
	1	Marker of appraiser's stores	540 00
	2	Watchmen	547 50
	1	Storekeeper of the port	1,500 00
	1	Superintendent of warehouses	1,200 00
	1	Assistant storekeeper	900 00
	1	....do	600 00
	2	Markers	540 00
	1	....do	480 00
	1	Weigher	1,485 00
	3	Assistant weighers	1,200 00
	1	Assistant weigher, (part year)	442 36
	1	Foreman to weighers	730 00
	3	Beamsmen	540 00
	1	Beamsman, (6 months)	271 48

No. 33.—*Statement*—Continued.

Districts.	No. of persons employed.	Occupation.	Compensation to each person.
Philadelphia, Pa.—Continued.	2	Gaugers	$1,485 00
	2	Measurers	1,485 00
	2	....do	1,200 00
	44	Inspectors	1,095 00
	1	Inspector, (6⅔ months)	600 00
	2	Special aids to revenue	1,095 00
	1	Special aid to revenue, (5 months and 22 days)	522 00
	8	Revenue agents	912 50
	1	Revenue agent, (10 months)	757 50
	1	Revenue agent	730 00
	2	....do	547 50
	1	Revenue agent, (10 months)	457 50
	1	Captain of night inspectors	800 00
	1	Lieutenant of night inspectors	650 00
	21	Night inspectors	547 50
	1	Night inspector, (9⅔ months)	439 50
	5	Night watch on wharves	547 50
	1	Night watch on wharves, (9 months)	411 00
	1	Temporary aid to revenue	547 50
	1	Temporary aid to revenue, (8 months)	360 00
	1	Messenger to inspector's office	547 50
	4	Revenue boatmen	600 00
Presque Isle, Pa	1	Collector	381 26
	1	Deputy collector and inspector	730 00
Pittsburg, Pa	1	Surveyor	3,964 20
	1	Clerk	750 00
	1	....do	600 00
	2	Aids to revenue	730 00
	1	......do	620 00
	1	Watchman	456 25
Delaware, Del	1	Collector	1,154 18
	1	Deputy collector	1,095 00
	1	Inspector	800 00
	2	....do	500 00
	1	....do	598 50
	4	....do	428 51
	2	Messengers	365 00
Baltimore, Md	1	Collector	6,000 00
	1	Deputy collector	2,500 00
	1	Naval officer	5,000 00
	1	Deputy naval officer	2,000 00
	1	Surveyor	4,500 00
	3	Appraisers	2,500 00
	1	Cashier	1,500 00
	4	Clerks	1,500 00
	1	....do	1,400 00
	5	....do	1,200 00
	3	....do	1,100 00
	7	....do	1,000 00
	1	....do	900 00
	1	....do	850 00
	1	....do	650 00
	1	Superintendent of warehouses	1,500 00
	2	Storekeepers	1,095 00

REPORT ON THE FINANCES.

No. 33.—*Statement*—Continued.

Districts.	No. of persons employed.	Occupation.	Compensation to each person.
Baltimore, Md—Con'd.	1	Storekeeper	$1,100 00
	1	....do	1,000 00
	1	....do	900 00
	1	Weigher	1,500 00
	1	Deputy weigher	1,000 00
	1	....do	730 00
	4	Laborers at scales	547 50
	1	Gauger	1,500 00
	1	Measurer	1,500 00
	1	Deputy measurer	900 00
	2	Laborers	547 50
	27	Inspectors	1,095 00
	2	Captains of night watch	730 00
	2	Vault watchmen	730 00
	24	Watchmen	547 50
	6	Messengers	600 00
	1	Superintendent of building	700 00
	6	Porters	547 50
	6	Boatmen	547 50
Annapolis, Md	1	Collector	310 00
	1	Surveyor	250 00
	1	....do	250 00
	1	....do	150 00
Oxford, Md	1	Collector	351 10
Vienna, Md	1	Collector	600 00
	2	Deputy collectors	345 00
Town Creek, Md	1	Surveyor	150 00
Havre de Grace, Md			
Georgetown, D.C.	1	Collector	1,774 00
	1	Deputy collector	800 00
	1	....do	821 00
	1	Temporary inspector	200 00
	1	....do	34 00
Alexandria, Va	1	Collector	520 40
	1	Deputy collector	1,069 00
	2	Inspectors—$1,095, $921	2,016 00
	1	Surveyor	441 16
	1	Boatman and messenger	360 00
Wheeling, Va	1	Surveyor	1,326 87
	23	Aids to the revenue	2,188 77
Yeocomico, Va		No returns	
Beaufort, N.C.		....do	
Beaufort, S.C.		....do	
Key West, Fla	1	Collector	2,083 90
	1	Deputy collector	1,095 00
	1	Inspector	1,095 00
	1	....do....Cape Florida	500 00
	1	Temporary inspector and night watch	63 00
Louisville, Ky	1	Surveyor	689 55
	1	Deputy surveyor and clerk	1,000 00
	1	Messenger and porter	400 00
Paducah, Ky		No returns	
Cincinnati, Ohio	1	Collector or surveyor	3,000 00
	1	Clerk	1,200 00
	1	....do	1,000 00

No. 33.—*Statement*—Continued.

Districts.	No. of persons employed.	Occupation.	Compensation to each person.
Cincinnati, Ohio—Con.	1	Warehouse clerk	$600 00
		Temporary aid.....................................	6,365 46
Miami, Ohio...........	1	Collector..	1,618 40
	1	Deputy collector.................................	1,000 00
	1	Inspector	800 00
	1	Messenger	300 00
Sandusky, Ohio.......	1	Collector..	1,680 07
	1	Deputy collector.................................	800 00
	3	......do...	200 00
	1	......do...	300 00
	1	Clerk..	365 00
	1	Porter	240 00
Cuyahoga, Ohio.......	1	Collector	1,618 42
	1	Deputy collector.................................	1,000 00
	1	Inspector	800 00
	1	......do...	600 00
	2	Aids to revenue	703 29
	1	Clerk..	800 00
	4	Deputy collectors and inspectors	240 00
	1	Porter	300 00
Detroit, Mich	1	Collector..	1,618 42
	1	Deputy collector.................................	1,000 00
	1	......do...	730 00
	6	......do...	240 00
	2	......do...	120 00
	1	......do...... and inspector	1,480 00
	1	......do..........do	1,095 00
	1	......do..........do	1,021 00
	1	......do..........do	745 00
	1	......do..........do	644 00
	2	Inspectors	480 00
	5	......do...	400 00
	2	......do...	360 00
	2	......do...	240 00
	3	......do...	120 00
	1	......do...	70 00
	1	......do...	60 00
	1	......do...	20 00
Michilimackinac, Mich.	1	Collector..	1,104 60
	1	Inspector and deputy collector...............	500 00
	1	Assistant	135 00
	3	Inspectors and deputy collectors...........	400 00
	1	......do..........do	118 68
	1	......do..........do	150 00
	1	......do..........do	224 71
	3	......do..........do	200 00
Evansville, Ind.......	1	Surveyor	2,961 78
	28	Aids to revenue	2,259 30
New Albany, Ind.		....	
Chicago, Ill......	1	Collector	1,400 09
	1	Deputy collector.................................	975 81
	1	......do...	300 00
	1	......do...	776 34
	1	Clerk..	800 00
	1	Inspector	600 00

REPORT ON THE FINANCES.

No. 33.—*Statement*—Continued.

Districts.	No. of persons employed.	Occupation.	Compensation to each person.
Chicago, Ill—Cont'd..	2	Aids......	$730 00
	4	....do	675 25
	1	....do	704 00
Madison, Iowa.........	1	Surveyor	838 16
	3	Aids to revenue	133 00
Alton, Iowa...........	1	Surveyor	350 00
	2	Aids	49 00
Galena, Iowa..........	1	Surveyor	474 16
Quincy, Iowa.........	1	Collector	350 00
	1	Aid to revenue......	169 50
Cairo, Iowa....			
Peoria, Iowa..........		No returns.	
St. Louis, Mo.........	1	Surveyor, acting collector	3,000 00
	1	Clerk......	1,500 00
	1	....do	1,200 00
	1	....do	1,000 00
	1	Inspector	730 00
	1	Janitor	480 00
	1	Aid	730 00
	1	..do	730 00
Hannibal, Mo.........	1	Surveyor	1,000 00
	1	Assistant inspector......	170 00
Milwaukie, Wis.......	1	Collector	1,250 00
	1	Deputy collector	1,000 00
	4	Deputies......	800 00
	2	Inspectors	900 00
	1	Watchman	480 00
Burlington, Iowa	1	Surveyor......	381 98
Keokuk, Iowa....	1	....do	175 00
	1	Clerk......	200 00
	4	Special aids	111.50
Dubuque, Iowa.......	1	Surveyor......	378 35
	2	Inspectors	39 00
	1	Watchman	14 00
	1	Collector......	1,200 00
	1	Deputy collector	800 00
Minnesota, Minn......	1	Occasional	33 00
Puget's Sound, W. T..	1	Collector	2,500 00
	1	Surveyor	1,000 00
	5	Inspectors	800 00
	1	....do	1,000 00
	2	Boatmen	720 00
Cape Perpetua, W. T..			
Port Orford, W. T.....	1	Collector	2,000 00
	1	Deputy collector	1,000 00
San Francisco, Cal		No returns.	
Sonoma, Cal..........		No returns.	
San Jonquin, Cal......		No returns.	
Sacramento, Cal		No returns.	
San Diego, Cal........	1	Collector	750 00
Monterey, Cal....		No returns.	
San Pedro, Cal........	1	Collector......	3,060 00
	1	Surveyor......	2,000 00

No 33.—PORTS FROM WHICH NO RETURNS ARE MADE.

Districts.	No. of persons employed.	Occupation.	Compensation to each person.
Richmond, Va........			
Norfolk & Portsm'th, Va			
Tappahannock, Va....			
Cherrystone, Va.....			
Yorktown, Va......			
Petersburg, Va......			
Camden, N. C.			
Edenton, N. C......			
Plymouth, N. C......			
Washington. N. C....			
Newbern, N. C......			
Ocracoke, N. C......			
Wilmington, N. C.....			
Charleston, S. C.....			
Georgetown, S. C.....			
Savannah, Ga.... ...			
St Mary's, Ga.....			
Brunswick, Ga......			
Augusta, Ga.......			
Pensacola, Fla......			
St. Augustine, Fla.....			
St. Mark's, Fla.			
St. John's, Fla.......			
Apalachicola, Fla....			
Fernandina, Fla			
Bayport, Fla....			
Pilatka, Fla.........			
Mobile, Ala			
Selma, Ala.........			
Tuscumbia, Ala.....			
Pearl River, Miss.....			
Vicksburg, Miss......			
Natches, Miss....			
°New Orleans, La....	(See below)...		
Teché, La..........			
Shreveport, La.			
Texas, Texas			
Saluria, Texas			
Brazos de Santiago,Tex.			
Paso del Norte, Texas .			
Nashville, Tenn			
Memphis, Tenn......			
Knoxville, Tenn.....			
Chattanooga, Tenn....			
Hickman, Ky....			
Columbus, Ky.......			
°New Orleans, La......	1	Deputy collector.	$2,500 00
	1	Acting appraiser......	2,500 00
	1	Entry clerk	1,800 00
	1	Cashier...... ....,......	1,800 00
	1	Register's clerk......	1,800 00
	2	Abstract clerks	1,500 00
	20	Inspectors	1,095 00
	3	Night watches......	730 00
	1	Keeper	900 00
	2	Messengers......	720 00

TREASURY DEPARTMENT, *Register's Office, Dec. 9, 1862.* L. E. CHITTENDEN, *Register.*

No. 34

Regulations concerning internal and coastwise intercourse, to which is appended the accompanying orders of the Secretary of War and the Secretary of the Navy.

[Act of Congress July 13, 1861, and an act supplementary thereto, May 2, 1862.]

TREASURY DEPARTMENT, *August* 28, 1862.

In pursuance of law, and by virtue of the authority conferred upon the Secretary of the Treasury by the act of Congress approved July 13, 1861, entitled "An act further to provide for the collection of duties on imports, and for other purposes," and an act supplementary thereto, approved May 20, 1862, and for the purpose of preventing the conveyance of arms, munitions of war, and other supplies to persons in insurrection against the United States, the following regulations concerning commercial intercourse with insurrectionary States and sections are prescribed.

S. P. CHASE,
Secretary of the Treasury.

I. No goods, wares, or merchandise, whatever may be the ostensible destination thereof, shall be transported to any place now under the control of insurgents; nor to any place on the south side of the Potomac river; nor to any place on the north side of the Potomac, and south of the Washington and Annapolis railroad; nor to any place on the eastern shore of the Chesapeake; nor to any place on the south side of the Ohio river below Wheeling, except Louisville; nor to any place on the west side of the Mississippi river below the mouth of the Des Moines, except St. Louis, without a permit of a duly authorized officer of the Treasury Department. And the special agents of this department may temporarily extend these restrictions to such other places in their respective districts, and make such local rules to be observed therein as may from time to time become necessary, promptly reporting their action to the Secretary of the Treasury for his sanction or disapproval.

II. All transportation of coin or bullion to any State or section heretofore declared to be in insurrection, is absolutely prohibited, except for military purposes and under military orders, or under the special license of the Secretary of the Treasury. And no payment of gold or silver shall be made for cotton or other merchandise within any such State or section. And all cotton or other merchandise purchased or paid for therein, directly or indirectly, in gold or silver, shall be forfeited to the United States.

III. No clearance or permit whatsoever will be granted for any shipment to any port, place, or section affected by the existing blockade, except for military purposes, and upon the certificate and request of the Department of War or the Department of the Navy.

IV. All applications for permits to transport or trade under these regulations shall state the character and value of the merchandise to be transported, the consignee and destination thereof, with the route of transportation and the number and description of the packages with the marks thereon.

V. Every applicant for such permits shall present with his application the original invoices of the goods, wares, and merchandise to be transported, and shall make and file with the officer granting the permit an affidavit that the quantities, descriptions, and values are correctly stated in said invoices, true copies of which shall be annexed to and filed with the affidavit; and that the packages contain nothing except as stated in the invoices; that the merchandise so permitted shall not, nor shall any part thereof, be disposed of by him or by his authority, connivance, or assent, in violation of the terms of the permit, and that neither the permit so granted nor the merchandise to be transported shall be so used or disposed of by him, or by his authority, connivance, or assent, as in any way to give aid, comfort, information, or encouragement to persons in insurrection against the United States. And, furthermore, that the applicant is loyal to the government of the United States, and will in all things so deport himself.

VI. No permit shall be granted to ship goods, wares, or merchandise *to* States or parts of States heretofore declared to be in insurrection, or to places under insurrectionary control, or occupied by the military forces of the United States, except to persons residing or doing business therein whose loyalty and good faith shall be certified by an officer of the government or other person duly authorized to make such certificate, or by a duly appointed board of trade therein, by whose approval and permission only the same shall be unladed or disposed of. And no permit shall be granted to ship merchandise *from* any such State or part of State in violation of any order restricting shipments therefrom, made for military purposes by the commandant of the *department* from which such shipment is to be made.

VII. Collectors or surveyors of customs, before granting clearances or permits, may require bond, with reasonable surety, in such cases as they shall think necessary to protect the public interests, conditioned that there shall be no violation of the terms or spirit of the clearance or permit, or of the averments of the affidavit upon which the same is granted.

VIII. No permit shall be granted to ship intoxicating drinks, or other thing prohibited by the military authorities, into territory occupied by the military forces of the United States, except upon the written request of the commandant of the *department* in which such territory is embraced, or of some person duly authorized by him to make such request.

IX. In order to defray the expenses under these regulations, a fee of twenty cents will be charged for each permit granted; and shipments permitted to and from States heretofore declared to be in insurrection shall, in addition thereto, be charged with the following fees, viz: five cents on each one hundred dollars over three hundred dollars on all shipments *to* such States or sections; fifty cents on each one thousand pounds of cotton, and twenty-five cents on each one thousand pounds of sugar permitted *from* such State.

X. No vessel, boat, or vehicle used for transportation upon or south of the Potomac river, or north of the Potomac and south of the Washington and Annapolis railroad, or to the eastern shore of the Chesapeake, or southwardly on or from the Ohio river below Wheeling, or westwardly or southwardly on or from the Mississippi river below the mouth of the Des Moines, shall receive on board any goods, wares, or merchandise destined to any place, commercial intercourse with which now is or hereafter may be restricted as aforesaid, unless the same be accompanied with a permit of a duly authorized officer of the Treasury Department, except as hereinafter provided in regulation number XIV.

XI. No vessel, boat, or other vehicle used for transportation from eastern cities, or elsewhere in the loyal States, shall carry goods, wares, or merchandise into any place, section, or State restricted as aforesaid, without the permit of the duly authorized officer of the customs, application for which permit may be made to such authorized officer near the point of destination as may suit the convenience of the shipper.

XII. No vessel, boat, or other vehicle used for transportation shall put off any goods, wares, or merchandise at any place other than that named in the permit as the place of destination.

XIII. Before any boat or vessel running on any of the western waters south of Louisville or St. Louis, or other waters within or adjacent to any State or section, commercial intercourse with which now is or may hereafter be restricted as aforesaid, shall depart from any port where there is a collector or surveyor of customs, there shall be exhibited to the collector or surveyor, or such other officer as may be authorized to act in his stead, a true manifest of its entire cargo and a clearance obtained to proceed on its voyage; and when freights are received on board at a place where there is no collector or surveyor, as herein-after provided in regulation XIV, then the same exhibit shall be made and clearance obtained at the first port to be passed where there is such an officer, and such vessel or boat shall be reported and the manifest of its cargo exhibited to the collector or surveyor of every port to be passed on the trip where there is such an officer; but no new clearance shall be necessary unless additional freights shall have been taken on board after the last clearance. Immediately on arriving at the port of final destination, and before discharging any part of its cargo, the manifest shall be exhibited to the surveyor of such port, or other officer authorized to act in his stead, whose approval for landing the cargo shall be indorsed on the manifest before any part thereof shall be discharged; and the clearance and shipping permits of all such vessels and boats shall be ex-hibited to the officer in command of any naval vessel or military post whenever such officer may require it.

XIV. To facilitate trade and guard against improper transportation, "aids to the revenue" will be appointed from time to time on cars, vessels, and boats, when desired by the owners, agents, or masters thereof, which aids will have free carriage on the respective cars, vessels, and boats on which they are placed, and will allow proper weigh freights to be taken on board without permit, keeping a statement thereof, and reporting the same to the collector or surveyor of the first port to be passed on the trip where there is such an officer, from whom a permit therefor must be obtained, or the goods returned under his direction. No permit will be granted for transportation into any insurrectionary State or district, except on cars, vessels, and boats carrying such aids.

XV. All vessels, boats, and other vehicles used for transportation, violating any of the above regulations, and all goods, wares, and merchandise shipped or transported in violation thereof, will be forfeited to the United States. If any false statement be made or deception practiced in obtaining a permit, such permit and all others connected therewith or affected thereby will be absolutely void, and all merchandise shipped thereunder shall be forfeited to the United States. In all cases of forfeiture, as aforesaid, immediate seizure will be made and proceedings instituted promptly for condemnation. The attention of all officers of the government, common carriers, shippers, consignees, owners, masters, agents, drivers, and other persons connected with the transportation of merchandise or trading therein, is particularly directed to the acts of July 13, 1861, and May 20, 1862, above referred to.

XVI. All army supplies transported under military orders are excepted from the above regulations. But this exception does not extend to sutlers' goods or others designed for sale at military posts or camps.

XVII. When any officer of the customs shall find in his district any goods, wares, or merchandise, which, in his opinion, are in danger of being transported to insurgents, he may, if he thinks it expedient, require the owner or holder thereof to give reasonable security that they shall not be transported to any place under insurrectionary control, and shall not in any way be used to give aid or encouragement to the insurgents.

If the required security be not given, such officer shall promptly state the facts to the United States marshal for the district within which such goods are situated, or, if beyond the jurisdiction of a United States marshal, then to the commandant of the nearest military post, whose duty it shall be to take possession thereof, and hold them for safe-keeping, reporting the facts promptly to the Secretary of the Treasury, and awaiting instructions.

XVIII. Where ports heretofore blockaded have been opened by the proclamation of the President, licenses will be granted, by United States consuls, on application by the proper parties, to vessels clearing from foreign ports to the ports so opened, upon satisfactory evidence that the vessel so licensed will convey no person, property, or information contraband of war, either to or from said ports, which license shall be shown to the collector of the port to which the vessel is bound, and, if required, to any officer in charge of the blockade. And on leaving any port so opened, the vessel must have a clearance from the collector, according to law, showing no violation of the conditions of the license. Any violation of the conditions will involve the forfeiture and condemnation of the vessel and cargo, and the exclusion of all parties concerned from entering the United States for any purpose during the war.

XIX. United States vessels clearing from domestic ports to any of the ports so opened will apply to the custom-house officers of the proper ports, in the usual manner, for licenses or clearances under the regulations heretofore established.

WAR DEPARTMENT,
Washington City, August 28, 1862.

The attention of all officers and others connected with the army of the United States is called to the regulations of the Secretary of the Treasury concerning commercial intercourse with insurrectionary States or sections, dated August 28, 1862.

I. Commandants of departments, districts, and posts will render all such military aid as may become necessary in carrying out the provisions of said regulations, and enforcing observance thereof to the extent directed by the Secretary of the Treasury, so far as can possibly be done without danger to the operations or safety of their respective commands.

II. There will be no interference with trade or shipments of cotton, or other merchandise conducted in pursuance of said regulations within any territory occupied and controlled by the forces of the United States, unless absolutely necessary to the successful execution of military plans or movements therein. But in cases of the violations of the conditions of any clearance or permit granted under said regulations, and in cases of unlawful traffic, the guilty party or parties will be arrested and the facts promptly reported to the commandant of the department for orders.

III. No officer of the army or other person connected therewith will seize cotton or other property of individuals unless exposed to destruction by the enemy, or needed for military purposes, or for confiscation under the act of Congress; and in all such cases of seizure the same shall be promptly reported to the commandant of the department wherein they are made, for his orders therein.

EDWIN M. STANTON,
Secretary of War.

NAVY DEPARTMENT, *August* 28, 1862.

The attention of naval officers is called to the regulations of the Secretary of the Treasury concerning commercial intercourse with insurrectionary States or sections, dated August 28, 1862.

I. Commanders of naval vessels will render such aid as may be necessary in carrying out the provisions of said regulations, and enforcing observance thereof to the extent directed by the Secretary of the Treasury, so far as can possibly be done without danger to the operations or safety of their respective commands.

II. There will be no interference with trade in or shipments of cotton or other merchandise conducted in pursuance of said regulations within any of the waters controlled by the naval forces of the United States, unless absolutely necessary to the successful execution of military or naval plans or movements. But in cases of the violation of the conditions of any clearance or permit granted under said regulations, and in cases of unlawful traffic, the guilty party or parties will be arrested and the facts promptly reported.

III. No officer of the navy will seize cotton or other property of individuals within the territory opened to traffic, and subject to the regulations of the Secretary of the Treasury, unless the same is exposed to destruction by the enemy or needed for naval purposes, or for confiscation under the act of Congress; and in all such cases the fact with all attendant circumstances shall be promptly reported to the department.

GIDEON WELLES,
Secretary.

AN ACT further to provide for the collection of duties on imports, and for other purposes

Be it enacted by the Senate and House of Representatives of the United States of America in Congress assembled, That whenever it shall, in the judgment of the President, by reason of unlawful combinations of persons in opposition to the laws of the United States, become impracticable to execute the revenue laws and collect the duties on imports by the ordinary means, in the ordinary way, at any port of entry in any collection district, he is authorized to cause such duties to be collected at any port of delivery in said district until such obstruction shall cease; and in such case the surveyors at said ports of delivery shall be clothed with all the powers and be subject to all the obligations of collectors at ports of entry. And the Secretary of the Treasury, with the approbation of the President, shall appoint such number of weighers, gaugers, measurers, inspectors, appraisers, and clerks as may be necessary, in his judgment, for the faithful execution of the revenue laws at said ports of delivery, and shall fix and establish the limits within which such ports of delivery are constituted ports of entry, as aforesaid. And all the provisions of law regulating the issue of marine papers, the coasting trade, the warehousing of imports, and collection of duties shall apply to the ports of entry so constituted in the same manner as they do to ports of entry established by the laws now in force.

SEC. 2. *And be it further enacted,* That if, from the cause mentioned in the foregoing section, in the judgment of the President, the revenue from duties on imports cannot be effectually collected at any port of entry in any collection district, in the ordinary way and by the ordinary means, or by the course provided in the foregoing section, then and in that case he may direct that the custom-house for the district be established in any secure place within said district, either on land or on board any vessel in said district, or at sea near the coast; and in such case the collector shall reside at such place, or on shipboard, as the case may be, and there detain all vessels and cargoes arriving within or approaching said district, until the duties imposed by law on said vessels and their cargoes are paid in cash : *Provided,* That if the owner or consignee of the cargo on board any vessel detained as aforesaid, or the master of said vessel, shall desire to enter a port of entry in any other district of the United States where no such obstructions to the execution of the laws exist, the master of such vessel may be permitted so to change the destination of the vessel and cargo in his manifest, whereupon the collector shall deliver him a written permit to proceed to the port so designated : *And provided, further,* That the Secretary of the Treasury shall, with the approbation of the President, make proper regulations for the enforcement on shipboard of such provisions of the laws regulating the assessment and collection of duties as, in his judgment, may be necessary and practicable.

SEC. 3. *And be it further enacted*, That it shall be unlawful to take any vessel or cargo detained as aforesaid from the custody of the proper officers of the customs unless by process of some court of the United States; and in case of any attempt otherwise to take such vessel or cargo by any force, or combination, or assemblage of persons, too great to be overcome by the officers of the customs, it shall and may be lawful for the President, or such person or persons as he shall have empowered for that purpose, to employ such part of the army or navy or militia of the United States, or such force of citizen volunteers as may be deemed necessary, for the purpose of preventing the removal of such vessel or cargo, and protecting the officers of the customs in retaining the custody thereof.

SEC. 4. *And be it further enacted*, That if, in the judgment of the President, from the cause mentioned in the first section of this act, the duties upon imports in any collection district cannot be effectually collected by the ordinary means and in the ordinary way, or in the mode and manner provided in the foregoing section of this act, then and in that case the President is hereby empowered to close the port or ports of entry in said district, and in such case give notice thereof by proclamation; and thereupon all right of importation, warehousing, and other privileges incident to ports of entry, shall cease and be discontinued at such port so closed, until opened by the order of the President on the cessation of such obstructions. And if, while said ports are so closed, any ship or vessel from beyond the United States, or having on board any articles subject to duties, shall enter or attempt to enter any such port, the same, together with its tackle, apparel, furniture, and cargo, shall be forfeited to the United States.

SEC. 5. *And be it further enacted*, That whenever the President, in pursuance of the provisions of the second section of the act entitled "An act to provide for calling forth the militia to execute the laws of the Union, suppress insurrections, and repel invasions, and to repeal the act now in force for that purpose," approved February twenty-eight, seventeen hundred and ninety-five, shall have called forth the militia to suppress combinations against the laws of the United States, and to cause the laws to be duly executed, and the insurgents shall have failed to disperse by the time directed by the President, and when said insurgents claim to act under the authority of any State or States, and such claim is not disclaimed or repudiated by the persons exercising the functions of government in such State or States, or in the part or parts thereof in which said combination exists, nor such insurrection suppressed by said State or States, then and in such case it may and shall be lawful for the President, by proclamation, to declare that the inhabitants of such State, or any section or part thereof, where such insurrection exists, are in a state of insurrection against the United States; and thereupon all commercial intercourse by and between the same and the citizens thereof and the citizens of the rest of the United States shall cease and be unlawful so long as such condition of hostility shall continue; and all goods and chattels, wares and merchandise, coming from said State or section into the other parts of the United States, and all proceeding to such State or section, by land or water, shall, together with the vessel or vehicle conveying the same, or conveying persons to or from such State or section, be forfeited to the United States: *Provided, however,* That the President may, in his discretion, license and permit commercial intercourse with any such part of said State or section, the inhabitants of which are so declared in a state of insurrection, in such articles, and for such time, and by such persons, as he, in his discretion, may think most conducive to the public interest; and such intercourse, so far as by him licensed, shall be conducted and carried on only in pursuance of rules and regulations prescribed by the Secretary of the Treasury. And the Secretary of the Treasury may appoint such officers, at places where officers of

Ex. Doc. 1——18

the customs are not now authorized by law, as may be needed to carry into
effect such licenses, rules, and regulations; and officers of the customs and other
officers shall receive for services under this section, and under said rules and
regulations, such fees and compensation as are now allowed for similar service
under other provisions of law.

SEC. 6. *And be it further enacted*, That, from and after fifteen days after the
issuing of the said proclamation, as provided in the last foregoing section of this
act, any ship or vessel belonging in whole or in part to any citizen or inhabitant
of said State or part of a State whose inhabitants are so declared in a state of
insurrection, found at sea, or in any port of the rest of the United States, shall
be forfeited to the United States.

SEC. 7. *And be it further enacted*, That, in the execution of the provisions of
this act, and of the other laws of the United States providing for the collection
of duties on imports and tonnage, it may and shall be lawful for the President,
in addition to the revenue cutters in service, to employ in aid thereof such other
suitable vessels as may, in his judgment, be required.

SEC. 8. *And be it further enacted*, That the forfeitures and penalties incurred
by virtue of this act may be mitigated or remitted, in pursuance of the authority
vested in the Secretary of the Treasury by the act entitled "An act providing
for mitigating or remitting the forfeitures, penalties, and disabilities accruing in
certain cases therein mentioned," approved March third, seventeen hundred and
ninety-seven, or in cases where special circumstances may seem to require it,
according to regulations to be prescribed by the Secretary of the Treasury.

SEC. 9. *And be it further enacted*, That proceedings on seizures for forfeitures under this act may be pursued in the courts of the United States in any
district into which the property so seized may be taken and proceedings instituted; and such courts shall have and entertain as full jurisdiction over the
same as if the seizure was made in that district.

Approved July 13, 1861.

AN ACT supplementary to an act approved on the thirteenth July, eighteen hundred and
sixty-one, entitled "An act to provide for the collection of duties on imports, and for
other purposes."

*Be it enacted by the Senate and House of Representatives of the United States
of America in Congress assembled*, That the Secretary of the Treasury, in addition to the powers conferred upon him by the act of the thirteenth July, eighteen
hundred and sixty-one, be, and he is hereby, authorized to refuse a clearance to
any vessel or other vehicle laden with goods, wares, or merchandise destined
for a foreign or domestic port, whenever he shall have satisfactory reason to believe that such goods, wares, or merchandise, or any part thereof, whatever may
be their ostensible destination, are intended for ports or places in possession or
under control of insurgents against the United States; and if any vessel or other
vehicle for which a clearance or permit shall have been refused by the Secretary
of the Treasury, or by his order as aforesaid, shall depart or attempt to depart
for a foreign or domestic port without being duly cleared or permitted, such
vessel or other vehicle, with her tackle, apparel, furniture, and cargo, shall be
forfeited to the United States.

SEC. 2. *And be it further enacted*, That whenever a permit or clearance is
granted, for either a foreign or domestic port, it shall be lawful for the collector
of the customs granting the same, if he shall deem it necessary under the circumstances of the case, to require a bond to be executed by the master or the
owner of the vessel, in a penalty equal to the value of the cargo, and with sureties to the satisfaction of such collector, that the said cargo shall be delivered at the
destination for which it is cleared or permitted, and that no part thereof shall be

used in affording aid or comfort to any person or parties in insurrection against the authority of the United States.

SEC. 3. *And be it further enacted,* That the Secretary of the Treasury be, and he is hereby, further empowered to prohibit and prevent the transportation in any vessel, or upon any railroad, turnpike, or other road or means of trans-·portation within the United States, of any goods, wares, or merchandise, of whatever character, and whatever may be the ostensible destination of the same, in all cases where there shall be satisfactory reasons to believe that such goods, wares, or merchandise are intended for any place in the possession or under the control of insurgents against the United States; or that there is imminent danger that such goods, wares, or merchandise will fall into the possession or under the control of such insurgents. And he is further authorized, in all cases where he shall deem it expedient so to do, to require reasonable security to be given that goods, wares, or merchandise shall not be transported to any place under insurrectionary control, and shall not in any way be used to give aid or comfort to such insurgents; and he may establish all such general or special regulations as may be necessary or proper to carry into effect the purposes of this act. And if any goods, wares, or merchandise shall be transported in violation of this act, or of any regulation of the Secretary of the Treasury established in pursuance thereof, or if any attempt shall be made so to transport them, all goods, wares, or merchandise so transported or attempted to be transported shall be forfeited to the United States.

SEC. 4. *And be it further enacted,* That the proceedings for the penalties and forfeitures accruing under this act may be pursued, and the same may be mitigated or remitted by the Secretary of the Treasury in the modes prescribed by the eighth and ninth sections of the act of July thirteenth, eighteen hundred and sixty one, to which this act is supplementary.

SEC. 5. *And be it further enacted,* That the proceeds of all penalties and forfeitures incurred under this act, or the act to which this is supplementary, shall be distributed in the manner provided by the ninety-first section of the act of March second, seventeen hundred and ninety-nine, entitled "An act to regulate the collection of duties on imports and tonnage."

Approved May 20, 1862.